Fragments of a Fractured

World

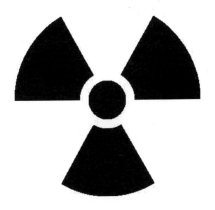

Edited by Miranda Kate and Michael Wombat

ISBN: 978-1-08969-353-6

Published by Michael Wombat

DEDICATION

to Miranda, without whom this book would not be spelt: write? Or have the correct.

Punctuation!

INTRODUCTION

Human 76 was spawned on an icy morning in spring when my family and I, with our German shepherd, stood shivering but galvanised in front of a tripod. We were adorned in war paint and post-apocalyptic fashion, brandishing weapons for an urban warrior family photoshoot in Pembrey Park's old, abandoned munitions bunkers. The camera clicked and even the dog was charged with post-apocalyptic energy.

One particular photo of my daughter, Bekah, caught the imagination of my writing community, revealing an urge to write for her character. A. E. Howard, author of Flight of Blue, caught the vision and from her initial idea Human 76 was conceived. With help from Michael Wombat, author of Fog, we began to create something special.

Bekah and I set about creating a post-apocalyptic backstory and world for Ghabrie and our writers, both published and unpublished, began to write tales set within this world. The only requirement: that their characters would cross paths with Ghabrie. Each story became a work of art, stitching our post-apocalyptic world together and telling a different story of survival. Ghabrie became a true legend as she wandered through her world of tales.

~ Lisa Shambrook, Wales, May 2016

EDITOR'S NOTE

This book came together in a remarkable way. Lisa has already told you of its beginnings in her introduction, but let me pass on a little more about the remarkable evolution that took place around the simple premise of a girl searching for her lost sister. At first, most authors simply got on with their own stories, but then slowly, almost organically, a new level of writing began to emerge.

As we authors chatted - in the Human 76 Facebook group, on Twitter, or by email - we began to pick up ideas from each other. We read and commented on each other's stories as they appeared in our common Dropbox folder. We became inspired by our peers, and edited our own work so as to include cool stuff invented by fellow Seventy-Sixers.

Eventually some of our tales became as intertwined as lovers (*Glint* and *Behind These Walls*), while others merely made amusing references. One story (*Sand*) was entirely inspired by another (*The Oasis*). This process of cross-fertilisation led to Ghabrie's world becoming very real to all of us. Of particular pleasure was the way that characters other than our sibling protagonists took on a life of their own. KJ Collard's David, at first a simple (though vital) walk-on part in her *Sheshwahtay*, now has a complex, moving story arc of his own. MS Manz's Leader causes ripples that even he would find difficult to predict. And Jeff Hollar's Hieronymous Planck eventually ... but let me not spoil the fun. You'll have to find out about him by reading the book.

So please bear in mind that, yes, what you have in your hands is a collection of tales - but it is also more than that. It is a single book-length story. The saga of Ghabrie, the girl and the myth, and her determination to make her own future in a fractured world.

You're still reading this? Blimey, get on to the stories already! Oh, but first let me say a special word of gratitude to Miranda, who threw herself into the project with astonishing gusto despite not having a story here. My admiration and thanks also go to all our authors. If you like what you read here, check the bios at the back of the book for links to more works by these extremely talented people. Finally, all hail the Shambrooks for giving life to our fractured world.

Thanks for reading Human 76.

- Michael Wombat, Lancashire, 2016

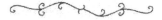

A note on Spellings - this collection features stories from authors all over this small blue planet, and each individual tale will retain the spellings and use of language natural to its author.

The map is loosely based on one found on freefantasymaps.org.

CONTENTS

PROLOGUE 9

LEAVING THE NEST 10

FOLLOW THE LEADER 32

WHERE THE WILD THINGS ARE 59

GLINT 78

BEHIND THESE WALLS 114

HIERO WORSHIP 144

HUMAN X 167

THE HUNTED 210

WHAT YOU PUT IN 230

UNDERNEATH 251

THE SONG OF AIDEN 264

SAND 304

THE OASIS 314

SHESHWAHTAY 322

THE BALLAD OF ASH & HUM 338

WE MAKE THE FUTURE 368

EPILOGUE 406

AUTHOR BIOS 407

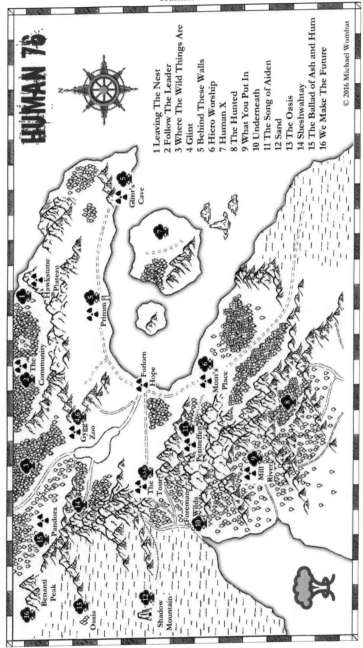

1 Leaving The Nest
2 Follow The Leader
3 Where The Wild Things Are
4 Glint
5 Behind These Walls
6 Hiero Worship
7 Human X
8 The Hunted
9 What You Put In
10 Underneath
11 The Song of Aiden
12 Sand
13 The Oasis
14 Sheshwahtay
15 The Ballad of Ash and Hum
16 We Make The Future

PROLOGUE

Lisa Shambrook

"Quiet, you fool! You're safe now!" Rough hands gripped Ghabrie.

A kestrel swooped but Ghabrie could not hear its call. She could hear only Nahria's shriek. Ghabrie strained to glimpse her little sister through the mass of rebellion warriors and Prometheans. The two sides were withdrawing, both claiming their spoils and retreating. Ghabrie thrashed: kicking, biting, struggling against strong arms that restrained her.

"Nahria, I'll come for you!"

The butt of a rifle thumped the side of her head as her words still echoed across the barren landscape. Ghabrie slipped into an oblivion brought by the hands of her liberators.

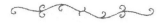

When she woke she swallowed her nausea, winced at her injuries, and wept at the loss of her reason to live. She vowed never to rest until Nahria was back at her side.

LEAVING THE NEST

Lisa Shambrook

Xanthe flinched as the kestrel swooped, but it was the resounding boom that echoed across the barren desert that caused her reaction, not the bird. She settled into the crevice, as if hiding, and gazed over kilometres of dust at the silhouette of the city. Usually Hawkstone hid behind a haze of dust and smog, a filth that clogged lungs and prevented the sun from touching the earth, but today the sky was clear and blue and the city shimmered on the far horizon.

Xanthe watched a plume, a spiral of black, rise and she shivered. The city was far enough away to feel comfortable, but when explosions rocked and flickering fires lasted well into the night, she felt fear chill her bones. Hopefully the unrest would stay contained and not spill into the desert. She swallowed her fear and stopped twisting what was left of her top lip with her fingers.

The bird in the sky keened, and his song of sorrow touched Xanthe. She shielded her eyes from the glaring sun and stared up at the bird. As she watched, her fingers moved back to her mouth and she unconsciously twisted her cleft lip within her thumb and forefinger again. A habit she'd never beaten. She sighed.

The kestrel danced upon the currents, gliding and swooping, punctuating his flight with notes of grief. Xanthe wiped away a tear that slid down her face. For a moment her own grief caught up with her and she struggled to stop her tears, but she sniffed and blinked and as the sun blinded her, and her thoughts disappeared into reminiscence.

A decade ago, she'd been climbing this very ridge, high on Hawkstone Plateau, searching for food. Both her children had been under ten-years-old and it had only been a few years since they had lost their father. Time out to gather luxuries — as that was what eggs had become — was rare and Xanthe always made the most of the few hours she got. Many of the compound's population were disabled, born with defects ranging from severe to the sort Xanthe suffered. Her fused fingers were the least of her worries, so Xanthe climbed.

She remembered pausing upon the ridge, staring across the ocean of dust to the far off hills and the city, feeling the same chill she felt today. She was one of the first surviving children born Post Blast. The ones born directly after the inferno had barely managed to live beyond their first few scrawny weeks. Radiation had flooded the land and even though hundreds had fled from the blazing city to the mountain's foothills a hundred kilometres away, only half survived ten years later. Twenty years later, when Xanthe was a teen, almost no children were born. When Xanthe was given to one of the original survivors, she was lucky to have conceived twice. She adored her two boys, born free from defects, but she relished her time out, time often spent scaling the mountain and returning with eggs and the occasional wild flower.

Xanthe shivered again as a fresh breeze rippled through her short hair and thin blouse. Climbing was hot work, and the scarf she wore around her neck would have been used to carry eggs, if she had found them.

She remembered tying the same scarf around her waist as the sun had beat upon her shoulders, and during that pause, the city undulated in the distance beyond the lake at the foot of the mountain in a shimmer of heat and dust. She had licked her dry lips and listened. It had been quiet, no bird calls, no warning tweets or squawks and she had hurried, pulling herself up the grey stone one crag at a time.

She had been close to where the birds nested, and moved gracefully until a nest, neatly woven, sat up in the crevice above her. She had pulled herself up the rock, carefully scanning the sky for angry mother birds, and gazed inside the nest. She had been too late for eggs. Inside sat a tiny bird, a bundle of white and grey fluff, and huge black eyes gazed right into her own. The two had stared at each other, until the bird released a pitiful squawk and Xanthe had backed away. Life was life, and if the bird had a chance in this harsh world she wasn't going to get in its way.

Xanthe sighed again, staring up at the bird now swooping in the blue sky. She recalled how she had stepped away from the nest, those years ago, and how her heart had dropped as she had almost stepped on a carcass a few feet down the mountain. The baby bird's mother was dead, just metres from her offspring. Xanthe had gazed back up at the nest resting not far above her head. Pathetic squeaks came from the nest and she had known the bird would not last the coming night.

She had wrapped the nest up inside her scarf, tied it across her back, and climbed back down the mountain.

That first night, after water and seeds to eat, the bird had cried. The scrawny kestrel had gained enough strength to grieve and resting inside the scarf cocooned at Xanthe's breast, he had cried all night. Xanthe had had enough tears of her own, and she had wetted the little bird's head with them.

Now she sat, with those same wet eyes, staring at the kestrel in the sky. Loss filled her heart as the bird soared.

Xanthe's own two sons had not had time for a scraggly baby bird; they had been too busy wandering the compound shadowing Alphaeus. Though in his seventies,

Alphaeus was still as strong as an ox and had a work ethic to match. The boys had taken to him as a father figure, or rather a grandfather figure, and that had suited Xanthe just fine. Alphaeus was a survivor, an original, and had been working at the shipyard before the Blast had hit. Since then he had run the shipyard, the compound, and the boys learned their skills from him.

She closed her eyes and sent her memories back to the day after she had brought the orphaned bird home. She'd been resting on her pallet bed, canvas curtains flapping in the breeze at the sawn-out windows, when a small face had appeared at the door. Xanthe had smiled and the face had quickly disappeared, then a hand had stretched forward, palm open and Xanthe grinned at the tiny worms wriggling in the hand.

"So, you heard him last night, did you?" she asked the child behind the door. "Come on in, and let's see if he wants a snack."

The child, grubby and thin, slid round the door and wandered into Xanthe's container. The shipping containers had quickly become homes. People had barely escaped with their lives, so the facilities at the shipping yard were luxurious and the Blast survivors had made the best of what they had found. For the first few months they had huddled in the caves dug out at the foot of the mountain, the huge, gaping storage depot. Then as they realised they had escaped to a pocket of land free from radiation at the foot of the huge Tinder Mountain range, they emerged to reclaim the shipping yard, its surrounding land and a compound they could protect and live in. The survivors had cleared debris, turned the hot, metal shipping containers into homes and built new homes with the timber, tin and breeze blocks salvaged from the warehouse. The stagnant lake protected the north edge. Nothing could traverse the lake and the ships still harboured there were lost as the sulphuric water corroded and ruined the iron. Xanthe had been able to see the rolling waves from the door as the young girl stepped closer to her bed.

"Do you want to see?" she asked the child.

The girl nodded and Xanthe beckoned. Soon the child was sat upon the bed and the baby bird, almost as skinny as the little girl, fed from her hand.

Nine-year-old Ghabrie had understood how it felt to be orphaned, and she had tucked the motherless bird beneath her own wings in the same way she had guarded her little sister. Ghabrie had come every day to feed the baby kestrel after spending hours in the dirt hunting for worms, grubs and insects, and every day the kestrel rewarded her. It had not been long before the bird was healthy and his fluff faded, replaced by feathers.

After a few weeks, when he was strong and plumed with slate and tawny feathers and only a little fluff remained, Ghabrie had followed Xanthe with the kestrel on her shoulder. Together they had climbed the ridge and sat upon a bluff overlooking the compound below. Ghabrie had pushed the kestrel from her shoulder to the sandy dirt on the floor and watched. She had refused to allow the bird back but had thrown grubs over the bluff. The bird shuffled to the edge and stared longingly at the grubs below. It had been Ghabrie, not Xanthe, who had pushed the bird over the edge. Panic had thrown out his wings and frantic fluttering had given him a rough landing, but he had come through unscathed and been compensated with grubs. A few more pushes and he had learned to fly.

Not only had the bird learned to fly, but Ghabrie overcame her own parental loss and blossomed.

Now, sitting upon the mountainside, Xanthe smiled, and let the breeze sift sand through her few unfused fingers. Ghabrie and the kestrel had been inseparable, and Xanthe's heart skipped as she listened to the bird's raw cries up in the cloudless sky. The kestrel missed Ghabrie just as much as Xanthe missed her sons.

Xanthe's attention switched back to the smoke rising far on the horizon. The disturbance unnerved her. Troubles from the city barely ever trickled into the desert, but it was not unheard of. With most of the young lost the compound was vulnerable, even Alphaeus could not protect everyone.

She cast her gaze down into the old shipping yard. From her perch she had a view of everything. The stagnant lake slapped the northern sides of the docks, the ruined ships slowly disintegrating in the toxic bay. The wide arc of barbed wire, the kilometres of no-man's land – planted with mines – and the olive groves, a strange but oddly beautiful sight against the stark, barren desert. Fields of corn grew parallel to the groves, and a deep, man-made lake protected the southern boundaries fed by the only mountain stream that had survived the Blast.

She watched the guards patrolling on tired, hot feet, and oil-driven motorbikes, dust trails betraying their locations. She did not want to leave the mountain, but she had had the best view of the new fracas and knew Alphaeus would want to know. She set off, delicately picking her way down the mountain, her feet as true as a mountain goat.

She had been up on the mountainside when they had come and stolen the children.

She had seen the vehicles approach like ants on the horizon, growing bigger all the time. She had watched and radioed down, but her radio had crackled and squeaked, and offered no communication. The cars, a combination of four-by-fours and two small buses, had grown closer

15

and as she had hurriedly scrambled down the scree, panic gripping her heart. They had known the path through the mines and that had terrified her. At the gates, gunfire had echoed and shouts had risen into the sky, reaching up to the mountains. She had lost her view for a bit as she had traversed the rocks, but as she had drawn closer she had heard the screams and the kestrel in the sky had swooped to attack.

In the forty minutes it had taken her to descend, the cars had driven off with their captives and left a trail of bloodshed and the surviving citizens locked inside the caves. Her fused fingers had fumbled with the locks and bolts, but as her people had flooded out of the caves, both fear and rage bubbling, she had searched desperately for her sons. Quinn, her oldest, had met her eyes with his own and the oily streaks of tears on his face revealed their loss. Levi, her youngest, had been abducted, along with twenty-four others, Ghabrie and her little sister, Nahria, amongst them.

Now, as she picked her way down the slope, the grief in her heart matched the kestrel's cry, high up in the sky. They both knew loss and its pain.

Xanthe found Alphaeus down at the dockside working on an engine, his hands thick with oil and dirt.

"Radding Hell!" he cursed beneath his breath and threw a spanner to the ground as she approached. It clinked and somersaulted, and Xanthe laughed.

"Excuse my language," Alphaeus spoke gruffly, but good-naturedly, and eased himself off his knees to his feet. He engulfed her in a bear hug and kissed her mussed up hair. "How about taking an old man away from all this?" he asked her.

She laughed again, the chuckle releasing her heightened tension. "Oh, Alph, you know I would if I could!"

"But not today ..." His laugh came from deep inside and rumbled, like an echo in the caves, and Xanthe smiled.

"Any news?" she asked.

Alphaeus glanced at the radio on the bench behind him and shook his head. "Not today."

"How long?" she asked. "How long will they be out there looking? It feels like I've lost everyone."

"Not everyone," replied Alphaeus, squeezing her hand. "I don't know. The only lead we had was Reilly, and he hawntched off with them. Always knew he couldn't be trusted." He leaned down to retrieve the spanner.

Xanthe's sigh caught the breeze and Alphaeus glanced at her. "They'll be back. Don't you worry. We've got our best out there searching."

"And Quinn," she whispered.

"He is one of our best!" he told her. "They've got Trent, Maddie – she'll never give up, you know – Petrov and Quinn... all the best, and with Krueger tracking, they'll find them. They've a whole army out there."

"And so have the Prometheans..." Xanthe's voice quivered. "And it's been three months, and there's trouble in the north..."

"I know." Alphaeus turned to stare across the noxious lake.

"What can we do?"

"We carry on, just as we have all these years. We carry on."

Xanthe shook her head.

"That bird still following you?" Alphaeus motioned towards the sky.

"Usually — he misses her — but an hour ago he bolted off across the desert, like a bullet shot from a gun."

"Can't believe it's still alive!" he grinned.

"He's pining. Like we all are. He wants Ghabrie back, just like I do, with Nahria, Levi and Quinn."

Xanthe shaded her eyes as she stared up at the sky, searching the clouds for the kestrel. Alphaeus crouched down to the engine and slid his hands inside its cogs. Another explosion echoed across the ocean of water and Xanthe jumped.

"What was that?" said Alphaeus, removing his hands and cocking his head.

"Another bomb or something…"

"No! Not that." He listened, pushing his steel-grey hair away from his ear. "That!" He raised his hand and pointed to the bench with urgency. "Pick it up, quick, Xanth!"

She followed his gaze and listened. The radio on the bench crackled and clicked. She grabbed it while Alphaeus wiped his grimy hands on his jeans. Voices buzzed and hissed, and Alphaeus held it to his ear. Xanthe leaned in close, trying to hear above the sound of the waves splashing the dock and the buzz of work going on in the yard.

Alphaeus held up his hand and the noise of the dock ceased. Expectant eyes gazed at their leader as they tried to determine his expression. His bushy whiskers and beard twitched, but betrayed none of what he heard crackling in his ear.

It was Xanthe's gasp that widened eyes as a familiar voice stuttered and sputtered. "Quinn!" she cried.

Alphaeus gestured for silence and a huge grin spread across his face. Xanthe held her breath and leaned as close as she could.

"We've got them!" The voice at the other end of the radio was triumphant and Xanthe's eyes filled with tears.

"They've got them!" she yelled, her own voice breaking with emotion. "They're coming home!"

A rapturous cheer rose throughout the yard and feet stamped in unison as Alphaeus raised his voice and responded with instructions. When he finally lowered the radio and grinned at Xanthe she threw her arms around him and kissed his furry cheek.

"Now, now, wait, young lady, and the rest of you — before you all go off celebrating — there's been a rescue, they found them, but, and it's a big but, there was a fight, a brawl, and not everyone made it out." Alphaeus paused as the yard sobered. "There've been injuries, on both sides, we didn't lose anyone, but not everyone got out."

"What d'you mean?" cried Xanthe, her cheeks pale beneath her ruddy blush. "Alph, what is it?"

"They still have some of our kids," his words were simple but effective. The crowd hushed. "Their information was right. They got there at the right time. Reilly switched sides when he knew we were onto him, but the snake held back. The ambush worked, but only half the group were being moved. Some weren't even there, and some got recaptured." He held up his hands as a man hurriedly approached with questions in his eyes. "Sorry, mate, couldn't tell you who's coming home, but we'll know soon enough."

As footsteps hurried away from the docks, spreading the news, Xanthe took her friend's hand. "Alph, what did he say? I heard Quinn…" she paused, "did he say anything? Did he…"

Alphaeus squeezed her hand again. "Levi's coming home with him." He kissed her forehead. "Both your sons are coming home."

Xanthe's tears slipped silently down her cheeks. Tears that encompassed both relief and guilt that she'd even asked the question. She could not stop herself. "Who else?"

Alphaeus shook his head and shrugged. "I don't know, I really don't know."

Xanthe returned to the mountainside in the hope of seeing their lost arrive home. She waited as the sky paled and the clouds began to brood tinged with pink. Spires of smoke still rose far across the lake as darkness began to invade and the glow of fire lit up the city beyond. She turned her attention west staring into the dusk as the orange blaze of sun gradually sank below the horizon. Some light still fell upon the mountain and Xanthe began to make her way down before it got too dark to see. Half way down a cry up in the sky made her stop, and her heart skipped. She stared into the gloomy twilight and a shadow circled above. Her ruined lip curled upwards and adrenalin surged. The bird cried again, this time delight echoed in his call and Xanthe nimbly bounded down the mountain.

The distant rumble of cars and bouncing grimy headlights, dirty and dusty, tugged at Xanthe's heart and she was soon at the foot of the crag. Excited voices and bobbing torches emerged from the vehicles and Xanthe watched as the crowd surged forward, everyone hoping to see a familiar face. Xanthe already knew her sons were coming home and the kestrel orbiting the compound told her Ghabrie accompanied them. She held back, listening to squeals of delight, tears of relief and cries of anguish, as the exhausted members of the rescue mission appeared.

The light faded, and flickering torches guided her forward as the throng dispersed. The injured were helped from the cars and her smile grew as Xanthe watched Quinn move efficiently through the remaining group. Her name echoed on the breeze and she spun round to see Levi leap to his feet as he saw her. Tears shone as he blinked and dashed across the dust into her arms. "I knew Quinn would come!" he cried, his voice breaking. "I knew it!"

Xanthe hugged him close, his hair tickling her nose and his cheek pressing hard against hers. She nodded, unable to speak, and loosed her own relief. The kestrel's wail interrupted their moment and Xanthe gazed over Levi's shoulder to Quinn. Her oldest son propped Ghabrie up as she stumbled towards Xanthe. Levi ducked away, and Xanthe stared at Ghabrie with horror.

"She was the oldest among us…" began Levi as if offering an answer. "They did more to her."

Ghabrie had always been slim, now she was emaciated and bruised – and alone. "Where's Nahria?" demanded Xanthe. "Where is she?"

Quinn shook his head and continued supporting Ghabrie.

Xanthe hurried forward and grabbed the girl's other arm, holding her tight as she and her son took Ghabrie home. She gazed over the girl's bruised forehead, ignoring the searing gash and the burns across her arms, and stared at Quinn. "Where is she?" she mouthed.

"We didn't get Nahria," he explained. "We almost didn't get Ghabrie. The fool fought us! She bit me! When they re-captured Nahria, Ghabrie fought like a mad dog, like a wild cat, and she almost got herself killed!"

Xanthe shook her head.

"We had to knock her out just to get her here!"

Xanthe brushed Ghabrie's hair from her face, gently stroking the cluster of bruises that decorated her cheek. "She's burning up…" She touched Ghabrie's forehead. "Get her back to the box."

The box was Xanthe's home, and the kestrel followed as they shuffled over the dusty ground, screaming as he swooped. Then as Ghabrie reclined on Xanthe's bed the bird perched outside and settled for the night.

As morning's sun filtered through the worn and torn canvas curtains, Ghabrie's kestrel whimpered outside the shipping container. He wandered up and down the roof, his talons tapping on the metal, singing a lament that Xanthe was sure would penetrate the girl's stupor. Ghabrie tossed and turned in a fitful sleep, and her adopted mother remained by her side.

Xanthe kept the sacking at the window closed, and small rays of sunshine shone through illuminating dancing spots on the walls. Levi and Quinn had stayed up late, talking through the Prometheans' experiments, until Levi had fallen asleep, his head on his mother's knee. Quinn had disappeared, only to arrive home in the early hours. After only a few hours of sleep, Quinn was gone again, and Xanthe knew Alphaeus had called the rescue band back together.

When Ghabrie finally stirred, the curtains lifted as her bird pushed through. He glided across the room to land on the blanket and sheets bunched up across Ghabrie's knees. Tears filled her eyes as she gently stroked her bird, her fingers caressing his soft feathers with the most delicate touch. Xanthe relaxed back and watched.

A deep, booming voice, as thick as gravel, resonated outside, and Xanthe glanced up at the open door. Quinn stepped inside, followed by Alphaeus. Ghabrie fiercely rubbed her eyes and her jaw set with grit. Xanthe watched the girl's fists tighten and her chest rise and fall with building ire.

"So glad to have you back, in more ways than one," began Alphaeus, with a cheery smile. "I've spoken to everyone, and I know how much you're revered." His voice softened. "You did much to shield the little ones, taking on responsibility and leadership. I salute you."

Xanthe glanced at Ghabrie, at her laboured breaths and the fury that glittered inside her dark eyes.

Alphaeus continued. "We'll never be able to thank you—"

"No, you won't!" Ghabrie's voice singed the air. She burned with anger. "You'll never be able to thank me enough."

The old man's brow furrowed. "We know what you did—"

"You'll never know what I did, or what I could have done!" She spat at him. "And what you've cost me."

"What we've cost you?" Confusion reigned in his eyes.

"Nahria!" Tears welled behind her rage. "You cost me my sister, all I have left! And I'll never forgive you."

"I'm so sorry…" began Quinn, stepping forward. "We tried—"

"Not hard enough!" she hissed.

"We're coming to the others — we've been talking, going over what happened," said Alphaeus. "We're sending the team out again."

Ghabrie shook her head and the kestrel shrieked. The bird's cry echoed throughout the metal house, and it rang in their ears. Ghabrie lifted her hands, and the bird leaped into the air sensing her wrath. He swept his wings back and forth and settled on a pile of crates behind the bed. Ghabrie pushed the bedclothes back and swung her legs out, placing her feet on the floor. She attempted to stand, but wobbled and landed back amongst the sheets. Her hands shook and tears slipped down her cheeks.

"It's too late," she whispered, "much too late."

Quinn stared at her, his eyes darting from the dirty girl to his mother, then to Alphaeus and back again. "But, Ghabrie—"

Vitriol poured from her voice. "Don't you Ghabrie me!" She hastily wiped the tears that welled. "Don't even speak to me! You all pulled me out of there like I was a sack of potatoes! With no thought for anyone else — you didn't even listen to me!"

"We had to get you out of there, all of you!" protested Quinn.

"But you didn't, did you? You didn't get all of us!" Ghabrie openly wept. "You left her there!" She gulped back the tears that clogged her throat. "You abandoned her, you made me abandon her! You… you don't know what'll happen to her now!"

"But, we're going back—"

"No, you're not, or even if you were, you won't find anything." Ghabrie paused. "Reilly's dead, you know that, and if they haven't already killed everyone you left behind, they'll be gone!"

"Gone?" Xanthe paled.

"They move, fast. The unit was set up with the ability to move. The Prometheans can close down in hours, shut down and destroy and be gone before you even knew they were there. They'll be gone." She crumpled upon the crinkled bedsheets. "They'll be gone and you'll never find them."

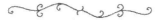

The rescue band left two days later to retrace their steps and save those they left behind. Ghabrie offered no support and only rancorous words. She rested, regaining strength, accompanied by both Xanthe and her kestrel.

The bird fussed, nuzzling and pushing and Ghabrie finally smiled behind her tears as she gently stroked his feathered head, feeling his fine feathers, soft and soothing beneath her fingers. Xanthe listened, standing in a flood of warm sunlight outside her shipping container home, as Ghabrie's grief rained down inside.

There was nothing she could say, her own anguish pooled within as much as Ghabrie's. Levi had joined Quinn and the band of saviours, and Xanthe was alone again. Only Ghabrie's sobs gave her reason to stay, reason to live, and the girl's sorrow matched her own.

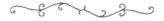

"Nothing helps." Ghabrie shook her head and winced. "Nothing helps at all."

Xanthe put her hand on the girl's arm and rubbed gently. "Try massaging your temples."

"I've tried that." She placed another citrusy feverfew leaf in her mouth baulking at the taste. "It's so bitter."

"That's why I've been putting the dried powder in your soup instead," said Xanthe.

"Well, it didn't help, which is why I'm trying the leaves." Ghabrie sighed and closed her eyes.

"Did you have the headaches before?" asked Xanthe, "With the Prometheans?"

"No. Well, not much," she replied. "We always had headaches with them." She touched the burns on her arm, and winced again at the pain that coursed through both her head and her mind. "It's not just pain…" she began.

"What is it?"

"Much more than that. My head feels like it'll explode, but then there are flashes and shocks that pulse through me." She paused and gazed at Xanthe. "And there's more…"

Xanthe nodded encouragement.

"I see things, shadows of things, shadows of people."

"Who?"

"Nahria."

"You see Nahria?" Xanthe's brow rose.

"I see shadows of Nahria…"

"I don't understand, what do you mean by shadows?"

"Just that, shadows. Blurry, dark, indistinct images of her." Ghabrie nuzzled the kestrel on her shoulder. "I see her."

"Where?" demanded Xanthe.

Ghabrie shook her head. "It's hazy, unclear and foggy," she tried to explain. "It's something they tried to give me."

"What d'you mean give you?"

"They tried to give me second sight." She picked at the blisters on her arm. "They *didn't* give me second sight, just this…" She indicated the healing blistered wounds. "These came from within, they touched me with nothing, but my skin bloomed with burning weals, and then came the headaches." She pounded the side of her head. "And they haven't stopped."

Ghabrie swept her hair back from her face and pulled it tight behind her head. She released a long sigh and Xanthe took the opportunity to lean in and hug her. The kestrel squeaked and hopped off Ghabrie's shoulder, swooping almost to the floor before fluttering and lifting up into the sky. Xanthe's open arms surprised Ghabrie and she let her hair drop to one side and relaxed into the hug. Their cheeks rested against each other and tears pricked Xanthe's eyes. A poorly healed tattoo peeped out from below Ghabrie's hairline. Still sore and scabby, the capital letters stood out in black ink 'HUMAN 76', and she shivered. Her thoughts raced and she wondered just what Ghabrie, Nahria, and the other children, including her own Levi, had actually been exposed to. Xanthe pulled away and gently traced the word and number with her fused fingers. Tears slipped down her cheek.

Ghabrie spoke softly. "I do see her, Xanth, she's there, on the peripheral of my vision." She sighed again. "I just don't know where."

"What do you see?" asked Xanthe softly.

"Shadows. Shadows and pain."

"How can you see pain?"

Ghabrie shrugged and bit her lip. "I don't know, but I can. I see purple, and purple is pain."

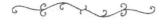

27

The mountain became Ghabrie's sanctuary. Xanthe watched the girl disappear in the early hours up into the dark mountain as the sun glanced over the horizon. The first time Ghabrie climbed out of the compound Xanthe followed, but the girl, lithe with her nimble feet, evaded Xanthe and vanished into the midday haze. The only clue that Ghabrie remained on the peak was the bird of prey that circled and sometimes descended into the swirls of mist. It was night, deep into the night, when Ghabrie returned. Xanthe opened a weary eye from her cotton pillow and watched the young woman slip into bed. The kestrel's claws scratched outside and the moon gazed through the partially drawn curtains. Xanthe let Ghabrie fall asleep. She did not sleep much herself. Her own mind whirled and buzzed with thoughts of relief, and anger, and care — until when she did finally wake again, as the midday sun rose high above the compound and mountain, Ghabrie was gone, once more.

After several days and barely a word from Ghabrie, a commotion arose on the outskirts of the shipyard. Xanthe left her work and hurried to the southern gates. Weaving through the mines a convoy wound its way. She hastily glanced back at the mountain, where a shadow hopped down the scree accompanied by a bird, and a continuous, excited call.

Xanthe watched the band of rescuers arrive back in town, but they came alone and with heavy hearts. Levi's eyes bled frustration, and Quinn's brow was even more furrowed than before. Words, almost whispered words, passed through the throng, before hesitantly, people left, their own hearts breaking again beneath the load of loss.

Ghabrie left dust in her wake as she reached the dissipating crowd. Her eyes beseeched Quinn and he met her with failure written in his own. He reached out, but she spun on her heels and was gone before he could apologise.

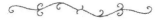

"I'm so sorry," Xanthe's words danced on the breeze as she climbed upon the bluff beside Ghabrie.

Ghabrie's knuckles were white and her lips sealed. She sat on a rock, the wind blowing through her purple and blue streaked hair. War paint smeared across her cheeks. Tears slipped silently down and Xanthe enveloped her in a hug. The girl was stiff and unyielding, but the woman held her tight and allowed the hiccupping gulps to escape. Ghabrie crumpled within her embrace and loosed her emotions. Her kestrel screamed with sorrow in the air and Ghabrie's loss consumed her.

An hour later, Ghabrie leaned close to Xanthe. Her body shuddered with the relief of emotions released and vanquished. "I see her." Ghabrie gripped Xanthe's hands within her own. "I see her, every day I see her."

Xanthe nodded.

"I know where she is," Ghabrie started, "but at the same time, I don't." She swept her hands out, encompassing the desert, stretching across the vista. "She's out there, somewhere, and I see her."

"Where, Ghabrie, where do you see her?"

Ghabrie shook her head. "That's the problem. I see it, I know it, but I don't recognise it. I don't know where…"

"If you can't tell, then…"

"Then there's nothing I can do?" Ghabrie turned to meet Xanthe's gaze. She shook her head. "Oh, but there is. You see, I promised I'd never leave her. I promised Nahria, I'd never leave her, and I did!" Tears glistened in her eyes like diamonds on water. "I promised her. And you know what? I'm not leaving her out there. This fog, this second sight, is clearing; slowly, but it is. And in time, I'll see clearly, I'll know where she is — and when I do, I'll be there, and I'll never leave her again."

"Then we'll raise an army, and in a while, when everyone's strong again, we'll go and search," offered Xanthe.

Ghabrie shook her head. "No, we won't. Nahria doesn't need an army — she needs me and I won't rest until I find her."

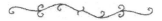

It was before the inky sky turned pink, when stars still dotted the night, that Xanthe woke to something that stirred deep within. She hurried outside with bare feet, and padded across the dust and earth. She followed a shadow to the compound gates.

At the gates she paused and watched as the shadow slipped past the guard, unseen, and moved beyond the safety of the shipping yard. The girl marched with determination, heavy boots on her feet. Her hips, clad in dark denim, swung with ease and her broad shoulders supported a rucksack laden with food and a bow slung across her back. Pistols rested, tucked into holsters against her thighs, and grenades hung clipped to her belt. Xanthe hoped that she carried the narrow dagger she had given her, and the advice she had shared.

With fear gripping her heart Xanthe wondered what on earth lay beyond those purple hills, until the sky lightened, and the stars faded, and Ghabrie was no more than a dot on the landscape.

"Follow your heart, Ghabrie, let it guide you."

In the distance, far, far away, a kestrel's cry echoed as dawn burst over the mountains and flooded the land with light.

FOLLOW THE LEADER

M S Manz

She huddled, whimpering in the corner of the small, bare room. Clutching her knees to her chest, she rocked back and forth to the rhythm of a tune only she could hear. But all the while she was listening, listening.

Listening for the approach of the footsteps that meant the hurting was about to start again.

She was starting to think she might not survive another session.

She was starting to think that might be for the best.

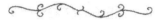

"… and I'm telling you I'm running out of patience. You promised me results. World-changing, earth-shattering results. And what do you give me? Cheap parlour tricks and 'a deeper understanding of the underlying principles at play'." Menace dripped like bile from the man's voice - a thin, dusty, whispery thing that was completely at odds with his solid physicality. "To hell with your underlying principles. To hell with your parlour tricks and, if I don't start seeing results, to hell with you, too."

She allowed the silence to stretch out uncomfortably, just long enough to throw off the rhythm of his anger. "Oh," she arched an eyebrow, "you've finished, then?"

She noted the rising flush crawling up his neck and allowed herself a derisive snort. "How quickly you forget. How truly short your memory must be. Have you grown so accustomed to the current state of affairs that you think things must always have been thus? Must I remind you? Your powers were so weak when I found you, your skill so non-existent, that you could barely control the three morons who were following you around at the time. Would you like to go back to that? The good old days before my 'parlour tricks' as you so flatteringly call them?"

She paused again, to let the implied threat sink in. When she continued it was more gently, in more conciliatory tones. "It hasn't yet been a full year since we began our little experiment here. How many souls now live within the compound? More than two hundred, isn't it? Is that not progress?" She smoothed down the front of her white lab coat, a relic from another age, and looked at him as though she was peeling off his skin in her mind, or possibly as though she had already done so and was now deciding what to do with him next. "Your natural abilities, such as they are, are a wild mutation and not something I've worked with before. Boosting them effectively without doing you permanent damage is a task that will require time, and patience, and experimentation." She smirked. "If you are in such a great hurry I supposed we could begin performing those experiments directly on you instead of the other test subjects? No? I thought not. Then let me work in peace and stop pestering me. The results you seek will come when they come. Now, if you'll excuse me, I have work to do. Subject 36 is almost due for another procedure, and the timing is important."

She turned and walked away from him, across the large, sparsely equipped laboratory to her desk, where she resumed her work on the notes she'd been writing when he'd stormed in moments ago. As she wrote, she kept one eye on him, in case he tried to do something foolish. He was not stupid. He knew how important she was to his plans. But he was also impulsive and often unpredictable, flying into a rage at the slightest provocation, real or imagined. She hoped she would not have to kill him. His abilities were subtle, and insidious, and more or less perfect for what she wanted. There had been more than one occasion when she had been very happy she had discovered how to make herself immune to mental powers.

After several moments standing in the doorway, he spoke. "You don't need to remind me of my humble beginnings, Doctor, but maybe I need to remind you who is the Leader here. I want results, and I'll have them. One way or the other, I'll have them." He turned and walked out of the room.

The doctor put down her pen and smiled. It was time for Subject 36 again, and that always cheered her up. She was pretty sure that she would learn nothing more from the little worm, but it was so much fun hurting her that she was in no hurry to move on to the next. She stood up and made her way past the polished concrete work surfaces towards the cells at the back of the lab. She had had some interesting new ideas yesterday, and she was looking forward to trying them out.

Ghabrie adjusted her position slightly where she lay in the long grass at the crest of a hill. It overlooked a walled settlement where she was hoping to do some trading, and it paid to be cautious. This far off the main routes the people could be a little … odd. They probably didn't get traders through very often, and might not react well to strangers. There was also a chance they would decide to just take what they wanted, and give nothing in return. If it went that way, there was a very good chance that what they wanted would also include Ghabrie herself. She was in a hurry - she was always in a hurry - but caution was sometimes necessary.

Like many settlements, the buildings themselves pre-dated the blast. She could not work out what the place had been used for in those distant days, but now it was set up for communal living. A handful of low, squat buildings were arranged overlooking a central space. There were paths between the buildings that might once have been paved, but were now overgrown with grass. The wall around the whole thing was a crudely built but effective-looking palisade made of sharpened logs, likely cut from the forest behind her.

The fence stood about twelve feet high in most places. The wall enclosed all the buildings, as well as a fairly large garden plot behind them. Some larger fields were being cultivated with cereal crops outside the wall, and there was a good-sized gate on that side to allow traffic to move back and forth. On the opposite side was a river in which a number of people were fishing with drag nets. Oddly, especially for a place as far out of the way as this one, the gate was guarded even during the day. Perhaps there were bandits in the area. She made a mental note to be more alert than usual once she moved on.

Speaking of alertness, perhaps she could get a better view of what was happening inside those walls. She quested out mentally, seeking her friend to get an aerial view, but he was still a ways off to the east. He had found himself a lady friend a few days ago and … well, she was sure he would catch up eventually, but for now she was on her own.

Okay, she had seen enough. The guards on the gate seemed slightly out of place, but it was not so terribly unusual and at least they seemed to be watching for intruders rather than escapees. That was reassuring. Most of the people she could see were going about domestic or agricultural tasks, and no one was obviously armed with anything other than farming implements. She would risk it, but again, cautiously. She would cache her trade goods in the trees, and come to fetch them if she made a deal.

She stood, dusted herself off, and began to make her way down the hill towards the settlement.

Ghabrie leaned against the logs of the palisade, and tried to control her impatience. She hated to be kept waiting, and she had been kept waiting a very long time. She was certain it was intentional. When she had arrived, she had been brought inside the gate by one of the guards while the other had run off, presumably to fetch someone higher up the food chain. The remaining man had not been willing to tell her anything other than Strangers could only talk to the Leader. She had been able to hear the capital letters.

She really did not care for the way the man kept looking her up and down and licking his lips.

From the hilltop she had noticed that the people here were all dressed in similar fashion; the men in simple trousers and tunics, the women in plain dresses, all of the clothing made from undyed cloth. As she watched people pass through the gate, she realized the clothes were not just similar in fashion, they were identical. All made from the same cloth, all unadorned. And the high-necked garments of the women were more like robes than dresses. There were very few children visible, and the ones she could see were dressed like the adults. Ghabrie's clothing must seem very strange to the gate guard. Perhaps that was what he was staring at.

Finally, a small group of people approached from further inside the compound. She hoped to whatever gods there were that this was the oh-so-mighty Leader, and that she was done waiting. She had her arms crossed over her chest and one leg bent so that her foot was also pressed against the wall. It was a position that looked relaxed and nonthreatening. Looks were deceptive. They wanted to play head games, she could play too.

The group of identically-dressed people walked up in a circular ... formation was the only word she could think of. In formation. When they were about ten yards away they stopped, as if at a signal she could not hear. They parted to reveal a heavy set, ugly man. He was broad across the shoulders and heavily muscled. His face was made up of a number of seemingly mis-matched features whose only unifying characteristic was a crude heaviness. Thick, rubbery lips seemed to support a fat, oft-broken nose, and the sloping brow was sheltered by a single, coal-black eyebrow that stretched from temple to temple. The man's hair, by contrast, was purest white, and stood out in shocks and patches.

The man's face broke out in the greasiest smile she had ever seen on another human being. "Well! What do we have here? Another lost soul come to join our little Community?"

"You must be the leader I've heard so much about," she smiled. "I'm afraid I'm only here to do some trading, if you're willing. I'm not looking to settle down quite yet. I'm on a journey and still have a long way to go." As she was speaking, his gaze fixed upon her forehead and he squinted in an unsettling way.

"A journey! Unthinkable! A young, defenseless girl such as you, traveling the wilderness alone?" She began to hear a buzzing noise, but could not tell what caused it. "No, no, no. You simply must stay with us. You'll like it here, I'm sure of it." And with that, the man started to turn away as if the matter had been decided.

"Again, thank you, but no. I'd really just like to trade and be on my way. I have some carved stones and some feathers suitable for jewelry. Or," she remembered that she had not seen a single decorative item of clothing or piece of jewelry here, "if jewelry isn't your thing, I saw evidence of deer in the woods. I'd be happy to trade most of a deer for some dried goods. Beans or corn ... or even better, flour if you have it."

The man had frozen when she had spoken, and a strange series of expressions had crossed his face so quickly she would have missed them had she blinked. Surprise, anger, puzzlement, curiosity - all in a flash. Then, just as quickly, the smile was back. "Well, perhaps. Perhaps ... we might be able to arrange a trade of some kind. As you seem to have noticed, we are not really 'jewelry people' here," the smile got bigger, "but we could certainly always find a use for venison. I have some other business to attend to right now; but perhaps we could discuss it over the evening meal?"

"My thanks once again, for your kind offer, but I'd really rather not have to travel by night." *And I really want to get some distance between us before I go to sleep,* she thought. "Is there anyone else I could talk to about trade terms?" The buzzing was back now, louder, but still with no discernible source.

"I'm afraid not, no. As Leader, trading for the betterment of the Community is one of my many duties. If staying for the evening meal will force you to travel by night, young lady, the solution is simple. Why not stay the night with us? I'm sure space can be found for you in the women's dormitory."

"Really, you are too kind, but I haven't--" she broke off as her head was filled with a wordless scream that almost drove her to her knees. It had a bilious green and yellow feel, shot through with bolts of purple.

"Miss, are you alright?"

"You didn't ... no, I guess not."

The scream had been mental; it had happened inside her head, and it seemed that no one else had heard it. No one had reacted, anyway, and they certainly would have. The voice in her head had been young, and female, and had carried with it an unimaginable amount of fear and pain. Unimaginable to someone who was not Ghabrie, that is.

"Actually, maybe I will take you up on your hospitality. It's been a long few days of travel and a day's rest might do me good. Also, if I'm going to trade venison, I should probably go and get myself a deer." She exchanged a few more empty pleasantries with the man, who had thankfully stopped squinting at her, and then made her way back through the gate with a promise to return before sundown for the evening meal. She intended to track down the source of that scream. She was all too familiar with the way that scream had felt. At least that annoying buzzing had stopped.

There were a number of things that bothered Ghabrie about the evening meal that night. The first thing was the long, tedious prayer that the Leader had intoned before anyone could eat. She was all for spirituality, and had nothing against people having some sort of religion if it made them happy, but this was something else. The prayer - more of a sermon, really - had been a meandering, self-congratulatory thing. It had taken her several minutes of listening to the monotonous droning of the Leader before she had realized that the prayer was not even addressed to a deity, but rather to the Leader himself.

He was trying to set himself up as a god, and these people all seemed to be buying into it.

Another thing that had bothered her, once the food had finally been served, was the huge difference in quality and quantity between the fare at the Leader's table and that being served at the other tables in the dining hall. It was awkward enough that the Leader's table was placed on a raised platform at the end of the room, but she felt acutely embarrassed at being offered salvers of roasted meats and fish, several different vegetables prepared in a number of ways, as well as soup and fresh bread, when what was being placed on the other tables was mostly bowls of thin porridge and little else.

When she asked about the disparity the Leader had chuckled. "Spiritual Growth through denial of the flesh. At the beginning of the Journey towards Enlightenment, a Brother or Sister has far to go, and so needs to deny the Pleasures of the Flesh as much as possible. As progress is made, the less dangerous the Pleasures become, and the more freely a Brother or Sister may partake without fear of falling into sin. It makes perfect sense, don't you think?"

Ghabrie decided to keep her thoughts to herself, and only smiled. She noticed someone entering the dining hall. The person seemed absorbed by a book, and was weaving slowly and absentmindedly between the diners towards the Leader's table. Something about her made Ghabrie's skin crawl. Whoever it was, she was dressed differently from the others as well, in a white garment that was almost blinding in comparison to the standard clothing. The smile froze on Ghabrie's face, then turned sickly as the woman got close enough for her to make out her features clearly.

Her! Blast! Blast, blast, blast! Well, she thought grimly, *that explains the screaming, earlier.*

At that moment, the newcomer looked up from her notebook and their eyes met. She froze in mid-step and swallowed convulsively. Without shifting her gaze in the slightest, she said in a quiet, but commanding voice, "Leader … might I have a word in private?"

The Leader put down his utensils, the only metal cutlery in the room that Ghabrie could see, and shifted his chair back from the table. "Of course, my child, of course. Whatever can be the matter?" The Leader walked smoothly over to where the woman was standing and turned her, putting his arm across her shoulders and guiding her several steps off to the side. They spoke for several minutes, their conversation punctuated by animated gestures on both sides, and with several very obvious gestures in Ghabrie's direction. Strangely, no one at any of the nearby tables paid them the slightest attention.

After several emphatic gestures and some obviously angry words, the woman shot Ghabrie one more venomous look and stalked off towards the door she had so recently entered. The Leader walked sedately back to the table and sat down again.

"No trouble, I hope." Ghabrie commented.

"Oh no, nothing serious." came the reply. "The Doctor was just conveying the results of some research she's been performing into … crop yields. She would normally have joined us, but she's not feeling herself this evening and has gone back to her quarters to rest."

"I understand completely. I'm feeling a bit restless myself, to be honest." She thought quickly. With the 'Doctor' here, she knew there would be a fight, and soon, but she wanted to control the choice of battleground as much as possible. "In fact, I think I may have to change my mind about imposing on you for the night. If it's all the same to you, I think I'll leave after the meal and see if I can't cover some ground tonight. I feel so rested and refreshed by your hospitality that I don't think I could bear not to be traveling this evening." Not the most convincing yarn she had ever spun, but judging by the relief on his face, the Leader was more than happy to go along with it.

"Of course, of course. For someone accustomed to traveling and sleeping out of doors, you must feel quite penned up inside. After we eat we'll collect your goods and I'll personally see you on your way." She breathed an internal sigh of relief, while trying not to let her feelings show on her face. She'd been worried that he would put up resistance and that getting out of the settlement would be difficult, or maybe impossible. If they weren't going to prevent her leaving … well, she was pretty sure she knew what they had in mind, and she could certainly use it to her advantage.

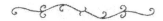

She noticed them following her almost immediately. Two of them, both men, both hopeless at tracking. It helped that she was expecting them, counting on them actually, but they really did not know how to move quietly through this sort of terrain. She probably would have heard them a mile off even if she had not been watching for them. It was all she could do to leave a trail they could follow without actually painting crude signs on the trees saying "This Way to the Gurl".

A small part of her was insulted that they had sent such incompetents after her, but for the most part she was relieved. It looked like this was going to be much, much easier than she had expected. Than it could have been.

Time to get to work.

He didn't like this.

It wasn't following the girl that bothered him, or the killing and so forth. He sure wasn't upset about getting first pick at the girl's stuff - he liked all that just fine. What he didn't like was being out in the woods at night like this. It was spooky, and he felt exposed. Like he was being watched.

"Jeb," he whispered loudly.

"Yeah, Ross. What?" came the hoarse response.

"Nothin', just makin' sure you're there. These trees are givin' me the creepies."

This wasn't the same as gate duty at all, and he felt out of his depth. They had spread out a bit, just out of sight of each other, to make sure the trail did not break off unexpectedly. The moon was full and bright, but it was cloudy and at the moment not a lot of light was making it to the ground between the trees.

"Pshaw! You're such a sheep. Scared of your own shadow. The only thing dangerous out here tonight is us!"

"I don't know, Jeb. Something don't feel right."

A snort of laughter came from slightly behind and to his right. "I'll tell you what's going to feel right. Once we catch up to that stranger girl …"

Ross waited for Jeb to continue, but heard nothing, not even the insects that had been chirruping only moments before. "Jeb? Jeb? You there? Aw, not funny Jeb. Come on." He turned and started walking towards where he'd last heard his partner's voice, using his arm to shield his face against branches he couldn't see. "Son of a ... come on, Jeb, this ain't ..."

The moon came out from behind the clouds, just in time to illuminate Jeb's body, spread-eagled and twitching in the darkly glistening pool of blood that was still pumping lethargically from his neatly slit throat. He felt a line of cold fire along his neck, just below his Adam's apple, and froze.

Nothing happened, nothing moved, nothing breathed for what seemed like a lifetime. He could hear a thin, high-pitched keening sound and realized he was making the sound himself. He managed to stop, and then pulled himself together enough to ask in a shaky approximation of his normal voice, "Who ... whoever you are p ... please don't kill m ... me."

"Whoever I am?" answered a female voice, "How many people do you think there are running around this forest in the middle of the night? I'm the stranger girl you were just planning to 'feel', you sicko creep."

He licked his lips. "Oh, not me miss," he stammered. "That was Jeb what said that. I'd never do anything like that."

"Well Jeb's already dead, so I guess there's no one here to vouch for your good character, is there?"

"Are you going to kill me, too, miss?"

"Yes. Yes, I am. But first you're going to answer some questions."

"I don't know anything, I swear!"

"Then I guess we can just skip the questions and go right on to---"

"Wait!" he interrupted, "I mean, umm, maybe I do know some stuff. Maybe. But how about we make a deal? How about I tell you what you want to know if you promise to let me go and not kill me. Okay?" The edge of the knife pressed harder against his skin. "I mean, why should I tell you anything if you're just going to kill me anyway?"

"You'll tell me what I want to know because there are so very many ways for a man to die, friend, and some of them hurt a lot more than the others. Take longer, too. Now, how many ways are there into and out of the compound?"

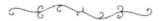

She paused to catch her breath, crouching in the darkness at the base of the palisade wall. At this point there were only a few yards between the wall and the river. This was where the man had told her she would find the secret entrance, the one that would take her directly underground and into the doctor's lair. He had used it sometimes to haul out what was left of the doctor's 'experiments' when she was done with them to dump them in the river. Sometimes they'd even been dead already.

Her questioning of the man had given her more information than she had wanted. Once he had started talking it had been as if a dam had burst, as though he had needed to unburden himself, and so he had. She had originally been planning to leave him bound in the woods until after … whatever was going to happen tonight, but the man had been a moral sinkhole, and had been responsible for any number of horrible and unforgivable deeds. In the end he had been so full of remorse that he had begged her to kill him, and by then she had been happy to oblige. She regretted it a little in hindsight.

But only a little.

Okay. To business. There was a young girl locked up in a basement cell, or had been as of this morning. Ghabrie needed to make sure she was still alive and, if she was, see what sort of condition she was in. Realistically, she wanted to ghost in and ghost out without the good 'doctor' ever knowing she had been there. Mostly she wanted that. A small part of her - the revenge fantasy part - wanted something else, but mostly she just wanted a clean rescue.

She sat down, cross-legged, with her back against the wall, and tried to slow her breathing and calm her mind. She had never done anything like this before, and had no idea if it would work, but it was worth a shot. She felt her pulse slow in response to her deep, even breaths and *reached* out with her mind, searching for the source of the scream that had hit her earlier in the day.

It was difficult; the mental equivalent of walking upstream while waist-deep in a slow-moving river. She had the impression of many minds around her, but they were muted and vague. None of them were the one she was looking for, of that she was certain. And then, suddenly, the girl was there, and Ghabrie felt fear. The power of the girl's mind was staggering.

Ghabrie wasn't exactly a weakling in the mental department. She could always feel her sister, of course, somewhere in the vague distance. If she concentrated she could touch the mind of her feathered friend, wherever he was at the time. And she could feel the surface thoughts and the motives of people who were physically close to her, well enough to tell if they were dealing honestly while bartering, for example. More than well enough to feel the need to bathe while interrogating murdering rapists in the dark forest at night.

At the moment she felt like a pampered house cat who had just been caught marking a tiger's territory.

46

And then she felt the nature of the mind behind the power and realized the girl posed no danger, either to Ghabrie or to anyone else. She was broken, her mind shattered and her sense of self destroyed. This girl had enough strength to destroy Ghabrie's mind on a whim, but she lacked any sense of focus or determination. Ghabrie would have to try and do something about that, or this rescue mission was unlikely to end well.

Well hello there, Sunshine. Having a good time, are you? Enjoying it there in your nice, damp cell?

wha … what? who? who are … you?

I was planning on helping you get out of there, but I'm starting to think you'd rather stay. Why else would you still be in there?

h … elp me please help me.

I'd be happy to help you, but I can't do everything myself. You're going to have to help, too.

nothing I … can do

Well now, that's just not true. There's lots you can do if you want to.

you don't … know … what she's like … too much

That's where you're wrong, kiddo. I do know. I've been through the same things and I came out the other side. So can you.

liar ! not true not true you're not real not … no one …

You know what you can do. I know you know. You can get out of there whenever you want.

can't use the power … it's evil … leader says … evil

*Power is power, my dear. It has no morality. What you do with it can be good or evil, but the power itself is neither. And hey, it's a part of you. If it's evil, that means you're evil, and you know you are not evil. I'll do what **I** can to help you get out of there, but if you don't do what **you** can, we're probably both going to die. Your call.*

… cant …

Ghabrie felt the contact fade as the girl's mind slipped away. Either she had lost consciousness, which was pretty likely by the feel of her, or maybe she had just lost track of the conversation and mentally wandered off. Either way, and whatever happened, Ghabrie would have to try.

She had thrown out any idea of avoiding a fight as soon as she had touched the girl's mind, though. Time and living had blunted the edge of her memories, and this had brought them back into sharp focus. She could not, in good conscience, allow that monster to continue to draw breath, could not allow her to do this to another human being.

It was time to face the demons of her past.

Even though she knew where it was and what to look for, finding the secret door had been the hard part. It was very well hidden. Once she had found it, though, she had discovered a flight of steps down and a straight, well-lit hall with no turnings; now she found herself beside the doorway that opened onto the doctor's latest laboratory. The bitch was in there now. Ghabrie could hear the scratching of a pen's nib on that blast-damned notebook of hers. She'd hated and feared that notebook. All the worst things had come from its pages.

"I know you're there, H76. You may as well come in."

She glanced back down the long, sterile corridor and realized just how foolish she had been. She could not see any cameras, but that did not mean they were not there. She could not see any poison gas jets or nozzles or dart-firing apertures either, but there was a steady, even source of electric for the lights, so … she would have to bluff and hope the few cards she had up her sleeve would be enough.

She stepped through the doorway, striving to appear calm and relaxed. "Dr. Stein. I can't say I'm pleased to see you, though perhaps I should be."

"So, you do remember me. So many of the H series block things out. A pity, really. It's important to know from whence you come."

"Of course I remember you. I remember everything. But don't expect me to fear you. I removed the last traces of you from my head long ago. You have no power over me any more." She was not idle while she was talking; she was also mentally mapping out the room. The doctor sat at a pristine chrome and steel desk. Her back was to the wall at the far side of the room. It was a large, squarish room, probably fifty yards to a side, with a high ceiling from which dangled various lengths of chain, wire and other, less pleasant, devices. To Ghabrie's right were several low lab benches littered with pieces of glassware and unusual looking flasks and vials. To her left was a wall-to-wall collection of ceiling high shelves holding assorted taxidermied animals, bones, skulls, rock samples, and more books than Ghabrie had ever seen in one place. Possibly more than she had ever seen, period. She would wager that the door to the cells would be on the other side of those shelves somewhere.

"Well, I'm certainly glad to see you, H76. It seems as though we have some unfinished business. I'm certain I'll be able to learn a lot from studying you, this long after your … development. Yes indeed, I'm already getting ideas for some wonderful new experiments."

"It's Ghabrie, actually."

"Sorry, what?"

"It's Ghabrie, not H76. My name is Ghabrie. And I'm afraid you won't have any time for experiments. You'll be too busy being dead."

"Oh, I don't think so, H76. I really don't—"

"Let me tell you how this is going to go down," she interrupted. "You're going to talk for a bit longer, trying to find some weakness in me. You won't find it, and so you'll attack me. In an underhanded fashion, no doubt. When that fails you'll panic and try to run, but you can't run from me. You aren't nearly good enough to run from me. You'll end up cornered and terrified. You'll try to hide it, but I know you at least as well as you know me and I'll see right through your bluster and bravado. Then ... well, then I'll kill you. More cleanly than you deserve, and more quickly, but you'll be dead and that's good enough for me."

The doctor laughed, and the laughter seemed genuine. "Oh ... oh my, you really should be on a stage somewhere." She wiped a tear from the corner of her eye. "I know your capabilities, my dear, down to the finest detail. Better than you do yourself, I would imagine. You haven't the slightest shred of precognitive ability, and yet you almost convinced me that you somehow knew what you were talking about." She walked around to stand in front of her desk. "And no, you don't know me nearly as well as I know you. You really have no idea what motivates me. No idea of the years of effort and toil that I have put into this great work of which you are only a very small part. You, my dear, are nothing but a very small piece of a very large, very complex machine - a machine that I helped build." She took two leisurely steps toward Ghabrie. "A machine that I am still building. That is necessary for the future of all humankind." She took another step, and the secretive smile on her lips took on a triumphant cast. "And oh, how Sisyphus suffered ..."

Ghabrie chuckled.

"I said," she raised her voice, "Oh, how Sisyphus suffered!"

Ghabrie took a step of her own, towards the doctor. "I heard you." They were now no more than twenty yards from each other, and Ghabrie was wearing a smile of her own. "I told you, you're not in my head any more. I rooted every last trace of you out of there - physical and mental. Your post-hypnotic control phrases, your programmed behaviors. That little explosive device behind my ear." She tilted her head to show the doctor the star-shaped scar nestled just behind her ear. "That one hurt, I don't mind admitting." She took another step, and was pleased to see the doctor take a half-step back. "You have no holds on me, now. You can't control me." Another step. And another. "You were right about one thing, though, I don't read the future." Her eyes flashed. "I make the future."

She charged, but had only managed to take three running steps by the time the other woman had pulled something out of her coat pocket and pointed it at her. She twisted and dove to her left, towards the bookshelves and, she hoped, the holding cells. Even though she had been expecting something of the sort, she narrowly missed being stuck by a bolt of something that moved too quickly for the eye to follow. An energy weapon.

She rolled, and managed to pull herself around the corner of a shelving unit just as another bolt of the stuff struck where she had just been. Paper pages and leather bindings exploded with a roar. She peered between a stack of books and the preserved skull of some sort of herbivore. The doctor was advancing slowly, her weapon extended in front of her. It was a thin metallic rod, as long as her forearm, and wrapped in leather at the end where she was holding it. The business end of the thing emitted an evil, humming sound, and was crackling and spitting with a purple energy. *Purple is pain ... purple is ...*

Ghabrie retreated as far down the row as she could, to the place where the aisle doubled back the way she had come. It was as she had suspected - a long zig-zag the whole length of the room. Not that it helped her any more. That weapon the doctor had was a game changer. A game ender.

As if summoned by the thought, the doctor stepped slowly around the edge of the shelves, kicking the still smoldering remains of a book out of her way. She stood at the entrance to the bookshelf maze, and pointed the rod at Ghabrie once again. Thirty yards, Ghabrie thought, give or take an inch. The doctor spoke. "You make the future, do you? I have to say you're doing a rather poor job of it so far. Perhaps you'd better leave it to the--".

There was a sudden crash from the main room, and an enraged bellow, "DAMN YOU, DOCTOR!"

The doctor's head flicked momentarily towards the noise, and Ghabrie's arm swept forward in a blur. The doctor snapped her attention back to Ghabrie, just in time to catch the thrown knife in her left eye. The metal rod clattered to the floor, and the doctor stood swaying in place for a moment, having just enough awareness left to register surprise, before collapsing in a heap.

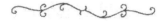

There was a rush of footsteps, then he was standing there, in the doctor's place. The Leader. Ghabrie cursed under her breath. She had only had the one knife, and it had been an incredibly lucky shot, anyway.

The man stood, staring down at Stein's body and panting like an enraged bull. He slowly turned his head to look at Ghabrie, his rage a palpable thing. "You!" he said, "You killed my men!" He glanced down at the doctor again, and then back at Ghabrie. "You killed my Doctor!" He turned to face her fully, still panting. "I still needed her. I still needed her and now she's dead." Something approaching sanity was starting to return to his eyes, "You'll pay for that, little girl. You'll pay dearly."

He stepped over the doctor and squinted at Ghabrie, the way he had done when he had first met her, and she once again heard the annoying humming sound. He must have some mental power; something that let him control people. She was not overly concerned. There had been many mentally capable people in the Promethean facility; none of them had ever been able to breach her defences, and not for want of trying. Mental abilities or no, the man was still big. Much, much bigger than Ghabrie. If he knew anything at all about combat, she would not stand a chance in an even fight.

She ran.

Back and forth between the shelves, away from the thundering footsteps behind her, trying to think of something, some trick or stratagem that would work against a man twice her size. She came to the end of the shelves all too quickly, into an open space between the shelving and the wall of the room. She turned right as she emerged from the shelves, went a few paces further, then turned to face her opponent. Chance or no chance, she would fight like a demon until the end.

The man came out from the shelves and stopped dead. He caught sight of Ghabrie, standing defiantly, hands up to fight, but instead of attacking her he turned to his left and ran towards the other side of the room, where there was a long table littered with various objects and equipment. Ghabrie chased after him, to stop him from getting his hands on another powerful weapon like the doctor's, but she was too late.

He reached the table and, with both hands, picked up what looked like a large bucket covered in coils of wire, and with metal spikes protruding at odd angles. She stopped, and got ready to dodge or run. He turned back towards her and lifted the bucket above his head. He lowered it over his head and pulled it down over his ears like a helmet. He turned a dial on the side and the annoying buzzing sound became a roar which built until she thought her head would explode. She staggered backwards, screaming and clutching at her temples.

The man turned the dial again. And again. And then the pain stopped. Now, though, she was filled with a turmoil of emotions. Fear, despair, self-loathing; every negative thought and feeling she had ever had returned, but a thousand times stronger. She sank slowly to her knees, no longer possessed of the will to move, or fight, or live.

The man's voice filled the space, "Poor child. It was always hopeless. You never stood a chance. You know it's true. How could one such as you ever stand against one such as me?" A small part of her recognized what was happening, knew that the things she was feeling were being imposed from outside, but that part of her was powerless to act, and the knowing in no way changed the way she felt. She wanted to kill herself, to disappear from the earth, to stop existing.

"It's not your fault, though." Now the emotional storm in her head took on a new harmonic, there was now a thread of hope in the vortex of despair that threatened to swallow her. The man took a step towards her and she scuttled backwards on her palms and heels. "Not your fault. You were misled. You shouldn't have been expected to know what to do, shouldn't have had to make your own decisions."

The urge to surrender, to give over her volition to the man in front of her, grew slowly, insidiously. But here, at last, was something which that small part of her could push against, could resist. The very idea of surrender was so contrary to Ghabrie's nature that even without volition her mind rejected it. The thread of suggestion snapped, and the man staggered back a step as if he had been struck.

"Too proud to bend, are you? Too sinful to submit?" He loomed over her now where she lay on the ground, pressed up against the wall beside the door she had been trying to reach in the first place. "Then you are no use to me." He closed his eyes and put a hand on either side of the helmet. Wave after wave of emotion poured from him, fear to grief to anger to self-loathing and back to fear again. She struggled against it, but she could feel her mind dissolving under the onslaught.

ENOUGH!

The mental shout was loud enough to make her teeth rattle as it cut easily through the tangled mass of the emotional assault.

IT ENDS NOW!

The door next to Ghabrie began to rattle in its frame, gently at first, but with increasing strength. She heard the squeal of metal on metal as first one, then the other hinge, pulled itself out of the steel door. The door shot away from the wall so fast that Ghabrie was tossed to the side by the wind of its passing. The door smashed into the man, who did not even have time to scream let alone get out of the way, and carried him through all of the bookshelves, and across the room beyond them, before smashing him into the far wall. The silence, both in the room and in Ghabrie's head, was deafening.

Ghabrie looked up at the doorway to see a girl step through. She thought it was a girl, although she was so covered in cuts and burns that it was hard to tell. She was wearing the tattered remains of a white robe, and both the shreds of her garment and what remained of her hair were writhing in the air, as if of their own volition. The girl looked down at Ghabrie where she lay, and smiled sadly.

HE'S GONE NOW. HE CAN'T HURT US ANY MORE.

"How ... how could you stand it?" Ghabrie managed.

THE HELMET? I ALWAYS FEEL THAT WAY. YOU GET USED TO IT.

With that, the young girl staggered and fell. Ghabrie rolled and somehow managed to get in between the girl and the ground, and then darkness swept in and claimed her.

"What is wrong with you people? The man who controlled your minds hasn't been dead three days and already you're looking to replace him? You know nothing about me except that we shared an enemy. I could be worse than he was for all you know." Ghabrie shook her head in disbelief. After taking a couple of days to recover from her ordeal, she had been getting ready to leave when three of the Community inhabitants - two men and a woman - had timidly approached her with the idea that she should take over as Leader.

"If you would look to someone for leadership, look to yourselves. Tell yourselves what to do, tell yourselves what is right and what is wrong. Or don't. Either way I will not accept responsibility for your lives. Besides," she laughed, "I wouldn't accept as a follower anyone who would have me as their leader."

She hoisted her pack up onto her shoulders, shifted it slightly to get the balance right, and started walking. But she headed away from the gate, not toward it. Instead, she headed toward the women's dormitory. To say goodbye.

The girl was sitting in a small, wooden chair; was tied to it in fact. Her face was slack and motionless and her eyes, though open, saw nothing. Ghabrie had assured the others that the girl was still in there somewhere, that she was not brain dead and that she would come back to them when she was ready. She had charged them with taking care of the girl's body until such time as her mind could mend.

Ghabrie placed her pack on the ground in front of her and rummaged through the contents. A parcel of trail bread, some leather tie-offs, a well-crafted flint and steel striker set, a … what was that? Oh yes, that thing. A lackey of the Leader had brought it to her "with the great man's compliments". A thin flat stone held by an ugly, lumpy frame. The lackey had called it a 'skystone', and had explained that it was able to track the position of the sun through the densest of cloud cover. Useful, if it worked. If not, she could always trade it.

Ah! There, underneath it was the thing she'd been looking for. It was a small wooden box which held a kestrel primary feather with the quill wrapped in delicate braided cord.

She took the feather and placed it in between the Thirty-Six's slack fingers. Then she leaned forward, closing her eyes and gently pressing her forehead against the other girl's. Silence, as before, but not an empty silence. A waiting silence. A listening silence.

I know you're in there, and I know you can hear me. These people will take care of you until you're ready to come back, but I have to go. There's someone else who needs me more than you do. Thank you. Thank you for saving me. If you discover later on that you don't have a place here, come and find me. Where I am, there will always be a place for you.

You could never be completely free of your past, but you could certainly decide how much it affected your future. As she straightened and turned towards the gate, her stride lengthening into the distance-eating pace familiar to those who travel long distances, she smiled. Her future was waiting to be made.

WHERE THE WILD THINGS ARE

Nick Johns

I was looking around for signs of pursuing Blasters when I felt Jake die.

Pounding back up the hill I knew it was my fault. I had left him there with orders to protect Laura. He had wanted to go with me like always, but I had ordered him to stay.

And what about Laura?

RAGE, snarls. PAIN! charging, closing the distance, teeth bared and leaping.

I drove my burning lungs and knotting calves to further feats of screaming effort. If Jake had died, then she must be in trouble too.

Snarl, teeth snap, taste of blood.

And I had seen the girl, bending close to him. Then nothing.

Just hold on. I'm coming.

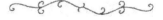

Tears washed dirt from my face even as my shovel heaped concealing earth on hers. I had seen the girl approach Laura, through Jake's eyes.

Stranger! Protect!

As Laura disappeared beneath the soil, my back creaked and ached and my arms became as heavy as my heart, but still I shovelled.

They had seemed easy with each other. Jake had scented no fear from Laura – until just before he died. If only I had not gone off to trace the other sounds we had heard, I would have been here with her. The girl must have turned on her. But how?

There must be some Blaster tech about her. Laura was the best of us; she couldn't be killed in a straight fight. It was Laura's gift. At the height of the assault, male and female Blasters had stopped in front of her, like they were asleep or something. I had chopped three of them myself as they stood there.

How had the girl done it?

Pausing only when the fresh-dug, damp soil hid Laura from my sight, I turned to add another body to the hole. The cause of the screaming silence in my mind.

I lowered Jake's body in on top of hers; defending her in death, as he had in life. I had not plucked the arrows from his chest as I had from hers. I lacked the energy to perform the same task twice. The shafts had gone deep into him. She must have fired from point blank range. Why did I not see her through him?

Our last link, before he saw the girl bending close, had been confused.

Stranger! Protect!

I'd felt his charge, teeth bared and leaping. But no image of who he was attacking. If the Blasters had found a way to overcome our strongest Talents, we were in real trouble.

He must have got close. I had pulled a swatch of ripped, bloodstained green and brown mottled felt from between his lifeless teeth. I tucked the fragment under my belt and took up the shovel once more. Soon, the brown of the earth mingled with the brown of his fur and he too disappeared from my view.

His absence within me ached, like a phantom limb itching. I would find this girl. If she was working with the Blasters, she must die.

I hammered the back of the shovel against the small mound: great overhead swings flattening the earth, venting my remaining anger and frustration. My knees hit the grass at the fringe of the hole and I toppled forward, face pressed to the earth, breathing in its loamy, decaying scent with ragged, gasping breaths.

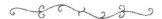

The faint rustle of the bushes half roused me, but I was unconcerned. Jake would know if there was anything for me to investigate.

Jake! Laura!

I jack-knifed to a sitting position and, fumbling for clarity, sought the cause of the sound. Like footsteps, stealthy and cautious, but not. I peered into the gloom, holding my breath and listening hard, struggling to hear above the blood pounding and singing in my ears. I closed my eyes and extended my Sense. I could only feel the faint, skittish thoughts of a few birds, high above me. I was forced to rely on mundane senses.

There! The sound I had heard before. A shuffle.

The sounds were moving away down towards the river and I rolled to my knees. I started in the direction that I had heard the movement receding, pausing only to sweep up my pack and long knife from where I had dropped them when I'd first seen Laura and Jake's lifeless bodies.

If I moved fast enough, I knew that whoever had crossed my path would be visible at the water meadow as they approached the water line. I raced, heedless of branches whipping my face and hands bloody, and brambles that tried to trip and snag me as I crashed through the woods. Sure enough, as I burst from the last of the trees, I could see a figure, moving fast towards the river bank. It was not easy to discern, clothing blending with the earth and grass. But the unmistakable shape of an unstrung bow hung loosely from one hand.

I reached out with my Sense. Stupid! I've never been able to Sense people. Laura did people.

I charged through the thinning undergrowth and careered down the slope towards Laura's killer, fighting to keep my legs under me as my momentum increased my speed to a headlong sprint. Belatedly measuring the closing distance between us, I recognised that the outcome of the race between my arrival and the intruder re-stringing the bow and firing was too close to call.

"Murderer!"

My screams caused her head to turn sharply. I was closer. The girl turned fully and I saw that I was second favourite in a contest that would leave only one winner alive. Betrayed by treacherously wet grass I slid, recovered my flailing balance, then tripped, crashing head first to the ground, winded. The girl stopped. And then turned towards the river once more.

I had her now.

Spring melt from the hill snowfall had supercharged the river into a roaring flood and widened the banks to twice its normal ten feet width. I scrambled toward her once more, raised my knife and prepared to deliver a killing, overhand blow.

The girl flexed her knees into a squat and then JUMPED.

I splashed into the shallows, the force of my intended blow carrying me forward to fall again, spluttering and thrashing in the icy water. I dug my knife into the mud to stop the flood from sweeping me away and looked up. From the far bank the girl faced me and raised her bow. I scrabbled for purchase, only reaching my knees, resigned now to seeing Laura and Jake sooner than I expected.

Then the girl smiled and waggled the still unstrung bow in my direction before turning on her heel and trotting off towards the woods in the distance.

I studied the river suspiciously. Impervious to my stare, twenty feet of water surged furiously between this bank and the far one. Yet the girl had jumped the river. In one bound. From a standing start. And just as puzzlingly, had not shot me when she'd the chance.

High above, a solitary windhover, silhouetted against the sky, quartered the tree line. I reached out for it with my Sense, hoping to use it to track her. And encountered nothing.

No, not nothing. It was more like hitting a shiny steel ball. My mind found no thoughts to link to, sliding off the surface, this way and that, slipping like a fawn on an icy pond. As if the bird's mind was not there at all.

Relying only on my eyes, I peered into the distance, seeking a sign of difference in this creature that I could plainly see but could not Sense. The bird hung for a moment, suspended, dancing on the wind, wings flickering, before swooping down to circle the girl's head.

That clinched it. She was a Blaster. Some of their fighters had animals with them when we fought outside their compound. Wolves, Hyenas; I had even seen a Bear. There had been rumours of them experimenting on people and animals for years. The girl's figure diminished as the distance between us increased, and I watched as she finally merged with the distant undergrowth. She vanished from view in the lengthening twilight shadows. Dripping and disheartened, I squelched back towards dry ground.

It took me almost an hour of walking upstream to find a fallen tree large enough to keep me afloat and almost half as long to make the crossing, punting with a makeshift staff. I was still swept far downstream before I reached the shallows on the other side. By the time I reached familiar ground again, I lacked the strength to continue.

As night fell, I wrapped myself in my damp blanket and shivering, let dark dreams take me.

A solitary tree root jabbed at my kidney, like a sneak thief's knife, and I rolled to my feet, muscles creaking and straining as I fought to regain my former upright posture. Dawn's flickering candles were forcing aside the reluctant night and struggling to herald the arrival of nascent day. Rolling and strapping my blanket to my pack I pondered the daylight reality of my task.

The girl had a head start on me, depending upon how long she had slept in the night. I knew where she had entered the woods yesterday, but nothing beyond that. But she was a Blaster. And she had somehow killed Laura. If the Blasters had found a way to do that, then the Leaders needed to know. Father had told me, the Blasters hadn't just caused the Blast, they had been the reason for the war.

Who, or what, was this girl? A leader? A scout? Or some new type of Blaster assassin? There were stories about Blaster hunters that killed people, even sometimes groups of people, and then they slipped away, vanishing like ghosts, unseen and, somehow, unSensed.

If she could jump a twenty foot river, what else could she do?

Should I follow her, or find the others? The stark thought of returning to sit beside the freshly turned mound at the top of the hill and waiting for others to catch up made my mind up.

I struck out for the trees. I cast around for tracks or other indications of her route, eventually finding a faint footprint heading deeper into the woods in the mulch beneath an oak tree. A little further on I found a ghost trail through a scattered blanket of snowdrops, leading in the same direction. I snapped some wood sorrel leaves and chewed them as I walked, eyes smarting at the tangy citrus taste.

At the first clearing, I had to pause, circling the edge for signs of any possible change of direction. Without Jake's scenting ability to follow, where tracks stood out like wet footprints on a dry earth floor, I felt almost blind.

A deep rumble from my stomach distracted me enough to veer away to pluck some mushrooms from a fairy ring. Snapping off the stems and blowing the gills clean, I popped a couple in my mouth and dropped the others into my pouch before resuming my search.

Another scuff on the ground straight across the glade indicated that she was not veering from her original path. The tracks didn't look that far apart. Not running then; they looked as if she was just out for a walk in the woods. Knowing now that I may well be moving more quickly than the girl, despite pausing to cast about for her spoor, I began to jog.

A moment later I heard a sound that caused my short hairs to stand up. The baying of a hound. Was this a pack of wild dogs, or hunters with a tame hound? I wondered which would be worse. Wild dogs would not generally be a problem for me depending upon their number, but they should be faced on the right ground. If I returned to the clearing, I knew that I could put my back to a tree and use my knife and Sense to drive them off.

One dog alone was not a serious threat to a full grown man, even without the Sense, and could be ignored while I pursued the girl. But if the one dog had a Blaster fighter following it, it would be a big problem, even for me, without Laura and Jake. They would need to be hidden from. I'd need to head for the deep bushes and hope that the dog was not tracking my scent.

So, two against one said back to the clearing. Once there, I pulled my knife from my belt and stood frozen with indecision, but listening hard. Just one dog, I decided.

Blasters or not?

I reached out with the Sense but found nothing. Too far, perhaps?

I ran across the clearing, diving into the cover of the greenest thicket, burrowing deep, then lay flat, knife pushed out in front of me, while I waited. I didn't have to wait long.

The hound was a huge rangy brindle, wolf-like ears pricked and hard on a scent. He was sleek and muscular, where Jake had been lean and rangy, and he wore a thick, black collar. A Blasters' collar.

I reached out to lightly Sense him.

Prey

His tongue lolled as he swept around with a questing gaze, air-scenting the clearing. His nose went down and he barked sharply, looking back the way he had come. He began scrabbling at something on the ground.

Prey! Blood! Prey! Come! Hunt!

It was the swatch of cloth that I had prized from Jake's jaws. It must have fallen from my belt when I had drawn my knife. The dog took a step toward my thicket and my breath stuck in my throat as his clear eye passed over me.

I reached out for his mind harder, intending to implant a stray thought of a bitch. At that instant, a deep, male voice called, "Freki!" from the trees and the dog turned back to indicate his prize to his master. He snuffled and clawed at the cloth, and barked once more.

The bushes parted with a crash and a man emerged into the clearing. Freki's head turned once more. I gripped the handle of my sweat-slicked knife with white knuckles. The man was big. Even from my prone position, I could see that he stood at least a head taller than me and outweighed me by at least the weight of the dog. He was wearing the black clothing of a Blaster fighter and carried a smooth backpack slung across his shoulders.

He slowed, walked straight up to the hound, and eased him aside. He bent to pick up the now slightly crumpled and dog-mouthed damp cloth. I could hear his breath, panting lightly from jogging behind the dog. He paused to examine the cloth more closely, turning it in his hands and smiling. Abruptly, he reached down, ruffled the head of the dog and rumbled "Good Boy!"

Looking up, he sought the limits of the clearing. He knelt and, holding the cloth over the nose of the panting dog, he hissed "Freki, Seek!" and pushed the dog away. The hound's nose went half down and he cast around in a wide arc, before lowering his head, ears forward, to lope in the direction I had been heading, scant moments before, directly on the scent once more.

Prey! Hunt!

He trotted out of the clearing on the opposite side, pausing only momentarily to bark eagerly at the man.

Follow!

The man swept the clearing with a cursory glance before jogging once again in pursuit of the dog and soon he too, disappeared from my view.

I let out the breath that I had not known I had been holding, and began to wriggle from my place of concealment. The man's voice froze me, half in and half out of the bush.

"Come on, keep up. She went this way. We are gaining on her."

I heard a rustling in the bushes off to the right of the clearing - the same shuffling that I'd heard yesterday. Feet dragging, or perhaps limping, through the undergrowth. No, not limping - whoever made those sounds was moving too fast to be injured.

I breathed out once again as the strange sounds receded in the direction that the man and dog had taken.

Pulling myself to my feet on a nearby tree branch, I faced another decision. This party were obviously hunting the same girl that I was. I could leave them and return to warn the others. I certainly didn't fancy tangling with that great man and his dog except from ambush; particularly without Laura to paralyse him. If there were more of them I might be content to leave.

Questions whirled though my mind. Were they tracking a group of us that had retreated after the assault on the Blaster compound? A rescue team or reinforcements for the girl? Had they found the location of the Haven? What if they followed the girl for some other unknown Blaster purpose? And the other noises that I had heard in the woods, was it one of our Seekers, following them for the Leaders? Or was this the sound of the Blasters' mysterious killer?

I had to know. The dog barked once more, urging the man on. The sound was fainter already and the distance dimmed my light sense. I set off in pursuit.

All through the day I followed, jogging when I could, pausing only for a handful of water at streams, eating the now wrinkled mushrooms from my pouch. Occasionally I would hear the dog bark. Too far away to Sense.

The undergrowth had begun to thin when I heard shouting up ahead and slowed to a walk. The Blaster fighter, I thought, but couldn't be certain. More shouts followed, then silence.

I slowed my advance to a creep, pausing behind every tree, listening before moving to the next. It took me a long while, inching forward, before the light began to brighten a little. Another clearing was ahead and I crept behind the last tree before the vegetation became just scrub, then grass. I peered cautiously out, lurking in the gloom of the tree line and looked closely at the clearing.

Five yards away, two bodies lay in the grass, not moving.

The only sound was wind rustling the leaves and the harsh 'chuff, chuff' of some nearby Jackdaws disturbing the peace of the evening.

The girl from the river bank was one of the bodies.

The big Blaster fighter was the other.

It didn't feel like any sort of a trap, but I suppose that was the point of traps – well, successful ones, anyway. They couldn't have been lying there that long, or birds would be there – even dogs if it had been earlier still.

It must have been the result of the shouting that I heard. The scene didn't look right, but I couldn't put my finger on why. I edged two yards closer, out from the shelter of the trees, heart pounding, searching for meaning in what I saw.

A slash across the girl's body looked deep enough to be fatal, but there was way too little blood, even if the dry earth had soaked up a good drop of it. The man just looked wrong - but why?

There was fresh blood on his knife, but I could see none on him. He lay face down, sprawled in the dirt. There was a strange pattern in the earth around him, as if an enormous foot had stamped the ground flat in two or three places around him. Or as if he had been picked up and smashed into the earth, again and again.

There were another set of marks behind him. Scrape marks, all leading towards the girl's body. It was as if he was trying to reach her, too stubborn to die, even with the Reaper clouding his eyes and stealing away his strength.

Who had done this to them? I started to move then halted.

A black shape drifted into the clearing, circling once before stalling to a graceful, hopping landing about three feet from the bodies.

The jackdaw took a jump closer then froze in a watchful pause, another hop, pause, then another. I reached out to Sense his mind and found the sharp, avaricious hunger I expected from his kind.

Hungry! Food!

Finally, he was close enough and took a tentative peck at the girl's outstretched hand. No movement.

Food!

Good. The attackers had done my job for me. I could claim some salvage and leave the birds to their meat. I eased myself further away from the trees, ears pricked to bolt at any foreign sound.

A swift shape swooped and bowled the Jackdaw over in a rolling flurry of feathers. His surprise sounded as a raucous squawk to my Sense. The jackdaw rolled to his feet and saw only the smaller, mottled shape of a windhover, perched on the girl's leg. I reached out for contact with its mind and bounced off the slick shield once again. Was this the same bird from yesterday?

I re-Sensed the Jackdaw. He gave an indignant 'caark' that quickly summoned others of his flock.

Food! Come! Food!

They fluttered to earth around him like a drift of black ashes settling after a fire. The setting sun gave their sleek black feathers an oily blue sheen. The lead jackdaw, emboldened now, strutted back towards the windhover and the two bodies, full of the pugnacious belligerence of his breed. I could feel his shock turning to hunter's confidence as his flock gathered around him. A cackling chorus of 'chuff chuff chuff' rose from his encircling black gang. The windhover responded: its 'kee-kee-kee' an asthmatic laugh at the advancing jackdaws.

I stepped out and strode toward the avian standoff.

The jackdaws halted their move toward the windhover, regarding me insolently, finally deigning to flap only a few yards away when I got close enough for my shadow to fall across them. I Sensed a diving buzzard into their leader's mind and he squawked sharply.

Danger! Fly!

He flapped away, the others following. The windhover still sat on the girl, watching my approach with unblinking, opaque eyes.

"Shoo!" I shouted.

The bird flicked it's wings to steady itself, but did not fly away.

My caution took me first towards the Blaster fighter. I scooped up his knife. He may be a corpse but there are two types of people in my world; the careful and the dead. I stepped back out of his arc to look at my prize. The knife was a beauty: two and a half feet long, polished and perilously sharp. It shone blue like pre-Blast carbon steel, but with no corrosion or wear, no thinning from fifty years of whetting and honing. It was as thick as if it had been forged yesterday. The riveted black handle, like horn but warmer to the touch and textured, was equally unmarked. I stabbed it into the ground, not sliding it alongside my own, shorter, worn knife, for fear it would slice through my belt.

The man's unfamiliar backpack was the real prize. It might have any amount of Blaster tech in it. Peering closer

I saw that it had a built in back scabbard, such as only a fighter would surely use. I knelt next to the body to ease the harness straps from his shoulders. I pulled at the first strap and stopped.

The body squished and flexed at impossible angles under my hands. This, then was how he had died. Almost every bone in his torso was broken, his rib-cage was concave and his head flopped freely when I moved him, telling of a broken neck. Had he been stomped, like the grass around him? By what? I looked up, but saw nothing.

I studied him once more. The man's boots were the shiniest I had ever seen and his belt was fine, thick leather. I pulled it free and fastened it around my linen trousers. Gathering the rucksack, I set it before me and slid the knife into the scabbard. It fit like they had been made together. Swinging it up on my shoulder I started for the tree line. And stopped.

Those boots.

Scooting back, I sat down and offered my feet up against his. They looked as if they would fit. I loosened the laces until one pulled free. Then the next. I slipped the boots on. The leather was hardly worn out anywhere and the thick soles had a grip pattern, half an inch thick. I marvelled at the strength of the laces that were not gut or hemp, but fine and strong, but slick.

I stood. But if the boots fit, what about his clothes? They were fine weave, not coarse linen like mine. His coat was short, ending at his waist, and both it and the shirt he wore were of the same sheer black material.

Getting a big, dead man out of his coat and shirt is no easy task and I was breathless and sweating once it was done. Shrugging myself into the shirt took only a moment, then the jacket. I began to fasten it. It had only two buttons, one at the bottom and one at the collar. In between, up the whole front edge, there were two jagged metal rows, like little teeth. I pushed them together but they wouldn't catch. I left the jacket hanging loose. I decided the trousers would be far too long for me, even rolled up. A cursory glance at the girl showed nothing worth salvaging, and I wanted to get away before whatever had killed them came back.

Standing ready in my new outfit, I stretched, deciding that the boots would soon mould to my feet. I turned to leave.

I heard a low whine and cast out my Sense.

The great dog, Freki, stood watching from the tree line, ears down, hackles raised. I reached for him with my Sense, finding no threat, only puzzlement and loss. Through our link I could see my scent rising up from the ground like a smoke trail across the field and felt the hunger; for food - and companionship.

I reached slowly into my battered pouch and threw a gnarled hunk of jerky that had been intended as trail food for Jake. He took a step back as it landed, cautious, then forward again to grab and gnaw at it. I walked towards him, Sensing him with calm and confidence.

He waited, chewing, wary tail swaying, allowing me to come under the shadow of the trees. Suddenly he started, jumping up; I caught the whiff of a harsh, foreign scent and felt his reaction.

Fear!

He bounded away, his panicked response ripping apart our fragile link. I heard a grunt from above and a weight fell on me from the tree. I crashed to the ground, winded. A hand closed around my ankle. Another clamped my arm, hauling itself hand over hand up my body.

I was turned over. Looking up I was confronted by the deep hazel eyes and sharp yellow teeth of a chimpanzee.

I Sensed out for its mind and was stunned by the backlash, like a child swatted by an adult. A raw wave of loathing surged through my mind, threatening to overwhelm me mentally. This was totally unlike any animal I had ever linked with; with a savage, cunning intelligence behind it.

I rolled and tried to scrabble away, but it pulled me back, dragging me on my arse while I kicked vainly to find purchase. Gods, it was strong. My arm began to tingle as the animal's grip cut my blood flow.

It pulled me up and I could see that something must have almost killed it. Livid, purpling, marks circled its throat, clearly visible even through the fine fur. Over one eyebrow and continuing down its cheek was a deep cut. But almost no blood.

The Chimp's other hand reached out behind and, swinging back toward me, long brown fingers levelled a short, shining crossbow at me. I recognised the fletching. These were the arrows I had pulled from Laura's chest. It shook me and then gave a weak, wet cough.

"The girl? The bird?" it lisped. I could barely hear it above the primal rage battering at my mind. I had never Sensed anything like it.

"Down there. Dead. Well the girl, not the bird." I gasped.

It sneaked a fleeting look, barely taking its eyes off me. Trees blocked our view. It gulped in air.

"Good. Help me ... return the body ... to the Centre." It was really fighting now for breath. Was its grip weakening, or was I imagining it?

"Why? She's dead. Just put her in the ground."

"No!" the grip tightened in a spasm that I thought would snap my arm. A torrent of red rage swept across my mind, blinding me.

"She must be ... des ... studied. All subjects must be studied ... even failed ones." The monkey regarded me through crafty, bloodshot yellow eyes. "There will be ... a rich reward."

"But she's a Blast ... well, one of your people ... Reward? Why?"

I was so intent on the answer that I heard a sound behind me too late – the blow fell on the back of my turning head and the evening instantly became night.

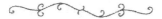

Red waves of light from my pounding skull woke me to dawn's stealthy approach. I turned my head to one side, paying dearly in flashing lights and throbbing for every movement.

The rucksack was still where I had dropped it when the monkey had grabbed me.

The monkey!

I struggled to my knees and, turning, saw that the animal was no longer where it had been. Nor was the knife. The Chimpanzee lay face down, the man's knife driven through its back, pinning it to the earth like a nail, only the black handle still visible.

I looked down into the glade. Through the thin low growth, I could see that the man lay where he had yesterday. The girl was gone.

Casting out for Freki, whom I could Sense skulking nearby, I sent a feeling of calm friendship. He trotted towards me, tongue lolling. Had he been watching what had happened? I re-established our link, strengthening and deepening it. I reached out to sense his memory, gently, cautiously. A dog's sense of time and of cause and effect can be confusing.

I sifted through his fading recollection of the monkey's death. It was like trying to read a picture book with some of the pages torn out. Just pictures, overlaid with simple, sudden emotions.

The girl hit me from behind, knocking me out.

Prey.

The monkey released me and bounded for the girl.

Fear ... Bad ... Run ... Fight ... Rage!

The girl caught the chimpanzee in mid leap and raised him above her head before, twisting, she smashed him to the ground.

Good. Kill! Kill!

She reached down and pulled the Blaster's long knife from its sheath in the back pack and drove it down, two handed, through the beast's back.

Good! Good! Kill!

I saw her slowly approaching through the dog's eyes. She offered a hand and he sniffed.

Prey ... Friend?

I pulled back from the great hound's memories and puzzled over what I had seen. Why kill the monkey and not me? I pulled the knife from the chimpanzee's body, bracing my foot against the corpse, straining until it came free, adding a swirling noise to my already pounding head. As I pulled, I noticed a lighter patch of fur at the base of its neck and a pale tattoo: 'HYBRID 17'. I tried to think through muddy waves of pain.

Think later; grab the stuff and leave.

The Blasters had clearly been hunting the girl. What was she to them? It was clear that she had saved me. I wiped the knife on the grass, scooped up the rucksack and the little crossbow. The arrows matched those I had pulled from Laura. The girl and I shared an enemy.

The great hound waited near me, tail swishing low and slow, friendly but unsure. I reached out and scratched the hair beneath his ear. He cocked his head, leaning into the scratch, and grunted in pleasure.

"You know, I think I'll call you Freddie."

His head twisted to one side, ears pricked.

"Freddie, the Leaders can do their own dirty work from now on. It's them that have the quarrel with the Blasters, not us."

I knelt beside him and, looking into his deep brown eyes, established a proper, full sensing link – like the one that I so missed with Jake. We regarded our path, Sensing once more with a companion of the mind. Looking through our eyes we saw a fading trail heading into the distance. Our path lay there.

We turned towards the fields in the direction that the girl had headed. The grass gave way to half-seen, mist-shrouded trees, greening with spring's new energy. Behind the trees rose the jagged mountains, still topped with snow at their heights. I had heard of a wonderful refuge called the Tour, high up above the snowline. We had never travelled that way before.

"Freddie, we've got a puzzle to solve. Come on, boy!"

GLINT

Michael Wombat

Jannery

Lauren strove to move, even to twitch. Her brain dispatched electrical impulses to motor neurons, but her paralysed muscles would not shift. She could not move a single millimetre; even her eyes were fixed straight ahead, gazing directly up at a grey ceiling. Her breathing, though, was unaffected, and her heart still pumped blood, reassuring her that her automatic motor functions continued to work normally. Peripheral vision showed white-coated figures moving about. They had told her that she would feel nothing because she would be unconscious during the operation, but they had been wrong. The back of her neck itched. Draughts caused by the bustling figures caused slight movements of the simple shift that covered her and stimulated her sensitive skin. She could feel. Terrified that they would cut into her while she was still conscious, she concentrated on moving even something as small as an eyelid to alert them. Nothing.

One of the figures reached above her and pushed a switch, turning on a bright light. The woman glanced down with a slight frown; perhaps she'd seen Lauren's pupils dilate. The woman leaned in close and, in a whisper that tickled Lauren's ear, said "You think we don't know that you're awake? Awareness is necessary for successful implantation. I know that is not what we told you, but to be honest we don't really care how you feel. Now, try not to struggle; it will do you no good at all. Besides, the pain will only last an hour or so."

The woman nodded and a second figure gave her something shiny. The scalpel flashed in the bright light as the woman brought it towards Lauren's face. Her mind thrashed helplessly, unable to make her muscles act on the frantic panic impulses it was flinging out.

A dark mass crashed into the surgeon, sending her flying out of Lauren's field of view. Loud shouts, thumps and crashes echoed in her ears.

"Glint!" screamed a voice, before a white-coated body crashed into the trolley on which she lay, sending it spinning. The ceiling revolved across her field of vision until the trolley crashed to a halt against a tall piece of apparatus. It fell across her, bringing the chrome clamps into her field of vision. They were smeared wetly with red.

A high shriek was cut short by a grunt, and silence fell, broken only by an occasional soft whimper from somewhere to Lauren's left. She was desperate to look around, but still could not move. She heard shuffling, small doors opening and closing, the clinking of glass, and then footsteps retreating quickly, leaving the room. They stopped.

"Damn it," growled a low male voice.

The footsteps approached again, and a figure leaned across her. It heaved her easily from the trolley. She was flung over a shoulder, a large hand gripping her backside to keep her in place. She could see little except the stranger's back. A camouflage jacket ended just above the man's knees, black denim covering the legs. The stranger strode quickly, and as she swayed she caught glimpses of the room they were leaving. Several bodies lay on the floor, some spattered with blood, none moving. They hurried down grey corridors, twisting and turning.

"Stop!" called a voice, but a soft *thwup* silenced it. The stranger stooped as he walked and Lauren glimpsed a hand pulling a crossbow bolt from a body. The man strode on. His strong grip dug into her buttock as they descended broken, rubble-strewn stairs and clambered through a jagged hole in a shattered wall. Ice-cold wind swept across Lauren's skin and she felt goose-pimples lift on the backs of her thighs. Her breath fogged in front of her. The back of her neck still itched but she could not move to scratch it. A dog barked.

"Quiet, Samson!" grunted her captor. Or was that the right word? Was this individual her captor, her rescuer, or worse? She was suddenly embarrassingly aware of the thinness of her simple gown, and of how vulnerable a position she was in. Suddenly alive to the fear of what he might want with her, her mind sent orders to her muscles to fight or to flee. Her body, however, continued to ignore the messages.

Her field of vision tilted and whirled, offering brief glimpses of shattered buildings blanketed with fresh snow. She was momentarily confused, until she realised that she was being swung from the man's shoulder and through the air. She landed hard on her front, and the breath left her body. From the little she could see, she had been thrown over a large object covered with fur, her arms dangling one side and legs the other. The object shifted and she caught a glimpse of a graceful leg covered with light brown hair.

Behind her the man climbed astride the warm back of the creature and urged it into rapid movement. As they lurched off, the man called out loudly, in a voice made of gravel.

"I am Fury! I am Glint! Maddie, Samson, let's go!"

At first she was uncomfortably aware of the front of the man's body moving against her side, but after some minutes her total discomfort took over her thoughts. Her back, and in particular her bare hands and feet, were freezing. Her stomach was pummelled by the backbone of the beast that carried them and she began to feel sick. Luckily, before this feeling came to its inevitable conclusion, the man slowed his mount to an easier walk. They rode on, their path twisting and turning.

"Why the hell did I go back for this one, Smith?" the man growled from above her. His voice was deep and old. There was no answer. "Last thing I need, a useless damned girl getting under my boots. Hey, kiddo – you still paralysed?"

She felt a hard slap on her buttocks, but was unable even to wince at the pain.

"Ha! I guess you are at that. Cold, too, or I'm a Dutchman, which I'm not." She felt warmer - or at least, less frozen - as a blanket was spread over her icy back. The man continued talking. "You'll be able to move a little soon enough, but don't for mercy's sake wriggle or you'll fall and break your damned neck. You can slide off when we reach the Fortress of Solitude. Allow me to reassure you here: I mean you no harm and I will cause you no injury. I was after the Alliance's LPA is all, but damn, when I saw you in there about to be mutilated I just couldn't leave you all helpless. Do you even know what they were going to do to you? Heh, probably not. The Alliance likes to keep things hidden; that's the way of 'em. Well, kiddo, they were about to implant you with a pretty nasty piece of tech which, among other things, is a bomb. You'd have made one wrong move after that, BOOM, there go your brains flying across the damned room."

The man chuckled at this grisly thought then fell silent. They rode on for perhaps half an hour. An odd distant sound, some kind of white noise, grew louder as the minutes passed. Lauren's arms began to ache, and her hands began to feel as though her blood was pooling at the ends of her dangling limbs. She wiggled her freezing fingers, which offered some relief.

Wait. She had moved her fingers. She tried bending her arms, and was rewarded by a twitch of her hands.

"Hey!" she called. "Let me down!"

"She lives!" mocked the man. Even above the rising susurration of white noise she could hear him clearly enough to sense his grin.

"Let me down!"

"Ah, take it easy. We ain't but a minute from the Fortress. When we stop you can get warm while I cook you up some food and Radbegone. How does that sound?"

"Let me down, you bastard! W... what are you going to do to me?"

"Not a damned thing, kiddo. When you've eaten and feel better, you can please yourself."

The rhythmical background hiss became louder, and the beast carrying them slowed to a halt. She felt the man dismount.

"OK, here we are. Maddie - guard duty! Now be still while I—"

Lauren was having none of that. She pushed against the rough hide of the creature beneath her and stumbled down to her feet. Her legs collapsed and she crumpled onto ice-cold shingle. She gasped at the sight of sun-glittered water stretching to a blue-mist horizon. Gentle waves collapsed onto the stony beach with a sound like whispered breath.

A loud fart sounded close by. Her head whipped around, nervously. The creature that had borne them loomed large above her. It stood maybe four feet tall at the shoulder, with an elongated neck adding another couple of feet. The animal had a rounded muzzle, with a mouth that showed an underbite and a cleft upper lip. The creature's feet each had two toes, with which it scuffed the small rocks about its feet as it eyed her curiously from large, long-lashed eyes. The whole animal was covered with shaggy, honey-coloured fur.

"What in glory is that, a camel?" she jabbered. Her mind whirled.

"Llama," said the man, behind her. "Well, mutated llama - or maybe llama crossed with camel. Smith don't right care what he is, long as he gets his grass and water and a song now and then."

"It looks like someone was knitting a sheep and forgot to stop." Lauren was beginning to feel a little hysterical.

"Ha, yeah, he kind of does at that. See now, you really should have waited for me to help you get down. You're not recovered from the anaesthetic yet. Let me help you up."

Lauren swung towards the voice to see the man stepping toward her, holding out a hard, calloused hand. She scrambled away from him in panic, and he straightened up. He was tall, with cropped grey hair and a grizzled, lined face covered with a white stubbly beard. To Lauren's young eyes he could have been any age between fifty and seventy. He wore sensible tough boots, black denim jeans, and a camouflage jacket covered with pockets. On his head sat an incongruous top hat. Something secured in the hat-band - Lauren could not make out what - glittered in the icy sunlight. His right hand held a small crossbow, his left still reached out to her, as if to help. By his feet sat a brown dog, a mastiff type that stared at Lauren anxiously. Behind the old man rose a high cliff-face, on top of which sat another, larger brown dog.

"People call me Glint," said the man.

"Not Fury?"

"Oh, that? Just a random thing I said once that stuck. Folk sort of expect it now. No, Glint's the name. Hello. Now can we get the hell inside? This cold must be freezing your chuff off." He lifted a saddle bag from the llama-creature.

Lauren was wary, but felt the Jannery air keenly through her thin shift. She clutched the man's blanket

83

tightly around her like a shield and followed him at a safe distance, teeth chattering, into a dark crack in the cliff face. The fissure cut maybe ten feet into the rock before dog-legging left. Glint lifted aside a blanket secured to the roof, and beckoned her inside.

She entered a large cave, barely lit by a dying fire. Glint set down his bag. It clinked. He took a log from a pile by the door and stirred the sluggish flames with it. Sparks and smoke spiralled up past a bubbling pot suspended over the heat, eventually escaping through a crack in the cave roof. He threw the log on the fire, feeding the wakened flames.

He grabbed a rough wooden bowl from the ash margin and blew on it, tipping out a spider and some grit before dipping it into the pot and passing it over to Lauren. She sniffed it warily. It smelled delicious. Her eyes narrowed.

"What is it?"

"Muskrat stew." The man smirked at Lauren's doubtful frown. "Never ate muskrat before, huh?"

"What does it taste like?"

"Squirrel." Lauren wrinkled her nose in disgust. "Aw, just eat the damned stuff, girl. You can't be flirting with Mr. Picky way out here."

"And then what?"

"Then you can do what you like, kiddo. I haven't exactly thought this through. Choose yourself some warm clothes from my extensive wardrobe and then stay or go, it makes no never mind to me."

Febbery

"Extensive wardrobe, my arse."

"What?" Glint looked up from his Superman comic, a relic of pre-Blast days.

"When you first brought me here you said I could choose from your extensive wardrobe. Two shirts, two coats and a ratty old flying helmet is not extensive."

"It is when you've got spit to wear otherwise."

"Ha! You're all hat and no cattle, old man!" Lauren ruffled Maddie's fur and the fat dog grunted happily, wagging its big tail against her leg.

"Shut your gob, kiddo. How's that Radbegone?"

Lauren peered into the pot suspended over their fire. She sniffed the acrid liquid. "Coming along. Needs a touch more LPA, maybe."

"How the hell you know that just from the smell is beyond me. Go ahead and stick some more in, then. I got plenty in last month's raid. Got more than I bargained for, too. Got a damned mouthy girl never stops nagging."

"What exactly is LPA?" Lauren asked, pipetting a tiny amount of the colourless liquid into the concoction.

"Lysophosphatidic acid," Glint growled, stumbling a little over the jumble of syllables. "Stuff contains a signalling molecule that buys your cells more time to repair their DNA after rad exposure."

Glint stood up, his grey hair brushing the cave roof. His once white T-shirt was now also greying with age. Blazoned across the chest were the words 'Montreal Canadiens'. He reached for his camouflage jacket.

"And where are you going, old man?"

"Out," he grunted, stooping to set his top hat on his head. The gewgaw sewn into the hat-band - a piece of gimcrack jewellery in the shape of a flower, fashioned cheaply from glass and faux-enamel - glimmered in the firelight. Lauren knew by now that 'out' meant Glint was off to scour the shattered post-Blast world for anything useful - food, random lost objects, maybe even the chems that he needed to cook his Radbegone, or other meds.

"Can I come this time? I'm ready, I truly am," she asked.

"Well," he spat in the fire. Lauren's nose wrinkled at the foul hiss. "You've learned the crossbow quicker than shit off a shovel, but you still don't know Mutant Army from Green Stripe. What do you think, Samson?" The dog wagged his tail enthusiastically. "Samson says OK. Come on then, kiddo, grab the gear and have a swig of your concoction. Let's go adventuring."

She swallowed a hot spoon of Radbegone, pulled her flying helmet tightly over her tangled dark hair and grabbed a small, single-handed crossbow. This would be exciting; Glint had not let her go with him before. He had always told her that she wasn't ready, but weeks of training with him had clearly brought her to an acceptable standard.

The llama, Smith, quite happily carried the two of them on his long back. Lauren sat behind Glint so that he could "see where they were damned well going". He rode them along the shoreline. The Febbery day was monochrome, and chill enough that she was glad of the soft old helmet hugging her ears. She stared at Glint's camouflaged back for a while, and the rear of his battered top hat, then relaxed into the rhythm of Smith's stride and watched Samson and Maddie playing along the water's edge to their left.

"Used to have three dogs, once," the old man told her over his shoulder.

"What happened to the other?"

"Named him Freki," Glint ignored her question. "Damn, I miss that dog."

"Why Freki?"

"Why the hell not?"

"What happened?" she tried again.

"He ate a lot," Glint said, cryptically.

"Old man, I am behind you. I will stab you in your bony arse if you don't start making sense."

"Freki was one of Odin's wolves. Means 'the ravenous one'. Got taken by the Alliance a three-month back. Shame. Damn good tracker." Glint fell silent and they rode quietly for several minutes, watching the waves. "Stupid dog," he added, in a tone that brooked no reply.

Occasionally they would skirt a ruined building or a broken pier, but mostly they were able to follow the coastline and the ride was uneventful. Gradually the devastation of smashed buildings to landward grew as they entered what had once been a small town.

"Primm," said Glint.

"What?"

"Name of this shithole - Primm." He fell into silence again.

Lulled by the sway of the llama, the slow tick of Glint's G-counter, and the sound of waves on pebbles, her eyes slowly closed and her mind drifted. She dreamed a tower, maybe a couple of hundred feet high; white in a red cage. There was a platform at the top with a square room at its centre. Somehow, she knew that the room contained food.

"Sod off!" yelled Glint, waking her from the reverie. He flung a rock from his pocket at a huge wolf spider that was daring too close. It skittered away under a pile of rubble. Smith snorted derision, and Samson and Maddie commenced a barking frenzy.

"Quiet! Creepy bastard," growled Glint, climbing from Smith's back. Lauren joined him. "Mutations get more extreme year after year - winged people, sentient trees and the like. Pre-Blast, you know, spiders were tiny. Years - hell, decades - of radiation exposure's grown them so now they're mostly as big as that sod; more than a foot across. Opportunistic sods, pouncing on the unsuspecting. That one'll not bother us now we know it's there. We might as well have a rest. Then we'll explore that old hotel about a mile to the north."

"Glint, is there a tower hereabouts?"

"Now, how did you know that, kiddo?" Glint's eyes narrowed. "I've only been that way but once myself. It's in a rad hot-spot, so normally I swing inland before that."

"I don't know. I've got a feeling there might be food there."

"A feeling?"

"I sort of saw it. In a sort of daydream. Sort of." It sounded pathetic now she said it aloud.

"Hmmm." The old man fingered his white beard, looking at her searchingly. "Given where I found you, kiddo, that's like to be information worth following up. Maybe we'll head there instead, have Samson and Maddie sniff out any food."

"What do you mean, where you found me?"

"The Alliance lab. You know you're not like most folk, right?"

"What the hell are you talking about, old man?"

"You don't know? Damn. I've just been assuming that you must be aware of your own nature. That you were just sensibly keeping real quiet about it. I mean, doesn't the tattoo give it away and all?"

"What is this stool water? What tattoo?"

"Sweet Baby Jesus and all his unicorns, you really don't know, do you?" Lauren shook her head. Glint looked around, and pulled a piece of broken glass from the pile of rubble. He set it against his black backpack, and took a hand mirror out of a side-pocket. "Take that helmet off and lift your hair."

It took some time to get the angles right, but eventually he was able to show her the back of her neck. There was writing etched into her skin.

"What does it say? I can't see."

"AVIAN 17."

"Meaning?"

"Meaning that you're different. The Promethean Alliance has been experimenting on people for some time. The mad bastards think they have a duty to complete God's creation or something; that if humans were created in God's image then until we have Godlike powers we are unfinished work. You're one of their attempts to make a god."

"But I'm just me."

"Like I said, they're mad bastards. Could be, though, that they inherited, or stole, or found knowledge that can enhance human abilities. Maybe they worked on you before I found you. That's why I think we should look into this vision of yours."

"But the radiation?"

"The Radbegone should last long enough if we head back right afterwards. We'll be fine. Any more fool questions, or can we get moving?"

"Who's Odin?"

Glint ignored her, and they mounted the grumbling Smith. Followed by the two dogs, they picked their way out of the ruins and along the coast once more. Now they passed through a once-tall city, keeping to the narrow beach that curved between steel-grey water and smashed buildings, now mounds of rubble interspersed with the gaunt metal skeletons of once-busy structures. The G-counter woke up, its ticks merging to a constant crackle. Soon afterwards Lauren spotted the tower ahead.

It looked exactly like the one in her daydream - a white circular tower with a rust-red staircase spiralling up the outside. How it had survived the Blast was anyone's guess but there it stood, though it tilted a little from the vertical towards the sea. They stared up at the bottom of the metal staircase, tantalisingly out of reach twenty feet above their heads. The waves lapped at their boots. Glint lifted his hat and scratched his head with the same hand. Lauren lifted her flying helmet and did the same.

"Grappling hook?" she suggested.

"We don't have one, you know that."

"Then we could tie the rope round a rock?"

"Don't be an idiot, we'd never manage to throw it accurately enough."

"Crossbow?" she suggested.

"Crying out loud, no! We have no thread for a start," Glint shook his head, "And the rope would be way too heavy for a crossbow bolt to lift."

"You could stand on Smith, and I could stand on your shoulders?"

"Give me a damned break," Glint sneered and raised an eyebrow at her; Smith made a noise that sounded suspiciously like a mocking laugh.

She frowned. "Well, if you're so clever, old man, you work it the hell out! You obviously don't want my help." She turned her back on him and sniffed haughtily.

"I'll go find something we can climb to get up there," Glint told her. "When you stop sulking, come help carry."

He headed for the nearest building. Lauren turned her head slightly and watched him go out of the corner of her eye. God, the old codger really annoyed her when he treated her like a child. He was an infuriating man. Exasperated, she glared up at the unreachable staircase above her head. She gritted her teeth and stifled a scream of frustration. If only she could get up there by herself. That would really show the arrogant bastard. Right now she wanted nothing more than to shove his mocking disdain down his throat. Tears of anger leaked from her eyes.

She felt dizzy and her head swam. The world whirled and spun across her vision - sea, pebbles, Smith, ruins, dogs, stairs, clouds; all glowing brightly and spinning rapidly past her bemused eyes, over and over. Sea, pebbles, Smith, ruins, dogs, stairs, clouds … if only she could reach out and … she grabbed the stairs as once more they swept past her eyes and hauled herself up.

"What?" she gasped. Her vision steadied, and she found herself standing at the foot of the stairs, twenty-five feet or more above the beach. The three animals below gazed up at her with wide eyes. Maddie gave a little yip of surprise.

Glint turned at the sound and his jaw dropped. "HOW?" he called.

"I'm full of no idea," Lauren jabbered. "The animals saw; maybe they can tell you. I certainly can't. One minute I was furious at you down there and the next I was here, wishing you'd throw the rope up so we can get up this tower."

"Uh, yeah, OK." Glint frowned, then sighed. "We'll figure it out later, I guess. Maddie, Samson - guard duty! Catch, kiddo."

Glint threw the rope and clambered up, then the pair spiralled to the platform at the top of the tower. A few steps from the top they paused. Muffled voices emerged from the white walled structure at the centre. They peered over the edge of the deck. The rotting door was closed.

"Damn," Glint cursed.

"How did they get up here?"

"Maybe they had thread. Or did … whatever the hell you did.

Suddenly the door flew open and a man fell out, crashing to the decking. He looked a little younger than Glint, though it was difficult to tell with the blood smeared across his face. A dark beard sprinkled with grey was matted with blood. His hands were tied behind him, and he was barefoot. Before he could struggle to his feet another man emerged and sat across his chest. This one wore trousers only. He was without any body hair, and his skin erupted with unsightly lumps and crevices. He wielded a blood-smeared knife. A second hairless, pock-marked man followed and grinned down at the poor bound unfortunate.

"Alliance?" whispered Lauren, trying to remember Glint's lessons.

"Mutant Army," Glint told her. "Not good. Not good at all."

The assailant raised his knife with a wild grin, ready to plunge it into his victim's neck. Without a thought Lauren leapt up the final few steps and in two strides was at the attacker's side. She attempted to knock the knife from his hand but was grabbed from behind by his accomplice, and her arms held in a fierce grip. She struggled, but was unable to free herself. The man with the knife stood up. Through the pustules that coated one half of his lopsided face she saw his lip curl in a disgusting leer. The two mutants looked her slowly up and down.

"A woman!" The one in front of her licked his lips. "Now we enjoy ourselves."

"Mutants!" growled Glint, just loudly enough to be heard. The mutants looked to the sound. Glint stood legs apart, arms extended, with a crossbow in each hand pointing at the mutants. The cheap jewel in his hat glinted in a stray shaft of sunlight.

"I am fury," he growled. "I am Glint. Now run."

Lauren's arms were released immediately, and the burly, malformed men hurried for the stairs, giving Glint a wide berth. He watched them go, then crossed to the man on the floor, and knelt to free him. "Where's the damned food?"

"The food would be me," the man answered. He looked up at them from dark-lashed eyes. The laugh-lines around them spoke of humour and intelligence. He spat blood and coughed. "They were about to eat me. Thank you."

Lauren indicated the stairs, from which they could hear the mutants nearing the bottom of the tower.

"How did you do that?" she asked Glint.

"Reputation."

"You're letting them go?"

From below came a cacophony of growls and savage snapping, until a single short scream shattered the still air.

"No."

Marsh

Glint left the Fortress to go and gaze at the sea, pebbles shifting under his feet. The early sun was shining and it was cold. He wore just a shirt, which wasn't enough when the wind blew, and suddenly that long-ago feeling was on him, like he'd walked into a cobweb made of all the childhood holidays before The Blast. It felt like a hundred years since he had been that boy. Footsteps crunched behind him and he knew that he wasn't alone.

"You know, Glint, if you hadn't saved me back then, given me your Radbegone ..." David left the thought unfinished. Glint said nothing, watching a storm petrel scan the breeze above the waves for a scent of food.

"Anyway, thank you again," David continued awkwardly. He paused for a beat, and looked at the grizzled old man with clear eyes the colour of chocolate. "You know she's ... different?"

"That's not her fault."

"I'm not saying it is, but there are some that would take it against her. Oh, don't worry, not me. She deserves help, not mistrust."

Glint looked sidelong at David, trying to judge the worth of the man they had rescued a week before. David's floppy hair lifted in the chill breeze and his eyes held an earnest look. Glint looked into them and came to a decision.

"She has ... abilities," he said, his gravel voice low. "She saw that tower before she even knew it existed. She got us to the top, and I swear to God I have no idea how she did it."

"She's talented, then. Most like her are."

"What do you know of her kind, David? You plainly don't share the common view that they are some ungodly horror come to destroy us all."

"Those like Lauren are just people, Glint. People who have been experimented on, almost always against their will. Occasionally, just occasionally, there's a crack in the Alliance wall and one or two are able to escape the system. I have, on occasion, been the cause of such a crack." He looked earnestly at Glint's weather-worn face. "We should be helping them, Glint, not fearing them. They escape from their torturers only to find themselves persecuted and alone, most likely hunted down by the Brotherhood. I want to change that, where I can. You could help a great deal, you know. You're a famous figure in these parts. Glint, The Huntsman, Alliance Bane – you have many names, but whatever people call you, they always say the same thing. You help people, where you can. You make the Radbegone for a start, and not just for yourself. Kids play at being you, for mercy's sake, running about shouting 'I am fury, I am Glint'. You're famous, man. You could use that fame. If you spoke out you could sway opinion, help people realise that they needn't fear these people who, you must have noticed, are appearing more often now. Perhaps even protect some of them from persecution."

"I'm no preacher. I'm certainly no saviour. All I'm trying to do is to survive this sod-awful world."

"Have you ever been in love, Glint?"

"Have you?" Glint narrowed his eyes, warning David not to dig too deeply.

"Oh, there was a pair of green eyes once, black hair lifting in the breeze, but … 'he who dares not grasp the thorn should never crave the rose' as someone once said." David caught himself, as if he were about to reveal something he'd rather stay hidden, then continued. "My point is, if it was someone you loved that was being experimented on, you'd want to save them."

"I told you. I'm not a saviour. I'm not rushing to save anyone."

"You saved Lauren," David pointed out.

"Yeah, and I'm still trying to fathom out why."

"Hey, Team Glint!" Lauren's voice pierced the still morning from the cave mouth. Samson, at her heels as he usually was these days, gave an echoing yip. "Are we going, or what? Oh, and you left your comic out, old man. Maddie's enjoying the taste."

"Damn that dog! That was one nine nine — Supes and The Flash."

"Stop whining, you've got plenty more. Now shift your scraggy old arse. You promised to show me The Barra. And why are you just standing there grinning, David? Get on your bike."

"Ha! Right away, ma'am." David laughed. He looked at Glint. "Fathomed out why you let her in yet?"

'Team Glint' presented an odd procession, winding their way through ruins that were only now, decades after The Blast, beginning to be overgrown by radiation-stunted vegetation. Smith happily carried Glint and Lauren, while David rode an old BMX bicycle that he had found three days ago on his first scavenging trip. All three of them carried backpacks full of Radbegone to barter at their destination. Maddie and Samson roamed nearby, and unusually for early Marsh the sun shone on them, lifting their mood. The ruined world seemed empty in the spring stillness, and their long journey was uneventful.

Clouds simmered at the rim of the sky as they approached the low mountain pass that cradled the trading post. The place had been a hotel complex once, but now served as home to a ragtag collection of permanent residents, temporary guests and fly-by-night ne'er-do-wells. Ramshackle corridors had been built out of a patchwork of different materials to run between the mostly undamaged buildings, partly to keep access between them in the winter and partly, Glint said, to stop paying guests from seeing too much of the trading post's more unusual activities. The place was known by many names, some of them uncomplimentary, though most locals called it The Tour. Glint called it The Barra, after the Barrantine Pass in which it nestled.

The trading post commanded a good defensible position that was well suited for trade. The residents bartered not only goods, but also - to people that they considered trustworthy - information that they teased out of those passing through. They accepted anyone as guest, as long as no-one was threatened or harmed. This policy gave rise to an always fascinating kaleidoscope of transients; a heady and volatile concoction of traders, bandits, slavers, brigands, travelling minstrels, mercenaries. The list was endless.

The sky darkened as they passed through the palisade that surrounded the place. The pass itself was still closed, and the stable that they settled Smith into still comparatively empty. As Glint chatted easily with the stable-hand, as if to an old friend, Lauren stooped to pick up a feather almost hidden in the clean straw scattered on the floor. It was about six inches long, chestnut-brown with pale buff flashes. She spun it round between thumb and forefinger as Glint chatted. The chill of the outside left as she stared at the spinning feather, and she began to see the stables as they were in the summer, when the pass was open. A glorious confusion of animals - horses, mules, oxen, camels and more - made for a noisome, cacophonous atmosphere. It felt so real that it made Lauren gag, and she felt hot and dizzy. She loosened her scarf, only for Glint to snatch her hand away roughly and tighten it about her neck again.

"Keep your neck covered," he snapped. The stable-hand was staring at her.

"Why?" she asked, looking around at the empty stable as if in surprise.

"Just do it, kiddo. We want to avoid trouble, get our trade done, and get gone. We'll stay here tonight, and you can look around while I'm bartering if you like, but keep your crossbow handy at all times and keep your tattoo hidden."

"He's right, Lauren," David told her, stepping up alongside Glint. "There's danger in that ink of yours. Best not to stir it up if we don't have to."

Lauren breathed deeply when they emerged into the fresh air, leaving Samson and Maddie behind doing tricks and eating treats given them by the stable-hand, who was clearly a friend to the dogs. The three crossed to an old caravan that was parked next to a two-storey building. The mobile home had long since lost its wheels, and had been repaired so often that the original walls and roof were almost completely replaced. Glint removed his hat and knocked on the door, just two short raps. There was no answer.

"Must be in the Guest Hall," Glint mumbled. "This way."

As they turned away from the caravan Lauren had a prickly feeling in the back of her neck, and glanced to her right. There was an unnatural-looking shape on the ground between the caravan and the wall of the building. She touched David's arm and pointed. He crouched, peering intently. The shadow remained still. Heavy drops of rain began to fall and Glint's G-counter began to crackle.

"Glint!" David called the old man back, and the three edged between the metal and stone walls for a closer look. It was the body of a man, crumpled on the ground. A tesla pistol lay in the corpse's right hand, an old sword by his left.

Lauren bent to examine him. No pulse, no breath. She felt cold drops of rain hitting her back.

"He's deader than bones," she said, and stood up. "No sign of any wounds."

"Look at this, though." David pulled the pistol from the dead man's grasp. Even normal guns were expensive, unreliable though they were, but this one had to be worth a fortune. David whistled in admiration as he examined it in the half-light. "Alliance-made, good quality. Must have cost him more than a month's food. The recharges wouldn't come cheap, either." David twisted the gun to catch the light, oblivious to the increasing rain. "Huh, empty. It's beautiful, though. Just look at the curve of the battery housing, feel the heft of it. I wonder what he was doing with it here?"

"Waiting for me," said Glint, without emotion. His companions looked at him, expecting more. His hat darkened as wet patches appeared from the thickening rain. The G-counter's crackle rose to a shriek. "That sin-ugly so-and-so is Shambrook. Looked like the backside of bad luck, but as clever as they came. Also a man with a lust in his soul to kill me."

"Why?" David raised an eyebrow. "What did you do to him, old man?"

"That's a long story that I'll tell you one day not this."

"Was a woman involved?"

Glint gave David a look that told him to steer well clear of that subject.

"Question is," he said, "why is he now face in the mud instead of shooting me in the head?"

"Firstly there's no charge in his pistol, so he'd have been stabbing you in the head. Secondly, how do you know that it was you he was after? That he was after anyone in fact?"

"Because he's here, where nobody would rightly be. He knew that I'd come over to the caravan first."

"And died of old age waiting?"

"Hmph. I guess there's no working it out for the moment," said Glint, shrugging. "Let's get out of this damned rad-soaked rain. There's someone I want you to meet."

David pocketed the tesla pistol and picked up the dead man's sword. "Katana," he whistled, "and a good one too, underneath all this rust."

"David!" snapped Lauren, "Getting wet here!"

The three made their way into the building. They passed under a rough sign that declared this to be the 'Guest Hall' and entered what had once been the entrance lobby of the old hotel. The walls had been curtain glass, the floor paved in imported marble. Much of the glass had now gone and the gaps had been panelled over, though some large panes remained to allow a sad, grey light inside. The floor was covered with old, worn woollen rugs. The vile smells emanating from these competed with the odours of sweat, smoke, and an unappetising smell of something cooking that was reminiscent of urine. Lauren wrinkled her nose. At one end of the room a bar served, according to a hand-written sign hanging above it. 'Booze – Clean Water – Barleybean Glop'.

Glint removed his top hat and scanned the smattering of people around the bar. A disappointed frown appeared on his weathered face.

"Come on," he grated, "they have hot showers here. And the food's dull, but it'll fill a stomach hole. If we're lucky we might scam some huiskee."

"Shouldn't we tell someone about the body?" Lauren asked.

"Given its location, no. Not until we find the right person."

Lauren was tempted to ask about 'the right person', but the mention of hot showers was now at the forefront of her mind. At the Fortress they had the occasional stand-up wash with sea water warmed over a fire, but mostly it was too cold for that and they just went dirty. After a bowl of warming pottage, which turned out to be a sort of flavourless grey goo, the hot shower was a glorious experience. She had no idea how the proprietors of The Barra had managed to get the showers working, but she had never been so grateful for anything in her life. Afterwards, skin tingling, she forgot all thought of socialising with strangers downstairs and simply fell asleep on her pallet in one corner of the women's dorm.

She slept well, and the following morning was well advanced when she woke. It was still raining, huge great drops pounding on the metal panel that replaced what had once been glass in the window. She found Glint and David sitting in the Guest Hall, staring at bowls of pottage and talking earnestly. She caught the tail end of David's sentence as she approached.

"… the authorities start to take notice."

"Take notice of what?" Lauren asked, sitting with the two men and spooning some of Glint's meal into her mouth. He didn't object, but nor did he answer. Instead he stared up at the staircase to one side of the room. His white beard cracked into a smile.

An old woman, her luxurious silver-streaked dark hair swept up into a bun secured by two skewers, balanced on the top step, seeming almost to float there. She was soft, round and pink, telling of a life spent indoors. She wore a dress of heavy blue wool and deerskin slippers. She glided gracefully down the wide staircase and towards them.

"Chaffinch!" boomed Glint, standing and holding his arms wide. The woman paused and her smile twisted into an irritated frown, which then dropped into a mischievous grin.

"How are you, Ramsbottom?" she asked, an amused look on her lined, still beautiful face.

"Ramsbottom?!" squeaked Lauren, and burst out laughing. "Ramsbottom, as in the rear-end of a sheep? That's your real name?"

"As in a valley where garlic grows. Shut up," Glint grumped as the woman gave him a hug of welcome. He sniffed the woman's hair. "From the ancient words 'hramsa' meaning garlic and 'bopm', meaning vale. Nothing funny about it, kiddo."

"I am fury. I am a sheep's arse," Lauren laughed. "I can see why you keep that quiet, old man." David's lopsided grin drew a "And you can shut up, too!" from Glint.

"I see that he's hidden that titbit from you," said the woman, giving Lauren a curious glance. She extended a hand. "Call me Chrissy. You here to trade, Rammy? Have you heard the latest story doing the rounds about you? That you can turn into a dog?"

Lauren got the impression that the woman was jabbering nervously. She took the small, surprisingly cool hand and shook. "I'm Lauren," she said.

"Ma'am," purred David, kissing Chrissy's hand. Glint shot him a look.

"Pleased to meet you," Chrissy smiled winningly. "How come you two are travelling with Ramsbottom?"

"This pair did me a favour," David smiled. "I just haven't moved on yet."

Chrissy turned to Lauren and gave her a quizzical look.

"So you were with Ramsbottom first?" she asked, calmly. "How on earth did that come about?"

"It's an interesting story, actually. I was—" began Lauren.

"A story that can wait," Glint interrupted. "I'm starving. This goo of yours is no fit food for a man. What are the chances of a good thick bacon sandwich?"

"No chance at all, I'm afraid. It's 'goo' or nothing," Chrissy answered Glint, though still eyeing Lauren curiously.

"Aw, c'mon, Chaffinch, give an old friend a break?"

"I already have done," Chrissy said, turning once more to Glint. "Rammy, I think you'd better just trade your goods and head out." She turned to leave.

"Chaffinch, don't ..." began Glint. Chrissy looked back over her shoulder, eyebrow raised. Glint seemed to catch himself before he continued. "Did you know there was a body outside?"

"Well, it's not the first and it won't be the last. I'll get it seen to," Chrissy said, and turned to leave through the front door.

"Well now," David observed after Chrissy had disappeared. "She didn't ask where the body was."

"Sod this for a game of soldiers," grumped Glint, pushing to his feet. "Let's get this done and bugger off home. Suddenly I hanker after the solitude of the Fortress."

They spent a good three hours bartering and trading goods, including most of Glint's Radbegone. Or rather Glint and David did. After an hour or so Lauren became bored and retired to the stables to play with Samson and Maddie. She was laughing at the two dogs, who each had a firm hold of the same stick, when the remainder of Team Glint joined her. Both men wore weighty backpacks, and David carried Lauren's, also heavy with traded goods. Glint, clutching a thin stack of comic books, gave a sharp whistle and the two dogs dropped their toy and loped over to sit by his feet. He idly scratched Maddie's head with his free hand.

"There's nothing more for us here," he stated flatly.

"Are you sure? What about tonight's entertainment?" asked David, eagerly. "Aiden's here, and Hurricane Lizbet! Two finer singers you've never heard, I promise. And Jorne will be juggling! There's going to be such singing and dancing! With fire poi!"

Glint shot him a look and David fell silent, his eager grin melting away.

"What's fire poi?" asked Lauren, stroking Samson's ear.

"Juggling with flaming chains," a woman spoke from behind them. Chrissy stepped down from the hayloft stairs, as gracefully as before but somehow harder, and crossed to join the trio.

"Come to kiss me goodbye, Chaffinch?" Glint gruffed, a twinkle sparking in his eye.

"Dream on," she said, though her face softened. "No, listen. Damn." She paused a moment. "It's as well you're on your way. I'm sorry," she continued, looking ... what? Puzzled? Surprised? Lauren could not decipher her expression. "It's not for me. You've always been a valuable friend to us, but there are limits," she glanced briefly at Lauren as she took a deep breath. "And if you go, I think there's a message your … friends … and you can carry." Glint raised his eyebrows.

"Some time ago," Chrissy said, "it was early, the pass was barely safe, and there was a party of Prometheans."

"Chaffinch has no love for Prometheans," Glint told the other two.

"No love? That puts it lightly. What they do, it's … it's not the time. A party came through, rough even for Prometheans. Nothing more than henchmen, no manners and no—"

"And no valuable information for you to worm out of them?" Glint said, tight-lipped. Chrissy gave him a glance. Now that was surprise, Lauren thought.

"They knew the road, not much besides. Not even how to look after their prisoner, a mo … a child. Injured, so I could take her aside. She called herself Nahria, and it seemed to me that she lived for a burning conviction that her sister would come for her, would rescue her, that she had only to survive. I've wondered about that, if hope was a true blessing, or only cruel and false."

"What has this to do with us?" David asked, an eyebrow raised.

"I'm getting to that." Chrissy was clearly tense. "She had the mark, on her neck, the Promethean brand. And I think … I think she saw things. Things not actually there."

"That's impossible," Glint stated. Lauren wondered why he was lying about something that he had seen with his own eyes.

"I'm just telling you what I saw. She healed remarkably quickly, too."

"We have to help this girl," David declared earnestly.

"What?" Glint asked, startled. "Why?"

"You know why."

"Not this again. We don't know her, or where she is," Glint sighed. "What would be the point?"

"The point would be that she's someone who needs help, and a group like that's going to get noticed. We ask; we'll pick up their trail."

Glint looked at Lauren and sighed.

"I'm game," she shrugged. Glint nodded and turned to a clearly impatient Chrissy.

"Can you tell us which way they went? Apparently we're going to track her down."

"Up through the pass, but she's not the point, she's the message."

"To whom? You don't mean there really is a sister?"

Chrissy nodded, a sadness creeping into her face as she continued. "She passed through a few weeks later. Called herself Gabby, I think. From her dress and her face she had to be kin."

"From her face? From her dress? You didn't speak to her?"

"I … I had reasons. I thought them good enough, at the time." A look passed between Glint and Chrissy. Lauren glanced at David. He shrugged – he, like her, was unable to understand the words that were being left unsaid. Chrissy spoke more easily now, as if she was relieved to be nearing the end of the conversation.

"The goatherds say – goatherds gossip, you know – that she headed north and east from the pass. It's a long road that. You'll need supplies, if you take it. I hope you've traded enough?"

"We'll manage," Glint told her. "Why exactly are you telling us this? What's your reasoning here?"

Chrissy shook her head.

"Must you know? It's a favour I'll pay off." Her lips lifted in a half-smile. "When you come back, maybe there'll be bacon. I might even run to a good wheat loaf."

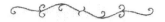

Apple

Glint stopped at the corner, holding up his hand. Lauren and David also came to a halt. There was a wide space between them and the building ahead. It stood relatively robust amongst the detritus of broken fences, scattered bones and the remains of a small kiosk. If anyone saw them crossing that space, the game would be up and they'd have no chance of freeing any captives inside.

"Samson," Glint hissed, "your turn. Go scout."

Samson gave Lauren's hand a warm lick and wandered out into the open space, sniffing the ground and glancing around as he did. To an onlooker, he looked no more than a wandering dog searching for scraps to eat. Lauren had seen him do this before, a couple of weeks ago when, following a tip that an Alliance party had been seen nearby, they had found that they needed to cross a city park that the day before had been crawling with Mutant Army cannibals. The dog had appeared to be interested in nothing but the scents under his nose, but in reality he was scouting. That time he had made three small, soft grunts and turned his nose to the east. Three men in that direction. Glint and Lauren had been able to step from cover and take them out with crossbows in a few seconds. David had still not mastered missile weapons, though he still carried his uncharged tesla pistol.

They had not found Nahria that day; the Alliance were keeping her moving, aware perhaps that people were on her trail. They had, however, found a boy, inexplicably left behind by the Alliance and tattooed like Lauren. He had sent them here. The boy was now back at The Barra -

or rather, with The Barra's goatherds in the high meadows above the pass.

Samson stopped sniffing the ground, looked back and wagged his tail. The coast was clear. Maddie left their side and ran to Samson, bumping heads in a 'well done' gesture. Team Glint crossed the open space to the double wooden doors, Glint and Lauren holding their crossbows at the ready, David wielding Shambrook's katana, now polished and sharpened until it shone.

The weathered sign above their heads read 'T__PIC_L HO__E' The doors opened easily, a sign they had been used recently. The air was still and dry in the small vestibule. It had a single display case to the left. A dirty notice told them that once this exhibit had held tuatara for visitors to admire. Lauren wondered what tuatara might be. There were more doors ahead of them. They went through warily, and all hell broke loose.

Men attacked them from all sides in a frantic blur. Glint sent one crashing to the floor with a fist to the nose while his crossbow bolt found a second's chest. David found himself in a desperate fight with a cudgel-wielding ruffian, twisting his blade to block and parry with the flat of his katana. Maddie and Samson launched themselves snarling at dark-clad attackers.

Lauren had no time to think. Instinctively she fired her crossbow at a man who was about to skewer David from behind. She had no time to see whether her bolt hit home as she was set upon by two Alliance thugs. The nearest grabbed at her coat sleeve and slashed at her with a wicked looking machete. The sleeve tore away and she felt a sharp pain as the blade shaved skin from her forearm. She dropped, whipped her dagger from her boot and stuck it deep into the man's thigh. He shouted an obscenity and fell. The second man swung at her with a club and she threw herself backwards. The club brushed her chin as she rolled back and up into a crouch, fists ready. She had a second dagger in her other boot but no time to get it out. From the corner of her eye she saw David still battling with his opponent, and she could hear the two dogs snarling savagely.

She threw herself at the second man before he could swing his club again, hitting him in the belly with her shoulder. If she could only get astride him, perhaps get a grip on his throat ... but even as she had the thought she knew that it wouldn't work. The man was too strong for her, and far too clever. He twisted somehow, and used her own weight against her, dumping her on her back. He raised his club to smash it down on her head.

Glint hit him from the side, sending the club crashing to the ground. Lauren looked around and saw David finally dispatch his opponent with a sweep of the katana that almost severed the man's head. Maddie and Samson, jaws foaming red, stood growling over at least four bodies, one of which had Lauren's dagger in its thigh. Glint, wrestling with the one remaining attacker, struggled briefly with him before manoeuvring the man round in front of him. One arm held the man's body tight while the other twisted his head, sudden and sharp. There was a sickening snap and the man fell dead. Glint stood erect across this last body, triumphant, arms outstretched. He smiled at Lauren.

"I am fury!" he crowed. "I am G—"

He gasped, and looked down in puzzlement at the arrow tip protruding from his chest. A spot of blood spread quickly across his shirt, erasing the words 'Montreal Canadiens' in under two seconds. His hat tumbled from his head, and he crumpled, the light gone from his eyes.

"Old man!" screamed Lauren. Horror twisted her insides. Tears flooded her eyes. David rushed to Glint's side, frantically feeling for a pulse. He glanced at Lauren and shook his head, then bent, against hope, to breathe air into the old man's dying lungs. Maddie licked the old man's hand and whimpered. Lauren's mind whirled with dizzying grief, and she stumbled. Her vision pulsed and glowed brightly. She sensed a presence above her, at the top of what was once a faux-waterfall, and arrowed through the air toward it like an avenging angel. There stood a woman holding a bow. Her eyes widened in terror as Lauren attacked, raking talons through her flesh and clawing out her eyes, sinking her sharp beak deep into the woman's hot throat and tearing away her life.

Lauren fell down, exhausted and empty. She sobbed on the high rock, chest heaving, nose dripping snot. It took David several minutes to find a way up to her. He put his arm round her and led her gently back down. They passed cages on the way, old zoo exhibits that had once held exotic creatures for people to gawp at. It was obvious that humans had been held captive there recently, but none were in evidence now. David opened a door marked 'Staff Only' and found a desk and chair in a small room. He sat Lauren down and looked at her arm.

"You'll be OK," he told her, "Though your coat's ruined. How did you get up there so fast? I … I couldn't save him. I'm sorry."

"I thought he was immortal," she whispered, finally beginning to get her tears under control.

"In one way, he is." Lauren had no idea what he meant and looked up at him with a puzzled expression. "I'll tell you something else," he said. "It's awfully clean in here."

Lauren looked around. He was right. There was no dirt, no cobwebs, no sign at all of the decades that had passed since this place was last a zoo. On the desk in front of her was a small box. She lifted the lid; it held scores of index cards. She took a couple out at random.

'Male, unnamed, newborn, birth weight 3.5kg, 46cm long, 32 fully formed teeth. Silent, always smiling. Recommend termination. Dr. Brightsmith.'

'Male, Tohmar, 13 years, 83% QR, NV, potential psi. Recommend FELINE. Transport to Northpoint. Dr. Boers.'

David met her eyes. "Look under 'N'," he said. Lauren fingered through the cards and pulled one out.

'Female, Nahria, 17 years, 97% QR, probable SS, potential psi. Recommend HUMAN 70 series. Transport to Benanti Facility. Dr. Brightsmith.'

Thank goodness for the Alliance obsession with record-keeping. Lauren gave the card to David. A wetness at her hand announced the arrival of Samson, licking her fingers either in sympathy or because he liked the taste of dried blood. She shook him off and walked back out to Glint's body. David followed and they stood together, looking down at the old man. Lauren wondered whether she ought to say a few words, but knew that Glint's response to that would have been "Shut your gob, kiddo."

The door opened and a slender woman strode in, dressed in black leather, dark hair tied in a bandana, face painted with a simple yet effective design. It was a young face, though the eyes seemed old. From the woman's dark hair sprouted short antlers - whether mutation or affectation was not clear. Lauren tensed, though not with fear. This was something else. David grabbed his bloody katana. It keened as he swung it towards the newcomer.

"David, hold," Lauren said. She sensed something about this woman. A kind of … kinship? No, not quite kinship, but something familiar. David stilled his blade, the tip hovering six inches from the woman's face. The newcomer did not flinch, nor even acknowledge David's threat. She gazed directly into Lauren's eyes, ignoring

David's bloody blade. Lauren laid her hand on David's arm and he lowered his weapon. She turned her back on the woman and lifted her own hair, showing her tattoo. The newcomer relaxed and Lauren turned once more to face her.

"You're Gabby?" she suggested, holding out her hand.

"Ghabrie. How did you … never mind," the woman said, touching Lauren's fingers briefly in greeting and staring blankly at the dried blood that covered them. "What happened here?"

"Damned Alliance," Lauren spat.

"I don't supp—"

"Your sister's not here," Lauren said.

"We were looking for her," said David, "We know your story – hell, it seems everyone does these days. We had a tip off that an Alliance group was here."

"I heard the same," sighed Ghabrie. "Damn. Back to square one, which, you know, what does that even mean?"

"A reference to old board games, I think," said David, "but we might be able to move you on to square two. Look." He handed Ghabrie the card they had found and her eyes brightened.

"Thank you!" she said. "There still is a trail to follow, after all. The Benanti Facility, any idea where that is?"

Lauren shook her head no. But David spoke up, more gruffly than usual.

"I wonder," he said. "There's a Benanti Peak, way up there in the mountains. I've not been there for, well, a lifetime. Might be worth a look." His eyes lost focus, as if he was remembering something long ago.

"I don't suppose you two would like to come with me?" asked Ghabrie, more in hope than expectation. "You look like you'd be useful, and I'm not happy about tackling the mountains alone. And the trail ... it gets lonely. Sometimes it would be good just to have someone to talk to. You said you were already looking for Nahria; why not carry on that quest?"

"Sorry, no," Lauren told her, "I've just lost ... well, my father. I need to take some time alone. We'll just head back home."

"Actually," said David, holding Lauren's look and speaking to her more with his eyes than his words, "I'd like to go along with Ghabrie, if she'll have me. Of course, I won't leave you if you need me to help with ..." He glanced at Glint's body. "I'm sorry, Lauren, but you know me. I'd hate to sit around just ... existing. For years I've been trying to help people like you, and what greater assistance can I offer now than to help look for this woman's sister? You're more than capable on your own, you don't need me."

Lauren returned his gaze.

"That's not your only reason, is it? Yes, of course you must go, and soon. They can't have left very long ago if their rearguard was still here. You'd better get moving. Come find me at the Fortress when you return."

"I'm not at all sure that I will return." David gave her a tight hug, whispering in her ear "Live well, Lauren. Take what you need, give what you can."

He turned to Ghabrie. "I'm David," he said, "shall we go find your sister?"

"Is that your llama-thing outside?" Ghabrie asked.

"Oh, I can do way better than that. I have a cool bike."

The two left and Lauren was left alone with her thoughts. She took off her ruined coat and threw it in a corner. She looked down at Glint's body, wiping her eyes dry.

"What the hell, old man?"

Glint's camouflage jacket wasn't too stained, and fit her well. She removed the sweat-inducing flying helmet from her head and flung it in the corner. When she retrieved Glint's top hat, the gewgaw sewn into the hat-band caught her eye. It was an old brooch, perhaps, a cheap and gaudy representation of a stargazer lily. She hadn't looked at it closely before. There were letters scratched on the back - C. H. Finch.

"Huh," she said.

The top hat was far more comfortable than the old helmet. The ride back to The Barra would not be accompanied by a sweaty head for a change. Smith was waiting where they had left him, but he was not alone. Three or four mutants circled the llama, trying to get a rope on him. He spat at them violently.

"Oi!" Lauren yelled, "Leave him alone!" To either side of her Maddie and Samson growled.

"Oh yeah?" sneered the nearest mutant from bulbous lips, "and who might you be?"

She looked up at the mutants from beneath hooded brows and growled.

"I am fury," she said. "I am Glint."

BEHIND THESE WALLS

Alex Brightsmith

"Once upon a time there was a house in the forest ..."
... and such a house it was! A great rambling place in the style of a chalet but blown out of all proportion, something that might have been the weekend retreat of a great man, or perhaps even a coaching inn, before the world changed and the forests took back their own. I can see it so clearly, all balconies and fretwork like a Christmas fantasy, but what would that mean to these children of ours, who know so much and have seen so little?

I can try, at least.

"Once upon a time there was a house in the forest, and in it lived the woman who was not a witch ..."

There was a tap at the door, and Chrissy dropped her pencil with a gesture that might have been irritation but might, though she would never have admitted so much, have been relief.

It was one of the guest hall servers, a slight, fair child. A child of Tour, Chrissy thought, too young to know that even the name had once been a joke, still young enough to be in awe of a woman so old that she remembered when things were otherwise, and yet fluent in three languages and already an expert – a line of blue stitching along the pocket of her trews, almost lost in the riot of colour, proclaimed it to the knowing eye – in botany. What did I know at that age, wondered Chrissy? So much more, and so much less.

What this child knew, now, was that a party of Prometheans was approaching, heading for the pass despite the season and the snows. They were a rough party, too, even by Promethean standards. Mere muscle, no one Chrissy was likely to learn anything useful from, but Chrissy was an old hand, and steady old hands were needed for a party this rough. They would not be served by guileless children or blushing maids.

Chrissy was so keen for any distraction, even one that promised a brush with her least favourite guests, that it took a stern look from the child to check her. She was rusty, for her services were not often required in the public hall these days.

She paused, emptied her pockets, and gave a slow turn for the approval of her chaperone. The child nodded gravely. Nothing went into the guest hall that hinted at the Tour's true reserves and capabilities. They were eking out a living, just like the rest – that was the party line. A good complex that they intended hanging on to, better than average inherited stores, the fat of the land, and a tithe on whatever their guests traded under their roof. Chrissy, dressed in goat wool homespun and deer hide slippers, her hair swept up, Geisha-style (though there were few enough left to appreciate that joke, either), with two slim rods of birch, matched the image perfectly.

Much of the detritus from her pockets would match the official image just as well. There was one very faded tin box, pre-Blast, containing five crudely pressed lozenges, one carefully hoarded pencil stub, a carved wooden mouse she had removed earlier from a toddler determined to swallow it, a rag of machine-knit jersey, once clothing, parsimoniously repurposed for spillages and snot, and a plastic whistle, removed from the same child. With the pills she was probably safe enough. It was unlikely in the extreme that any guest would have the interest or the capability to analyse them, and so find out what the Tour's laboratories were still capable of synthesizing, but ... Tourists, those who lived here, were careful. It was in the bone, and she needed the pills less in this cold weather. The plastic whistle, she thought, was the only dangerous thing, and not because of what it was but because of what she knew it meant. It might easily have been picked up in trade, or from the complex's eclectic stores. There must be thousands gathering dust in little stashes all across the world, still mint, and no one need look at it twice. But a second look, a casual glance, might show the practiced eye that the whistle had been printed, and even that it had been printed as a little as a week before, and that had wrapped within it facts that the Tour would rather not have known.

It was doubtful that they had the last 3D printer still working, and where there was knowledge to run one there was almost certainly the knowledge to run it on a cellulose based program. Raw materials would not be the problem; power would be the problem. That the Tour could generate electricity was no secret. It would have been too difficult to conceal perfectly, and a lot of places had solar cells that still functioned and even stores of fuels that would run generators – it would have seemed unlikely that the Tour had not. That they had not only solar cells and batteries but the ability to renew and replace them; that they had the printers and the power and the maintenance skills that they could print off a child's whistle cavalierly, for fun ... that was a secret to be guarded.

Her musing brought her to the landing at the head of the guest hall, and as she passed through the last swing door into the open space she shivered. The extent of their reserves being a jealously guarded secret, the hall was just warm enough to be comfortable to a well-dressed man. She looked down, and though she shivered again it was not because of the chill. In summer, with the hall full, she could see it as it was, and forget. In winter, and even in this season of treacherous thaw and false hope, she saw the bare room, and remembered.

Space, that had been the luxury they took for granted. Warm, light, space, at any season. This had been only an entrance hall, the walls of curtain glass, the floor paved in imported marble, a tiny corner given over to the reception desk, a third of the remainder occupied by a zen garden of boulders and stone chips (faintly, very, very far away, her father whispered Silfurberg, see that honey? Icelandic spar, it's come even further than you have). Desk and boulders too had gone, as had much of the glass. Large panes remained, and made the hall easy to light in summer but difficult to heat, but at least half had been panelled over, and the glass removed to places it could serve more usefully (there would be salads sown in a week or two, she knew, thanks to those panes, but they would not be served here – another secret) and the floor was covered over with woollen rugs to deaden the clamour of a hundred guests and to aid in insulation, rugs in their last incarnation before they were broken down, and went into the vats for viscose or onto the fields as shoddy. Chrissy wrinkled her nose instinctively, even after so long. Some spills were unavoidable, but deep inside her the child raised in pre-Blast sterility gagged at the thought.

Her party were still at the doorway, and she scanned them automatically as she descended the stairs that had once been unremarkable, and were now shabby to her and awe-inspiring to their younger guests. A dozen tough riders, mired from the road; so familiar a type that her glance barely lingered. She almost missed the last member of the group, but as they moved into the hall she saw a young girl hesitating behind them. One of them turned, snarled an insult and tugged at a cord Chrissy hadn't noticed. The girl staggered and then came on, one arm out to keep the cord that tethered her to her master from tripping her, and for a moment Chrissy too stumbled. She had thought she was proof against that; she had seen worse, but for a moment horrified pity had overwhelmed her. We allow this! We could insist on better. If the child had been left in the stables she would have been better treated. Even as a Modern, she would have been better treated.

The thought sobered her. Yes, a Modern, else she would not be travelling with the Built. Not a girl, not a child, a Modern. A product of the Promethean's laboratories, an unknown danger, and none of your concern, Chrissy, be about your business. Obeying her own stern injunction, she slipped into the kitchen before the Built' patience could be tested.

Abigail was there before her, less than half Chrissy's age and a hand's span taller. It would begin to be noted, soon, that Tourists bred tall youths, but there was nothing to be done for that. Well-fed children grew into tall and comely youths, they would just have to hope that envious eyes put that down to breeding, and not to resources that might be snatched. For now it was just another advantage to be played for all it was worth. Abigail's thick black hair was simply plaited, for it didn't do to seem to be trying, but the same homespun that covered Chrissy, when modestly draped on Abigail, revealed her curves rather than concealing them, and that owed more to art than chance. Fifty years ago, when those who now called themselves Tourists had been split very clearly between actual tourists and staff, there had been some skilled seamstresses on that staff, and their talents had been valued and passed on.

The effect would doubtless be entirely wasted on the Built. In expansive mood, they would leer at the plainest wench. Otherwise – and from Chrissy's brief inspection this party's mood had been very much otherwise – they were taciturn and inward looking, speaking little even between themselves, hungry and ungracious, and noticing who served them only if that service was slow. Little risk of that today. Abigail was moving with practiced efficiency. She'd already stirred the fire into new life, and moved aside the lid of the cauldron that permanently hung above it.

There was a stew of barley and pulses, helped out by a little fat bacon and a hint of game stock, sustaining but dull. Good enough for Prometheans. Too good for Prometheans. Abigail clearly shared the thought. She had stirred the stew thoughtfully, added some water from the jug standing by and stirred again, watching carefully as it came back to a slow seethe. She met Chrissy's eye with a conspiratorial grin that turned to unconvincing penitence.

"I won't spit in it, not this time. It's early yet, there might be others on the road as wouldn't deserve it."

Chrissy didn't argue. For other travellers, however distasteful, she might have chided Abigail, but she was willing to let her standards slip for Prometheans.

The Prometheans were already restless by the time they brought out the bowls and a basket of small loaves, roughly quartered. She'd misjudged it, Chrissy acknowledged to herself as she set down the basket and began passing out bowls. Whatever reason had brought them out into the pass so early had left them in a worse than average mood.

Perhaps it was the presence of the child – the Modern – they were being required to escort. They certainly weren't treating her as an honoured companion. With so much space to share they hadn't prevented her from settling tentatively onto the long bench, but she sat hesitantly, poised for flight. It wouldn't surprise her, Chrissy judged, if she found herself eating off the floor. Even the bowl she might consider a bonus. For now she seemed almost forgotten. She took the bowl that Abigail handed her almost furtively, without eye contact or apparent gratitude, and attacked it urgently. Abigail showed no offence. That was a lesson they learned early in the guest hall, but she didn't even release her feelings when they fetched flagons from the bar.

It was too early in the year for the bar to be staffed, but other guests would have fetched ale from the barrels for themselves. For Prometheans, and especially for Prometheans in so grim a humour, allowances were made. Even so, as they fetched the flagons Chrissy was surprised to see Abigail reach for a jar of huiskee to warm the brew. It came from the north – rarely, and at expense. Chrissy raised an eyebrow, and Abigail gestured to the Modern.

"If we keep them warm and pleased they'll let you take the girl without an escort," she said, evidently surprised at Chrissy's obtuseness, "hadn't you noticed the gall?"

Chrissy hadn't, and she studied the Modern more carefully as they filled beakers from their flagons. There was a raw patch on her wrist, a slight enough injury when Chrissy had been that age, but an invitation now to fever and death. Despite the Modern's evident worth, they had done no more than transfer the rope to her waist and tie a rag around her wrist. It was clear that better attention was required, and it was clear that by the Tour's own rules they must provide the treatment. That was enough to account for Abigail's interest. Of course it was.

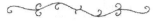

It wasn't enough to account for the way the Modern haunted Chrissy, not just that evening but well into the following day. Except that it was not the Modern, she decided at last, who haunted her. It was her own reaction. She didn't pity Moderns, not this way. If she pitied them she pitied them as she pitied any deformed newborn, and would have given them the same mercy that the Tourists gave a five legged calf or two headed foal, the mercy of a quick end and the lime pit. If they made her more uneasy than a helpless, mewling, stumbling thing in the stable yard, it was because despite their wrongness they might one day rule the world, and fear trumped pity. What could there be in one more damaged Modern to disturb a Tourist? Hadn't Chrissy seen enough?

The Tour had always accepted any guests who came. It had been a matter of policy from the earliest times. They had been lucky, very lucky, in the talent assembled there when the hammer fell, and twice lucky – no, a dozen times lucky – in the books and equipment they had been able to scrounge, adopt and flat out steal whilst they still had fuel for their vehicles and ammunition for their weapons, but they had always known that there were vast holes in their knowledge. They had never felt able to be squeamish about the guests they welcomed, when any guest might be able to plug a hole. Some guests, after much tentative sounding, had stayed. Many more had been fed and warmed and found themselves served the Tour's deceptively strong ale by a bright, interested child or a sympathetic maid. The Tour clung to obsessive secrecy over their knowledge, but very few of those experts who passed through, experts whose expertise seemed suddenly to be no more than gilt on gingerbread, had seen any reason not to relax and be expansive, to tell fables from a time before the world changed to a wide eyed audience they never dreamt could sift and evaluate those tales.

There was little enough pre-Blast knowledge to harvest now, but the policy remained, and gleaners still passed amongst the guests, learning more of the world as it was as they fought to retain an image of the world as it had been. Chrissy wondered, sometimes, if they should place a higher value on themselves, and insist on a higher standard from their guests, but it was mere idle fancy. She had been reconciled for a long time to guests who beat their pack beasts, their wives, and even their children. If a human child had reacted so badly to her sterile little clinic she would have felt a stab of sorrow, might perhaps have prescribed herself a shot of huiskee to ease it, would in time have managed to suppress it. That she had felt the same pity for a Modern kept the sorrow sharp in her mind, and she could not settle to her proper work.

Eventually she found an excuse to go up to the central tower, which most visitors nowadays assumed had given the Tour its name, but even the widening view as she climbed could not distract her.

She thought of the Modern, following her with resigned docility, casting a yearning glance at her half empty bowl and unmollified by promises that she could eat her fill in comfort. She had recoiled on the threshold of that little clinic room, and for the first time Chrissy allowed herself to wonder just what these children – these Moderns, Chrissy, not children, not humans, whatever their masters sometimes tattooed across their necks – had experienced to make a bare white room smelling faintly of raw alcohol and soothing herbs a source of terror.

Even more, she wondered that a child so young, human or otherwise, could overcome that fear and hold herself so poised in such circumstances. She had tried to find an answer, and it had not strained her guest hall training. Nahria – that was her name – was willing enough to talk, on her own terms. As she allowed her wrist to be dressed, suspiciously rather than gratefully, but without protest, she had spoken with simple confidence of the sister who would come for her. She was certain that escape was possible, even without assistance, if she were careful and patient and sharp, but it was not a thing to be rushed into. These were strange lands, and not to be ventured alone. Promethean servitude could be tolerated, because it would not last for ever. The fabled sister would come, helped by whatever friends she could make along the way, by the birds and the beasts and by the forests themselves.

She was a tracker, Chrissy interpreted prosaically. She would have to be a good one, and close behind too. It was not the season for tracking.

Nahria's quiet confidence had been, in its way, impressive, but Chrissy had been too frustrated to be impressed. As she grumbled her way up the steps of the tower she found that even the frustration had passed. All that lingered was a sense of tragedy. Was this what stories were good for? For false hope?

She reached the viewing gallery in time to watch the Prometheans make their way up into the empty stretches of the pass. They were mounted, except for the Modern. They had tethered her to the packhorse, and she followed on foot, dogged, docile, delusional.

As they dwindled into the distance, Chrissy remembered Nahria's confidence that she could escape at a time of her own choosing. Maybe her delusion that her sister would come for her was not so bad a thing. She certainly had something that the children of Tour did not; maybe what she had was a hero to believe in.

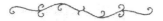

"The hunter had been aware of the house for some time, and on the day that he finally approached it he came in a wide, unhurried spiral. At first glance he might have been a searcher, but whatever he sought, he sought it with a light heart, and he moved through the forest with the confidence of the forest born, not the recklessness of the lost. Even so, it was not his forest, and for all his appearance of ease he did not go unwarily.

It was evening before he reached the curtilage wall ..."

This time the only thing that kept the pencil from flying across the room was the knowledge that there were fewer pencils in the entire complex than Chrissy had once grasped carelessly in one pudgy fist. The hunter was everything she was sure a hero should be, good and bold and strong, as handsome as the day was long and as smart as a cocky little jay bird. He was also, and there was no avoiding the fact, about as interesting as ox dung.

A corner of Chrissy's mind rebelled at that. She knew some really fascinating things about ox dung, though she'd be the first to admit that they didn't make for good mess hall conversation. Very well then, he was less interesting than ox dung. That didn't help much, except that ox dung led to oxen and oxen led to the stables, and to the thought that the stables were always warm and welcoming, and often interesting, even so early in the year. She put her precious scraps of paper carefully aside, and headed for their embracing warmth.

Chrissy hadn't always loved the stables. For a long time she had avoided them entirely, much to the frustration, as she remembered with a smile, of more than one young man. Before that, there had been a day exhausted in fruitless tears, in childish determination that they could not, would not ... what? It was gone. The tears she remembered. The original purpose of the building she did not, only that it had seemed a gesture of complete defeat to strip it out, to cannibalize its equipment and to fit it with the rails and partitions of a stable. It had all been so very long ago.

It was impossible now to think of it as fulfilling any other purpose, much less that she could have thought that purpose worthier. In summer, with the pass at its busiest, it was full of horses and burros, oxen and camels, all eating their heads off in a fug of their own making and leaving their own payment to be scraped from the concrete floor, but even at its busiest there was an underlying calm that radiated off the great beasts and the sureness of their handlers, and it was that peace that Chrissy sought. She didn't expect to find any more than the Tour's own plough team, the goats if they had not yet been released into the higher meadows, and the overwintering boar and sow grumbling contentedly in a corner.

What she found, to her surprise and briefly to her delight, was Smith.

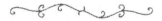

Though the meadows above the Barrantine Pass were goat country, Chrissy was familiar with sheep. Sheep were fluffy abstractions in nursery stories, and she was almost certain that at some time in the long distant past she had held a wriggling lamb in her lap and squealed when it tried to suckle from her fingers. When it came to the size and temperament of the adults her hazy memory was of little use, but she was almost sure that the various woolly beasts driven and ridden by their guests were not sheep. What they were, that was another matter. Monks, paccahs, llamas she had heard them called, but the names meant nothing to her. They were at best an uncomfortable reminder that she no longer inhabited the world into which she had been born; worse than that – that even she, who had seen more of it than most, could no longer say with any certainty what was an authentic remnant of the real world and what belonged wholly to this brave new alternative.

And then there was Smith, who was not, in Chrissy's opinion, the best of anything. He was, as far as she knew, one of a kind, whatever he was, though he seemed to take his solitude cheerfully enough. She made no effort to pet him. He was resistant to the treatment, and seemed quite above such things, and in any case it was not Smith, in his own self, who had raised that reflexive grin. Smith meant Glint, as sure as the sky was blue, and Glint meant ... well.

She sunk onto a hay bale, and tried to decide just what Glint did mean. She had little hope of succeeding; she had never found an answer before.

Glint – his name had been Ramsbottom once, but he had embraced the name that he earned from the bright glitter of a trinket in his hatband – was valuable in that he had LPA to trade and interesting in that he had the knowledge to brew it into the concoction he called Radbegone. For that knowledge he had been her preserve since she was first considered old enough to handle him, but by that time he had been far too canny for her to learn what she had been sent to learn from him – not the recipe for his jollop, which was three parts snake oil, as their analysis had already shown them, but where he had learnt it from, and what else might be locked within his head.

There were Tourists who considered that allowing that head to roam into danger was akin to leaving an untended fire in a library, but she was reconciled to the loss of whatever he knew. His learning was as inaccessible as a book printed in the Korean characters that no Tourist could read. Worse than that; inscribed in Linear B, for it was clear that to Glint whatever knowledge he had locked away was as irrelevant to him as the temple records of ancient Crete. He kept what was useful to him, like his chemical knowledge, and what amused him, like his garish magazines, but the rest he let drift away from him like chaff in the breeze.

She had tried cunning, she had tried wheedling, she had blazed at him in fury that he was throwing away what mankind had once been and might yet be again, and at last she had acknowledged her helplessness and asked that others might be sent to deal with him.

They sent him pretty girls now. She saw it with amusement. As far as she knew they had got no further than her, and certainly she never had to prescribe for them after his visits. She should have been disappointed in that, for the sake of Tour, for the sake of knowledge, but she could not deny that it gave her a quiet satisfaction. It was juvenile, she told herself, to be pleased to see them fail as she had failed. She would have confessed the fault readily, if her childhood had trained her for confession. It would have been a very skilled confessor who saw beyond that conventional flare of jealousy, who understood, though she did not, that her reaction was the inverse of the disappointment she would have felt for an old friend if he had lowered himself to take casually what was so cynically offered.

There was one reaction that she could not hide from herself, and that was the surge of joy that came from seeing Smith in his accustomed stall, and knowing that Glint had come safely through another season. She might have explained even that away as the reassurance of continuity, of the evidence that life went on, but that could not account for her corresponding sadness at his departure. It was a loss, always. One did not look too eagerly for the return of any who left Tour, even if that return was promised, and Glint made no promises he could not keep.

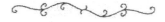

"Hey Merz Finch."

It was George who startled her from her reverie. Anyone else and she might have retreated in confusion, but she and George had been children together, and she answered him with reflexive mockery despite her troubled smile.

"Hey yourself, Merz Jones."

The title had enjoyed brief currency in their youth, when the Tourists had considered themselves a new republic and tried to vote themselves new mores. Some had stuck, some had faded away. Honorifics, except those that sprang from blood, were little use in a community so small. Chrissy was Aunt, and Ma, and Nana, but had never been Mrs, and was Merz only in jest. George settled beside her, casting a glance at the llamoid and misreading Chrissy's unhappiness.

"He's in more trouble than he knows, that's sure enough."

Chrissy had been trained for the guest halls. It was second nature to behave as if his comment was expected, to ask an open question so naturally that he would never doubt she had known all along.

"You don't think he'll ride this one out? He's been in trouble enough before."

"With that little Modern in tow? And you know Glint. Even if they'd met at the gate, he'd not abandon a companion to save his skin."

She was glad he ran on. Even that guest hall training was barely enough to cover her shock. Glint? Travelling with a Modern? If she had been less rigidly trained, the thought might have been 'shacked up with', it was there in George's tone, but she had too little data for the assumption. She groped for the keys in what George had told her, his own easy acceptance tearing away from her their lifetime of easy companionship.

"She," but had he said she? Had Chrissy only assumed it? "She's definitely a Modern?"

"Any odds on it. Them above haven't made themselves sure of it yet, but they didn't see her with Maddie."

At the sound of her name a mastiff roused herself from some hidden corner and ambled over for attention. Chrissy occupied her hands gratefully in giving Maddie the all over scratch she craved, but her attention was all on George.

Glint had come with two companions, a male traveller known to the Tour and a girl they had never seen before. There was some suspicion about the girl; though with her neck covered and her mouth closed there could be no certainty about her. Even so, one developed a feel

Human 76

for Moderns. It would be the end of Glint's easy relationship with the Tour if she proved to be what she had seemed.

"It may be that yesterday we did the last free favour we'll ever do for him."

He had known her long enough that, guest hall training or not, he could see that she had not heard. Or perhaps the shocks had accumulated to the point that she was beyond dissembling.

"It wasn't done for him, as such. That man Shambrook has been here a week or more. Had a tesla pistol he hadn't declared, so one of our sharp boys gave it a tweak. Seems Shambrook knew where Glint was likely to go, seems he lay in wait. Seems his heart wasn't strong enough to take the jolt his pistol gave him when he tried to use it."

"Shambrook? Well he's no loss, and he knew the rules well enough."

"You might want to make them a touch clearer to your friend Glint, from now on. He'll not get the allowances he once had."

She rose, her joints grumbling a little.

"I'll tell him, but she might not be a Modern. There's human girls on the road."

"She's a Modern alright, and he knows it. She had a turn, and I glimpsed her neck as she loosened her neckerchief. Glint was fast enough to get her covered again."

"A turn?"

"A moment of second sight, you must have seen how it takes them."

She was already leaving as he said it. She said dismissively "Oh, so she's wyrd."

It was as well that she couldn't see his face as he said sadly "Some folk call them talented."

130

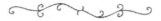

Chrissy's confidence had faded by the time she reached the guest hall. Glint and a Modern? She hadn't wanted to believe it, and it was true that there were girls on the road, but she had no grounds to doubt George's judgement. Glint and a Modern. It wasn't as if she had ever been able to count Glint as a friend, but he had been part of her life for a long time, and he had been part of the world before it changed. He had adapted to the world as it was, he had made it his own, but she had never seen it as his home. It was a greater loss than she had ever expected to find that he was willing to embrace a future she was still trying to avoid.

She had only meant to get a better view of Glint's party, but it was too late for breakfast and too early to trade, and the hall was too quiet to allow her to pass unnoticed. Glint had caught her eye and hailed her over before she could retreat.

He had greeted her as Chaffinch – an old nickname, and one she detested – but introduced her as Chrissy 'an old friend who's going to rustle us up some bacon sandwiches.' She'd denied there was bacon in the stores, and it was true enough that it was that cruel season when the weather was full of hope and the larder was full of empty drums. Glint had accepted it, or at least had appeared to. The girl had not. She had said nothing, but Chrissy was sure somehow that she'd been caught in the lie.

She had turned her attention to the third traveller. She had been hoping that he would give her a solution from the moment she first glimpsed him, because she knew the man. David, a traveller, a searcher, a man who was known to have unfortunate views on the place of

Moderns in the world. She had asked innocently when he and the girl had met up with Glint, and she had cursed herself for having no answer ready when he broke her world apart all over again with his simple explanation that Glint and Lauren – Lauren, at least the girl had a sensible name – had been together when he met them.

It put her on the wrong foot, and she couldn't disengage herself fast enough. Glint had wanted to talk, about his plans, about his friends, even about Shambrook, cooling in the yard. She'd squelched it, and she'd run, but she hadn't been able to run from her thoughts.

It was Nahria who came to mind, the Modern who had seemed to be no more or less than a child in need of protection. That was easily dealt with. Even wolf cubs are cute – didn't Glint know that?

She couldn't see the connection with this party until she remembered that David was a searcher, though whatever he sought he did not ask the Tour's assistance with his search. Nahria too, had been sought.

The first time Chrissy had seen the older girl – Gabby, was it? No, some modish, broken name with no history and no meaning. The first time Chrissy had seen her she had seen nothing more than a searcher, and even that was something she saw only at a second glance. The look of a searcher was one that she had known well, once, but she was a child then, and a lucky child, and they had all been so much older than her, immeasurably older in their loss, even when she topped them in years. Searchers had grown rarer, with the passage of time. Old bonds were fading, and new peoples were forming, settled peoples able to defend their own, nomad peoples inured to loss, all manner of peoples. There would always be searchers amongst them, all the same, as long as there were people such as the Prometheans to prey upon the weak.

Chrissy had been busy on the evening that she saw Gabby across the hall, and she hadn't spared any more than that second glance until her own party were preparing to leave. Then she had seen that Gabby was still in her place, alone in the sparsely occupied hall. Chrissy had wondered why she lingered, for the dormitories were warmer, but then she had seen the girl's face. For a moment it was a mask of fear and pain. That faded as quickly as it came, but it made Chrissy take a proper look, and what she saw was an image of Nahria with a few years' growth, and that old familiar look of the searcher.

So Nahria did have a sister, and that sister was looking for her. Chrissy had taken the correction in her stride, had left the hall by another door, and had tried to put it out of mind. Moderns, Chrissy. No concern of yours. Could a Modern be a searcher? Surely not. A trick of the light, perhaps.

It was harder to put out of mind a second time, harder to put out of mind now that she had seen Glint treat Lauren as a real girl. Glint, she thought, would have expected her to pass news of Nahria to her sister. Glint could go to hell. Glint was wrong.

She held on to the thought fiercely, but it did not seem to help.

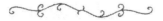

It was impossible to settle to her work. She sent a boy to excuse her from the laboratory, and sought solace once more in the stables. George had seemed to greet her with all his old warmth, and had ushered her up into a tack room off the hay loft before he let her see that he was in no mood to offer unconditional support.

Her conversation with Glint had been public; George knew that she had not passed on the clear warning that she had promised. They had quarrelled then, as bitterly as they had quarrelled long ago when their blood was hot and yearning fuelled the fight. They were older now, and the bond between them was not a proud and fragile need but a long fondness that neither was ready to shatter in a moment. She knew that it was a point that he would never agree to differ on, and his intransigence and certainty were another sharp wound to everything she believed. To her shame she had flung at him

"What do you know of it anyway, George Jones, out here in your stables?"

"I know the animals love them, and that's good enough for me."

"Which animals? Not this nonsense about all the birds of the air and all?"

"You think it nonsense? No, never mind."

There was something in the way he said it that tugged at her memory. Something about pepper vines, and flowers in the tropical dusk, but George had gone on, bitterly

"Here's one you can understand. The dogs love her."

"Dogs love their masters."

"If they're the only masters they've known, yes."

She didn't argue. Her response had been automatic and, she knew, essentially unfair; the dogs were Glint's. She softened a little, and George took his chance.

"I know you're afraid of the Moderns, Chrissy. I'd hoped you weren't. But if you can't grasp anything else, don't you at least know enough to show a stray dog what kindness is?"

"You know I do!"
"Do I? You're hardly showing it now."

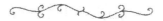

It had gone downhill rapidly from there, and she had left in haste. She was on the stairs before she remembered why his disappointment had reminded her of peppers. They had been very young, and he had been very earnest that night. He had talked of the people of the Barrantine Pass, "we who call ourselves Tourists, though we have forgotten the joke. We make it our business to know everything, and we are proud to have goods from the ends of the earth, but what's the profit in that, closed in on ourselves, within these walls? It's not enough to have silk if we never saw the moth that laid the eggs. We have pepper in our food, but it's a wrinkled black seed, not a glorious flower, heady in the tropical darkness. There's salt in the cellar there, but can we even begin to imagine the sun sparkling off the flats, the warm water, the powder crusting on the ankles of the workers wading there? Okay, we can live within these walls, we've had to. But we must not live within our heads. That's exactly the mistake our fathers made."

And she had laughed. She had been very young, but that hardly excused her. She had laughed, and she had told him that peppers grew on a vine with boring white flowers, as if that changed the essential truth of his argument.

It was very vivid to her as she came down the stable stairs, and she was entirely unprepared to find Glint and his companions, ready to leave. She never knew quite what she said to them, much less why. She mentioned the girl who needed their help, she knew that, and she promised Glint bacon, next time he came. But that was an old promise. There had always been bacon sandwiches next time for Glint, and it never seemed to dent his optimism that it was always barley and beans today.

She watched them until they had dwindled into the distance, thinking about heroes. Who was she to tell tales of heroes? Who was she to judge what qualities to endow them with? Better that the children should have tales of Nahria and Lauren and their kind. True tales – or nearly true tales, at least – that would coalesce around them as the need arose.

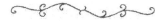

"The forest was young, but the house was old. There had been a time when things had been otherwise, when the forest had been ancient and the clearing in which the house stood had been new and raw, but the house had been both a beginning and an end. It had been a rich man's fancy, a ... "

Chrissy paused, and rocked the pencil restlessly between her fingers. What's a rich man, Nana Christina? What's money? Why gold?

" ... it had been built by a powerful trader, a strong man with a long train, as a place of safety to retreat to in the winter months. He had chosen the place for its solitude, but money attracts company ... "

Sakes Chrissy, there's a thousand stories they can read if they don't mind picking round references to a time when the world was otherwise. This is supposed to be one they can understand.

Chrissy had told herself a hundred times that the world had no need of her stories, but still they came. They were little trifles about the world she had lost, and they seemed to amuse the children, which should have been enough, but somehow she came back, time and again to the one tale that she couldn't seem to tell, to the house in the forest, the nameless hero, and the woman who was not a witch. She was, as ever, pleased to be distracted from it.

It was no guest hall servant who came for her, this time. It was a boy from the stable, and if he was welcome simply as a distraction he was doubly welcome when his breathless Merz Finch proclaimed him as a messenger from George. There was only one message that George was likely to send in haste, and she did not wait for the boy to recover himself sufficiently to deliver the message in full, but picked up a package she had waiting and went on ahead of him.

Glint, the boy had managed. And he's alone ... She had hoped, as spring blossomed around her, that when Glint came he would come alone, but she did not find the relief she expected in his solitude. She supposed it was David whose presence she missed. A friend to Moderns he might be, but he could be a good friend to Glint for all that, and it had been a comfort to think that Glint was no longer facing the world beyond the walls alone. Perhaps, she told herself brightly as she crossed the last inner yard, David had found what he was looking for. She would have liked to believe it, but her life had not trained her for optimism.

She slipped into the stable, to be waiting for him. There was a good view from the stable tower; she knew she would be well ahead of him. She'd had plenty of time

to settle her nerves by the time she heard Smith's
distinctive puffing and snorting at the door. She wasn't
really listening, but away in thoughts of her own. Even so,
she must have heard something awry in George's greeting,
and in the barely audible reply, because she found that as
the door swung open she was suddenly on edge again.

It meant that she was watching closely as Smith was
led in, and because she was watching closely she saw
beyond the hat and the jacket, saw at once that the stride
was wrong, and that there was no sparkle on that hat brim,
not even when a stray beam of sunlight caught it. That
gave her a moment's preparation she might not have had,
so that she was not entirely surprised when Lauren threw
Smith's reins over the rail and turned to face her, but even
half-prepared as she was, she was too torn between grief
and anger to respond. That saved her. Shock stilled a
tongue that would have been quick to accuse, and allowed
her to see the girl's defenceless face before rash words
could erase what was written there. For what was written
there, brought out in all the sharpness of a new wound by
the knowledge that in telling what she had come to tell she
must live the loss once more, was the fathomless grief of a
child.

A human child? Who could say? What monster
would care? A child, and full of human doubt and human
sorrow. In the second, greater shock of understanding it,
Chrissy's words came more harshly than she meant

"Why did you come here?"

But the words and the tone meant nothing. All that
mattered was that Chrissy was on her feet, catching the
girl by her elbow, guiding her stumbling legs to the hay
bale and settling her at rest. The girl was ready to be
steered. It was as if in coming here she had obeyed some
final command, and in coming to the end of her
instructions found no road ahead of her, and must now

face the grief she had suppressed. She managed to stutter out

"I thought you'd want to know."

She didn't have to explain what her news was. Chrissy said, more gently,

"I would. I do. I'm grateful."

She offered water, and saw the gentle flare of Lauren's nostrils before she drank. A corner of her mind screamed *She doesn't trust me! Doesn't trust the Tour's hospitality!*

But the outrage snapped off like an electric light before it could break through the surface of a life time's habitual serenity.

She's right not to, she acknowledged to herself, watching as the girl drank and repossessed herself. Our policy, that can change on a vote, on a whim, that's her life. And what kind of life is that for these poor wretches, trusting no one?

There was a mocking answer to that. It was a Tourist's life, safe behind these walls, trusting nothing that came from beyond them. But at least they had one another, as Lauren had had Glint, for a while. She was talking now, in broken phrases, about their search and the place that it had taken them to, about their last skirmish with a Promethean rearguard, about Glint's death in that broken, misused place.

He should have died in the sunshine! But Chrissy had a child to tend, and her own turmoil never showed. If she asked questions, she did so only to ease Lauren's telling of her tale. This was personal, and not Tour business. So it never came into the Tour's records that there were Promethean stock cards, and who knew what other secrets, blowing freely around the wreckage of a zoo, or that David, who might have been a searcher, or might not, had gone on with the Modern known as Ghabrie into the far north, whence the huiskee came.

At last she found herself asking "And what about you? Are you going on?"

"What else is there?"

"I don't know," Chrissy had been certain once that she did know, but this was not the time to say so, "whatever there is, I think you'll find it."

Chrissy was surprised to find that she really did have that faith in the girl, though she doubted that anyone could find the path alone. She was more surprised when Lauren asked "Did Glint know?"

"I don't think so."

"But you did know him?"

There was an urgency in the question that prepared Chrissy for worse. Before she could answer, Lauren had swept on with a childish impulsiveness that she would have to lose.

"I've wanted to ask you about him, who he really was, where he really came from."

Chrissy stalled. "What makes you think I'll know?"

For answer Lauren pulled a cheap hair slide from her pocket, a slide that would have appealed to a girl who dreamed of princesses in pre-Blast days. Chrissy had owned several, once, but she'd outgrown them. She hadn't even realised, until she held it in her hands and recognised it for the flashy trinket that Glint had worn his hatband, how similar his trophy was to the ones she had once worn. She still did not understand how this one connected them, until she turned it over in her hands and found her own name scratched there in her own childish writing.

For several minutes she turned it over and over in her hands, lost in a tangle of thoughts without words, until Lauren must have doubted that she would get any more answer than Chrissy's shocked reaction.

"Yes," Chrissy said at last. "We both came from the same place."

She wouldn't have said so, before the Blast, but before the Blast was so long ago now that all places there were one country. She continued painfully, hardly knowing her own thoughts until she heard them fall from her lips.

"But that ... it doesn't matter where, it doesn't mean anything, any more. I've wanted to go back there my whole life, but Glint, he belonged here. He made it his own country."

"But what kind of man was he?"

As if Chrissy knew that. Lauren knew the man better, in a few short months. Chrissy had been too busy her whole life trying to hide herself from him to really see him clearly. And what a chance was lost in that – for the Tour, yes, but she was surprised to find the greater loss was hers.

"He was a man who knew ... when to the let the right one in."

That earned Chrissy a very sharp look. Lauren's head cocked on one side, like a songbird.

"You thought that? But you didn't think I was the right one."

"I was wrong."

To cover the pain of the admission she brought out the parcel of bacon.

"I put this aside for Glint. I've owed it him a long time. You can have it and welcome, though God knows you've no reason to trust me."

Lauren took it gravely and Chrissy saw the twitch of her nostrils once more. Some folk call them talented, George had said. Well at least this one had learnt to use her talents with discretion, but the thought that she had expected to bring comfort came instead with a stab of pain. It wasn't nice to understand, and to know that she had been part of the reason that such discretion was so urgently required. The thought came and went in an instant, and their eyes met.

"I'm beginning to have one."

"I hope I can learn to deserve it. Glint was a good man, a good judge. He chose you, and I hope you choose so well."

Lauren accepted it in silence, slipping the bacon into her pack and gathering up Smith's reins.

"You're going?"

"I'll be back when I've aught to trade."

"That's more than Glint ever promised."

That got a smile at last, as they passed out into the yard together.

"I'm still learning."

She vaulted easily onto the llamoid's back, and Chrissy found herself loath to part. They walked down together to the gate in the palisade, Chrissy watching the girl sidelong, Glint and not Glint. Hardly knowing what she did, much less why, she tucked the trinket into Smith's harness. It almost surprised her to see it sparkling there; it certainly surprised Lauren.

"Glint needs a glint my girl. Every story needs a push. Chin up now."

There was a glint in Lauren's eye that matched the sparkle in the harness, but tears would pass. She nodded, tucked the clip back into its accustomed place, and then, like Glint, was gone.

It was evening when the Huntsman reached the house at Falls Edge for the first time. He had a haunch of venison over one shoulder and two dogs ranging casually ahead of him, but there was nothing casual in his approach. The dogs led him to an unlatched

door tucked away amongst the accretion of sheds and lean-tos that meant the working end of the house, and he found himself in a cavernous kitchen. There was a hook for the venison and a hearth for his fire, and if he noticed that the hearth was still warm he gave no sign of it.

An hour later there was a stew bubbling on that hearth, and the Huntsman's attention seemed entirely taken up in the gaudy magazine that he had unrolled from his pack. The woman who was not a witch watched from the shadows, savouring the smell of the stew but hungrier for company than for meat. She never knew that his hand was on his crossbow all the time she waited there. She never knew what sound she made that finally betrayed her. She certainly never knew what made her comply when he looked up, straight into the eyes he could not have seen, and said gruffly

"Might as well come out of the shadows, kiddo, and share this while it's hot."

Despite herself she smiled, and settled warily onto the bench, ready to find out what manner of man the world had sent to her."

HERO WORSHIP

Jeff Hollar

- ➤ **System Initializing**
- ➤ **Nanobot Capacitors … Fully Charged**
- ➤ **Nanocomp Capacitors … Fully Charged**
- ➤ **Nanocomp Boot Sequence … Successful**
- ➤ **Cybernetic Implant Systems Diagnostics Initializing**
- ➤ **Cybernetic Implant Activation … Successful**
- ➤ **All Systems Check … Optimal**

Planck regained consciousness in a preternatural state of awareness and infused with a deep sense of well-being and completeness. Though fully restored, he remained motionless and allowed himself a brief period of introspection and invocation before all else. His rituals to the Brotherhood satisfied, he returned to his obligations as a Retributor.

Pressing the tip of his tongue against a back tooth, he activated the satellite uplink that allowed him data-sharing with the mainframe computers of the Benanti Abbey. Using the visual acuity input of the display, he blinked out the access code provided to him by the Abbot himself. Rarely did Planck find himself under the specific authority of a given member of the Brotherhood hierarchy, but his current field assignment was not … typical.

His mission brief had indicated that the presence of no less than two and perhaps as many as seven Apostates of the 7-Series of Novitiates had been confirmed. As yet, Planck had only gleaned vague references to validate the initial intelligence provided to him. Still and all, in a world no longer graced by immediate confirmation of facts via an interlinked network, such apocryphal data was worthy of further investigation. Thus his presence here in the Fringe Lands.

He uploaded such meager updates as his investigation had so far yielded and was only nominally disturbed to find no new intelligence data to further his quest. He was a resourceful and proven field operative accustomed to unearthing leads himself, rather than being spoon-fed operational guidance. Faith and perseverance were the hallmarks of a proper servant of the Brotherhood and so Planck would forge onward, confident in his belief that his cause was just and destined to be fulfilled to the benefit of all.

Severing the data connection, he remained immobile and reached outward with his augmented senses for guidance forward. He received little of encouragement. Two days prior, he had received confirmation of a raid on an Alliance outpost responsible for the development and exploitation of one of the Augments currently on his tracking list. As was often the case, the laboratory files conflicted in several telling ways with the reports they had filed with the Abbey.

The subject, a young adult female, was confirmed to have entered the facility as a Level Two Novitiate, indicating she had successfully completed both the initial physical and psychological screenings necessary to validate consideration for the Protocols. Of these, there were five, as Planck was well aware having submitted to and survived such as part of his Brotherhood commitment. Those Protocols involved serums to augment five specific requirements: strength, agility, speed, intelligence and healing. Completion to that point designated a Novitiate as 7-Series. From there, the advancement became ever more discerning and demanding.

While a significant percentage of applicants failed or, sadly, perished in the completion of the five core Protocols, it was at Level Eight that very meticulous consideration was taken to determine which subjects were most deserving of and most likely to survive the next phase. Of any given group of ten Novitiates selected, it was considered extremely successful if any more than a half dozen were able to be termed "operational". Planck knew all too well the fascinating capabilities and the inherent risks of carrying the Implanted Nanocomputational Module or INM. Though it had been decades since he had undergone the procedure he still recalled his fear, his pain, and his utter confusion when the module was fully installed and activated.

The INM, or nanocomp as referred to in Alliance medical/scientific circles, was one of the most advanced Post-Blast technological achievements ever conceived and actually implemented. The surgical process alone took nearly twelve hours to complete. It began by slaving the device directly to the recipient's heart with ancillary connections to all of the internal organs. Additional linkage was made between the device and specific areas of the subject's brain. This included the installation of an external data jack that would be used to directly input data, skills sets and such, in Novitiates determined fit for field duty. As a precautionary measure of control, a pellet of compressed thermite was additionally installed at the base of the brain stem to guarantee Alliance control of the nanocomp by remote or, in extreme situations, to allow captured operatives an 'out' before interrogation/exploitation.

After the nanocomp was installed, activated and assimilated the Novitiate received perhaps the greatest boon the Alliance had to offer - the nanobots. Of microscopic size and limitless potential, the nanobots offered the promise of near-limitless lifespan, unwavering health and virtual indestructibility. One million of the self-replicating micro-machines were implanted and placed directly under the control of the advanced capabilities of the nanocomp. The nanobots additionally maintained the ability to function independently of the nanocomp in the event of temporary disruption of signal linkage. They also had the benefit of being able to service and repair such damage as might be inflicted upon the nanocomp that did not directly kill the individual.

When tasked by the nanocomp, these diminutive protectors had the ability to screen out toxins of both natural and chemical nature. They purified the recipient's body, repaired the inevitable wear and tear of travelling through areas of extreme contamination, and extended lifespan by retarding the degradation of those organs and internal systems most susceptible to the ravages of time. Thus no Radbegone, hedge witch remedies or fumbling non-Alliance medics were ever required.

When an operative decided or the nanocomp determined a sufficient level of hostilities or physical risk existed, the nanobots became the most advanced form of personal body armor ever conceived. When imminent threat was detected, the 'bots formed an ingenious technological equivalent of lamellar armor. By massing and emitting specific electromagnetic patterns, they made the body impervious to damage by conventional handheld weapons of a low-tech nature (knives, clubs, etc.) as well as insuring non-penetration of standard kinetic projectiles and the output from nearly all man-portable energy devices. Truly a boon to any devoted follower of the Alliance.

Beyond Level Eight, candidates might receive additional cybernetic enhancements of various sorts before being elevated to Level Ten, or Full Field Operative. As a result of nearly three decades of service to the Brotherhood and its objectives, Planck boasted an impressive seven cybernetic augmentations making him a Level Fifteen or F.R.I.A.R. (Fully Re-Engineered Infiltration Agent Retributor). He knew instinctively and in practice that he had little to fear from a group of Level 7 Apostates.

No longer able to resist the primal need to serve the Brotherhood and thus the Alliance, Planck opened his eyes and rose to his feet with sinuous grace. Naked but for a pair of thin Lycra shorts, Planck was an impressive specimen. Topping two meters in height and massing 120 kilos, his body was heavily muscled and devoid of scars, wrinkles or other detriments. Clean-shaven, bald and devoid of any trace of body hair, his skin a bronzed copper hue, he radiated physical power and potentiality.

After donning his dun-colored skin suit and heavy knee boots he felt less exposed to view, as the chameleon-tech clothing blurred him to near invisibility. He folded his Rad Lizard-skin duster and his trademark hat into his pack as unnecessary accoutrements until he re-entered civilized lands. He strapped a wide belt of the same Rad Lizard hide about his waist. Pouches on the belt held various necessities like trade commodity gems and such. Lastly he slid Constant into a loop of his belt. She, Constant, was his lifelong companion and most prized possession.

She was one of the only weapons of her kind still in existence. Not at all impressive to look upon, she was, nevertheless, not an item whose worth was to be gauged in appearance alone. She took the form of a tube approximately one half meter in length and composed of a shining grayish metal that was, in point of fact, nano-infused iridium. Constant predated the Blast and was still every bit as functional as the day the Brotherhood's Knights Marshal took possession of her and placed her into their secure artifacts armory.

She was a Coherent Beam Refractory Amplifier, or C.O.B.R.A. Bonded to her user by a DNA-specific encryption, she could only be wielded by her champion. Her nanite component allowed the weapon to be controlled directly by the conscious will of the user as channeled to the nanos by electronic impulses. At will, she projected a beam of coherent energy or plasma capable of taking the form of whatever weapon the user deemed most appropriate. In the blink of an eye she could alter her output to manifest as a sword, an axe, a spear or really any conceivable hand weapon. Planck still recalled, as if it were yesterday, the exact moment they had bonded.

He had entered the Promethean crèche system at the tender age of six years old. It was only the fifth year Post-Blast and the times were … chaotic. His parents had been killed by a team of Reclamators seeking tech that was held by those deemed unworthy to have it. With little ceremony and even less belief in his viability, he had been handed over to the Brotherhood for training. From that day forward he was no longer the person he had been and invoked the privilege of choosing for himself a new name - a Promethean name. He became Hieronymus Ignatius Planck.

Ten years later, that small, malnourished boy had attained his full growth and survived the first tentative Protocols. He requested Trial by Combat to prove his worthiness to become a full Brother and performed on a level only hinted at in the oldest archives of the Brotherhood. Squaring off against a round dozen competitors in single combat, the final three being Masters of Arms, he triumphed while not sustaining even the slightest injury. He was, within hours, awarded his Brotherhood and was led to the Alliance Armory to choose a Blessed Weapon from the amassed horde.

He was drawn to her as a moth to a flame and was so steadfastly determined the Knight Marshal was unable to convince him otherwise. Upon proving he actually could interface with the artifact (for no one had in the annals of the Armory), he was presented with an unexpected quandary. The Knight Marshal, with a wry grin, had demanded to know what name he intended to give to his now-lifelong companion. Hiero had been confused and so bold as to ask what value there was in naming a tool.

The Knight Marshal had cuffed him about the head for the affront of calling such a precision instrument a tool. He reminded the startled lad that, as he should well know, there is power in names. Thus the "fiery one with the blessed name ... that of a maker of science" was no more a "tool" than was the C.O.B.R.A. Suitably chagrined, Hiero had thought for only a moment before whispering that she was to be named Constant. Since she would be his only weapon for all of his days and with him at all times, it was only fitting. The Knight Marshal mused on this for a moment before bursting into a full belly laugh, while inscribing into the Armory annals that the weapon was to be henceforth known as Planck's Constant.

So lost was he in the random thoughts and flashes of the past, that Planck was startled to be snapped back to the here and now by his nanocomp requesting a status update for his inactivity. Shaking off the query and annoyed at his wool-gathering, he returned to his preparations. A glance to the west confirmed the advent of early night. He had slept the day away allowing his cybernetic systems to recharge via solar radiation as the meat portion of him rested. Digging into his pack, he extracted and quickly consumed four of the Alliance's packaged field rations. He would need to move hard and fast and hoped the 6000 calories ingested would be sufficient to sustain him. As they were all he had left of his initial stores, they would have to do.

Taking a bearing from his nanocomp of his target's last known location and projected direction of travel, he nodded in satisfaction. They had not changed course while he rested and could be headed to only one destination. Shouldering his pack, Friar Hieronymus Ignatius Planck, Retributor Prime of the Holy Promethean Brotherhood set off into the burgeoning night at a brisk run.

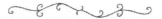

Hiero's face contorted in an involuntary spasm as his nanocomp flashed another warning to his ocular implant. As outstanding a piece of technology as it was, the nanocomp could sometimes be a bit too persistent in its task of monitoring his status. It wasn't as if he didn't already realize his cybernetic systems were operating at minimal levels due to depletion of his power reserves. He wasn't unaware of the bone-deep pain in his joints and muscles that presaged complete physical shutdown if he didn't ingest a massive amount of calories in very short order. In his three decades as a field operative of the Brotherhood he had depleted himself before, albeit seldom to this degree. Still, it was only pain and pain was transient. Pain was confirmation the body still functioned and as long as function persisted and fortitude remained, Hiero could ... would prevail.

Two days of omnipresent rain had wrought more havoc on him than he had anticipated. He had allowed the promise of success in overtaking his quarry to cloud his judgment. The 7-Series he pursued was definitely to be found at a trading post nee hotel but a scant twenty kilometers from his present location. The Barra, the Tour - by whatever name it was known - was not an unfamiliar way-post to him. He had been sent there some years ago to conduct covert surveillance and evaluation of the threat potential the place presented to the Alliance and its interests.

He was well aware there was far more than met the eye in the ramshackle structures and outbuildings. Even at this distance, his nanocomp could detect in the air the trace elements associated with the production of electrical energy. He could almost smell the hydrocarbon emissions of some sort of refined fuel oil. His recommendation to the Council had been that, while the continued existence of a metaphorical nest of techno-snakes in what was clearly Alliance territory was troublesome, their meddling had not developed to such levels as to pose a serious threat at the time. He welcomed the opportunity to reassess the threat level as a side effect of his hunt.

With a renewed sense of purpose and still undaunted in his faith, Hiero redoubled his pace, the consequences to himself be damned. He would survive. He would fulfill his task. He would not allow hardship to overcome him. He was a Promethean. Nothing short of total commitment could be permitted. By Einstein's Frizzled Hair, he would survive!

Two kilometers from the periphery of the outpost, Planck paused to put on his duster and the wide-brimmed slouch hat he always wore when in unfriendly territory. It obscured his features and obviated the need for him to expend energy by activating the holo-illusion to mask the harsh red glow of his ocular implant. With his impromptu disguise in place, he shrugged his pack back on and stealthily covered the remaining distance to his objective.

His power reserves down to a niggling five percent he paused in the shadow of a collapsed garage to prioritize his systems usage. The tracking subroutine confirmed that the Apostate was within the hotel and stationary. He shut down all of his targeting systems as non-essential for the moment and was rewarded with an undeniable decrease in energy consumption. Swallowing down his pain he made his way to the mouth of the narrow alleyway that he sought.

Still unobserved by any of the myriad life forms, human and otherwise, in close proximity, he crept into the service walkway and proceeded forward until he was no longer visible from the main thoroughfare. The next few minutes promised to be fraught with risk but his need to replenish his systems was unavoidable. That his siphoning of electricity from the concealed sources beneath the hotel would go unnoticed was unlikely. He could not imagine such a covert operation was not actively monitored from some sort of control room.

He was relying on the fact that the producers of said electricity could hardly make a public outcry over the fact their systems were being pirated. To do so would be laughable and likely to make them a priority target for Alliance reprisals as well as the target of unsavory predatory elements of all sorts. He intended to secure sufficient to return him to full operability in as timely a manner as possible. He anticipated a high probability he could do so and depart the area before any watchmen could investigate the source of the power drain.

He stopped at the midpoint of the alley and initiated an active scan for electromagnetic emissions. His ocular implant overlaid a target reticule that indicated a cable of some sort ran directly through the wall before him. Steadying his hands he proceeded with even more caution. Drawing Constant from its holster, he willed a tight-beam output sufficient to cut through the wall and expose the conduit. Grasping the thick cable in a tight grip, he directed his nanobots to initiate the power transfer.

Despite knowing what to expect, Planck's expression waxed euphoric as the surge of energy flooded through his veins. He tamped down his enthusiasm as inappropriate and concentrated on the heads-up display for his nano systems. The levels rose steadily but far too slowly for his liking. He hadn't been aware the nominal output of the facility would be so ... weak. Two minutes later, he had achieved full recharge and let the cable fall from his grip. Wasting no time, he left the obvious proof of system intrusion behind him and returned to the main street.

A rumble in his stomach reminded him of his next priority. The dour expression on his face had less to do with his gnawing hunger than it did for the compromises he would have to make to fulfill that need. Even without the necessity to be unobtrusive as a result of compromising the power grid, he didn't dare take the chance of alerting the 7-Series to his presence in the area. That meant dealing with one of his few known connections in this squalid demesne.

Shambrook was a thoroughly odious though somewhat useful creature. A scavenger and a jackal, his measly form bore the scars of too-frequent forays into the poisoned areas of the Fringe. The weeping sores gave him a most unpleasant odor and did little to improve his sullen disposition. But, by Curie's Lead Apron, the little squidge would have access to food in the staggering quantities Planck currently required. Quelling his disgust, Planck made his surreptitious way to the back alley most commonly known to be Shambrook's favorite haunt.

Planck crossed his arms over his broad chest and stared at the body lying face down in the stinking mud. It would appear he had located Shambrook a tad too late to satisfy his needs. Glancing about and seeing no one, he knelt to examine the body. Seeing no obvious indications of foul play, Planck laid a hand on the exposed skin of Shambrook's arm and initiated an active bio-scan. The man had died, so the nanocomp indicated, of cardiac arrest with an 89% probability it had been as a result of an energy discharge that disrupted the man's bioelectrical field. The Tesla pistol lying next to the body might well explain his death.

Planck had no more than picked up the weapon when his nanocomp flashed a hazard warning not to attempt to use the pistol. Allowing his ocular to survey the device, he immediately saw the two wires that had been crossed to create a fatal discharge upon activation. His suspicions confirmed, Planck wasted no prayers or sympathy on the carcass of the vile creature he had known as Shambrook. After rifling the body for any items of value or worth, he rose to his feet and went in search of that without which he simply would not survive … food.

Head down to mask his face and olfactory enhancers active, he soon located what his sensors indicated was a source of sustenance. The small shop was closed but the smells were unmistakable. Planck isolated two life readings within and moved quickly and decisively. Crossing the threshold with a burst of speed, he kicked the door closed behind him. Before either of the occupants could do much more than utter surprised exclamations, Planck had snapped their necks like twigs. Over the next hour, he consumed every bit of sustenance in the place. Slipping quietly out the door, he was once more concealed in the shadows and moving to the far edge of the settlement. Setting his internal chronometer for an hour before dawn, he dialed down his cybernetic systems to minimal and slept … fully fed and free of dreams.

The sun arose with Planck lying on his belly on a low promontory to the north of The Tour. He wasn't entirely sure who he was looking for, but his nanocomp, as well as his intuition, indicated that today would see contact with the Apostate he had been tracking for the last several days. He knew her to be female and barely mature. He strongly suspected she would have acquired allies in this land so sparsely policed by Alliance troops. He was pleased when the motley trio of subjects rode past his very location with no indication that he had been detected.

Planck's ocular scanned the faces and compared them to known anti-Alliance subjects. Glint! By Nobel's Dusty Beakers, it was Glint! The man was considered to be a target of opportunity to be neutralized with extreme contempt. A holo appeared in Planck's display of a warrant bearing the seals of both the Alliance President and the Brotherhood Prelate Marcus. This … man … was directly responsible for countless raids on Alliance research laboratories as well as the deaths of no fewer than thirty Alliance scientists.

And what was this? A blinking icon directed him to another file. The photo bore little resemblance to the man riding the unusual beast but his nanocomp indicated with 86% certainty it was him. Ramsbottom Elias Crippin, Professor Emeritus of Organic Chemistry, University of Manchester. He had vanished in the first few years Post-Blast and was believed to have perished during the period of unrest. Planck now had reason to believe that reports of the good Professor's death had been greatly exaggerated.

The second individual was identified in the Alliance database merely as 'David'. A known anti-Alliance sympathizer and probable terrorist. While not the catch

Ramsbottom might well be, he was still a thorn in the Alliance's side deserving of removal.

Finally, the girl. 'Lauren' she was tagged in the research file. Though she was listed as a 7-Series, he got mixed readings when he scanned her. The energy signature was somehow … wrong. It was quite possible her forced removal from Enhancement had somehow mutated her into someone … something else. She would be of great interest to the Alliance's Forensics Research facility. Forensic since Planck now had no reason to believe that the trio deserved anything other than the ultimate expression of retribution … death.

Now that their unique bio-signatures were stored in his nanocomp, Planck felt no need to dog them too closely. He was now able to isolate their location to within meters via his satellite uplink. Their projected course would lead them into the area of the defunct Gygg Zoo which disturbed Planck greatly. These fools had no way of knowing Alliance scouts had declared the area Extremely High Risk due to confirmed reports of Mutant Army rabble in the immediate vicinity. Although, Planck mused, if he were careful and patient perhaps the M.A.'s would do the wet work for him. He could not allow harm to befall the Apostate as she would be of far more value to the Alliance if taken alive. He resolved to follow them at a discrete distance and watch how events unfolded before making a plan of action.

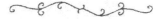

Planck had again taken a position of high surveillance on a windswept dune and watched Glint and his party blithely wander into the Mutant Army ambush. How had Glint managed to survive so long when he was so oblivious to the dangers around him? It beggared explanation. Planck opted for discretion as the better part of valor and settled for high-definition video recording of the events that unfolded.

He would have preferred Glint to face an Alliance firing squad after a very publicly viewed trial but was satisfied enough by the man's demise to admit it served the greater good of all regardless of how the defiler had met his end.

He was left speechless when the Apostate demonstrated paranormal abilities of both teleportation and shapeshifting. She had, indeed, mutated beyond what might normally be expected as within the realm of 7-Series abilities.

The high point of the whole affair, however, was the appearance of the second 7-Series. It was Ghabrie herself! An infamous Apostate figure, indeed. She had made a mockery of the Brotherhood and of the Alliance by spitting upon the gifts she had been so generously given. He now knew who his priority must be. When Lauren, David and Ghabrie broke company he knew he must apprehend Ghabrie and leave Lauren for another day.

Planck took a drink of the tepid home-brewed beer and said a silent prayer to the great Saint Semmelweis that his bio-filtration system was equipped to counteract the various toxic contaminants in the beverage. Seated as he was at a bench in the back of the way-house, the beer was more of use as window dressing than as any means of satisfying thirst. His thirst now was to corner the elusive Ghabrie and offer her retribution.

He scanned the crowd inside the dimly-lit bunker known as Mom's Place. The proprietor, the Alliance database had informed him, was former Free States Alliance Colonel Jerome "Mom" Mombersly. Though the redoubt enjoyed a rather dangerous and unscrupulous clientele, Mombersly was the only subject Planck considered to be any sort of threat. Mombersley was indeed an anachronism in the Post-Blast world. He was an Augment.

Conceived in the latter days of the war between the Free States Alliance and the Confederated Nations, the Augment Project had been a last-ditch effort by the FSA to combat the numerical superiority of the CN by use of the advanced technology of the FSA scientists. Little factual information was available on the Augments other than that they were some sort of genetically-engineered super soldiers of unknown capabilities. Their actions in the Great War were ultimately without purpose as both the FSA and the CN had vanished in nuclear firestorms.

Mombersly was as tall as Planck and perhaps even more massive. Muscles rippled under his sleeveless leather vest and he projected an air of silent and unquestioned control. That he appeared quite hale and hearty when his age must be more than seventy years was impressive to a warrior of Planck's experience. In the event that his capture of Ghabrie might result in a physical confrontation (a strong likelihood), Mombersly would bear watching. He was armed with another anachronism. Planck recognized it as a Mark VII crew-served railgun that had been modified into an enormous pistol-gripped weapon. Weighing in at over twenty kilos even stripped down, Planck noted it did not seem to hamper the big man's mobility in the least. Yes, he would, most certainly, bear watching.

Planck's nanocomp beeped an alert that he could almost have anticipated without its assistance as three red blips on his proximity scanners approached from various directions. Ghabrie and two other Apostates had arrived. In his latest downlinked update from Alliance Intelligence, he had been made aware of conclusions gleaned from a variety of sources that Ghabrie was organizing her fellow Apostates for an expedition to recover her sister from the Benanti Research Facility. The Brotherhood's mandate was predictable. Ghabrie and confederates must not, under any circumstances, be permitted to pursue their objective. Planck was to subdue and incarcerate as many of the Apostates as possible. Given the unknown variables of the exact nature of the subjects' mutated abilities, casualties were to be expected. No animus would fall on Planck were it necessary for him to put the Apostates down rather than pursue capture. He was uncertain of the outcome of the impending confrontation but had faith that his skills as a Retributor Prime would not see him fail this night.

With their arrival imminent, Planck elevated his nanocomp to Passive Combat Mode. It would take mere seconds to place the unit in Full Combat Mode but it was best to prepare when seconds might mean the difference between survival and failure. Additionally, he projected an undetectable subsonic carrier wave that would act as an avoidance shield. Essentially, while he made no special effort to conceal his presence, the avoidance shield would render him invisible to those within the field's range. Even if they looked directly at him, the carrier would induce them to look elsewhere. It was a capability possessed by only a handful of chosen F.R.I.A.R.'s and so would not, he hoped, be anticipated by the Apostates.

Ghabrie sauntered through the front entrance with a brazen display of nonchalance. While there were numerous Alliance warrants in effect for her and roving troops of Promethean security forces tacked up posters of known Apostates everywhere, she clearly felt no fear.

Planck was both impressed and disgusted by the blatant effrontery of the girl. He vowed then and there to offer her the opportunity to surrender, but would not hesitate to designate her as his primary target if push came to shove.

He watched her walk to the bar and exchange pleasantries with Mom before taking a tankard and seating herself with a clear view of the entrance. If she had any hint of Planck's presence it was not evident in her body language. She slid into a seat, placing her fabled bow within easy reach. The lithe play of her muscles as she pushed back a strand of her dark hair portended strength. He found her intricate facial tattoos and the faux antlers to be curious affectations and wondered if they had any significance or were worn merely for effect.

So intent had he been on her arrival he had not initially noted the presence of David. His tousled hair and reserved looks caused him to fade into anonymity beside his companion. Planck noted, with some interest, Shambrook's scabbarded katana across David's back and he wondered if the man had become any more proficient with the blade than the Mutant Army encounter indicated. Planck considered the man more of an annoyance than a target and so had attached no importance to his presence. He promised himself not to be so dismissive in future.

As Planck observed, two more individuals entered the redoubt from the back entrance. The first he recognized as Amnet Singh, designated Reptiloid 78 in the Alliance database. Planck had, of course, heard of Reptiloid subjects but never actually encountered one. The youth was on the short side but strongly built. From his belt hung a curved short sword and an antiquated slug thrower that belonged more in a museum than on the belt of an Alliance Apostate. His body language was relaxed but his face belied a tenseness Planck could understand well.

His companion had no name listed in the files and was merely designated Felinoid 77. Lean and sporting a mane of wild orange hair he moved with the sinuous grace of a dancer. He was festooned with a wide assortment of knives of varying sizes and lengths. Having trained to Mastery in close quarters combat, Planck knew those knives in the right hands could be deadly. The man appeared to possess those right hands.

As with Ghabrie, neither of the lads appeared to have any clue of Planck's presence. They took drinks from the bar as well and seated themselves at the same table with Ghabrie. Neither of them took measures to guard their backs or to take advantage of the bar's setup to adopt a defensive posture. After exchanging greetings with Ghabrie the three drew closer together and seemed intent on their private conversation.

Planck's nanocomp had marked and designated the three primary targets, with Mom and David tagged as secondary targets. His hand slid slowly to his side as Planck drew Constant from his belt. He kept the weapon below table level as he considered his various attack options. While Constant was primarily a hand weapon, she did have the capability to launch plasma bursts to lethal effect. This, he mused, might perhaps be his best option. While 7-Series subjects were fast he felt certain his training and experience would still provide him the edge. The avoidance shield gave him an enormous advantage as he would be striking with the confidence of complete surprise in his favor. While he would be seeking non-lethal hits, he had no delusions they might not be necessary after his initial attack.

Ready as he was to begin his attack, Planck paused as an unavoidable feeling of unease washed over him. Years of combat-honed reflexes kicked in and he scanned the room with all sensors active in an effort to identify the source of his agitation. He saw no obvious reason for ...

no, wait! He was being watched. A scraggly-haired girl of no more than eight years was staring directly at him. Her face was hideously scarred by radiation, the skin seeming to have melted like candle wax. A bulging mass of keloid tissue covered what would have been, on any ordinary face, the place where her eyes would be. So, although the ragamuffin was blind, she was clearly oriented facing him and her body language left little doubt she saw something.

Before he could react, the child scampered through the crowded bar more quickly than could any sighted child. Ducking and weaving, she placed objects and bodies between her and Planck in an effort to thwart his attack options. She stopped at Ghabrie's table, tugging at her arm as she pointed directly at Planck. She was gibbering madly and though Ghabrie could have heard little more than guttural noise, she seemed to immediately grasp the meaning. She pushed the child behind her as she snatched up her bow and nocked an arrow.

Her companions reacted nearly as quickly. Singh threw the table over and their unnamed companion dove to the other side. Both figures shimmered with waves of distortion and in their places stood an enormous Rad Lizard and a feral Death Leopard. The lizard began snorting and pawing the floor, its lethal tail arcing back and forth. The leopard dropped into a crouch, baring all of its claws and exposing a mouthful of pointed teeth and two enormous fangs.

The lizard spun and launched a dozen six-inch spikes directly at Planck's presumed location. He ducked and rolled, his plasma bolt striking the reptiloid squarely in the face. The spikes rattled against the wall with tremendous force. Planck dropped his now-unnecessary avoidance and sought an unobstructed second shot. It was then that Mom chose to assert himself by drawing his railgun and firing in the same motion. Superheated projectiles of kinetic energy struck the lizard broadside, gouging hunks from its hide in a spray of indigo-purple blood. Enraged and mortally wounded the beast spun about and in its dying throes stitched Mombersley with a salvo of spikes. Impressively, the titan held his feet against the force of impact. His mouth dropped open in a silent scream and he fell to the floor thrashing spastically as the venomous spikes ended the life of the anachronism. Singh crashed to the floor as well and reverted to human form. His body was an oozing mass of blackened flesh and charred bone.

Planck's hand blurred through the air as he caught Ghabrie's first arrow, snapping it in two and casting it aside. Her second arrow struck his chest and shattered against his nanite armor. Before she could fire again, the Death Cat yowled out its challenge and bounded towards Planck, launching itself into the air midstride.

Rising to one knee, Planck ducked under the airborne cat, lifting Constant upward and projecting a three-foot lance of glowing blue energy. The weapon took the monster squarely in the chest sinking deep into the hard-muscled flesh. Using every iota of his cybernetically-enhanced strength and the attacker's own momentum, he arced the beast's body over his head and slammed it to the floor with crushing force. He twisted his weapon free, deactivating the force and advanced on Ghabrie. Realizing the futility of a bow in quarters this close she had discarded it and now held a pair of foot long serrated knives in her hands.

Frowning his disapproval, Planck dodged her first frenzied double thrust. He lashed out backhanded, splitting her lip and dropping her to the floor with a sound akin to a thunderclap. He straddled her prone form and raised Constant over his head. A curved blade of force emerged as he made to end her life.

He heard rather than felt the blow as David entered the fray, striking at Planck's seemingly unprotected back.

The razor-sharp blade screeched in protest against his lamellar armor before it snapped off leaving David with but the hilt and a few inches of jagged, broken metal. Planck whirled about, his eyes smoldering with menace. He dropped Constant where she struck point first and stood upright in the floor. Planck grabbed David's unarmed hand slapping it flat against the table and holding it there. Crushing David's other hand in his grip, he spun the man's wrist about and skewered the hand he held in place. David's eyes were unavoidably drawn to the tableau of his one hand having so grievously injured the other. He wrenched at the sword's stump, tears streaming from his eyes as he howled with pain.

Satisfied that David would not be a factor anymore, Planck returned his attention to Ghabrie. Snatching Constant up he turned, only to be caught by the metal-shod toe of Ghabrie's right boot in an obviously non-enhanced part of his anatomy. His breath whuffed out of him and he bent at the waist barely retaining his hold on his weapon. Ghabrie scrambled out from under him and rose to her feet with an impish grin and a mock curtsey. Turning, she fled out into the darkness.

Planck stumbled back upright and painfully limped after his target. Switching his ocular implant to infrared he scanned the immediate area. He saw absolutely no sign of Ghabrie in any direction. How was that even possible? He'd not been ... incapacitated for more than a handful of seconds. As if in answer, the silence of the night was split by the raucous screech of an avian predator. He glanced upward and saw the glowing red form of the kestrel wheeling about the sky. In a blur of feathers and wings the bird swooped low over his head before arrowing away to the north.

Planck sheathed Constant and saluted the fleeing kestrel before rendering a court-perfect bow. He chuckled with chagrin and whispered, "Round one to you, my dear. Well played … well played."

HUMAN X

Michelle Fox

Is this real? I take a deep breath and feel an irritating tickle deep in my chest. I cough and attempt to move, but I am being weighed down by something my numb body can't make out. Stale air looms and stalks my senses, slowly creeping into my nostrils without my consent. My eyelids flutter but refuse to open, forcing me into darkness. With infirm senses, I have only my mind to look to for answers. I see images of a bright, arid landscape and three men hauling wooden handcarts filled with scrap supplies and plastic containers of water. Heat-distorted, bare craggy mountains dot the horizon. Everything else is unclear. *Why can't I remember?*

Thu-boomp Thu-boomp goes my heart. The palpitations are all I can hear. *Am I buried alive? Were we caught in a storm? Were we robbed? Am I bleeding out? Am I going to live? Am I going to die? Thu-boomp. Thu-boomp.*

Muffled, disembodied voices hush my beating heart. *Are they real?* I'm not sure at first, but they are growing louder and clearer.

"It's a shame," a strident male voice says. "The barrens are rough."

"I found some water," another male voice chimes. His voice is deep and controlled; dramatically different from the first.

"We should burn them," a reverent female voice says.

Burn who?

"Burn them?" the first sounds shocked.

Hey, wait!

167

"Yes, burn them. We should at least have the decency to do that."

I'm here! Help me! I'm here!

"They had the Scar, too," the second says, still controlled. "I agree with Pri. We should burn them."

Help! Can't you hear me? My voice barely escapes my throat. I realize that there is no way they are going to hear me.

Plop! Something is thrown on top of whatever I'm buried under. *Plop!* I gasp. The extra weight is crushing my torso, threatening to suffocate me.

Every muscle in my body tenses as I struggle to move. I grit my teeth and attempt to lift the weight off of myself. Splinters dig into my hands, but I have to push through the pain. No use. *Thu-boomp, thu-boomp, thu-boomp.*

"Rest in peace," controlled male voice says.

I claw and beat the wooden surface above me and cry out as splinters burrow further underneath my fingernails. But I can't stop.

"Did you hear that?" Pri's voice comes to my rescue.

"Hear what?" Strident voice says.

I beat and claw with everything I have left in me, which isn't much. I have to hope that it will be enough to alert them to my presence.

"I think someone is buried under there!" Pri exclaims. "Quick! Help me with this!"

I take a deep breath and sink into the mess of wood and debris beneath me. The clatter of wood is like a lullaby to my weary ears; soothing and sweet.

It doesn't take long for the strangers to reach me. Several hands grab hold of me, drag me out of the rubble, and carefully roll me on my back. I groan as my atrophied muscles stretch for the first time in … well I really don't know how long.

One of the strangers lets out a big, exaggerated sigh. "How does someone get *that* big during a famine? Ridiculous."

I squint and cover my eyes as bright sunlight seeps through my eyelids. My tattered clothing has left some of my skin exposed, which is scorching in the sun.

"You are lucky to be alive," the controlled male said. "Your comrades were not so lucky, I'm afraid. You would have joined them had we not found you."

An awful, sinking feeling erupts in my stomach. "They're dead?" I breathe. "Are you sure?"

There was a small pause.

"There ain't no mistaking *that*," strident male remarks.

I let out a heavy sigh and nod. Tears burn my eyes, but do not shed. Death is as familiar to me as loneliness — a sting I have grown numb to but a sting nonetheless.

"We are sorry," Pri says, her voice empathetic.

"Thank you," I say as sincerely as I can. I attempt to open my eyes again, but my vision has not changed. I blink over and over again, but still no change.

"What's your name?" Pri asks.

I rub my eyes and blink several more times. "Are my eyes open?"

Another pause.

"Yes?" Strident male sounds confused.

No! Sweat beads down my scarred, bald head and pools in the corner of my mouth. My chest rises and falls faster than I can control. I blink a few more times before I accept the truth: *I'm blind.*

I shake my head and clench my fists. My thoughts are like electric shocks which zip through my mind, burning everything in their path. "I can't see anything!"

"May I take a look?" controlled male asks.

I shake my head and instinctively guard myself with my hands. *He'll surely notice.*

"You can trust Narron," Pri reassures. "He knows what he's doing."

Even worse.

"Forgive me, but you are in no condition to protest," Narron points out. "You will need my help if you wish to recover."

Damn. I lower my hands in surrender, but my muscles remain tense.

Gloved fingers tickle my cheeks as they gently steady my face. Narron's breath feels hot and irritates my skin, but I don't complain. Narron makes guttural noises in the back of his throat as he repositions my face.

"What is your name, by the way?" Narron asks.

"Ael."

"Well, Ael, there doesn't appear to be anything wrong with your eyes," Narron explains. "You have no apparent injuries." He pauses and moves my head from side to side. "I don't...WHAT THE—!" Narron's hands disappear from my face.

"What?" Pri and strident male ask at the same time. His voice rings louder than hers.

"This is remarkable," Narron continues in a breathy voice.

Someone blew a raspberry. "Geevus, Narron!" strident male exclaims. "Learn to express your emotions appropriately. I thought he was gonna go all psycho mutant on us and I was about to have to kill somebody."

"Calm down, Rob," Pri chides. "It's not all that serious."

"If you startle a bear, it's gonna kill somebody. That's all I'm sayin'."

"Anyway, you were saying, Narron?"

"You survived the Scar," Narron continues. "Extraordinary. In all my years I have only seen one person survive it. Her skin was so badly damaged that she barely looked human. But you — at first glance you just

170

look like anyone else from the barren. It is not unusual to see someone with scars or burns here. Were you given medication or treatment, or did you survive it on your own?"

"You aren't even scared!" Rob's shrill voice slices through the air.

"Survived it on my own," I say, trying to ignore Rob.

"Extraordinary!" Narron says.

"That's not the point, Narron!"

"Rob …" Pri warns.

"What if he's got mind powers or something? Survivors of the Scar are scary powerful, I hear. There's this chick that escaped from the Prometheans a while back—"

SMACK!

"Get it together, Rob," Pri scolds. "How are we going to face our families when we get home?"

"What the crap, Pri!? That hurt!"

"I SAID get it together! We don't have time for your lack of control. Can't you see we have an opportunity, here?"

Opportunity? I don't like the sound of that.

"I agree with Pri," Narron says. "When he recovers, he can be of use to us."

His comment raises alarms in my head. "No!" I wheeze. I panic and thrash about as much as my battered body will let me. I can't control myself — I have to get out of here before someone uses me to do harm again. "Please!" I beg. My wrists and ankles burn — irritated by the memory of restraints.

"Oh, I didn't mean …"

Narron's voice fades. My stomach churns as a rank smell attacks my nose. *I have to get out of here now!* I struggle with my body harder in an attempt to flee, but my muscles fail me. I realize that I'm not really moving much at all, despite the rush I feel. Still, I have to try before it happens again.

"Ael! Snap out of it!" Pri's voice cuts through the noise.

I try to calm down, but their voices won't quiet! My whole body is moist with perspiration. The more they scream, the faster my heart beats. I want them to go away and leave me alone.

A pair of gentle hands stroke my shoulders. "It's okay, Ael. Whatever it is, you're safe." The tenderness in Narron's voice eases my anxiety. Much to my relief, I feel myself calming down.

"What was that about?" Rob questions.

I wearily shake my head as I struggle to catch my breath. My head pulses and throbs, blinding my thoughts as much as my eyes. I open my mouth to respond to Rob, I can't make out an articulate thought through the darkness in my mind.

"Leave him be," Narron orders. A pair of hands cradle my head and lift it off the ground. Something soft is placed underneath my head. Though the fabric is slightly irritating, the supple support it provides is very welcome.

"You should rest," Pri suggests.

"Yes," Narron agrees. "Rest will do you good. I suspect your body will recover quickly."

I take a few deep breaths and push out, "Will I see again?"

There is a pause before Narron answers, "I'm not sure. Honestly, I don't understand why you can't see at the present moment. I'm interested in examining your eyes again after you rest."

I sigh and try not to think about my blindness. The uncertainty of my situation makes me anxious, but my body has reached its limit. I feel myself drifting off into a deep, dreamless sleep.

What is that smell? Is that food? My stomach growls and moans as an acrid, gamey smell fills my nostrils. Stretching my arms out to the side, I overcome my drowsiness and come into awareness. Cool, crisp air gnaws at my skin and whistles through the quiet. I take a deep breath and feel dizzy, as though I only received half the air I actually took in. The air is so thin that I have to breathe in deeper to satisfy my lungs. *I must be in the mountains,* I conclude. I wonder how long I have been asleep to have made it this far.

Am I still blind? I blink a few times and frown. My world is still enshrouded in darkness. At least I'm moving with relative ease.

I release a heavy sigh and try to listen for the others. All I hear is the whistling wind. I strain my ears and catch soft whispers mixed with the wind.

"I don't know about this. The place looks … creepy," Rob says in a low voice. "I mean, I was expecting it to be a little run-down, but that … that's some messed-up stuff."

"We don't have a choice," Pri says. "Rob, Isa will die."

"Don't talk to me like I don't care about our daughter, Pri!" Rob's voice raises. His sudden burst of anger shocks me. "I know what's at stake!"

"I didn't mean—"

"Yes, you did! Yes, you freakin' did!"

"Rob!" Pri barks. "You're overreacting again! Calm down!"

"DON'T TELL ME TO CALM DOWN! What? You're smarter than me so you get to control how I feel? You think—"

I spring to my feet and shout, "Hey! I think you should lower your voice."

"Stay out of this!" Rob roars.

"You best calm down," I advise firmly.

Something shuffles. *Whisp.* I can feel the pressure change as something comes at me hard and fast. I raise my arms and catch the blow before it lands on my face.

Pri gasps.

"How did you … ?" Rob stammers.

I am just as shocked that I caught his fist and don't answer.

A tender hand touches my arm. "It's okay, Ael," Pri sooths. "Rob is just a very passionate, very angry person. You just got to let him get it out."

"He'll never hit Pri, anyway," Narron says with a chuckle. "He would not last very long."

"Ha, ha," Rob groans. His arm relaxes, so I release his fist. "Been blind for five minutes and you're already creepy."

"Don't mind Rob," Narron says. "He's just emotional."

"I'm not *emotional.*"

"You most certainly are. And stubborn, might I add."

"And smart-mouthed," Pri adds.

"Ah, I see how it is. Not one of you understands me."

"It'll be all right, Rob," Pri sniggers.

I don't understand anyone. The drastic change in the mood gives me mental whiplash.

There is a moment of silence before someone exhales. "I'm getting more stew," Rob announces. "You want some stew, Creeps?"

Is he talking to me?

"Ael. You want some stew or not?"

"Sure."

"It's actually not bad," Pri says as someone places something heavy and cylindrical in my hands. I think it's a mug, but I'm not sure what it's made out of. "My goodness, your hands are freezing. Hey Narron? Do we have enough kindling to restart the fire?"

"It's best we not draw any attention to ourselves at this hour," Narron says. "A fire would surely be seen now the sun is gone."

"Oh, fine," Pri moans.

"I'm all right, really," I reassure, although I suspect that she isn't as concerned about my comfort as she is her own.

Plop. Something is dipped into liquid, most likely the stew. My mug grows hot as someone pours me some stew.

"Here ya go," Rob says.

I bring the mug to my lips and sniff. The stew smells so pungent that I can't make out its ingredients. I slurp the hot, briny broth. It trickles down my throat and warms my insides. Chunks of gamey meat leave an unpleasant aftertaste in my mouth and yet it is so satisfying that I barely pause to breathe between sips.

"Whataya think?" Rob asks.

"Not bad."

"*Not bad,*" Rob imitates in a sarcastic tone. "That's the best you're going to get under the circumstances."

"We all appreciate your food, Rob," Pri encourages.

Rob scoffs. "You better."

"Anyway, I take it you are still completely blind?" Narron asks.

"Still blind."

"I'll take a look at your eyes in the morning. There isn't enough light right now."

"We could rebuild the fire?" Pri offers.

"No fire!" Narron's voice raises with irritation.

I tip my head back to gulp the rest and swallow the last bit of food. Someone pours me some more before I can ask.

"Thanks," I say.

"You're welcome," Rob says. "By the way, I've been wanting to ask you about those people you were traveling with. Who were they?"

A lump forms in my throat and their faces pop into my head. "They were friends."

"I'm sorry," Pri says, sincerely. "Did you know them, long?"

Yes. I unconsciously rub my wrists where shackles once were. I can still hear the clinking of the chains as they sway back and forth; back and forth to the rhythm of our marching feet. I can see their eyes — those lifeless, sullen eyes that can only belong to someone who has lost their soul.

"Ael?" Narron inquires. "Are you all right?"

Thu-boomp. Thu-boomp. The mug in my hands shakes and splashes hot liquid. "I ... I ..."

"Geevus, Creeps, you all right?"

"Ael?" Pri sounds concerned.

I grit my teeth and steady myself. "I'm all right. I'm all right."

"Are you sure he's good for this?" Rob fails to whisper.

"You're so loud!" Pri snaps.

I knew it. There are always strings. "Good for what?" I mentally brace myself for the answer.

"We need your help," Pri says. "We need it bad. The stakes are high on this one."

"We've lost over half of our clan to the Scar," Narron explains. "The other half is either suffering from it or standing here before you. The disease is beyond our ability to control. We need medicine."

"Promethean medicine," Rob clarifies.

"So you want to steal from the white coats?" I ask. "Nope, nope, nope, nope, nope. That's stupid."

"Now hold on, Creeps," Rob persists. "Hear us out. We ain't trying to get caught by no mad Promethean scientists. No offense, Narron."

"None taken."

"We heard there was an abandoned Promethean lab somewhere in these mountains," Pri continues. "If we can get to it, we might have a shot."

"So what do you want me to do? I'm blind."

I can tell by the silence that I'm not going to like the answer.

"With your permission, I would like to run a few tests," Narron treads carefully. "Your body might hold the key to finding a cure for the Scar."

A warning shiver shoots down my spine. "What sort of tests?"

"I understand your apprehension …"

"I highly doubt that," I bark.

"We have a rare opportunity here," Pri pushes. "We have access to Promethean technology, someone who knows how to work said technology, and a natural survivor of the Scar. It's meant to be, Ael."

"So, let me get this straight; you want me to go with you to this abandoned lab and let some former Promethean scientist run experiments on my body? And you want me to trust someone who used to be a Promethean?"

"I know this is an extraordinary request, but consider the circumstances," Narron says. "The odds of finding you, a natural survivor, are just astonishing."

"What were you going to do if you didn't find me?" I counter.

"Scavenge and hope for the best," Narron counters back. "Arguably, I could pose a similar question to you, Ael."

"We saved your life," Pri points out.

I was waiting for this. "Oh, here we go," I grumble.

"What? It's true. What would you be doing right now, anyway? Not much, I can promise you that. Look. Your butt is blind. Your only real chance at survival is with us."

I'm annoyed with Pri's candor.

"Hey, man, stew every night," Rob jests.

I don't want to, but I smile.

"You could have worse company," Narron chimes.

I let out a heavy sigh. Pri is definitely right about one thing: my chances of survival on my own are slim to none.

"In any case, your best chance at regaining your eyesight is with me," Narron points out. "I highly doubt you will encounter another person with my skills as long as you live — well, at least not one you can trust."

Damn. I have no choice but to acquiesce. "Fine. I'll go."

Someone claps their hands. "My man," Rob says.

"Thank you," Pri's gratitude is genuine and sincere. "You just gave our daughter a chance."

Someone pats me on the shoulder.

I nod, though I'm still uneasy about the situation. I put my mug down on the ground beside me and shiver. With no more stew to warm me, I am left to the whims of the mountain air. But the cold is not as biting as the ominous feeling I have in my gut.

A small fire cackles and snaps as it greedily consumes thick chunks of wood. There is nothing around

— just the fire and Grillock. I can see, so I figure this is a dream. I feel strange knowing that I am dreaming — like I have just entered into another dimension. The fact that Grillock is dead makes me feel more existential.

His disfigured face glows golden-red through the firelight and his lean frame is hunched over the fire. Scraps of dirty cloth hang from his edgy limbs and tease the flames.

"Is it better on the other side?" I ask.

Grillock doesn't respond. His face remains vacant.

I sigh and toss a rock into the fire. "I don't remember what happened." A part of me feels really guilty for this. I wonder if he is angry with me because I survived and he didn't. Was there something I could have done to save them? Not knowing is tearing me up inside.

Grillock's jaw drops and he lets out a raspy hiss from deep within his throat. He holds the hiss like a bad note and fixes his eyes on me.

My spine tingles and I want to look away, but his eyes are holding my gaze. My muscles tense as I say, "Stop it." I'm afraid to show any more defiance than that — as though I would provoke something darker and stronger to act.

Blood pools in one of Grillock's eyes and drips down his face, yet he does not blink or even flinch. He slowly leans towards me until he is over the fire. I expect him to stop, but he doesn't. Instead, he leans onto his hands and begins to crawl into the fire to get to me.

My arms prickle as goose bumps rise. I'm paralyzed with fear and can't move. His body catches on fire, but he is not hindered. Still hissing, he reaches for me. The heat from his blazing arm burns my face, but I just can't move.

"Keeeee," he gurgles. His eyes widen and turn black as the flames eat his flesh. And then his mouth twists into an inhuman grin.

The hairs on the back of my neck stand and I realize that my mouth is open, making the same hissing noise as his.

I have to die! Kill yourself! Kill yourself! Kill yourself before he gets you!

"Gi … ve … me …" Grillock exudes menace. His fingertips scrape my nose. A bolt of electricity strikes my brain and everything goes black.

Am I still asleep? I can't tell. My blood rushes, urging me to take flight, but I can't move. The feeling lingers a little longer and slowly dissipates.

I take three deep, calming breaths. My blood stabilizes and I become aware. Bright sunlight seeps through my eyelids, creating circles of color in the darkness. I yawn, rub my eyes, and gasp. *Is that …?* Amidst the color circles is what looks to be the faint outline of rock. I stretch my hand out in front of me and press my palm against the cold, jagged mountain wall. I release a suppressed laugh as I stroke the wall. My lips coil into a smile. *There is hope.*

"You fall in love with the wall, Creeps?" Rob yawns. "It's cool. Just I took you for more of a tree type."

I turn to Rob's voice and see a partial outline of a tall man. "I think I can see a little," I declare.

"You *think* you can see? You either see or you can't."

"It's hard to explain," I begin. "It's so faint I can't tell if what I'm seeing is real or if it's just the light."

"That's too … beyond me," Rob says. "That stuff is Pri and Narron's area. Not mine."

The longer Rob speaks, the more detail appears. Deep eyes and a small, slender frame materialize where I believe Rob is lying. The image is so distorted, though; I'm not sure if I'm imagining it or not. But it's something.

"Your eyes … are sort of on me, man. Like, you are violating me with your face."

"Oh ... sorry ..." I'm put off by Rob's choice of words.

"When Narron gets back, he'll have to check that out for ya," Rob continues.

"Where did he go?"

"He and Pri are checking supplies and refilling the water jugs," Rob explains. "They shouldn't be long."

I nod and turn my head from side to side to test the limits of my vision. No use. All I can see are outlines so distorted and faded that I really don't know what I'm seeing.

"How far from the lab are we?" I ask.

"We are literally above it," Rob answers. I hear a series of *whisps* as he talks, which tell me that he likes to use his hands when he speaks. "Like, if you were to take a few steps to your left, you would fall right on top of it. Of course, you would also die."

"What does it look like?"

"Like an old, white box," Rob says. That doesn't tell me anything and it must show on my face because Rob adds, "It looks pretty worn out. If I didn't know any better, I'd say that it existed before the Blast. It looks that old. Also, it's positioned right smack dab in between all these mountains with no visible roads or anything. I don't know how they got in. I don't know how *we* are going to get in, to tell you the truth."

My arms tingle and become restless. I have an overwhelming desire to run, but I have enough presence of mind to keep myself still. My blindness is fuelling my anxiety. The thought of being so close to death and yet so unaware of it frightens me.

Pull it together.

"The place is freakin' creepy," Rob continues in a low voice. "I'm not completely sure, but it looks like there's dried blood splattered all over one side of the building and the ground."

Oh freak, shut-up, Rob! My head begins to swell.

The shuffling of feet relieves me. *That must be Pri and Narron.* I turn my head toward the sound of their feet and think I see their outlines. One of them is clearly taller than the other, but it's hard to say which.

"We're back." Pri announces. "There's a small stream not far from here that has the best tasting water."

"Freakin' apocalypse and you're picky about your water," Rob pokes.

"Nothing picky about appreciating water," Pri replies.

"Anyway, now that you are awake, Ael, I would like to take a look at your eyes," Narron says, upbeat.

I am surprisingly relieved and energized that he is back. I am anxious to hear what he has to say about my eyes now that they have changed a little.

A distorted figure of a man draws near my face. *There's Narron's breath, again.* I can't make out his features, but I think the darkest spots in my vision are his eyes examining mine.

"Something's different about my vision," I begin. "It's really faint, but I think I can see your silhouette or … maybe your outline? I can also see light a little better."

"Hmm." Narron's voice sounds quizzical. "I don't understand. I can't find anything wrong with them. I think …"

A hooded cloaked figure walks into my vision span. I can't think; I can't hear. I don't understand what's happening. My heart stops. My blood freezes. I don't know if I'm even in my own body anymore.

Its hood consists of a long cone with a sharp point at the end. It extends over its head and Vs in the back. It has a harrowing, beak-like snout jutting out of its head. The hood hangs loosely from its beak and frays at the end, hiding the hideous snout like a well-known secret. The tips beg to stab — to spill blood, to cause harm. The nightmarish cloak is loose and bulky, leaving my mind to wonder what lies beneath. Nothing about this figure is human. Everything about it means me harm.

It slowly turns to face me. *No eyes.* It lifts one of its long, bony arms. Long, sharp claws peek out of its massive bell sleeves and point at me. Fear seethes through my veins, poisoning my body. My abdomen writhes in pain in anticipation of its claws or beak.

"Gi … ve … me …" it whispers menacingly. Its beak is touching my nose and its claws are digging in my upper arms. "Get out!" It growls. "GET OUT!"

If I don't break out of this paralyzing fear, I'm going to die. Ropes of terror bind my nerves and cling tighter and tighter to my body, but I fight my way through them and raise my fists to defend myself.

"AEL! STOP IT!" Rob's voice pierces my ears.

The cloaked figure dissipates and I realize that my hands are squeezing something pliable, yet firm.

"Ael, let him go!" Pri shrieks.

I can't let go. My nerves are on fire and won't let me stop. Something rams into me and knocks me on the ground. "Get a hold of yourself, man!" Rob barks.

Someone gasps and chokes for air. "I'm all right," Narron wheezes. "I'm all right."

"What the heck was that all about?" Rob demands.

I thought Narron was a demon. "I'm sorry … I don't know … what happened …" I'm only half lying.

"You just freaked out!" Rob exclaims. "Your eyes glazed over and everything!"

"You looked scared," Pri observes. "You reminded me of Azus."

"Yes, Azus," Narron chokes. He clears his throat before continuing. "He was very troubled, indeed."

"Yeah, the Prometheans messed that dude up," Rob puts in. "They like, gave him something that made him want to eat people. He ate his freakin' father and they watched him do it!"

"That's right," Narron says. "When we first found him, he would break into a feral rage for no apparent reason. After working with him, I determined that he was responding to triggers: for example, if someone said something that reminded him of the lead researcher who conducted the experiment on him."

That's not what happened. I really just want to stop talking right now. I don't like where this is going.

"Did you eat your family, Creeps?" Rob asks.

"No, I didn't eat my family." *Ridiculous.*

"Did something really awful happen to you? Were you captured by the White Coats? Did they do unspeakable things to you?" I'm not sure if Rob is being sarcastic or not.

"No," I lie. "Let it go."

"This isn't the first time this has happened, Ael," Pri chimed in. "This is, in fact, the third time you have acted weird, hostile. Those times you didn't actually hurt anyone."

My face grows hot. "I'll be all right." *Please just leave me alone.*

"We all got problems but we don't all go homicidal, ya feel me?" Rob says.

"Rob's right. We can't afford for you to freak out on us like that," Pri adds. "You gotta tell us what's going on with you and get it over with."

My heart begins pounding. *I really don't want to talk about this.* I can already feel the mental walls going up.

"Come on Ael," Rob encourages. "Just spit it out."

My limbs begin twitching. *Why do people always think sharing this stuff helps?* I feel as though the world will cave in if I utter any words.

"It's ok," Pri reassures. "It can only help."

I swallow hard and take a deep breath. *They aren't going to understand.* "People like me … we … we will never be able to be part of any tribe or clan. Survivors. If people aren't running away from us, they are trying to use us." I gulp and fight the urge to run away. "I got the Scar when I was 11 years old. My parents abandoned me. Western slavers found me. I escaped. Can I stop talking now?"

Silence.

"You escaped the slavers?" Pri exhaled in disbelief. "I have never heard of anyone … wow."

"Yeah, well, they have a nasty habit of capturing people that grow up to be much stronger than they are," I add. "Are we done?"

"I heard that they deal with the Prometheans," Rob says, despite my attempts to shut the conversation down.

"Everyone deals with the Prometheans," I correct. "The Prometheans are bad people. The slavers are bad people. People are bad people. This is a messed-up world that frankly, I don't want to be a part of anymore."

"Ok, Ael," Pri grumbles. "We can stop now."

"No, you wanted to know what has me all *messed up*," I say with intensity. All the emotion I have kept bottled up inside of me comes to the surface. "Have you ever seen a child put up for auction? Hmm? They are put up on stages — chained, crying, and naked. You know who bids on them? Not just Prometheans. They are the scum of your tribes and clans — scum with something to trade. If they are lucky, the children will be sold to tribes for slave labor. The unlucky ones … unspeakable." I pause to contain my emotion. It has come up too quickly. Shaking my head, I continue, "I did what I had to do." My voice is cracking. *Oh no … tears.* "I had to save them. I did." Unoccupied faces pop in my mind, sending chills down my spine. Heat rises from my neck and burns my cheeks. My brain is flooded with memories of blood spilt by my hands — my bare hands. Their screams pierce my eardrums and resonate through my mind. "If I didn't ... if I hadn't, they would have all been sold to ..." I can't say anymore without weeping, so I don't.

They are all quiet as I stifle my sobs. I really wish someone would say something so I wouldn't have to hear myself.

Someone sucks air through their teeth. "That's ... intense," Rob says.

"I'm so sorry," Pri breathes.

There is another moment of silence. I shake my head and rub my eyes. I need to change the subject, but my mind isn't cooperating with me.

"What did you do?" Pri asks.

Why? Just why?

"Nah, that's enough," Rob says. "I think we need to get this mission over with before it gets dark."

Thank you, Rob. I am relieved to have something else to think about.

"Indeed," Narron says. "Shall we?"

Someone slips a bare, muscular arm in the crook of mine. I assume its Rob, but then Pri whispers, "I'm sorry for prying," in my ear.

"It's all right." I forgive her.

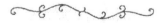

After a few hours of stumbling along an uneven path, I am ready to sit down. My feet are throbbing from stubbing my toes and my nerves are on edge, scraped raw by my poor vision. Wherever we are, there is not much sunlight. The path is smoothly descending, like a ramp. Our footsteps echo off the walls of what I believe to be some sort of tunnel.

"Just a little farther," Pri assures, sensing my discomfort.

"I see some light," Rob says. "It's not far."

"Thank goodness," Narron complains. At least I'm not the only one.

The ground levels and we are no longer descending. Pri's grip on my arm tightens and she slows her pace. "Is that ... blood?" she gasps.

"Goodness me ..." Narron breathes.

"What?"

"There's blood ... everywhere," Pri shrills. "All over the walls, the fountain, the ground ..."

"I don't know about this," Rob says. "I don't know what to think about blood all over a Promethean lab."

"This is rather unsettling," Narron agrees. "Perhaps we should camp up in the mountains for a while and observe the lab before we proceed."

"No." Pri decides. "No, we can't wait any longer. Isa can't wait."

I shiver as an ominous feeling settles in my chest. Having no actual visual to work with, I immediately think of the old stone cells the slavers used to 'break' defiant slaves, the walls of which were covered in both dried and fresh blood.

"She's right," Rob reluctantly agrees. "Let's just get in and get out."

Debris crunches under our feet as we continue walking. "What are we stepping on? If it's bones ..."

"No, no, it's just shards of stone-like stuff from damaged walls," Rob says.

Oh that makes me feel so much better, I think sarcastically.

"Look! Something's written by the entrance!" Pri exclaims. She hastens her pace, dragging me along with her.

"What the heck?" Rob puzzles.

"That's not real words, is it?" Pri says. "I mean it's letters, but they don't make sense."

"That's because it is a different language," Narron explains. "Our tribe has not really left the lowlands since the Blast, so it is understandable that you do not recognize different languages."

"Is a language how you write?" Rob asks.

"Well, yes, but also how you speak," Narron answers. "The words you use and how you use them."

"People talk like *that?*" Rob says, astounded.

"Diaboli … volun … voluntatem carnis dat nobis virt … virtutem ad inferos," Pri sounds out. "What in the world does *that* mean?"

"I wish I knew," Narron sighs. "I've never seen this language."

I hear multiple whispers in my mind. "The will of the flesh giveth the spirit of the devil power to bring us down to hell," I blurt. I rub my temple as my head begins to spin.

"How did you know that?" Narron says, taken aback.

"I don't know," I answer, honestly. *Did they tell me?*

"Okay, THAT is creepy," Rob remarks. "Seriously, anyone else freaked out right now?"

"Perhaps a slaver spoke this language to you," Narron suggests.

Not likely. "Perhaps," I say.

"Are you good?" Pri asks me.

I nod. "Yeah," I answer. "Yeah, let's just get this over with."

"Not anyone?" Rob presses. "No one is worried about Ael's random knowledge of a language Narron doesn't even know? No? Okay then, let's just waltz into this blood-stained, abandoned lab with disturbing messages over the entrance."

"No one is comfortable right now," Pri says. "We just don't have time to freak out. Besides, whatever is in there, I'm sure we can handle."

"Ya'll are lucky I'm here," Rob mumbles as we begin walking. "Ain't no psycho sneakin' up on me. No sir. I'll go straight for the eyes. You take out their eyes, they ain't coming for you."

We cross over a threshold and pause.

"Wow," Pri breathes.

"What the—?" Rob stops short.

"What?"

"Is this really a lab?" Pri questions. "It looks like a bunch of narrow halls. Where are the doors?"

"Clever," Narron admires. "It's a maze. The Prometheans must have hidden something special here — something they didn't want people to find."

"What's a maze?" Rob asks.

"It's basically a mess of halls and corridors that lead to nowhere," Narron explains. "A puzzle, if you will. We have to choose the correct paths in order to reach our destination."

"They went to a lot of trouble to hide something," Rob observes. "Maybe we should leave it alone."

"That's the truth," Pri concurs.

"Don't worry. They wouldn't keep the supplies and their secrets in the same place," Narron reassures. "They wouldn't risk unauthorized personnel stumbling upon 'need-to-know' information."

Our footsteps reverberate off the barren walls — the sound bouncing further and further down the halls. The stale air feels empty and lonely, eager to consume us. There is something horribly wrong with this place. Something I don't think any of us can fathom.

Bang! Something falls in the distance.

Pri jumps and releases my arm. "What was that?"

We pause to listen.

"Probably nothing," Narron says, breathing a sigh of relief.

A faint, human-like sound enters my ear. "Wait … listen," I whisper. "Do you hear that?"

They all fall silent again and I am able to hear the sound more clearly. Someone is moaning. An androgynous voice is twisted as though in pain. But there is something inhuman about the voice that sends chills down my spine.

"Is someone here?" Pri whispers. The moaning stops.

The hairs on my arms begin to stand and I reach for Pri. I graze her arm and she jumps out of my reach.

"That was me," I whisper.

Heavy footsteps head towards us. "I NEED YOUR FLESH! GIVE ME YOUR FLESH!" It is moving impossibly fast: too fast to be human. The sound ricochets in too many directions to work out where it is coming from.

"This way!" Rob belts out.

I grab hold of someone's arm and take off with them. My deep, heavy gasps for breath are making my lungs feel sour and my chest hurts from my heart palpitations.

"Slow down!" I gasp. No response.

"Ael!" Pri's voice calls from somewhere on the other side of a wall. "Ael, where are you?"

My skin crawls. *Whose arm do I have?* I release my grip and slide to a halt. I place my hand on the wall next to me and use it as a guide.

"Where are you going, Ael?" it hisses from behind me. It releases a hideous, piercing laugh.

Something sharp glides the length of my spine. I spin around swinging and end up punching air.

"I'm here," it whispers in my ear.

"Get away from me!" I scream, swinging madly.

Long fingers grip my upper arms and claws dig into my triceps. Grunting, I wriggle and fight to free myself. My skin tears in the process, but I manage to escape. Despite the pain, I bolt in the opposite direction.

WHAM! I bounce off a wall and land on my back. It feels like someone hit my face with a cement block. The sudden, shocking pain stuns me into a stupor, as though my brain cannot process what is happening.

Measured footsteps approach. *Get up.* I roll over onto my side and stagger to my hands and knees, but the pounding pain in my head halts me.

"Don't move," it taunts in a spine-tingling, inhuman hiss. It clicks its tongue every so often as it speaks. "Let us have it. Let us drink it. Let us bathe in it."

Crawl away! Wait … I can't move. I know that I am sending signals to my muscles to move, but my muscles aren't responding. *No. Move, damn it! Move!*

Its cackle stabs my ears. A foreign *presence* enters my body through my feet. It creeps up my legs and leaves a cold burn in its wake.

"GET OUT!" I cry. No. Nothing escapes my lips. I am completely frozen in darkness. The presence works its way into my abdomen and digs into my gut. I feel it … violating. This thing — this vile, unnatural, evil thing — wants something sinister beyond my comprehension.

I won't let you. My arm quakes as I struggle to bring it up to my mouth. Summoning all the grit left in me, I sink my teeth into my wrist and tear through my flesh.

"You won't do it," it taunts.

You don't know me. Fear gives me the strength to bear the agony as I rip a chunk of meat out of my wrist. It screams and snarls, "You dog! Stop it! Stop it! Curse you and your mother's nakedness!" My body is thrown against a wall by an invisible force. As soon as I recover, I rip through more flesh. Metallic, salty blood oozes from the wound and seeps into my mouth. I catapult to the opposite wall and slide down to the floor. My back cracks as it is forced to arch. I grunt as my head is pushed into the ground and my back arches even more. "Get out!" I howl.

Someone is approaching. I turn my head toward the sound of their footsteps and see the vague outline of a figure with a cone-shaped head. My skin crawls when I remember the hooded figure from before. My elbows snap straight as my arms press against the floor. I am completely immobile and helpless. My heart beats my chest so hard I think it might burst through.

Cold, bony hands grab my wrist where I bit into it. A spine-tingling hiss erupts as my skin burns. I clench my jaw tight and grunt as the burn intensifies. "GUHAHH!" I cry. Lights flash in my mind as waves of searing pain burrow into my skin. My eyes are beginning to roll behind my head and I think I might pass out.

A chorus of feet stampedes in my direction. "Hey!" Pri screams. "Get off of him!"

It lets out a cry that sounds like a combination of a screech and a roar and then releases my arm.

Whoosh! Pri utters a curse.

"Wha ... where did it go?" Rob stammers. My body seizes and I am dragged away from Pri by my feet. Someone grabs my arms and I cry out. Their grip on my wrists causes me blinding pain. I am caught in a deadly game of tug-of-war. The skin around my gut stings as it is being pulled apart, but I would rather be torn in two than be taken by the fiend. I have to push through this pain, somehow.

The thing inside me growls as it releases me. It slithers out of my body leaving me heaped in an awkward fetal-like position, feeling disgusted and violated.

A pair of trembling hands rest on me. "Geevus," Rob sighs. "That was messed up, man. Really raddin' messed up." Rob continues talking, but I don't listen. My dry eyes beg me to blink, but I don't. Every sense is paralyzed. Every thought is dark. I can still feel the thing's vile vestiges poisoning me with despair.

I have seen the worst humankind has to offer — slavery, rape, murder — but this thing, this evil thing that thirsts for my being, is something on a level that transcends humankind. It is original evil. It is death. It is agony. It feeds on life and violates for pleasure.

I hear someone snap their fingers. "Ael, can you hear me?" I blink.

"Hey man, you gotta snap out of it," Rob insists. "Stay with me, Ael."

I shut my eyes and bear with the smoldering pain in my wrist.

"There's a room right there!" Narron exclaims. "Let's take him there!"

Strong arms lift me under my armpits while someone else grabs my legs to keep them from dragging. My stomach churns as my body bounces with their unsynchronized trots.

"Hold on a little longer," Pri reassures in a soothing tone. "Narron will help you."

I doubt that. We need to leave.

I clamp my eyelids down harder as bright, artificial light soaks through. They hoist my body on top of an elevated, cold, hard surface. I can feel heat emanating from them as they crowd around me. Someone turns my wrist out and straightens my arm.

"Good lort, Creeps!" Rob cries.

"What happened?" from Pri. I don't have the energy to respond.

"Hmm," Narron ponders. Light fingers probe my arm and my jaw. "The wound is perfectly cauterized. Curious. I've never seen anything like this."

"What was that thing?" Pri asks. No one responds. "Narron!" she snaps. "What was that thing?"

"Oh!" Narron becomes alert. Fingers return to my arm. "Probably a Gegen."

"Genshin?" Rob says. I'm not sure if he mispronounces it on purpose, or whether he is going deaf. "What's that?"

"Gegen, Rob," Pri corrects. "You know, the experiment people."

"Yeah, yeah! Like that Gabby or Gibbie chick I heard about. You know, the one with mind powers."

"Ghabrie," Narron's voice trails off.

"You think that thing was a Gegen?"

It wasn't a Gegen.

"Whatev, let's just do what we gotta do and get outta here," Rob mumbles. "This place is freakin' creepy."

"The malevolent Gegen complicates things," Narron says. "Even with Promethean equipment, making a cure is very time consuming."

"Let's just grab what we can and get out of here," Pri says with a hint of disappointment. "We can regroup in the mountains."

"Let's get this thing goin'," Rob says. I can hear them all stride away from the table. A series of clicks and clanks irritate my ears.

"Do you need help looking for anything?" Pri offers.

Something pings. "Thank you, but no, not at the moment." BANG. "Confound it! Whoever worked in this station was sloppy!"

Pri inhales through her teeth. "That looks like that hurt. I'm gonna help you with that."

Their muddled noise upsets my ears which are weary from trying to distinguish sounds.

"Hey, what's this?" Rob asks.

"Let me see it," Pri says. "Project Abraham?"

194

Someone, I assume to be Narron, trips over objects as he stumbles toward where I heard Rob's voice. "Let me see that!" he barks.

"Sheesh!" Pri says as something exchanges hands. "What's Project Abraham?"

"A failed project that supposedly led to the Gegen Experiments," Narron replies. "It was an urban legend of sorts amongst researchers." Pages flip.

"Okay. What?" Rob sounds confused.

"Where did you find this?" Narron ignores his question. The energy in his voice is somewhat unsettling.

"It was just sitting out right there."

"Hmm," Narron hums. "This is very old. It's hard to make out …"

Pause.

"Human X moved two spaces today," Narron reads. "Upon return, his blood pressure rose significantly and he had to be sedated. Other than that, his vitals were fine. We can continue with the project." Narron gasps. "Human X?" Pages turn. "Human X moved eight spaces today. We had to use considerable pain in order to coax him into teleporting. His will is much stronger than the others, but after we broke him he finally moved. However, time between launches and returns has increased by three seconds. I am curious as to where he is during this time. Is his body breaking down into microscopic particles? Currently, there is no way to test this theory."

Pages flip.

"There is something about this project that makes me very nervous. Today, Human X moved from one side of the containment field to the other. Time between launch and return was five seconds and upon return, he was drenched with saltwater. How? This unanticipated development makes me wonder if he is actually moving through time and space."

More pages turn.

"Something happened to Human X today. Upon return, he was unusually quiet. I think he smiled at me, but not in a friendly way. He clearly has more control over his powers, which frightens me. No one else seems to be concerned." Pages flip. "That looks like the end of it. Wait. There's something scrawled ..."

"What is it?" Pri sounds concerned.

Silence.

"Narron!" Rob snaps. "What's wrong?"

"It says 'evil'. It's written in what I think is blood."

Cold claws dig into my spine and send shivers up the back of my neck. A light catches my eyes, but I can't make out what it is that I'm seeing. A screen?

Hiss. Crackle. "Subject is ... *hiss* ... vitals ... *crackle* ..."

"What is that!?" Rob shrieks.

"How did that turn on?" Narron screeches. "There's no power!"

"Human X appears to be stable ... *crack* ... now," a level female voice continues, crackling with static.

"Geevus," Rob breathes. "That's one of *them*."

"Poor soul," Pri's voice is quiet with genuine concern. "What are those wires they have him hooked up to?"

"Some of them are to measure his vitals and the others are likely meant to cause him pain," Narron's voice is deadpan.

Unrecognizable shadows move about the screen, teasing me. "What's happening?" I ask, frustrated.

"They are prepping a man for an experiment," Narron answers. "By the looks of it, they are about to test his abilities. That glass dome he's in is a very formidable force field."

"Help me!" A desperate man cries in the background. The bangs I hear must be him trying to break free of the force-field. "Promethean pieces of SHIT! I'm a human being!"

"He's clearly agitated, but vitals are still good," another voice states, unaffected by the noise in the background. "We are ready."

"Don't do this!" the subject screams.

"On three ... two ..."

"Oh God, Please don't!"

"One ... now."

Equipment hums and beeps. "AAAAAAAAARRRRRRGGGGHHH!" The blob on the screen that I suspect is Human X shakes violently.

POP! The blob disappears and the noises cease.

"Wha—? Where did he go?" Rob asks.

POP! The blob reappears on the other side of the dome and is silent. After a few moments of quiet, one of the figures cries, "Vitals are good! He's stable!"

The other figures begin clapping. "We did it!" one exclaims.

"Hold on, there's something wrong," a male says. He does not share in the others' triumph. "He's all wet. Is that ... is that seaweed on him?"

"One step at a time, McBride. Make your notes and we'll continue tomorrow."

"But ..." McBride objects.

"Make your notes, McBride!" One of the figures shuts him down. Silence. The figures scuffle around and slowly exit. The screen crackles again and then a lone figure appears.

"We are about to conduct another experiment," he whispers. His voice trembles with anxiety. "I don't have much time. Look at my notes. Human X ... he is turning into something ... I don't know. Look at my notes."

The screen crackles again and when the image clears, it reveals several figures standing around the dome.

There are more figures this time and they are all talking amongst themselves.

The familiar blob of Human X is where he was before, only he's not moving.

"Vitals?" An authoritative voice asks.

"Good," someone responds.

"Sir ... I don't like this," a cool, female voice says. "He's ... smiling. Why is he smiling?"

Human X snickers.

"Are we ready?" the authoritative one asks, unconcerned.

"Nam et vasa furoris irae Dei pati morti ..." Human X hisses.

"What's he saying?" McBride asks. "Sir ... something's wrong."

"We will proceed with the experiment. Any more objections and there will be serious consequences."

"... in aeternum cum diabolo et angelis eius!"

POP!

Everyone falls silent.

"I didn't press anything!" one of them shrieks.

"He did that on his own?"

A deep, spine-tingling rumble builds and shakes the force field.

POP!

Human X returns. He's silent.

"Restrain him!" authoritative figure roars.

Human X laughs with multiple voices. "You cannot restrain ME!" The force field shatters and all the figures take flight, toppling over each other in apparent panic.

Three or four figures bolt to Human X and are thrown backwards by an invisible force. Their agonized cries are cut short by chokes as they are denied air. Something cracks and breaks. Crimson spews out of the figures nearest to Human X and they are cast aside like rag dolls.

Chaos breaks loose as the remaining figures struggle to escape Human X. A few get away and lock the doors behind them, leaving stragglers futilely screaming and fighting for a way out. The image disappears and we are back in darkness again.

"What was *that*?" Rob gasps. "Was that ... real?"

"We need to leave," Narron says. "Ael, can you walk?"

Not really, but I'm getting a surge of adrenaline at the thought of getting out of here. "I'll figure it out."

"Wait! We can't leave empty handed! Please! My Isa," Pri objects.

"We won't give up, Pri," Rob reassures. "We will find another way. Let's just get out of here for now, ok?"

"No! We can fight it! We don't have time!" Pri is sounding almost hysterical.

"Priconly! We must not engage that thing, do you understand me?" The pressing tone in Narron's voice is alarming. "It is not what we thought!"

"But ... Isa," she desperately argues.

"This isn't over, Pri," Rob says. "I won't let our daughter die like that! Ain't none of us good to her if we're dead."

"He's right," I chime in. They fall silent, making me feel tense. "You didn't feel it *inside* of you. And it's not alone."

Quiet.

"All right," Pri concedes. "Let's go."

"Let me help you, Ael," Rob says as he grabs my upper arm. He helps me off the table and onto my feet. I am unable to hold my own weight, though, so I lean on Rob for support. Finally, we are getting out of this awful place.

"Do you remember how to get out of here?" Pri asks.

"I believe so," Narron says. "If all else fails, we can just solve the maze."

The silence is unsettling.

You can't goooooooooo! A cold voice screeches in my mind.

I can hear my heart pounding against my chest. It's near, but I won't let it stop me. I push through the pain and sourness and pick up speed. Our footsteps reverberate off the walls as we round a corner and speed down another hall. The fluidity of our movement makes me hopeful that Narron is confidently leading us the right direction. We round another corner and our pace suddenly slows.

"What's going on?" I ask.

"You don't know where we are, do you?" Rob says.

"Impossible. I have an excellent memory and sense of space. I am sure that this is where we came in."

"You're lost, Narron," Rob spits.

"No, the exit should have been here," Pri begs to differ. "Narron's right."

I hear hiss-like cackles in the distance. The sound bounces in every direction, overwhelming my ears and ability to gauge space.

"Oh snap!" Rob's says. "Ya hear that?"

"We have to move!" I insist. "Go! Pick a direction and go!"

We speed forward, pushing through doors and making aimless turns. Rob's grip on my arms grows tighter and tighter, but I don't complain. I have no choice but to hope that we'll happen upon a way out. I'm not sure how long we've been running, but the acid in my legs tells me that I am reaching my physical limit. I slow down a little, but I refuse to stop.

We are going down a hallway that has doors every fifteen feet. Pushing through them is slowing us down much more than I'd like. Suddenly we come to a skidding halt. A familiar odor enters my nostrils. It is a foul combination of blood, mold, and death. The air feels different here, too. It's heavy with moisture and filth. I cringe as it coats my skin.

"What? Why are we stopped?" I demand, though my body is secretly grateful. They don't respond at first.

"This is the place …" Narron chokes.

Thu-boomp. "This is what place?" I don't really want to know the answer to this.

"Geevus …" Rob gasps, "this is where they messed him up."

My skin crawls as though seized by millions of tiny, hairy insects.

Why?

SLAM! The doors shut and lock behind us.

"Can't say that I didn't see that coming," Rob says.

"Aaaaeeel," something rasps from a short distance.

"Da Ffff …" Rob stammers.

"Show yourself!" Pri growls.

Footsteps drag toward us. I automatically turn in the direction of the sound and see a cloaked figure emerging through the darkness. I know that baleful sharp beak and cone-shaped hood. *Thu-boomp. Thu-boomp.* When I briefly glance at Rob, his form is still extremely unclear. Some cruel twist of fate is allowing me to see the figure that has haunted me since I set foot on the barrens.

"Get back!" Pri warns.

"Don't provoke it!" I whisper.

It stops and raises its bony arm at me. "Gi … ve … me …" it croaks. It clicks its tongue as it speaks. "A … Ael.."

Rob's arm quakes in mine, but he doesn't let go.

"What do you want with me?!" I cry.

He doesn't know! He doesn't know! a chorus of whispery voices chant from the corners of the room.

"You … must … get … Human … 76," it continues. "We … must … reunite."

Reunite?

Reunite! Reunite!

"Ae …?" Rob breathes.

"Wha— I don't know what it's talking about."

Its sharp finger slips out of his black cloak and points at me. "Re … member!" It screeches.

Black liquid gushes out of my eyes. It feels hot instead of wet and seeps into my mouth and nostrils. Panicked, I try to wipe it off with my hands, but I don't feel anything — like I'm trying to wipe away a shadow. As it engulfs my body, I am completely cut off from my senses. I think I'm screaming, but I can't hear anything. If my comrades are trying to help me, I can't feel them.

I'm not sure where I am anymore. Everything is dark and silent. It doesn't feel like I'm in the lab anymore — I'm somewhere else. The darkness is strangely comforting. It embraces me like a warm blanket and coaxes me deeper and deeper into this world of never-ending night.

"Get Human 76," a weak disembodied voice breathes. I'm actually not sure that the voice didn't come from me. *Did I think that?* I don't really care. I just want to sink deeper and deeper into nothingness.

How long have I been here? I can no longer gauge time. I also realize that I can't feel anything. When I try to wave my hand in front of my face, nothing happens. *What happened to my arms?* Panicked, I try to move my legs, but nothing happens. *I'm nothing. What's happening? Am I dreaming? Where am I?*

But I'm not dreaming, am I? *Wait … is this my voice or someone else's?* I've been here before. I know what this place is. I will never escape. I'm neither alive nor dead. I barely *am*.

That wasn't me. I didn't think that. I have to get out of here! This can't be real! I exist! You're wrong! I am alive!

A clean-shaven, bald man appears before me. He has brooding crystal-blue eyes that remind me of a dream I can't remember. Underneath his crooked nose is a pair of thin lips. His skin is so pale that it's almost translucent. It is difficult to look upon him, but I cannot avert my eyes.

"Who are you?" I ask.

"I am you," he replies.

I'm not sure how to respond. "What do you mean?"

"We had a family, once. Remember?"

An image of a tawny-skinned woman with black eyes pops in my head. Seeing her sunny face stings my heart. And then I see two children: twin girls with wild ringlets and rosy cheeks. These images make me feel something I've grown numb to, a pain so beautiful that it can only be love.

But this doesn't make any sense. I spent most of my youth as a slave. When did I have a family? That couldn't have happened.

But those images stir inside me an emotion that I cannot fake. They feel real to me as well.

"The Prometheans took us from them. They experimented on us. They did unspeakable things to us. We begged them to stop, but they refused. But because of their arrogance, we were given a great power, a power that enabled us to pass through time and space; a power they would never understand."

"You are making no sense," I say, though a part of me knows exactly what he's talking about.

"One day we traveled somewhere we weren't supposed to. *They* offered us revenge if we took them back with us. So we did. They gave us our vengeance. We gave them our body."

My head is spinning. "But if you are me ... how am I in this body?"

"When they took our body, you traveled the realms for countless of years. You were searching. And then you found a boy who was about to succumb to disease and asked for his body. You said his spirit could move on while you made his body strong. And you did. You made his body very strong, didn't you?"

"No ... no that's ... that's ..." I stammer. *This has to be a dream.* But somehow I know he's telling the truth. I remember everything — the Promethean's false promises, the sting of separation, the unbearable physical pain they put me through, traveling to other worlds that challenge the imagination. I remember *them.* Hungry for vengeance, they offered to satisfy my deepest desires and I gave them everything. Those things have been connected to me ever since. They were there in the barrens.

That's right. Me, 98, Warrick, and Grillock escaped the slavers and were traveling through the barrens in search of a better life. But really, I was leading them back to the lab. I didn't know it at the time, but I was being summoned. As we drew near to the mountains, *they* came for me. They took Warrick first. Then Grillock. Then 98. Their joints became unhinged. They gnashed their teeth and came at me. I felt conflicted when I defended myself, but in the end, they all died by my hand. I made a burn pile out of the broken handcart and dry brush that was scattered about. I was going to bury them, but with them gone, the fiends came for me. My fight with it ended with me in the bottom of the burn pile.

It feels like I've been punched in the stomach.

"You remember."

I nod.

"Then it's time for you to return to your body," his voice — my voice — is unusually smooth. "There is a girl who is trouble for us. She must be stopped. Reuniting with your body will give you the ability to escape her sight."

He wants me to kill just like everyone else. "You aren't me," I say.

He chuckles under his breath. "Of course I am."

"No you're not. Who are you?"

His expression fades into a grimace. "I am the one who gave you vengeance." His voice is slightly higher in pitch. "I am the Lord of eternal night. I will see all mankind brought to their knees in every world in which they exist!"

His pupils dilate until they overtake his entire eyeball. "We will devour this world," he hisses. "No one will escape our wrath." His skin evaporates until there is nothing left but darkness. After a few moments pass, shapes and figures surface. The familiar foul odor assaults my nostrils. *I'm back.*

I blink several times as I regain feeling in my body. When I open my eyes, I am face to face with its beak. The fiend's claws are buried in my torso and it's laughing maliciously at me.

"Ael!" Pri cries.

"Stay back," I choke. "Please."

Now I'm feeling pain. My entire torso is on fire.

"Do not fight me," it says triumphantly.

Faces flash in my mind as I contemplate my next move. *Do I protect myself? What can I even do?* The death it brings has no grave for the soul to rest. Defiance might provoke it to unleash malevolence beyond my comprehension. The very thought of it brings me to my knees.

But there is great power in boldness, though it often comes with a price. There is nothing more terrifying than understanding the cost of nerve. But to pay nothing would be to receive nothing, so I must forfeit it all.

Do it now! "Get out!" I shout. "Get out! I command you in His name! Get out!!!!"

It cries out with cringe-worthiness of a thousand cawing crows at their death.

"GET OUT!" I command with more intensity. I place both hands on its claws and push as hard as I can. "GET OUT! GET OUT! GET OUT! GET OUT!"

To my surprise, it releases me. I fall in a puddle of my own blood and instinctively cover my torso.

"I got you!" Rob yells.

I turn my head and see three people running to me. *I can see.*

Rob, a middle-aged man with sun-burnt skin and red hair, pounces to one side of me while Pri, a bronze-skinned woman with green eyes and wild brown hair, steps to the other. They lift me in a basket-like hold and attempt to carry me away.

The demon roars and leaps several feet into the air. It lands right behind us and swings, barely missing.

Narron swoops in from the side and punches the demon hard in the face. When he does, its hood and beak are knocked off, revealing a wrinkled man with crystal blue eyes.

It's Human X. Me.

Human X screams and cowers backwards. "Aaaaeeeel!" It cries.

"GO!" Narron roars. He helps Pri and Narron kick down the double doors and we bolt down the hall.

I look over my shoulder and catch a glimpse of Human X with his aged head thrown back and laughing before the door closes behind us. *You will never really escape me, Ael,* his voice laughs in my head. *Soon.*

Lights flash in my head as I start to lose consciousness. Perhaps it's because of the immense amount of adrenaline surging through my veins or maybe because I'm about to pass out, but the gaping wound in my gut doesn't bother me.

Every time I start to black out, something pulls me back into consciousness. I don't know how long we've been running. I stopped feeling a while back. I'm fairly certain Narron has been trying to talk to me this entire time, but I've not responded.

I close my eyes and see my beautiful Reya. I'm not sure if this is an actual memory or just a dream, but it is a welcome vision indeed. She is playing with our spirited twin girls in a place with green grass and trees — a place that no longer exists.

Much to my chagrin, I'm pulled out of that fantasy. A blast of crisp mountain air touches my skin, healing it. I take in a deep breath and allow the freshness to sooth my lungs.

"You're going to make it, Ael." Rob says.

I nod and close my eyes. As much as I want to gaze upon the mountains, I am too exhausted to keep my eyes open.

I can still hear the faint whispers of the demons calling to me. I wonder if I will always hear them. I wonder if I will even survive my wounds.

Time passes and we put more and more distance between us and the lab. The farther away we get, the more the voices fade until they are completely gone.

We finally stop and they lay me down on the hard stone ground of the mountains. My eyes sting when I try to open them, but I bask in the colorful sunlight as long as I can before closing them again.

"Do you think they are going to follow us?" Pri asks.

"Let's hope not," Narron says.

We sit in silence for a while before I muster the energy to say, "We cannot … cannot let them out."

They all turn to me with blank looks on their face. "What do you mean? How?" Rob asks.

"First, we have to get as far away from them as we can," I say. I take a few deep breaths before continuing, "We have to find Human 76: Ghabrie. They are coming for her and it's only a matter of time before they do. They are afraid of her. She must have the power to stop them."

"Stop them?" Pri inquires.

"They are pure hate," I say. "Somehow, humans are the target of their loathing and they want us to suffer."

They fall silent and look out toward the barrens.

"If you intend to find Human 76, you should know that the Prometheans won't be far behind," Narron warns.

"I know," I admit. "But I have to try."

"You'll fail," Narron says.

His words catch us off guard.   Narron laughs under his breath and turns to me. His pupils dilate until his entire eyeballs are black. My muscles freeze with fear. Pri and Rob both gasp, but they don't move.

"Pity," Narron continues. "Your body was most certainly preferred, but I gotta admit that this one is more agreeable."

"Wha ... what happened to Narron?" Rob breathes.

He throws his head back and laughs. "Ha! Narron is no one." Suddenly he is speaking with multiple voices. "I am Legion! I am many!"

Pri pounces toward Legion, but he jumps on the mountain wall and clings to it like a spider. He hisses a laugh and starts crawling up the wall with unnerving ease.

"Narron!" I scream. "Narron, I know you're in there!"

Legion blows a raspberry and calls, "Narron is no more! And if you want to save your precious world, you will get to her before I do. But of course, you would have to survive, first."

"What do we do!?" Pri panics. "Narron! NO!"

But Legion is gone. Pri and Rob turn to me, horrorstruck. "Ael! Ael what do we do?" Rob pleads.

My mind hasn't caught up to what just happened. Physically inept, there is nothing I can do, anyway.

Rob grabs my arm and wraps it over his shoulder. "Come on," he says to Pri. "We can't let that thing have Narron."

She grabs my other arm and they lift me again. Exhausted, they tremble under my weight.

"You should leave me," I say.

"No, we need you!" Rob argues. "You are quite possibly the only one in the world who understands what that thing is, so you are going to have to live."

I shake my head. *They'll never catch up.* I look around for something, anything, I can use to change their mind.

"Don't try anything stupid," Pri cautions. She pauses before adding, "Narron is our friend. We can't let this happen to him and you are our only hope of both saving that Ghabrie girl *and* getting Narron back."

She does have a point.

I sigh and sink into their arms.

Ghabrie, if you can hear me, something is coming for you. Something more sinister than the Prometheans. That they are targeting you tells me that you have the power to defeat them. Don't forget this! And don't let your pain consume for they will use this against. Hold on, child. I'm coming.

THE HUNTED

Steven Paul Watson

The rope bridge swung violently from side to side with every overly-cautious step. Waya grimaced. His heart roared in his chest; he pictured himself plummeting to his death in the foggy cavern below. He closed his eyes and held his breath until the bridge halted its violent movements. His stomach churned with each screech and shrill whistle. He thought he might vomit, though it had been over a day since he had last eaten and there was nothing in his stomach to lose. The wind pushed up into his face, blistering his exposed skin.

Biting his lip he looked back the way he had come, shifting his body to secure his uncertain position. There was little in this world he was truly afraid of: the main ones being heights, and the loss of his family and home. He could still see the smoke from the ridgeline reminding him that he had lost his home already. He knew the cause of the smoke; years of hard work gone up in flames.

The howling of his pursuers broke his vision of memories floating against the sky. Emerging from wilderness, they spotted him immediately, their yells echoing louder than the wind. He focused again, placing one foot in front of the other, over and over. He felt the advance of the first hunter, as the bridge shifted harshly beneath his feet. His pursuer rushed on, showing no caution. Waya smiled, and hurried forwards, away from the man, but lost his footing and slipped. He gritted his teeth, holding tight, not allowing himself a breath until his feet were again secure on the rope.

The man was closer now. Waya turned to face him, and braced his trembling feet, waiting. He told himself not to look down. He could feel his knife resting against his lower back. It would be easy to pull free, but he knew how the hunter, a blade gripped between his teeth, planned to attack. Waya forced himself to wait, and tried to quieten his vertigo.

When the hunter was close he released one handhold and took the knife from between his teeth. Waya gripped the rope above him and kicked out at the approaching hunter's leg, managing to unbalance him. The knife fell from the hunter's hand as he tried to hold on. Waya again kicked, keeping his own hands tight on the braces. The hunter slipped down, frantically trying to get a grip on something, but only catching air. Waya watched the man's terrified expression as the hunter disappeared into the dense fog below. The other pursuers yowled impatiently as they realized that he would not be an easy meal.

Waya turned again, towards the far end of the bridge. Safely across, he hurried into the wilderness.

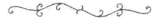

Waya pulled the cloth cover over his mouth, trying to hide the mist of his breath. He was struggling, having put a mile between him and the bridge, and every muscle in his body ached. He made no attempt to go quietly; he just wanted to put distance between him and the hunters. He knew that the path he was leaving was easy to follow.

From his vantage point in the tree Waya watched the brown, dead undergrowth for any sign of pursuit. He could hear no sounds of pursuit. He leaned back against the tree trunk and examined the blood-soaked scarf tied tightly around his bicep. Despite the silence, they would be coming.

Something made a sound behind him, and he twisted his gaze away from the direction of pursuit. It had been barely noticeable, but he was sure he had heard the flurry of wings. He frowned and turned to look behind him. Had the hunters circled him? The tang of fresh water teased his nostrils, but there was another scent carried on the slight breeze, a cleaner odor than the rank smell of the hunters.

She was easy to spot, kneeling by the stream that tumbled through the undergrowth nearby. Dark hair on pale skin that glowed in the filtered sunlight. His mother had spoken of angels and demons; he'd seen many demons in his life, but no angels. This woman was different from any he'd seen in his long life. He ran his hand through his thick, greying beard, checked back for any sign of the hunters, then returned his gaze to the girl.

He could not continue to lead the hunters on without at least warning her. He knew all too well what would happen to her if he just left her there in their path. She stood and looked around, frowning. Somehow she knew that she was being watched. He dropped down slowly, quietly, and moved towards her.

When he emerged into the clear area by the stream, she was gone. He examined the area carefully; her tracks led into the water and then … nothing. She had left no trace of the direction she had gone. He could not waste time; he had to lead his pursuers deeper into the wilderness. The girl would have to fend for herself.

He jumped the small stream with the aid of a protruding rock, making sure that he left a deep imprint on the bank for the hunters to follow. He dug into the earth on the far side as he left the stream behind him. Another easy path for them to follow.

Waya hurried through the trees and dense scrub for almost a mile before he paused to catch his breath. If they came upon him now, he would be easy prey. The sky was changing to deep dark red and purple, streaking the horizon. Darkness would come soon, and with it the frigid night air. He needed a fire; he was not dressed warmly enough to face the night.

He climbed the steep embankment in front of him, rock to tree to rock, slipping back several feet on numerous occasions. At last he managed to scramble to the top, from where he would be able to hear them coming in plenty of time. He would camp here for the night and hope they would do the same somewhere in the valley. He knew all too well the chances. They were dressed and conditioned to survive the coldest of nights, something he was no longer able to do. He had lost that edge many years before.

Waya used his small axe to gather arm loads of wood and laid them along the crest of the embankment - another obstacle if they came for him in the darkness. The horizon was a deep, violent purple as the sun disappeared. The drop in temperature on his exposed face blistered his flesh and made his eyes water. Even with a small fire, the night would be icy cold.

He struck rock against flint over and over until he made a spark. He let the kindling catch fire, then stacked small lengths of wood against the flame. He sat back, gathering a pile of dead leaves around him. He stroked his beard, watching the flames grow, feeling a brief moment of comfort from the warmth.

Waya pulled the book from his cloak. He flipped to the last page, running his hand down the paper as he closed his eyes, lost in a happy memory.

"You're being hunted."

Waya opened his eyes. He had dozed off looking at the drawing on the page. His fire was nearly out, and darkness distorted his surroundings making everything seem alive.

He sprang to his feet, looking for the small axe still cleaved in a nearby piece of wood. Before he could make a move towards it an arrow struck the wood by the blade. He still had his knife tucked into his belt, but he could not see his assailant and that gave them an extreme advantage. He decided on caution, and merely rested his hand on his hip, just inches from the knife hilt.

"Who's there?" he growled.

"You're being hunted, you make no attempt to hide your trail, they'll be on you before the sun rises again, and yet you stop and take the time to build a fire." He could hear almost a laugh in her voice at his foolishness – or perhaps what he heard was pity. She stepped into the light, the girl from the stream, no older than twenty years he guessed. Waya glanced at the surrounding darkness. Was she alone? A rustling sounds in the branches above him suggested not.

"You're leading them," she said. "Either into a trap … or away from something." Waya finally met her eyes. "Your pursuers are too concerned with killing you to realize it." She displayed no reaction to his own yellow, wolf-like eyes. She must have met mutations before. "So I can't help but wonder," she continued, "which is it?"

"Who are you?" Waya asked.

Her face remained expressionless. How easily she had found him. She had made no sound until she had wanted to be heard. An uneasy chill crawled across his skin. She had shadowed him since the stream and he had never noticed.

"My name's not important," she said.

Waya sat down again in his pile of dead leaves. The bed crackled with dry sounds at each movement he made, each breath he took. "I'm Waya," he said. He settled comfortably, carefully placing his thick matted hair over his shoulders. He fingered his thick beard; his habit when trying to calm his nerves. His other hand found his place in the book.

The young girl smirked. "You're being hunted and you take time to read a book?" The smirk persisted; that at least he could see in the dim glow from the fire. That and blue markings under her eyes, one reaching from her chapped lips to the edge of her soft chin. As she studied him he noticed a necklace around her neck, the bullet hanging just above her cleavage. She showed no reaction to the chill in the air, and she was far less covered than him. Somehow he knew that she could be as deadly as she was beautiful.

Waya leaned forward, setting his elbows on his knees. "This book, it was my mother's. She was alive before this new world. Before the sky rained death upon everything. When people could live something of a normal life." Waya smirked, trying to cover his partial lie. He could see the tension in her lips. "I know how I look: the thick hair, the beard. I was raised in the mountains. My mother would applaud my willingness to look beyond what I was ... applaud that I see another way."

"Serpents don't change," she replied. "They just slither out of old skin into new, still the same deceivers underneath," she replied.

Waya grunted. His eyes traveled up and down her, settling on her neck bone. He could barely even see when the girl took a breath, so calm and calculated was she.

"So you're her?" Waya couldn't contain his laugh. "You're no more than a--"

"A what?" she growled, sounding almost bestial.

"A kid." He did not refer to her years - he knew he was almost twice her age – but the young woman before him reminded him of another.

Her lips curved into a charming smile, one he'd almost consider beautiful, but it caused goosebumps to rise on his arms. He had heard the stories, from his people, from traders and travelers alike. Tales of a young nomad looking for her sister. Tales of her coming to the rescue of those who needed it, whilst to others she was death. Deadly with her bow at a distance. More unpredictable, and twice as deadly, up close.

"You're Ghabrie," he whispered almost afraid to give her name life. Her smile did not change. Waya leaned forward to feed the fire. "You're her."

"If I am?" she replied. He could see the tension in her ease a little. Waya positioned himself so that she had every advantage – a sign that he meant her no harm. He had no reason to provoke the nomad. He only wanted to rest his eyes.

"You have no reason to trust me," Waya leaned back, closing the book and letting it settle close to his heart. "But I don't mean you any hurt. I'm not sure that if I did that it would matter." He sighed. "Yes, I know I am being hunted. My mother used to call them wasps. They swarm across our lands, killing almost everything in their path. Those they do not kill, they ... have other uses for. Women, they rape, even breed from. Children ... they swell their ranks with the young. And anyone who resists them, they kill, and even feast on. I was separated from my mother in my ... tenth ... no, maybe my ninth year. I forget. It has been so long now. I was one of them for a time ... three years I was a mule for them before I slipped away in the night."

He took a deep breath, his lungs still aching from the day's exertion. "You have no reason to trust me, but tomorrow I will likely die. And I am going to sleep now. I will not die from exhaustion, and I intend to take as many of them with me as I can when I go to see my mother again." He closed his eyes and immediately fell fast asleep.

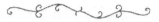

Waya woke; it was still dark, and his fire was almost dead. He was as surprised to realize that he had slept as he was to see Ghabrie still there. She slept just at the margin of the firelight. He sat up and pushed the last of his gathered wood into the fire. He held his hands out and warmed his aching fingers. He eased to his feet, smiled and pulled his axe in one smooth motion. He circled the fire, treading carefully. Ghabrie was not sleeping peacefully; she fidgeted in her slumber, twisting and turning. He bit his lip and tightened his grip on the axe.

He had thought the stories were just that, stories told to scare people. People like him. He stepped back away from her, putting the axe back in its place on his belt. It had been a big mistake on his part leaving it in the log. If she had been a hunter he would be dead now. He prowled around the fire, stoking the flame.

"Nahria," the young woman muttered, catching Waya off guard. He turned and looked at her, still asleep in the midst of a nightmare. "Nahria," she said again. Waya studied the young woman. She reminded him of another - innocent, but completely capable of taking care of herself. He heard the flutter of something out of sight, causing him to peer out into the darkness, but he saw nothing. He again took his place across the fire from her, nestled back into his make shift bed and quickly fell asleep.

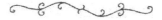

When Waya woke again, the sun was rising. He had made it through the night. The hunters still had not come for him. He nervously stood, and looked back along his path of the previous evening. His heart raced; he could see the mess he had made. It should have been easy for them to follow but they still hadn't come. He ran his hand through his hair pushing leaves from the braids.

"Where are you?" he muttered. He had failed. They must have turned back. His chest was tight with disappointment - he had failed again. He turned, looking for the young woman by the fire, but she too was gone, leaving him alone. He would have to turn back, and expect the worst.

He slowly gathered his few possessions. He had been so hopeful. They had to come for him, surely? So why hadn't they? He checked the scarf wrapped around his arm. The blood had dried in the cold of the night but he could smell it, and he knew that the hunters could too. Perhaps they had feasted on one of their own the night before and slowed their pursuit of him. He had not seen any fires in the night, however - they were close enough that he would have seen the ember glow, had they lit any. He grumbled inside. There was no room for failure; it would cost him everything he held dear.

The dragonfly caught his eye. It lingered, its wings fluttering at a speed even his eyes could barely see. It floated out in front of him, circling him around to his backside. He tracked it, twisting, stalking the curious little creature. Holding out his hand, he watched it gently settle onto the grimy fingertip that protruded from his fingerless gloves. He smiled at the simple beauty of the creature.

The man came from his right, axe already arcing through the air. Waya bounced from his position, throwing himself onto his back, and the blade narrowly missed his face. He smiled. He had not failed after all.

Waya rolled as the attacker pulled the axe from the ground. He was a large man, with exposed arms and chest. He raised his axe to strike again. Waya launched himself horizontally and kicked the man square in his chest, knocking him down the steep embankment. Waya could hear another, somewhere in the undergrowth. He pulled his own axe from his belt. A shrill scream from below drew his attention for a moment. The first attacker had lived through the fall.

Waya growled. "Come on!" He could hear a second attacker moving in the thick undergrowth, out of sight. Waya slowly moved sideways, trying to get a better perspective to peer through the bushes. The noise stopped as his eyes caught movement.

A deer, mutated with a vestigial third eye in the middle of his forehead, gave a growl that exposed enlarged canines. Its antlers dripped with blood, its jaws were covered with crimson. At its feet lay a second attacker, gored to death. The animal twisted its head, looking beyond Waya, then startled and disappeared into the wilderness.

The mutant deer had taken care of one attacker; that left, he figured, at least two others for him to worry about. But where were they? He turned, trying to see what had scared the beast off. He carefully approached the top of the embankment but heard nothing. "Ghabrie?" he called softly. There was no answer.

Waya traveled back the way he had come. In contrast to his headlong rush of the day before, he moved slowly through the dead forest, careful with his steps, trying this time to avoid leaving a trail, listening acutely to every sound. There were at least two others hunting him, maybe more by now.

When he arrived back at the bridge he crossed slowly, and carefully, and alert for any sound. He reached the other end half expecting to see the hunters leap out of hiding to attack.

Unmolested, Waya crossed down a small overgrown path to the left. It led, he knew, to an old temple. He was in a hurry now but could not risk moving too quickly. He needed to be ready if the hunters appeared anywhere close to him.

The door to the old church was missing. He moved slowly inside, holding his axe ready. Crossing the room, he found the old door leading to a back chamber, just as he remembered. He pushed against it. It was still blocked on the other side.

Waya smiled. "Ahyoka," he whispered, and paused for a reply. None came.

"Ahyoka," he said a little louder. He waited, his pulse rapid. He was sure he had been loud enough for her to hear.

"Ahyoka," he called, louder still. His voice echoed inside the dark chamber. Time stopped; his blood pounded in his ears, and he held his breath for a long minute.

"Ahyoka, can you hear me?" He pressed his ear against the door, tense and on the edge of tears. He heard movement, finally, and years seemed to replace seconds until the door opened. He grinned broadly as he saw his young daughter. She had obviously been asleep, and was pushing brushing the crimson hair from her eyes. "Can you travel?" he asked her.

"Yes," she replied with a half-yawn.

She stumbled through the door. Her skin was pale, and she clearly could not travel despite her answer - she needed food, water and rest. At the moment, he could only give her the last of those, and the warmth of a fire. He caught her on her second stumble, carrying her into the body of the church until he found a place they could sit amongst the rubble.

He smiled as he noticed that she still had a tight grip on her bow and quiver. Waya lifted her shirt to look at her stomach. "It stopped bleeding," she mumbled.

She unwound the scarf from his arm. They had used it to mop blood from her wound the day before, and he had used the scent of it to lure the hunters away from her.

"You're still weak, daughter," he muttered. He rummaged through the contents of his bag, looking for anything for her to eat.

Ahyoka took a sharp breath and her eyes darted to the door. He jumped to his feet, axe raised in defence. The doorway did not hold the hunters he had expected, however.

"Ghabrie," he muttered. She held her bow high with arrow notched. Waya stepped forward, putting his body between the nomad and his daughter.

"Your prize is a girl," Ghabrie stated.

"My daughter," he replied quickly.

"And the men hunting you?" she questioned.

"We took one of them in. I never realized what he was until my mate … she went missing. I was a fool. We barely escaped, and Ahyoka was injured." Waya looked down at his daughter. She held her own small bow raised, but her hand trembled. His daughter was a better shot than he had ever been with a bow, but she was weaker than he had thought. "Do you have food?" he asked. "Water?"

Ghabrie released the tension on her bow and put the arrow back in its quiver. She crossed the room and dropped a bag in front of them. Waya kneeled and looked inside. There was a skin filled with water, and a handful of nuts. He pushed it over to his daughter.

"I'm sorry there is so little. I have just returned from a fruitless expedition. The place was abandoned," Ghabrie told him. "You know there are still two more of them out there?" Ghabrie told him.

Waya sighed. He had hoped they were long gone. He put the axe back in his belt. "I had thought there might be more. Still, she can't travel, not yet. Even two is too many."

"They'll close in on this place after noon," Ghabrie said, walking inside. "The light will favor them then." Waya moved to the open doorway. They needed to barricade the door somehow. "You cleaned her wound?" Ghabrie said. He looked back to see the nomad inspecting the wound on his daughter side.

"Yes," he told her, "with clean water. I used the scarf to lead them away from here. They followed the scent of her fresh blood on the scarf."

"Smart," Ghabrie smiled. "Listen. There are some roots. They'll be hard to find this time of the year, but maybe ... maybe we can get lucky. They could give her some strength, enough to move. How far do you need to go?"

Waya frowned. He did not like depending on a stranger. "A little over a week ago, our home was a day's walk south of here," he replied, warily.

"Hidden near the cliffs?" she said.

Wait - she'd seen their home? This made Waya feel uneasy, but he nodded. "A traveler came, asking to trade as often they do. We welcomed him, bartered for food, gave him a place to sleep ..."

He turned, feeling his face flush with anger, on the edge of tears, as he repeated his story in more detail. "My wife, she went to get water ... I heard her scream. I rushed out to help her, but all I found was blood ... so much blood. When I heard my daughter scream I ran back as fast as I could ... the man we had given a place to sleep ... he had cut her, he was licking the blade ... while ... while a second man held her down." Waya's voice cracked with the pain of memory. He looked away and took a long, shuddering breath. "When I saw them there, I lost it. All I saw was red. I killed the one that held her, while the other slipped away. I carried Ahyoka away from that place for as long as I could, until we came here. But the man had followed us, and brought more like him. I waited near the bridge, then made sure they saw me and led them into the forest, making sure they would follow me ... away from my daughter."

Ghabrie smiled her approval. Waya turned to look back out of the door. "And now we are here."

"I will see if I can find what your daughter needs," Ghabrie disappeared as fast as she appeared.

Ghabrie had been gone almost an hour. Waya sat with his daughter's head on his knee. He watched the light from the fire reflect from her face. She had her mother's smile. So much about the nomad reminded him of his own daughter; he could only hope that Ahyoka would grow to be as powerful as Ghabrie.

"Where will we go?" she said. He hadn't realized she was awake.

"There is colony, somewhere in the mountains to the north," he ran a hand through his daughter's hair. He had heard tales of the community. They used wind power, and there were homes there still, like the ones his mother had told him about when he was little. At one time he had thought it was just a dream.

"They have power. Lights as bright as stars," he smiled. He had told her this before, as bedtime stories when she had been barely old enough to walk. "Running water they have, beautiful flower gardens, everything you could hope for. A place for you to draw, use those gifts you were given." His free hand went to the journal at his side. "There are soldiers there, to protect those in the community. Brave knights sworn to protect the innocent." He felt her shiver. He twisted, throwing a couple more small logs onto the fire. "And the homes! Heat, warm beds like you have never experienced, my princess. Lush gardens of produce. Plenty of game for hunting … we'll never go hungry again." His own stomach growled with just the thought of food.

"Mom would have loved it," she again closed her eyes.

He forced a smile. He could still remember the last time he had seen his wife. Her smile before she had disappeared into the darkness. "Yeah," he replied. "She would have loved it. And I know she will be just as happy knowing you are there, safe." He ran a hand through her hair. She was still pale, but her skin was warmer to the touch now. "I promise you."

"Do you think she'll come back?" the question caught him off guard. He could not be certain that his wife was dead. He had seen only blood, lots of blood.

"Your mother …"

He saw the sadness overtake her expression as she opened her eyes. She had her mother's eyes, light blue, but bloodshot now. "I meant Ghabrie," she explained. "But Mom?" He knew then his daughter had the same fear as he, that his mate was gone forever.

"I don't know," Waya replied, looking toward the open door and then back to his daughter. "I hope so."

"I think she will," she replied, closing her eyes again. Ahyoka was nearly fourteen; they had done their best to keep her safe. To keep the evils of this world at bay. Both he and his wife had grown up seeing bloodshed and violence often. He continued to stroke her hair until he was certain she'd fallen asleep. He reached and tugged the blanket tight up over her shoulders.

Waya's stomach growled again. It had been days since his last meal. He opened the journal, flipping through the drawings and writings. Some were his wife's, others his daughter's. He found the drawing of his wife - her long flowing brown hair, her wild blue eyes that looked more mysterious in the drawing. There was the smile, the twitch of her nose, the dimples – every time he closed his eyes he could see her. His stomach twisted thinking of her, warming his entire body with the memory of the woman he loved and her infectious smile.

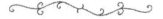

A maniacal laugh in his dream jolted him awake. Waya had not intended going to sleep. He scrambled to his feet, the journal falling from his lap to the ground, close to the fire. He had fallen asleep as he had gazed at the drawing of his wife, as he had the previous night. He put the journal back safely in the bag near his daughter. A cold sweat engulfed him. The fire was all but dead. He quickly pushed some of the remaining logs into the flames and looked towards the open door. Daylight was almost gone and Ghabrie had not returned; but he could understand why she might not want to. Ahyoka was not her problem, and she had her own nightmares to deal with.

Another insane laugh echoed through the church. He groaned; it had not been his dream after all. He gripped the axe tightly. "Come on, then," he muttered as another cackle echoed through the temple. The last of the daylight disappeared as Waya waited.

The howl of laughter sounded again, louder now, seeming to come from all directions around the old abandoned temple, and he realized with horror that there were more than two hunters.

A figure emerged from the darkness like a shadow made flesh, looming in the low light of the fire. It was him. The stranger to whom they had offered a place to sleep and a warm meal. Waya watched as he licked his blade. A scramble behind him told him that his daughter was awake and had pushed herself against a nearby wall.

The hunter licked his lips and looked past Waya, at Ahyoka. "I can still taste you, wild flower," the man hissed. He pointed his large blade towards them. "Your woman may have gotten away …" Waya's heart skipped. His wife might still live. "… you two will not. I will feast on your bones." The man was larger than Waya, a head taller and his shoulders almost twice as broad. His thick beard was caked with blood; he must have feasted on one of his own as Waya had suspected … unless the cannibal had killed Ghabrie.

Waya steadied himself, and even gave a slight smile he stepped forward. His wife was alive, he was certain. The same warmth of love that had helped him to sleep now fueled his anger. He would see her again. And he would reunite his daughter with her, no matter how many men he would have to kill in the process. They would be reunited.

"You will die this night," Waya told the monster. Another laugh from somewhere above him, but this one was cut off abruptly. He heard the body fall somewhere out of sight, and he knew that the hunter had not feasted on Ghabrie. She had returned, and he was not in this fight alone.

Waya grinned. The man charged, dual knives swinging wildly at Waya, but with each thrust, each slice, Waya blocked with his axe or dodged. The larger man grunted in frustration as his blows continued to miss their target. And now Waya found himself the one laughing. He thrust his free hand into the man's throat, forcing him backwards to the ground. Without hesitation Waya slammed his axe down, but the man was too fast, scrambling back to his feet and scrambling away, holding his throat.

Waya went on the offensive, swinging madly at the man, sloppily in his rage. He knew he had made a mistake even before the knife slid across his cheek. Waya skipped away, holding his free hand on the cut, blood seeping through his fingers. The man smiled, licking the knife. "Not as sweet as your daughter. A little too aged and salty."

Waya took a deep breath. He would not make the same mistake again. He backed away. He could hear his daughter's panicked breathing. "It's going to be alright," he gave Ahyoka a quick smile, paying little attention to the cut on his face now. He could feel the blood soaking his beard. Waya moved left and the hunter did the same. The two men circled each other warily.

When the hunter's back was to his daughter, Waya nodded, and she raised her bow. It was not as big as Ghabrie's, and she had never used it for anything more than hunting small animals. "You underestimated us," Waya said, "and most of your people have died for it." Waya said.

"I'm still alive--" the hunter's words ended with a gurgle as the broad head of the arrow emerged from his throat. He glanced down at the blood covered stone arrowhead, twisting as he fell to look at the young woman who had killed him.

Waya strode over to the man. Dead eyes stared up at him. He had not wanted this. He had never wanted Ahyoka to have to take a life. But they both knew it had been unlikely that he would have beaten such a large opponent. He ran a hand across his face as he approached her, and rested his other hand on hers.

"We're okay," he said. "We are all okay." He heard the footsteps, and turned to see Ghabrie in the church doorway, her bow held ready.

"The others?" Waya asked.

"None of them survived," she told him. "You all did."

He helped his daughter to her feet. The young nomad had a curious smile on her face, and when they moved towards her and she stepped aside he saw why. She emerged from the darkness behind Ghabrie, her light blue eyes shining in the light of the fire. Her smile made him weak. Olathe, his wife. Streaked with blood, her own axe, a twin of his own, hanging from her belt.

Waya could not make his legs move. He had hoped beyond hope that Olathe had escaped, but he would never have thought that Ghabrie might bring her back to them. His daughter left his side and rushed to her mother's arms. The woman twisted her around in a hug.

Waya watched her as she came to him. There were no words spoken between the two of them; he simply took her in his arms and gaze down into her eyes. The warmth was back, and his heart rejoiced as he kissed his wife's lips.

"Where will you go?" The question broke them from their kiss but their eyes did not break contact.

"North ... some travelers have said there are communities there. It is obvious The Wilds are no longer safe; every year there are more strangers. The next time we may not be so lucky," Waya told the nomad.

"What will you do?" Ahyoka asked Ghabrie.

"I have my own nightmares, my own journey to finish," the nomad replied. Waya remembered the nomad's dream by the fire.

Waya gave his daughter and wife a glance before looking to Ghabrie. "If there is anything I can do to help you ... you've given me so much. You've given me my life back."

Ghabrie smiled. It was a smile full of confidence and beauty, but her eyes spoke a different story. She was lost in her own journey. "Take care of your family, Waya. Family is everything."

Ghabrie brushed past them, but before she could escape the young girl grabbed her, wrapping her in a hug, bringing a new warmth to the young nomad's eyes. As the two young women separated, Ghabrie was gone as quickly as she entered their lives.

WHAT YOU PUT IN

Julia Rios

It was hot in the grinding house, but Kayera didn't mind. And she didn't mind the hard labor of it either. Every day she spent there made her more a part of Mill River. She patted the sack of grain three times as she tipped it into the grinder, a ritual for luck. You get out what you put in, she thought.

She liked working here because people didn't talk much while processing grain into flour. They were too busy feeding things in at the right speed, getting everything into containers, and hauling the finished product out to the staging area so it could be sorted at the ration house. The grinding house was not a lonely place, but it was also not a talkative one. Not usually.

A soft bump from behind reminded Kayera that today was an exception. Eneri from Dome 2 gave an exaggerated laugh, too long and loud to be genuine. "Oh, I'm so sorry, I didn't see you there."

"No problem," Kayera said, refusing to meet the woman's eyes. She turned back to her work in silence.

Eneri's post was in office administration, but she had managed to get herself reassigned for today and she stuck to Kayera like glue. She hadn't done half the work Kayera had, and she had stopped Kayera from working to her full potential. It was hard to keep a rhythm while constantly tripping over someone.

It wasn't as though they were friends. Eneri had two decades on Kayera, and she lived in a different dome. Kayera was still in Dome 6 where newcomers lived for their first year. Normally the old-timers gave the new settlers a wide berth, waiting to see if they were

230

trustworthy, but because Kayera was a young woman with dark hair that had not happened for her. Every week it seemed someone else wanted to chat her up, hoping she was someone other than who she claimed to be.

When she had first arrived, she had not known who Ghabrie was. In the city she had come from, the name of Ghabrie was not known to every household. When she had arrived at Mill River's front gates after a day of wary circling, trying to judge the lay of the land and the politics of the place, she had thought they mistook her for one of their own who had gone missing.

"Ghabrie?" the on-duty watch had asked. It had been reverent. The sort of tone one used for a child long missing. "Is it truly you?" Kayera had shaken her head, sorry to disappoint, but unwilling to impersonate someone probably long dead.

When Eneri tapped Kayera on the shoulder, Kayera flinched.

"Sorry, I didn't mean to startle you," said Eneri. Kayera nodded, wary of what would come next. "It's just... I transferred here for the day because I wanted to ask if you would consider using your gift to help me."

"I'm not her," Kayera said. "I don't have the gift."

"I can pay," said Eneri. "I'll give you credit or work in trade. You could take some time off."

"I'm sorry." Kayera turned away and hefted a sack of grain to pour into the grinder. Even if she had the gift, she had no idea what she would do with time off. Work kept her sane, gave her something to focus on.

"Just listen, please," said Eneri. "I want to find my baby. My Sheila. She was taken from me when she was six. That was six years ago. I just want to know she's all right. Even if she can't come home."

Tears streamed down Eneri's face, and Kayera felt terrible for her, as she did for everyone who had lost someone. But there was nothing that Kayera could do to bring Sheila back, or even to find out where she had gone. She could be with the Alliance, or she could be anywhere else. Most likely she was dead. It was not a nice thought, but it was probably the truth.

"I'm sorry." Kayera spoke more softly this time, as softly as she could over the roar of the grinder. She made eye contact with Eneri, willing her to know that if she could help she would. "I'm not her. I don't have the gift. I'm just a girl who's willing to do hard work. That's all."

Eneri grabbed her arm. "But surely if you try—"

"No," Kayera said. "I have tried. I don't have it."

When the last of the grain spilled from the sack into the grinder's hungry maw, Kayera took it to the pile of empties and then signalled to the foreman asking to go on a break. "Please don't follow me," she said to Eneri. "I need to be alone."

Outside the grinding house it was not as hot, but thanks to the western wind, the air burned all the same. Kayera ran to Dome 6 for shelter, hoping for five minutes of peace and quiet. But it was Jenna's nursery day, so the dome was full of children, all under the age of five. There would be no peace there.

Sighing, Kayera stepped into her collecting gear and made her way to the registration office in Dome 1. It was a brisk seven-minute walk, and with the gear on it was hotter than the grinding house, but at least the wind wouldn't burn her. Plus walking outside in gear was quiet because you had to undo the face shield to talk.

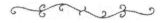

Across the river lay the scrub. After a brief stop to pack a lunch and put it in her backpack, Kayera set off. In either hand she held a nylon bag for any weeds she came across. They would be shoved into the textile mill and turned into clothing, curtains, containers, sails, or any number of other useful things.

Collecting scrub was one of those gruelling tasks that no one really wanted to do, but did because it was necessary. Inside the gear, Kayera was already a sweaty mess, but to take it off while pulling scrub was asking for illness or injury. The weeds would get detoxed before they went through the mill, but in the wild, they could be full on lethal.

Kayera took one of the rafts tied loosely to the dock by the Dome 3 gate, and used a long pole to push herself across the muddy water. On the other side, she hopped off and pulled the raft ashore, mentally marking the place in relation to where it sat in line with the mills. If she lost the raft, it could take ages for someone to notice and come across to look for her; days even. And although in some ways the thought of not having to deal with people seemed nice, Kayera knew better than to imagine the reality would be anything other than miserable. She had been halfway to starving when she had come to Mill River and didn't fancy being that way again.

She thought about the time before she had left the city as she walked, particularly in contrast to how empty the scrub was, and how strange she would have found that emptiness six months ago. In the city she had lived in a big housing block. She had shared her unit with Gran, who was old enough to remember the world before. Just barely, but it was enough to make her one of the authorities in the block. Sometimes they had gotten meals or other little things out of the other residents in exchange for Gran's stories of the before.

There had always been noise in the city. Workers, traffic, people going about their daily lives. It was worlds away from Mill River, where even on a day like today, when Kayera was feeling stifled, the only noise outside the domes was the whipping wind. When she had first arrived she had found the quietness eerie. She was growing more used to it now, though. It was reassuring in a way. Kayera knew that if anyone came to cause trouble, all of Mill River would hear, and they would have time to mount a defense from inside the domes.

Kayera had left Gran's because they had had no way of knowing exactly when trouble would arrive, and no real ways to fight back. People whispered that the Promethean Alliance was searching for young and healthy subjects to test, maybe to make into super soldiers, but no one knew when or how they might attack. When Kayera heard that they had raided a block just a few minutes from hers and killed anyone who had tried to protect the people they had wanted to take, she had known that she had to leave, and to wipe out every trace that she had ever grown up there. It was not just to protect herself, but because no one was going to kill Gran – not if she had anything to say about it.

They had cleared out her room before nightfall, giving anything that looked like a young person's possession to the community center collection point. She had helped Gran to move her sewing table and knitting supplies in there to look like it had always been a workroom. Gran made enough scarves and gloves and hats for the block that it was plausible they would have given her the space.

They told their immediate neighbors, trusting them not to give Gran away, and Kayera had left under the cover of darkness that same night. She remembered feeling scared, but also half invincible in a way that only the ignorant can. She had grown up in the city, scampering through the streets, knowing every alley and all the places to score food; how to bargain and barter. She had left with scarcely enough food to last her two days.

Looking back, it was a miracle she had managed to survive.

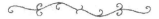

A rustle in the brush brought Kayera's attention fully into the present. She braced herself for fight or flight, dependant on the source of the noise. Then the girl stepped out. Kayera knew it was her the moment she appeared: the antlers, the face paint, the aura of something different.

This was Ghabrie.

It was not like looking into a mirror. They did both have dark hair, but that was where the similarities ended. Ghabrie was pale-skinned where even in deep winter Kayera was light brown. Ghabrie was elfin compared to Kayera's solid frame.

Kayera unfastened the face plate and pulled her helmet off. Her breath caught in her throat and she stood stock still, staring.

Ghabrie cocked her head to the side, gauging. Her kestrel swooped in from overhead and landed on her arm. When it had settled, and Ghabrie seemed to make up her mind about the safety of the situation, she spoke.

"I'm looking for a girl named Nahria. Younger than me, but similar in looks. Have you seen her?"

Startled out of her silence, Kayera blurted the first thing that came to mind. "You're Ghabrie."

"Yes," Ghabrie said. "So people know of me here?"

"They mistook me for you when I first arrived," Kayera said. "I didn't know if you were real."

Ghabrie laughed softly, ruefully. "Oh, I'm real."

"Can you really see the future?" Kayera asked. When Ghabrie frowned, Kayera took half a step back.

"I'm sorry. I didn't mean to pry. You don't have to answer."

Ghabrie shook her head. "It's not that. I'm just not sure how to answer. Maybe? Sometimes? It's inconsistent and vague. I am certain of one thing, though: I *make* the future."

"I haven't," Kayera said. And then, feeling foolish, added, "Seen your sister, I mean. She's not in Mill River."

Ghabrie did not sigh or deflate, which surprised Kayera. If she had been searching for her own sister, she would probably be heartbroken not to find her. But Ghabrie simply nodded slightly, keeping her chin high and shoulders back, a fierce warrior, dignified and stoic.

"I will move on then, toward Foreman Wilds," she said.

"We have food," Kayera offered. "I'm sure they'd be happy to give you supplies if you come back with me."

Ghabrie held Kayera's gaze, challenging her to understand. "They think you are me," she said.

"Yes," Kayera said, uncertain.

"You see then why I can't go there."

"Oh," Kayera said, understanding. She did not say more. It was not necessary. Ghabrie could not come back because it would slow her down. The price of supplies would be handholding, soothsaying, and any number of celebrations and delays. Kayera took out her untouched pack lunch, and offered it to Ghabrie. "Take my lunch, then," she said.

Ghabrie closed her eyes for a moment, considering. Kayera could not read her well enough to know what she was thinking, but thought she might be considering the price of taking it. "It's free," she said. "I can go back and get more food at the settlement. You can't."

"That's very kind of you," Ghabrie said. "I can't take it without offering something in return, though."

"You said you're heading to Foreman Wilds. That's south of here, right? Have you been to the city a few days to the north? It's where I'm from."

"I came from there," Ghabrie said. "Nahria was not there."

"I wonder if maybe, in exchange for the food, you can tell me what's happening there?" Kayera asked.

"Yes," Ghabrie said. "That's a fair deal. Let's find a rock to sit on. We can share food and trade information."

Kayera's stomach rumbled in response. She hoped it wasn't audible. She picked up the nearly full sack of weeds she had set down earlier and began walking. "This way," she said. "I've already cleared it of weeds, and there's a nice flat boulder."

When they had sat and divided the contents of the packed lunch between them, Ghabrie asked, "What do you want to know?"

"Is the PA still there? I guess maybe not if Nahria isn't?"

"They've left. The Green Stripes are in control of the city now. Have been for the last six weeks." Kayera's heart beat faster. The Green Stripes. Why did that name scare her? Not knowing what else to ask, she told her story, letting words spill out in a great rush until she had laid her life bare for Ghabrie's perusal. She finished by saying "When I left, seven months ago, the PA was stealing kids to experiment on, and they were hurting anyone who tried to protect them. I lived in a block with my grandmother, and left to protect her."

"The PA apparently found everyone they required," Ghabrie said. "Or it may have been that they got word that there was trouble at their headquarters. They left overnight in a hurry. Nahria may have been there before that. I don't know. But if she was, you did well to escape."

"Is the city stable? I haven't heard from Gran, but of course I couldn't have because she doesn't know where I've gone. I didn't think it would be safe to tell her."

Ghabrie paused between bites of sandwich. Then she set the sandwich down, and looked Kayera in the eye. "You are right to be secretive. Information is valuable, but it can also lead to bad things."

Kayera nodded, once again feeling like there was a deeper meaning to Ghabrie's words that she was missing.

"The city is …" Ghabrie shook her head and started again. "Stable is a strange word. The Green Stripes care more for environmental reform than human testing. But … they value the young over the old. They believe the older generations have not helped to heal the world. Do you understand?"

"I … I think so," Kayera said slowly. But she was not sure she did understand. "Are you saying that Gran might be in danger?"

"I don't know," Ghabrie said. "She might be considered valuable. Does she garden? Or have other earth healing skills?"

"We all gardened some, in the community plots, but no, it's not Gran's chief role. She sews and knits mostly."

"Hmmm." Ghabrie didn't say anything more, but ate the rest of her sandwich in silence. When she had finished, the kestrel swooped in and nipped the last bit of crust from between her fingers before flying off again.

"This feels silly, but I can't help thinking I've heard that name before," Kayera said. "The Green Stripes, I mean. And it scares me, but I don't know why."

Ghabrie looked away for a moment. The kestrel flew in a low circle around them and made several short sharp trills as Ghabrie listened intently. Finally, without looking directly at Kayera, she said, "Take my hand."

Kayera had stripped the top half of her gear off before sitting down to eat, so her hands were bare. She was simultaneously excited and worried about what touching Ghabrie might do. Everyone said she had superpowers. Was she dangerous? Gingerly she put her hand forward. Ghabrie took it and held it firmly like they might have a handshake, except without the shaking part. At first it didn't feel like anything much, but then Kayera felt a jolt and a warm tingle spread up her arm and over her whole body.

Images too fast to catch flashed through her mind. It was strange and unsettling, and she felt dizzy. Then, abruptly, everything stopped. In a daze, Kayera realized that Ghabrie had let go of her hand. The world came rushing back to fill Kayera's senses: the breeze against her skin, the sound of the Kestrel trilling overhead, the dull, baking heat of the mid-afternoon sun. Everything felt simultaneously distant and hyper-real.

"What just happened," she asked.

"I tried to use the sight," Ghabrie said. "It's not easy."

"Did you … see anything?" Kayera asked.

"Tell me what happened to your parents," Ghabrie said.

Kayera frowned. "Is this about them? What did you see?" It was frustrating to have her question answered with another question. Why couldn't Ghabrie just be straightforward? But if it had been anything like the flood of images Kayera had experienced, maybe she didn't know how to explain what she had seen.

"I don't remember much. I think they both had dark hair. My mom's was lighter than my dad's, but we all looked alike. They were happy. We would go to the community garden together. But then when I was five, they were gone, and Gran took care of me."

"Do you remember them leaving?" Ghabrie asked.

"I... I don't know."

Ghabrie put her hand on Kayera's arm and the images came flooding through her mind again, but this time more slowly: her parents laughing, her tiny young hands working a trowel into the soil in the garden. Her mother helping her plant a seed, and saying, "Give it three pats for luck, love, and growth. You get out what you put in, Kay." Kayera had forgotten that her parents were the ones who had taught her that work ethic, even that they used to call her Kay. What else had she forgotten? The memories plunged on: her mother blowing her a kiss goodbye as Kay watched two men walk her away from the block. Had there been tears in her eyes? Why?

"You know the penalty for disloyalty," one of the men was saying.

Gran telling her everything was fine and that they were going to be a cozy home of two now. Gran cutting up the shirt Kayera's dad had left behind with three green stripes on one sleeve, and giving the pile of rags that resulted to the community store instead of keeping them. "I couldn't have it in the house anymore," she said. "Not after they took them from me like that."

"Your parents were with the Green Stripes," said Ghabrie.

Kayera nodded slowly, feeling sick. "I think they were. I think... I think maybe they tried to leave, but they weren't allowed. Do you think they're still with them?"

Ghabrie looked away, but didn't say anything. She didn't have to. Kayera understood it was as she had always feared. They were dead. Killed by the organization they had tried to help.

"If they know Gran was my mother's mother, they'll kill her for sure. She's old and she doesn't support them." Kayera sucked in a sharp breath. "I have to go back."

Ghabrie called her kestrel to her and stood. "We will go our separate ways, then. Be careful, Kayera."

"As careful as I can be under the circumstances," Kayera agreed.

"Mill River is independent and peaceful?" Ghabrie asked.

"Yes," said Kayera. "I'm sure if you wanted to go there they would give you supplies."

"No, I have to keep searching for Nahria. I can't afford delay." Ghabrie's eyes went to a faraway place, and her voice shook. "She's in pain."

"I'm sorry," Kayera said. "It must be horrible sensing that."

"Worse than you can imagine," Ghabrie agreed. "But I will remember Mill River and your kindness."

She strode off southwards, and Kayera watched until she could no longer distinguish Ghabrie from the kestrel on her shoulder. Then she pulled her gear back on and picked up the full bag of weeds. She would normally stay out later, but instead it looked like she would be spending the afternoon resting and gathering supplies for her journey back to the city. She would leave at moonrise.

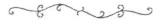

The way back to the city was easier than it had been when she had come the other way. Kayera was equipped with a map, knowledge of the area, and enough supplies to see her through without starving. On the way out she had wandered for over two weeks, but this time she arrived at the outskirts of the city just as the sun was setting on the eighth day.

The atmospheric change was startling and familiar all at once. Smoke, sewage, food, and other accumulated scents of daily life made her realize how pristine the wilds were. In the city dogs barked, and she could see the barrel fires of the street vendors glowing even before she made out individual landmarks. As she drew closer, she started to distinguish individual blocks in the jumble of tall buildings that made up downtown. One of them was her block.

The thought of returning had felt abstract until now, more like a dream than like something she was actually doing. Now Kayera's heart beat staccato and hard, and her palms began to sweat.

She found a wall to lean against and adopted a nonchalant pose, as though she was carefree and loitering after a workday, perhaps avoiding evening chores at home. She had done enough of that before leaving — that was easy to fake — but inside she was in turmoil. Her emotions shifted in tumultuous heaps: guilt, shame, anger, fear, and just a tiny bit of elation.

She had grown up here. This was home. In so many ways it felt right to be here. But she had left. When she had gone, she had told herself it was self-sacrifice, an act of courage to save her closest loved one. But was it? Or had it been selfish? She had been itching to see the world, to see what might be possible outside the sphere in which she had grown up. And now that she was back, she wondered if the city would have been better for her staying.

You get out what you put in.

Had she put in enough here? Could she have put in more?

She waited for full dark before making her way through the maze of streets to her block. She figured it was better to approach under cover of night; she did not know what the Green Stripes had changed, and she did not want to run into them.

The block was quiet, with just a few solar lamps glowing, but less electric hum than she remembered. Kayera let herself in the back way, and scurried up the fire escape to Gran's floor. There were ledges enough that she could climb into her old room if the window was open. Of course there was no reason to think it would be.

There was no reason to think that she should not just knock on the front door. Except...

What if Gran wasn't there? What if they had taken her? Or Gran had moved to a different place? Kayera resolved to climb along the ledges just to see if it still looked like the home she remembered.

She left her pack on the fire escape so it would not unbalance her. It would be easy enough to grab if she needed to run back down.

It had been over a year since she had last done something like this. She had gone to a concert that Gran had forbidden her to attend. She had not been caught, but she had felt so guilty about sneaking out that the idea that she was doing something wrong clung to her even now, even though this time she was doing exactly the right thing; or what she hoped was the right thing.

She steeled herself not to look down and focused on the shapes of the bricks as she sidled across the first ledge. By the end of the second ledge, her confidence had returned and she felt more sure of her course. Just two more to go. So far all the windows had been dark, which was simultaneously helpful and unsettling. Was everyone out? Did people not live here anymore?

There was light coming from Gran's place, though. That was a good sign, surely?

At the edge of what had been the living room window, Kayera paused and took a deep breath. Up to now she had been able to imagine that it was the same as always; that Gran would be inside making tea, or perhaps sharing dinner with one of the neighbors. But as soon as Kayera looked, she would know the truth. If everything had changed she would know that this was no longer home. Was she ready for that?

She had to be.

Kayera leaned her head against the brick wall and squeezed her eyes shut tight. She counted backwards from ten before opening them again. Time to face the new reality.

Cautiously, she edged over enough so that she could peek into the window. The curtains were open and solar lamps lit the kitchen where three people were seated at the table. One of them was Gran, her hair shorn, instead of the familiar long silver braid. The other two were no-one that Kayera recognized. All of them wore the Green Stripes uniform. Gran served salad from a big bowl, heaping the others' plates, and reserving a smaller portion for herself. She was smiling, but Kayera could tell that the smile did not reach her eyes.

This did not look good. Kayera needed to know what was going on here, and the only way she could find out was by going over one more ledge to see what had become of her old room. It had been set up as Gran's sewing room when she left, but the sewing machine in the living room suggested that was not the case now.

The living room was dark, and the diners were not facing the window directly, but moving across it was still a big risk. If she made a noise, or if one of them looked, she would be found out, and then what? Probably nothing good.

She held her breath as she tiptoed across, sighing with relief when she reached the other side. Stepping to the next ledge, she felt a smidgen safer. The room was dark, but she had a flashlight with her. She would have to risk the noise of cranking it enough to give a little light.

The people inside were in the next room with a thick wall between her and them. She could not hear their voices. That was enough to persuade her to take the risk.

She fished the light from her pocket and turned the crank slowly, letting it hum low and weak. It would take a bit longer to get a charge, but she did not dare to risk the shrillness of a fast crank – plus she worried that she would lose her grip on the ledge if she moved too quickly. The cranking seemed to stretch on forever, and Kayera strained to hear signs of people inside approaching. There were none by the time the light had charged and she projected the weak beam through the window of what had once been her room.

It was a bedroom again, but definitely not Kayera's. Bunk beds lined two walls, a small dresser between them. The beds were made up with perfect square corners and each one was covered with a blanket that showed three green stripes. There was nothing else in the room. No personal mementos stood atop the dresser. There were no pictures on the walls. It was uncannily spare and sterile. Somehow this scared Kayera even more than finding Gran pretending to be cheerful with strangers.

The place was like a military base, not a home. And from the look of it, at least four people were living here with Gran, not just the two she had already seen. Kayera worried more than ever about Gran's safety. She had to find a way to get her out of there, and she suspected knocking on the front door would do more harm than good.

She had almost finished folding the light and stowing it in her pocket when she heard a thump, followed by the sound of the living room window being opened. She had to get out of there. Kayera could not go back the way she had come, so she edged as quickly and quietly as possible across the ledge to the one outside the next apartment.

"Do you hear something out there?" a male voice asked. Kayera froze in place, and held her breath, praying that someone would not look outside the window.

"Other than the normal sounds of dirty city life? No. I'll be glad when we can leave this place." This voice was female. It sounded like both the Green Stripes had come to the window together.

"No," said the man. "I mean, like a scurrying or something. It's stopped now, but I swear I heard it before."

"Probably a rat," the woman answered. "The city's full of them."

"Hmm. Probably," the man agreed, but he sounded unconvinced. Kayera pressed herself as flat as she could against the wall, wishing she could melt into it and disappear.

"Close the window," the woman said. "It stinks out there, and it's not like you can see the stars here anyway."

The window did not close, but the voices receded, suggesting that the pair had walked further into the apartment. Kayera took it as her best chance to move, and turned her attention back to sliding along the ledge. She made it two more ledges down before she found another open window.

This was the apartment that had previously belonged to the Chung family, and it looked like might still be theirs. The room she let herself into was the kids' bedroom, and it still looked like a room kids lived in. Their two-headed lizard, Mr. Chuckles, was even in his terrarium. Kayera breathed a long sigh of relief. She was out of immediate danger, but she still had to get herself back out of the building, and figure out how to save Gran.

Kayera didn't have long to think. The door opened, and Danny came in. He would be seven by now, and in the past months he had grown up quite a bit. He was taller, but he also looked sadder and harder than the happy-go-lucky kid Kayera remembered. She wondered what he had been through since she had left.

Danny's eyes grew wide when he saw Kayera, but when she put her finger to her lips he nodded and didn't say a word.

"Danny," she whispered. "I don't want anyone to know I'm here, but I need to get a secret message to Gran. Can you help me?"

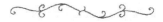

Gran arrived at the community garden at noon just as Kayera had asked. Kayera nonchalantly pulled weeds as though she belonged there, as though she had never left.

"Good afternoon," she said. She hoped Gran would understand that she was trying to make it seem as though they didn't know each other. Gran nodded and took a position next to her.

In a barely audible whisper Kayera said "We need to leave the city as fast as we can. I met someone who told me that things are looking bad. And I don't like the way that your house is occupied."

Gran put down her trowel. "If you have time for a walk, I'll show you one of the tricks of irrigation that we've been working out."

A walk. Kayera knew this might mean their chance to escape. "That would be great." She said the words loudly and in a carefree manner as though she was interested in growing food and irrigation. But under her breath she added "Do you need to get anything before we leave the city?"

Gran shook her head slightly, just enough so that Kayera would notice, and they walked briskly out of the community garden. Gran explained irrigation to her as they went. To the casual observer they looked like regular city dwellers, but Kayera knew that Gran was walking faster than she might normally.

Kayera led the way to the edge of the city where she stopped to retrieve the pack of supplies she had hidden when she had first arrived. "I don't know for sure there'll be enough for both of us," said Kayera, "but hopefully it'll see us through."

"I brought a sack of beads and coins for barter," said Gran, opening her gardening bag to reveal some supplies of her own. "I couldn't take too many things out of the house, but I brought some summer squash, since it's coming out of our ears, and a picture of your parents."

"You're wearing sturdy clothes," said Kayera. "That's the main thing. We can share the bedroll, and I've got enough food that it should be okay, especially with extra squash. We can save the seeds for replanting."

"You've grown up so much, Kayera," Gran said.

"Funny," said Kayera. "I thought the same thing about Danny when I saw him."

"All the children grow up too fast these days," said Gran. "It's not right."

"Will they be looking for you?" Kayera asked, ignoring Gran's comment. Now was not the time to dwell on sentiment. They needed to move.

"Not yet," said Gran. "Maybe not until tonight."

Kayera hoisted the pack onto her shoulders and strapped it around her waist. "Then let's go as far as we can before then," she said.

When they slipped out of the city down one of the side streets, no one paid them any attention. Kayera's long journeys through the wastes and the wilds had paid off; they were soon hidden from view by brush and scrub.

The journey back to Mill River took some time, but they made good progress considering Gran's age. Nothing attacked them and they were able to forage along the way.

It gave them a chance to catch up on all the things they had missed in each other's lives. Kayera told Gran about life in Mill River, about people thinking she was Ghabrie and demanding to hear the future, as well as her experience with the real Ghabrie. And Gran told Kayera about the Green Stripes' plans to fight other groups for control, not just of the city, but of all the surrounding lands.

"They never paid me any mind," she said. "I was old and frail to them. Someone worth keeping for the housework and knitting, but not a soldier or a deep thinker."

"They were idiots if they didn't see how competent and amazing you are, Gran," said Kayera.

"People will see what they want to see," said Gran. "And it suited me fine. Better to be ignored and learn about how things are than to be the center of attention and always in danger."

"It will be different from now on," Kayera promised.

There were long stretches of amiable silence, too, during which Kayera thought about Gran's words and Ghabrie's, and about the constant refrain in her head: you get out what you put in.

On the last morning of the journey, as the domes were just becoming visible on the horizon, Gran stopped and took Kayera's hand in hers. "Is that it?" she asked.

"Yes," Kayera said, giving Gran's hand a gentle squeeze. "We'll be there by midday."

"What will you tell them?"

Kayera looked down at their joined hands, both darkened to a richer brown than usual from days in the sun. "I will tell them I've brought you to help us. That this is where I plan to put down roots."

"Will they accept me?" Gran asked.

"They'll love you," Kayera said. "You have so many skills. In Mill River, you'll be an asset to the community, not a frail old woman. You'll love them, too, if you try. You get out what you put in."

Gran smiled sadly. "You sound just like your mother."

"I think that's a good thing, isn't it?" Kayera asked.

"She was a wonderful person. I miss her. So many people lost over the years."

Kayera had no answer for that, so she simply bowed her head in acknowledgement until Gran spoke again.

"And you?" Gran asked. "Do they love you?"

"They tolerate me," said Kayera. "But we can be happy there. We can rebuild our life."

Gran squeezed Kayera's hand this time. "You are a good girl," she said. "But will it be all right? What if they keep asking you to be a soothsayer?"

Kayera squared her shoulders, channeling Ghabrie's warrior stance. "I will tell them I have seen the future and that it requires defense lest the Green Stripes try to invade. I won't let it happen. Mill River will stay independent."

Hand in hand, they marched towards the domes.

UNDERNEATH

Denise Callaway

Sleep, elusive sleep. Cievette shoved herself out of the makeshift bunk. How she missed soft mattresses and the luxury of pillows, especially now as she wrapped herself in a blanket that resembled glorified tin-foil, cold and clinical. She wrinkled her nose. She would love to bring her own bedding when on assignment but impracticality overrode such desires. It was comfort she missed more than anything, but comfort was a luxury tunnel rats could rarely afford. Eisle glanced over from the flickering screen. "Awake already?"

"That statement implies sleep."

"Ha! Don't I know it? I've barely hit REM once, maybe twice, in the last two weeks. And now I'm hearing voices and wondering if it's the radio or my own insanity."

Eisle stood wearily and stretched. His long arms seemed to lack definition, however Cievette had seen him fight. He had a gift for finding and exploiting his opponent's weakness – unless that opponent was a computer monitor.

This was Cievette's specialty: a role she stepped into with ease. She could traverse the landscape of these systems with the grace of a dancer across a stage. Her codes were elegant, tying up loose ends seamlessly. So when Eisle had been assigned to her unit, she had stared at Commander Harkins with incredulity: he expected her to teach this lunkhead? But to her surprise, Eisle had turned out to be quite teachable, at least to a degree, and he provided the necessary physical protection required on topworld assignments.

251

"I'll be glad when this project is complete," responded Cievette dully.

The tunnel rats had a knack for thievery, stealing anything from food and clothing to power. They only found independence in the deep spaces beneath cities. Over the years, they had learned to network with the rats in other cities, sharing skills, trading resources. Cievette's skill was one of those resources, and it held her in rare regard. Her assignments were often dangerous, but fortunately having Eisle with her had gotten her out of a tight spot or two.

Taking over at the code screen, Cievette studied what Eisle had managed to unravel. "Not bad, Eisle. Keep this up and they're going to start sending you out on your own."

His quiet laugh rumbled as he settled in near the door. Commander Harkins had made it clear that Cievette's safe return was to be Eisle's only concern. He had only learned to rattle a bit of code to pass the time. Besides, Cievette was a patient teacher for all her complaints. She glanced his way as his eyes closed, appearing to be asleep, but he was watching her through veiled lids as she dug through the code. The projected image of the interface glittered around her fingers like jewels. Where his code barely scratched the surface, she would dig trenches through those seemingly impenetrable fields.

The sound of a hatch opening startled Eisle. He gracefully rose into an alert stance, assessing the situation. "Yes!" came a triumphant cry and he realized Cievette had managed to crack the code. The warm air from above whooshed inside, vanquishing for a moment the dampness of the underneath. She met his eyes, challenge dancing in their depths. Did she know about his feelings for her?

Straightening, he approached the ladder that led to the topworld, an area known as Foreman Wilds. He knew that she loved this part, that she craved adventure, but the risk involved kept him tightened up in knots. The cover of night greeted him as he peeked through the hatch. Good, he felt at home in darkness; it gave them an advantage. Of course, the topworlders would recognize them as tunnel rats: their pale skin and enlarged eyes, adapted over time spent living in the shadows, always gave them away when they were topworld.

He reached down to give Cievette a hand up. She gazed about her in wonder, transformed into an innocent child; her eyes crinkling with joy. He looked around for dangers and threats, while she looked for treasures and experiences. It was as if she had never known pain. Eisle still remembered the day that she had cut her hair, a symbol of the shedding of innocence among their people – all free-spirited children ran with their hair long and wild. Cievette had been on her third mission, and when they'd returned, she and another team member had dragged their partner, Clave, into the hatch. But it had been too late. Death had been imminent, yet she had not been able to leave him out there. At his funeral they had all walked by, saying their goodbyes before the cremation. She had been silent as she'd approached him, and with knife in hand, she'd made the first cut of her hair, dropping the curls across his body. It had been a sign of honor.

Eisle had requested to be her guard that same day, drawn to her by her honor display. He told Harkins that she was too valuable an asset to risk on shoddy mission handling. Her focus needed to be on the code. Breaking a hatch was always the first leg. The topworlders used extensive security protocols to lock them down. If one did not handle the codes correctly, the topworlders would be alerted and would be upon them within moments. Cievette did not make that kind of mistake.

Shadowing through the groundcover, the second phase was the mission at hand. They were assigned to break into a power hub in order to redirect trace amounts of city resources. The plants always had residual energy. The rats harvested this energy to use in their own cities. Efficiency was necessary for the survival of the tunnel rat hives although topworlders seemed unconcerned with waste.

As they skulked closer to the plant base the constantly moving security lights raced around forcing Cievette and Eisle to dance to avoid detection. They successfully traversed the open space undetected to reach the grating that would let them into the base. It gave into a sewer that ran beneath the plant. Topworlders could not handle exposure to the radiation from the plant without special suits. Rats, however, absorbed the energy. As they dropped down into the tunnel, Cievette stopped briefly, taking in the energy hit. As she acclimated, she began to assess the system. Watching the tunnels was much like watching the code that directed them.

They ran through the peripherals with caution, following the merging byways to reach the core. There, topsiders in protective suits were working on a ruptured conduit. Cievette and Eisle wore close-fitting dark clothing that helped them to hide in the shadows. They managed to remain hidden as they sidled closer to the core. Once in range, the transponder on Cievette's arm vibrated. Pulling it off, she began to communicate with the computer. This was much quicker than the hatch code. She was in the system within minutes. Eisle stood guard, keeping an eye on the workers so that Cievette could focus. Within a few minutes she had redirected the residual to the ground systems, where tunnel rat engineers below could pick up the current and take it into the hive. It was time to leave.

They pulled deeper into the shadows, pleased to be undetected, when a surge caught the arm interface. A curse slipped out of Cievette's mouth, barely above a whisper, but enough to alert the workers of their presence.

An alarm blared. Without delay, they began sliding through the maze to the edge of the network, but now all of the access gratings were under guard. They were gradually herded towards one of the grates, where they were picked up by the outer guard.

"I'm sorry," Cievette whispered to Eisle. He waved off her apologies. He could read the pain in her eyes.

"You need to take that off." He reached for her interface, but the guard's gun lifted to point at his head. He dropped his hands helplessly.

The detention center operated on a number of manual systems, with the exception of the hand scans. Cievette noted the technology weaknesses as they were led inside. Eisle's eyes simultaneously scanned for physical weak spots. It would take both of them to escape.

They were placed in a clean room and commanded to strip down. The guards watched Cievette closely as she removed the damaged interface. It was gingerly taken from her, followed by their clothes. The burns on her arm blistered only slightly, but Eisle knew the burns went deeper. They slipped into the provided tight-fitting jumpsuits, which allowed nothing to be hidden on their bodies. Cievette pushed the sleeve above her wound to relieve the pressure.

Another series of hallways led them to the general detention center. A single, slight figure in the corner appeared to be sleeping. As the door shut behind them, the figure stretched. It was a woman.

"Hello." She greeted them, but remained guarded in the corner. "I am Ghabrie." Eisle nodded, as he studied the room, which held a door at either end. The white walls glared harshly under bright lights.

"I am Cievette and my friend is Eisle," responded Cievette as she shifted uncomfortably, squinting and holding her damaged arm.

Ghabrie came to her feet. "Oh. You are hurt. And of course our captors don't have the decency to tend to your injuries."

"I ... suppose they think it will show some sort of weakness," Cievette said, trying to calm her breathing and maintain her focus.

The girl nodded and moved closer. "I ... I haven't seen your kind before. Are you ... an experiment?"

Startled by the question, Cievette looked over at Eisle, uncertain how to answer. Eisle laughed quietly, "Well, Cievette might be." That comment earned him a punch in the gut. He grinned. "Glad to see your injury hasn't totally dulled your senses. Actually, we are from below. Most call us tunnel rats. Our eyes, our skin, they are natural adaptations to our environment."

Ghabrie nodded, "I ... am not a natural adaptation. I would like to escape before I'm handed back into the hands of my enemy – any ideas?"

"I think escape is something we can agree on. Tell me, have you ever considered becoming a tunnel rat?"

Laughing, Ghabrie said, "Unlikely, since I've only learned of your existence this second. However, if it helps me get out of here, why not?"

Cievette spoke quietly. "The closer drop will likely be guarded since they've discovered an incursion. However, the one in the eastern forest should let us in. Security is so much easier to bypass from this direction."

Ghabrie remained silent, having no idea what they were talking about.

Eisle nodded in agreement. "It will be the easiest ... but that one drops into a different district. How do we stand with Lorvaine?"

Cievette made a face. "We'll be fine. He hasn't got a clue that I am not interested in him, despite my repeated dodging of his affectionate advances."

Eisle grinned. Lorvaine held more affection for himself than anyone, but Cievette had caught his eye a few months back and he had decided she would be a fine trophy for his entourage. Thankfully, Cievette knew how to play the game – a talent which served them well in this situation.

Their plan depended on Cievette reaching a computer interface, but the hand scanner would not do in this situation. She needed something more. She needed to gain some trust. But for now, though, she needed rest and clear her mind.

Eisle had already found a corner to lean into, one knee drawn to his chest and the other leg stretched out. She curled up beside him, his arm resting around her protectively. She knew he cared deeply about her. She just wasn't ready to open that part of herself up, clinging to her childlike ways to give herself time. For now, she allowed him be her protector, her guardian. Caring too deeply could lead to mistakes. Bringing Clave back to the hive had cut into her soul. If she had to carry Eisle back in the same way, it would break her. She felt his hand slide gently over her shoulder. She suspected if the roles were reversed, he would be equally broken.

Somehow she found sleep. Broken fitful dreams tormented her as she shifted restlessly. A movement shook her out of her dreams and as she slowly found her feet, disoriented, she realized that she was being led away from the group. She looked towards Eisle in fear. He was being held back by several armed guards. Ghabrie was also being subdued. Cievette gave a subtle nod to the others, intended as reassurance. This could be the opportunity she needed.

She was led through a door opposite the one they'd entered. She immediately took in her surroundings and studied different interfaces. She need only get close to the right one and she would be able to use her cybernetic implants to create a link. They passed through two more doors and she found herself in another bright white room.

To her surprise, a clinician checked her wounds and began to treat the burns on her arm. He spoke harshly to her, but then pressed a note into her palm. Did they have friends among these people? "Take her to the sonic chamber and leave her. It will accelerate the healing of her wound."

"When do we return for her?" one of the guards inquired.

"Half an hour should do."

She was lifted up off the table and to her feet. Soon she found herself in a chamber and the door was securely closed. She hoped there were no cameras. Opening her fist, she read the note.

"Do what you must in the chamber but don't give me away. I have several friends Underneath. Drop this note in the incinerator before you leave."

Looking around, she realized that she had just what she needed. The computer interface allowed her to make a subtle link to the system. She would be able to remotely connect through her enhancements. Quickly she disposed of the note and started to work. The healing chamber hummed and she saw that several interfaces were built to entertain patients during treatment. However, they also provided a way into the system for a skilled coder. She began to worm through the entertainment data and drill her way into the security system. She wanted to stay on the minor systems so that she could open doors and divert sensors without alerting the guards, but she didn't want to make them aware of her presence in the system. Placing a few subtle markers, she backed out of the network.

Twenty minutes remained and she relaxed while the treatment continued. Half an hour later, she was returned to the holding cell.

"I'm okay," she told her friends, "they were seeing to my wounds. The clinician had heard I had an injury that hadn't been attended to and insisted they bring me to him."

"Hmmm," responded Eisle. "A topworlder with a heart."

After they settled into the corner, they talked in low voices. "Did you accomplish anything?" Eisle began. Her nod encouraged him and his face brightened. "Can we move forward?"

"Let me check security logs." Cievette closed her eyes as she dug through the logs. She promptly found the schedule she was seeking. "There will be a security change in about an hour."

Ghabrie interjected, "What about our clothes and appearance?"

"Our clothes are oddly very similar to what they are wearing. I saw a nurse take off her lab coat and walk out the door wearing basically the same thing. If we can grab some of those coats as we exit, that will help with the rest."

"And you can open the doors?" Eisle asked.

Cievette grinned. "You doubt me?"

Eisle shook his head. Ghabrie opened her mouth then closed it. Cievette answered her unspoken question with a grin. "You asked earlier if I was an experiment. Eisle's tease held more truth than lies. I have had some enhancements. They allow me to take advantage of certain systems."

"Then why ...?" Ghabrie trailed off but nodded at the arm that now held only the memory of the injury.

"It was a job specific interface and shortened the task at hand."

"I suppose I'm the last one to question someone about their differences," Ghabrie said.

Eisle shook his head quietly. "Trusting strangers is difficult … especially if they hold information back. We've worked together for some time and it did not occur to us to explain."

They lapsed into silence as the minutes slowly ticked by until the scheduled guard change. Finally, Cievette stood and approached the door. The hand scanner accepted her palm and the door slid open. No outer guard awaited them. They moved into the shadows and followed Cievette who accessed a map of the facility. Following the map, she sought their escape. The drain grate was right where she thought it would be. They removed it and slid into the pipe. It was damp but it headed in the right direction. They would soon be out of the building and into the forest.

Activity overhead alerted them that their escape had been discovered. They moved through the drains until they reached an area of decreased activity. All looked quiet in the woods through the grating beneath which Cievette had stopped. She crouched for a moment, checking to make sure she was on the correct path through the maze. The others were relying on her. When she nodded the other two pushed the grate open. Eisle pulled himself up with a muffled grunt, reaching down to assist Ghabrie. Cievette required a bit more assistance. Once they were all free of the drain, Eisle replaced the grate to cover their exit.

They moved to the edge of the wood and entered the undergrowth realizing they were not alone. Wordlessly, Eisle motioned eastward. They shifted their trek to avoid the guards. The air was hot and they had to duck down for cover on several occasions. Approaching the access point, Cievette hissed an expletive. It was guarded. Ghabrie placed a calming hand upon her shoulder. Then placing her hands over her mouth, she mimicked a kestrel call perfectly.

The bird of prey came out of nowhere and swirled around the guards, diving aggressively at them with talons extended. While the guards were distracted by the kestrel, Ghabrie and Eisle managed to subdue them with blunt force. Cievette leaped on the opening and decoded the hatch. The three allies soon slipped into the tunnels. Ghabrie called the kestrel in after them.

"Secure the hatch," hissed Eisle. Cievette entered the interface immediately to jam the signal. It would take someone with great skill to break the coded lock she placed on that hatch.

"Now for Lorvaine." Eisle grinned. "But at least the worst is behind us."

Cievette's look could have melted the rock around them. He dodged her attack and laughingly jogged ahead of them.

Ghabrie had been quietly observing them. "He's quite fond of you."

"I know."

"Not interested?"

"I'm fighting my own demons. Maybe one day."

Ghabrie considered Cievette's comment for a moment before answering, "That one would fight your demons for you."

Glancing at her feet, Cievette smiled softly. "Perhaps ..."

After a moment, Ghabrie changed topic, "Anyway ... my friend here is going to grow restless in these tunnels. Can you get me to a safe exit?"

Grinning, Cievette responded, "But of course! After ..." She visibly shuddered, "after ... Lorvaine."

They continued through the tunnels, Eisle and Cievette taking the twists and turns in their stride, not noticing Ghabrie was getting dizzy and lost. After a little over an hour, the tunnel broke into a wide expanse of caves, with running water from a natural spring and some interesting architecture made from found objects. Ghabrie was impressed at how they had made something out of nothing. And soon, she learned what Cievette's shudder had meant.

"Why, what an unexpected surprise! Cievette! And you have brought friends." The man's voice held a greasy quality. The colorful robes seemed out of place in the drab tunnels, but perhaps no more so than the strong perfumes that seemed to be competing for their attention. Ghabrie took a subtle step back. She was impressed that Cievette accepted his outstretched hand without hesitation.

"I knew my old friend Lorvaine would welcome us. I was hoping you would allow us to pass through to the western tunnels."

He looked shrewdly from one to the other. "Well, I know the two of you. However, who is this upworlder? I'm responsible for the safety of the other hives as a perimeter city."

Cievette nodded. "She is a friend, Lorvaine. We bumped into her when we got into a minor scrape."

Lorvaine narrowed his eyes. "A scrape? Just what were you doing topworld?"

Cievette grinned. "Now, you know I can't reveal all of my secrets. Where would the mystery be in that?"

"I can't have a fugitive from the above in my city. They might send someone after her."

"Fugitive?" Cievette laughed. "Look at you jumping to conclusions. I merely meant that Ghabrie had skills that came in handy in my last job. If you are concerned, though, I will be happy to escort her to an exit. Perhaps NW72?"

Lorvaine considered the northern hatch. It was a fair distance from the city and the path went to three other hives. "Can you ensure she won't be traced to this hive?"

"Of course. And the hatch will be jammed once I get her clear of the tunnels."

Lorvaine nodded sharply. "If you return this way within the week, now, dearest, I can assure you a place at my table for the Taboran festival."

Forcing a smile, Cievette answered, "Of course. I'd be honored to join you. We'll work out the details on my return."

As they exited the city into the next series of tunnels, Cievette explained to Ghabrie that this hatch would open into the Nunsen district above. For the most part, scavengers and nomadic traders filled the zone with a scattering of very small villages.

"That sounds perfect. Thank you so much!"

This hatch was not well secured. Cievette unscrambled the code with ease and the door released. Ghabrie sent her winged friend first and his cry sounded through the breaking dawn. Turning to her new friends, she smiled. "It is good to make friends for a change."

The couple nodded, and Eisle responded, "I hope you find what you seek."

THE SONG OF AIDEN

KR Smith

"Hurry, Maeve! We don't want to miss the show!"

"But, Kendra, I'm supposed to finish my chores and put away the clean laundry. Your mother will be furious!"

"Never mind that," she laughed. "If we get there too late to see Aiden, I'll never forgive you!"

"Oh, all right! I'm coming! And he'd better be as good as you say. He's all you've talked about for the last week."

"He is! You'll see!"

Kendra took her hand, giggling as she pulled Maeve through the doorway and down the street.

A crowd had already gathered in the dusty square at the center of the village when the girls arrived. Snaking their way through the gathering, they approached an impromptu stage which was little more than empty carts tied together, with a stepladder for access. Atop them stood a single man, young and tall, his hair a tangle of brown wavy curls. He held up his hand and smiled to the crowd, and after they quieted, he began to sing.

Maeve watched his fingers move over the strings of the instrument he held, their tones soft and rhythmic, carrying the words to her ears. As she listened, her mind traveled to places she'd never been, never known, into dreams that seemed too real. It was so different from the little music she had heard before. There were no hymns of battle, no chants of warriors facing death, no drums beating out a march. Words of warm evenings, of passion and love, of romance lost to time danced through the air. He glanced over the crowd as he sang, and when he looked at Maeve he smiled, or so she thought. When he stopped the words and melodies still filled her mind.

"I need to rest my voice for a while," Aiden shouted, "but I'll continue again after the noon hour. Until then, allow me to offer my hat for any small token of appreciation whilst our acrobat and world-famous juggler — I think his name is Jorne, or something like that — entertains you!" Rising from his seat to begin his performance, Jorne mocked tossing one of his juggling pins at Aiden as the two smiled at one another. "And to soothe my dry throat, I'll gladly accept the donation of a mug of ale." The crowd laughed when he added, "Or two."

The girls waited as Aiden passed among the townspeople, graciously accepting any offering. He was soon standing in front of them, a well-worn hat in his outstretched hand.

"Anything for the bard today, ladies?"

Maeve shook her head and said, "I'm sorry. I don't have anything. I've only recently come from the Northlands and—"

"There's no need to apologize." Aiden pulled the hat back and placed it over his chest. "Times are difficult, and I understand. In any event, the rare sight of a girl with hair like yours is payment enough. I believe I've only seen one other with red hair in my entire life. Well, except for …"

"Except for the mutants," Maeve said, finishing his sentence.

Aiden paused, looking directly into Maeve's eyes. "I'm sorry. I shouldn't have mentioned it."

"That's all right. I suppose I stand out a bit from the crowd."

The smile on Aiden's face grew larger. "Yes," he said softly. "Yes, you do."

Kendra interrupted the awkward silence that followed with, "I have something!"

"And what might that be?"

Kendra reached into her pocket and pulled out a piece of fruit.

Aiden's eyes grew large. "Two surprises in one day! I haven't seen an orange in years. I won't even ask what you had to do to get this. Are you certain you wish to give it up?"

"It was nothing as exciting as you think. My mother has a small shop. We make soap and grow herbs to barter for what we need. A man passing through traded two oranges for one small bar of soap."

"You've made a good deal."

"I hope so. Our village is so remote we seldom see rarities like this."

"If you're sure you won't miss it, I'll gladly accept your kind contribution." Aiden placed the orange in his pocket, and patted it. "And if you don't tell anyone," he added in a quieter voice, "it may be my breakfast tomorrow. Thank you."

"You're welcome!"

"Will you stay for the afternoon show?"

Maeve and Kendra exchanged glances.

"I think we'd best return to the shop," Kendra said. "We have a lot of work to do."

"Then perhaps you can come tomorrow. Our troupe will be here for a few days."

"Oh, yes, of course!" Maeve turned to Kendra, her eyes begging permission. "I mean, we can, can't we?"

Kendra sighed. "It sounds like you've already decided."

"Very good! I'll see you then." Aiden waved his hat as he waded off through the crowd. As Kendra turned to leave, Maeve stood motionless, watching him.

"Maeve?" Kendra waited for a response. "Maeve?"

"What?"

"We have to get back to the shop."

"Oh, all right."

"I had to drag you down here," Kendra complained as she took Maeve's hand, "now I have to drag you back."

"I'm coming!"

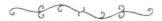

The next morning Maeve and Kendra were already at the wagons before any of the other villagers arrived. They sat directly in front as the show began, not moving until it was over. When Aiden's part was finished, they followed him around as he made his pitch for donations from the crowd. After he delivered the offerings to another member of the troupe, he asked them what they thought of his performance.

"I love listening to your songs," Maeve replied.

"Even the ones you heard yesterday?"

"I've never heard music like yours, so I don't mind hearing them again. And my chores are finished, so I'm free for the entire day. When does the next show start?"

"The others will probably begin in another hour or so. You can stay, of course, but I'm afraid I won't be here."

"You're not singing this afternoon?"

"No, there's someplace special I need to see again."

Maeve's smile disappeared. "Someplace? Or someone?"

Aiden put his hand on her shoulder, but she wouldn't look at him. "Someplace." He took a deep breath, then paused before continuing. "I'll tell you what.

If you promise not to divulge the location, you may come along if you'd like."

Maeve raised her head, a smile beaming across her face. "Of course! I mean, I won't tell anyone!"

"It's quite a walk. Are you sure?"

"Oh, yes!" Maeve nearly jumped into the air before noticing Aiden's attempt to suppress his laughter. With her face nearly as red as her hair, she said with a forced calmness, "Yes, I would like that."

"All right, then. Let me get my pack and we'll be off."

No sooner had Aiden left than Maeve turned to Kendra, her face buried in her hands, groaning. "I acted like a complete idiot, Kendra! He must think I'm some silly child!"

Kendra shook her head. "I doubt that, or he wouldn't have asked you to go with him."

"Do you think so?"

"I saw the way he looked at you ... which makes me wonder if you should go. You barely know him, Maeve."

"You're the one who insisted I come with you to see him sing!"

"Listening to songs is far different than trotting off into the countryside with a stranger."

"I'm not trotting off and Aiden wouldn't hurt anyone. Didn't you listen to his music?"

"Of course, I did. But even if Aiden is harmless, it's dangerous outside of the village, especially for girls."

"I made it here all the way from the Northlands on my own. Or nearly so. Besides, I'll be safe if Aiden is with me. I'm sure of it."

Kendra said nothing for a moment. "Promise me you'll be careful."

"I will."

"And don't do anything you shouldn't."

"Kendra!"

"Well, not too many things you shouldn't."

Maeve giggled, the blush returning to her face.

"Hush! He's coming back," Kendra whispered.

Aiden held out his arm and asked, "Are you ready?"

Maeve glanced at her cousin and said, "Yes."

As she accompanied Aiden down the dusty road leading from the village, Kendra watched as she bounced along, nearly skipping, in an attempt to keep up with Aiden's long stride. She shook her head and smiled. "Lucky brat!"

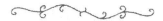

For some time they said nothing as they walked, with Aiden seemingly indifferent to Maeve's company. Once they were out of sight of the village, however, she broke the silence.

"Now that we're by ourselves, I don't suppose you can tell me where we're going, can you?"

"It doesn't have a name. But I know how to get there."

Everything else that came to mind to talk about seemed silly, or personal. Maeve bit her lip and fumbled with her fingers, and she noticed a trace of a smile on his face. He brought up a new subject.

"Why don't you tell me about yourself while we're walking? You said you're from the Northlands. How did you end up here?"

"It wasn't a hard decision to leave. There are so few people left. Those that remain have such a hard life. I was told the farmers slaughtered their livestock to survive the dark winters after the Blast. Many of the farms and towns had simply disappeared by the time I was born. It was always a struggle to find enough food. There's not much of a future in a place like that."

"I must say, I was surprised when I saw you. Your hair caught my eye. How did you survive the plague?"

"The plague? We knew it as the 'red curse.' My earliest memory is of hearing that I wouldn't live for long, because of my red hair. Nobody knew what caused it or why it only seemed to strike people like me. Everyone told us to be prepared to die, and many did," she paused, "including my parents. I was still very young then. It's difficult to see any beauty in life while looking through a cloud of death."

"You seemed to have come through it well."

"Not that I escaped completely, mind you. I remember being sick for a long time, but I lived. I have no idea why."

"Perhaps you're stronger than you know."

"I hope so. That's better than discovering you're a mutant. I didn't even know about them until I came to see Kendra. You should have seen her face the first time we met!"

"Really?"

"Even though most mutants don't have red hair, enough of them do that I had to do a bit of talking to convince her I wasn't one. Do you know if the plague affects the mutants with red hair?"

"I don't know. Still, I'm surprised anyone would think you're one," Aiden said. "It's obvious you're not."

Maeve smiled.

"You say your parents died when you were very young. You couldn't have been old enough to care for yourself."

"Another family who had lost their own daughter took me in. They were good people. Still, I was another mouth to feed. They barely had enough for themselves. When another family decided to leave, I went with them."

"Why here?"

"There were stories of the southlands, and how life was easier there. My mother had mentioned a cousin, Kendra, who lived there. So, trading work for my passage, I rode along hoping to find her. I knew little more than her name and the village where she lived. I didn't even know if she knew of me. It was pure luck to find the village where she and her mother lived. It's good to have someone near my own age to talk to, and Kendra is teaching me how to make soap and grow herbs."

"It seems the two of you get along quite well."

"It was rough at first, but we soon worked things out. I think she's glad to have someone to talk with, too. Life isn't perfect, but it is better."

"You don't miss the Northlands, then?"

"I miss the snow. It can be so beautiful. I guess I haven't yet adjusted to the heat. And it's so dry. I should have brought some water."

"You'll be able to quench your thirst soon enough."

"Soon? How much farther is it?"

"We're there, or nearly so. It's just down this trail."

"All I see are briars and vines. This is the special place?"

"Follow me."

Aiden made his way into the trees stretching away from the roadside, careful to avoid the thorns and twisted vines hanging over what remained of a path. The dense canopy formed a tunnel sloping down into darkness. She followed Aiden closely until the vegetation cleared enough that he could stand. He stopped, holding out his hand to present a lush glade spreading out before them.

When Maeve stepped into the opening, cool air rushed past her face. Beyond was an expanse of emerald moss, speckled with sunlight, carpeting the banks of a small stream. Wildflowers sprouted, flashing delicate yellow and purple hues between the dark rocks that rose up one side to where a waterfall splashed from an overhanging ledge of stone; above, the trees arched together into a patchwork of green leaves and blue sky.

"It's the most beautiful place I've ever seen!"

"If you're thirsty these falls are as pure as any you'll find. No radiation, no poisons, nothing but water." Aiden cupped his hands and filled them with the sparkling liquid, then took a long drink. "It springs from deep within the hill, so the Earth has filtered out anything harmful."

Maeve followed, letting the water flow over her hands. "It's so cold!"

"You can even step behind the waterfall, beneath the overhanging rocks," he said as he demonstrated.

Together they enjoyed the beauty of the glade, refreshing themselves in the mist from the falls, and admiring the vibrant colors of the flowers. They rested on the cool carpet of moss and shared the food Aiden had brought in his pack, including Kendra's orange. Though he had no instrument with him, Aiden sang to her, his voice echoing among the rocks, giving it a depth that wrapped Maeve in its magic. Finally, they laid back on the moss, staring at the leaves and sky above.

"It's starting toward dusk," Aiden noted. "I can even see the moon just above the horizon," he said, pointing below an overhanging branch to an ivory disk low in the sky.

"Does that mean we have to go?"

"We've already stayed longer than I had planned. I didn't have the heart to suggest we leave."

"How did you find this place?"

"A girl showed it to me."

"Oh?" Maeve watched him out of the corner of her eye. "You were here with someone else? Was she pretty?"

Aiden smiled and shrugged. "Of course."

Maeve looked away.

"Her name was Deirdre. She was the most beautiful girl in all the world, with the greenest eyes, and long, dark hair that fell almost to her waist. She could dance and sing like ... well, so much better than I ever could."

"So, why isn't she here? Did you grow tired of her?"

"It was nothing like that." Aiden took a deep breath. "It was nearly three years ago. She was killed just a day's walk to the west, not far past those hills in the distance."

"Oh, Aiden, I'm sorry. Do you know what happened?"

He shook his head. "Not the details. Only that she died. She was with friends looking for new places to perform. They were caught between two groups fighting over, oh, who knows what? It doesn't really matter. Some were killed, some captured. A few escaped. They told me she had died."

"But if they were there, surely they could tell you how."

"Yes." Aiden gave a slight smile. "Yes, they could."

"Then why didn't they?"

Aiden's eyes closed briefly. "Because their faces told me I shouldn't ask, and they were wise and kind enough not to say."

Maeve's head bowed. "You loved her, though, didn't you? I can hear it in your voice."

"And I always will."

Maeve bit her lip, only turning to face Aiden when she felt his warm hand on her arm.

"She was my sister. Older by two years."

Maeve's mouth fell open, but she had no words.

"And so, here I am with another beauty!"

Maeve frowned. "Hardly. My hair looks like it comes from one of the mutants."

"True, red hair is rare, which makes it all the more special. And you're not a mutant."

"And my skin," she complained, holding up her arm, "is all covered with these ugly little blotches, probably from the radiation."

Aiden laughed. "Little blotches? I can assure you they're quite natural."

"No one else seems to have them."

"They go with your red hair. They're called freckles."

"Freckles? What a silly name. You made that up, didn't you?"

"No! That's what they're called. I swear! I saw it in a book."

"You can read?"

"A little," he said with a nod. "Enough to know what freckles are."

"Well, whatever they are, I wish they'd all go away."

"Really?" Aiden leaned toward her, squinting. "Let me take a look at them." He eased closer until his lips touched softly against Maeve's, pausing just long enough for the intention to be clear.

"Aiden!" Maeve lowered her face only enough to end the kiss, though not so far as to preclude the possibility of another. "Why did you do that?"

"It's a warm summer evening," he said, raising his hand toward the sky, "the moon is rising, and I'm here by the falls with a beautiful young woman. And beautiful young women should be kissed on warm summer evenings — even more so when the moon is full," he added, cocking his head slightly to the side, "if they wish to be." Aiden brushed the loose strands of hair away from her eyes. "Did you mind?"

Maeve only smiled more as she tried to hide her blushing face.

"I was hoping you would feel that way."

They sat in silence for a moment before Aiden said, "We should be leaving here, though. They say this place is visited during the full moon. I'm not sure we'd be welcome."

"Visited?"

"Perhaps it's only an old tale, but I'd rather not take the chance, especially with you here."

As he started to rise, Maeve put her hand around his neck and drew herself close enough for a brief kiss.

Aiden smiled. "I wasn't expecting that!"

"Did ... did you mind?" Maeve's head bowed. "I know I shouldn't have. It was stupid. I mean, I've never kissed a man before." Her voice turned into a whisper as she rambled on, "I don't even know if I've done it right—"

With his fingertip gently on her lips, she stopped speaking. His hand brushed lightly across her cheek and into her hair as he looked into her eyes. "Of course you did. It would impossible for you not to." He glanced up at the sky. "But it is getting late," he added, "and you are very young."

"I'm not that young!"

"You're young enough that your cousin will be worried. And as I mentioned, we should go before the moon is high."

Maeve smiled and nodded. "You're probably right."

The long walk back to the village was filled with Aiden's songs, their laughter, and more than one warm glance.

When they reached the shop, they stood facing each other in front of the door. As Aiden and Maeve started to draw closer, the door opened and Kendra stepped out holding a candle.

"Is someone there? Who is it?"

Maeve rolled her eyes. "It's just me, Kendra."

"Oh. And Aiden. I didn't know—"

Aiden laughed quietly. "It's late," he said to Maeve with a smile. "You should go."

"But ... oh, all right." She turned toward the door, her fingertips lingering in his, reluctantly parting.

Aiden couldn't help but listen as the girls went inside.

"Honestly, Kendra! Would it have hurt to have waited a little longer before coming out?"

"I'm sorry, Maeve! I didn't know who it was. But you have to tell me all about it!"

He smiled as the voices disappeared behind the closed door and began to walk toward the troupe's camp in the village square. When he reached the end of the street, two men blocked his path.

"We've been waiting for you. We have some business to discuss."

"Who are you?"

"We represent a group that would like to pay you for your services."

Aiden couldn't see their faces. "It's rather late and I'm really not interested."

"We think you are."

One of the men pulled back his jacket. The moonlight reflected off the grip of a large revolver.

"There's a truck waiting," the man said, his hand indicating a direction away from the village square.

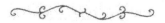

It was morning when the truck stopped. The town was not one Aiden recognized. His newfound companions led him to a room inside an old building.

"Have a seat," one of them said before leaving and locking the door from the outside. Aiden didn't have to wait long. The man who entered was tall and very thin. His dark, sunken eyes stared out from a face covered with rough stubble, his hair short and bristly, with a touch of gray.

"Good morning, Aiden. I apologize for the way you were brought here, but I may be leaving this quaint little place soon and what I have to discuss is urgent."

"What would that be?"

"You're very popular with the people," the man said as he circled the chair where Aiden sat. He then walked over to a window and gazed out. "They like you. They listen to you."

"And?"

"I think that could be beneficial to us both."

"Us? I don't even know you."

The man turned and smiled. "I'm Jarek."

The color drained from Aiden's face. He didn't know the man, but he knew the name.

"I like to think of myself as an entrepreneur. When an opportunity arises, I seek to make the most of it. Currently, I'm working with the Alliance. They pay well, and if you work for me, I'll be generous in passing some of that on to you."

"The Alliance?" Aiden shook his head. "I don't think I'm interested."

"Hear me out first. It's a simple request. The Alliance has a bit of a public relations problem. The people are unsure of their purpose. That can make things difficult for the Alliance. Instead of working with them, they resist, often quite stubbornly. That doesn't help anyone, now does it?"

"From what I hear the Alliance is the one causing the problems. If they left the people alone, there wouldn't be any problems to solve. In any case, what do you think I could do about it?"

"As I said, the people listen to you. Perhaps during your act you could tell people how the Alliance has helped make the world a better place by providing safety and stability in these uncertain times. A few good words from someone they trust could go a long way toward easing their fears. You might even write a song about them. The people do like your songs, don't they?"

"Safety and stability? So, you're asking me to lie."

Jarek shrugged. "If necessary. Trust me, it can be quite profitable."

"I'm not interested. And it's time I was leaving. We have nothing to discuss."

As Aiden attempted to rise to his feet, Jarek put a hand on his shoulder and pushed him back into the chair. "If I can't persuade you, perhaps my associate Krieg can."

"Face it, Kendra. He's not coming back. He's already missed two shows. I thought he—"

"Don't talk that way, Maeve. The rest of his group is still here, and their wagons. He wouldn't leave all that behind, would he?"

"I suppose not. But then, where is he?"

"I don't know. Let's go down to the square. The troupe should be starting soon. We can see if he's returned."

"And if he hasn't?"

"Perhaps someone will have news." Kendra got behind her and gave a nudge toward the door. "Come on,

Maeve, let's go! It seems I'm always pushing you through this door one way or another!"

Maeve's labored steps fit her mood. As they turned the corner onto the street leading to the square, they could see a large crowd gathering ahead of them.

"Look, Maeve! He must be back! See all the people coming?"

Maeve's pace quickened with each step. The crowd in front of her was oddly quiet.

"Aiden? Is Aiden here?"

No one answered as she pushed her way through the people gathering at the square. The crowd had formed a rough circle around the troupe's wagons. In the center was a form, crumpled and bloody, face down. Maeve stopped when she saw it.

In a soft and trembling voice, she spoke his name. She turned to Kendra with tears in her eyes.

"It's Aiden, Kendra! Why is no one helping him?"

As Maeve started toward him, Kendra put her arms around her, holding her as tightly as she could.

"No, Maeve! He's there for a reason, and you don't want to be a part of that reason."

"We can't leave him there!"

"Not now, Maeve! Later … maybe."

"We don't know if he's alive!"

Kendra looked at her and shook her head. "Maeve. He's not."

"No! He can't be dead! Why?"

Kendra scanned the crowd. "My first guess would be Jarek," she said in a low voice. "Perhaps the Alliance. Or both."

"Jarek? Alliance? Who are those people?"

"Keep your voice down," Kendra said through clenched teeth, "unless you want to end up like Aiden!"

As they spoke, a hazy darkness fell over the center of the circle. Slowly it sharpened into a shadow, circling

Aiden's body. A woman in the crowd pointed to the sky as someone whispered "It's the windhover!"

A pair of surreal wings, backlit by the sun and disturbingly motionless in the air, floated above Aiden's lifeless form. Those closest took a step away from the body.

"Kendra, what's happening?"

"It just got worse. The windhover means she's near."

"Who is near? Tell me what's going on!"

"It's the demon-girl, Ghabrie."

"Who? I don't understand!"

"She's a girl warrior, as much beast as human. The bird is her familiar."

"Did she kill Aiden?"

Kendra grabbed Maeve's shoulders, giving her a shake. "You're asking questions I can't answer, Maeve. All I know is we're in danger here. We should go."

"I can't leave Aiden!"

As the girls faced each other, the silence overwhelmed them. Opposite to where they stood, the circle began to part. Just beyond the gap a young woman waited, her dark hair swept back, the markings of a warrior on her face.

Kendra whispered to Maeve, her voice quivering, "It's her! Don't look into her eyes, Maeve! If you do, she'll kill you!"

Ghabrie entered the circle, walking deliberately, silently, toward Aiden. When she reached him, she gave his body a slight push with her foot.

Maeve glanced back at Kendra. "What is she doing to him?"

"It doesn't matter now, Maeve!"

"Tell her to let him be!" She tore away from Kendra's grasp and ran screaming, "Don't touch him! Let him be!" Maeve launched herself at Ghabrie, but the deft swing of a muscled arm sent her sprawling in the dirt. Ghabrie grabbed her collar and lifted Maeve onto her knees.

"Look at me!"

"They said you would kill me if I did. Please! Please don't hurt him!"

"I may kill you if you don't. Look at me!"

Maeve looked up slowly, the blades and bow of the huntress stark reminders of her precarious position.

"You're the girl who was at the falls a few days ago. Was this the man with you?"

"Yes," Maeve nodded, "but we meant no harm."

A softer voice replied, releasing her grip on Maeve, "I know."

"Did you kill him?"

"No. He had done nothing to me."

"Then who?"

"I would guess Jarek's group of thugs, but this is brutal even for them."

"May I hold him?"

Ghabrie indicated as much with the point of her bow. Maeve ran her hands over his back, fighting tears as she did so. When she put her arms across Aiden to pull him face-up, Ghabrie knelt and put her hand on Maeve's.

"It would be best if you didn't." She squeezed Maeve's hand and said, "Trust me."

Maeve closed her eyes and wept.

Ghabrie stood up and shouted, "I don't suppose one of you fine people would have a piece of cloth for this man's shroud?" The only answer was the sound of shuffling feet. "It would be helpful if at least one of you were as brave as this girl."

Jorne, the juggler, stepped forward. "There are cloths we drape over the wagons during our shows. I can get one of those."

"That's better."

Ghabrie held up her arm and the hovering bird descended, landing on her gloved hand. She raised her bow with the other hand and pointed at one of the men in the crowd.

"You. The tall one. Come here."

"Me?" the man replied. "I've done nothing!"

"It's better for you to come to me than for me to come to you."

The man looked to his friends. Several of them backed away, while another pushed him forward. He edged toward her, stopping a few arm's lengths away. She motioned him closer with her finger. When he was within reach, she placed the bird on his shoulder.

"My friend needs a perch. You'll do nicely. And try not to flinch. He hasn't eaten today and he's attracted to movement."

Ghabrie helped Maeve to her feet. She told the juggler, "Once his body is wrapped, place him on the wagon. He should be buried quickly."

Maeve wiped the tears from her eyes. "You said a person named Jarek did this."

"That would be my guess."

"Why would he?"

"Jarek has never needed a reason to kill. It's nothing more than an amusement to him. But I would think your friend did something he didn't like."

"Aiden was a musician. He was kind and gentle. Why would Jarek hurt him?"

"If it was Jarek, only he knows. It may be a warning to the town not to cross the Alliance."

"Do you know where this Jarek is? I need to understand what sort of person could do this."

"He's a dangerous man. It would be best to avoid him."

Maeve looked directly into Ghabrie's eyes. "I need to know."

Ghabrie stared back at Maeve turning her head slightly, her eyes narrowing. Those close enough to see exchanged nervous glances. Ghabrie nodded slightly, then spoke. "Take the road that leads to the south. Follow it to the river, about two day's walk. The road splits at that point. Take the branch leading west. Not far along that road is Pentreffen, an old industrial village. The last I knew, he was there."

Maeve closed her eyes and whispered the directions under her breath, then looked back at Ghabrie. "Will you come with me?"

"No, I have my own quest. I do have advice, however."

"What is that?"

"Try not to end up like Aiden."

Maeve slumped, her hair falling in front of her face. "It doesn't matter."

Putting a finger under her chin, Ghabrie lifted until she could see her eyes. "It always matters."

Ghabrie turned to the man holding the kestrel. "Still alive? You've done well." She held out her fist. The bird jumped up, flapping a few times, and landed on her hand. As she walked away, she looked back at Maeve. "Good luck."

Maeve nodded. Ghabrie said nothing else as the crowd parted in front of her. Walking away from the village, she soon blended in with the dusty brush along the road, disappearing from sight.

Kendra hurried out of the crowd.

"Maeve! I was so frightened! Weren't you scared?"

Maeve looked away for a moment before answering. "At first. But after she touched my hand ... no."

The next morning Maeve, Kendra, and the troupe buried Aiden in a field at the edge of the village. There was no stone marker for the grave, so Maeve planted a tree instead. As the two girls walked home together, Maeve said, "I'll be leaving here in a few days, Kendra. I may not return. If I don't, I want you to have everything I own, though it isn't much."

"Please don't go, Maeve! There's no need for you to die, too."

"I need to find the man who did this. And I need to know why. I won't rest until I do."

"Even if you do find Jarek, what would you do if he admitted killing him?"

"I don't have to do anything. I just need to understand."

"Does it matter?"

Ghabrie's face appeared in Maeve's mind as she whispered, "It always matters."

Once they returned to Kendra's house, Maeve began her preparations. Clothes, chosen for their durability, included a hood fashioned from lightweight cloth to hide her red hair and protect her from the sun. She picked well-worn, comfortable, boots. Black leggings, covered by a short skirt, were the final pieces. When her outfit was assembled she was amazed at how much it looked like Ghabrie's, minus the leather and weaponry. She packed a small bag with whatever dried fruit could be spared. An old bottle became a canteen. A couple of bars of soap were wrapped in cloth and added for her to use or to trade for supplies.

The next morning Maeve was up early to begin her journey. Kendra waited by the door and made one last attempt to dissuade her.

"Maeve, you can't go. You have no idea what waits for you out there. You don't even know if Jarek is the killer."

"Then I'll search till I find the one who is. I need to know what sort of person can do what was done to Aiden."

"Everyone liked him, Maeve. He brought a little light into our lives, but you barely knew him. There wasn't time."

"I know enough. His life — and his death — are all I can think about."

A tear traced a line down Kendra's cheek. "You're going to die and I'll never see you again."

Maeve answered, forcing a smile, "I'll try my best not to." She grabbed the rope binding her pack and swung it over her shoulder. With no more words she hugged Kendra, picked up the bag of supplies, and walked out into the rising heat of the day.

Though the village soon faded into the dusty hills behind her, Maeve's progress across the parched land seemed abysmally slow. Heat shimmered on the horizon as she passed the rusted hulks of old machines, some whose purpose was no longer apparent. It took a two full days to reach the river Ghabrie had described, and she saw no other person during her time on the road. She spent the first night hiding in the brush and the second along the banks of the river. She made no fire and created as little sound as possible, fearing it might alert others to her presence. A few trucks rumbled by during the second evening, all full of men with weapons. She had no idea if they were friendly and didn't want to chance finding out.

Even more trucks passed by once she reached the outskirts of Pentreffen. Maeve hid in brush or ditches whenever they passed. The few people out along the road avoided her as eagerly as she avoided them. She hoped that once she reached the town, blending into the crowds would be easier.

It wasn't long before the shacks and grubby lean-tos on the outskirts gave way to proper buildings. The town was larger than the village where Maeve lived, with many buildings of brick and stone. Trucks sped down the main road, oblivious to anyone walking, causing them to scurry for safety every time they passed.

Maeve approached an old man intent on scavenging bits of metal from a corroded piece of machinery by the road. He watched her as she drew near, tracking her movements out of the corner of his eye.

"Excuse me. Could you tell me where to find Jarek?"

The old man stopped for a moment, then turned slightly and said, "Jarek? Nobody wants to find Jarek." He gripped the rusty wrench in his fist tightly. "And you'd best pray he doesn't find you, mutant. He doesn't like your kind, so I hear."

"I'm not a mutant."

"Yeah, sure. Nobody ever is, are they?"

"If you don't know, I can ask someone else."

The old man grumbled. "What do I care? One less freak in this world's no cause for concern. There are three red brick buildings left standing along the main road. Two on the left going west, and one on the right. Try the one on the right."

"Thanks," Maeve said as she started to walk away.

"You won't thank me once you meet him," he shouted. The old man shook his head as his attention returned to dismantling the rusted contraption. "Stupid freak."

Inside the town proper, the road was paved still, but it was cracked and broken in most places, matching the buildings on each side. There was an odd smell to the place: a combination of fermenting trash, urine, and diesel fuel. Still, people were out and doing business, such as it was; they were bartering for food, gossiping, and staring — especially at Maeve. A group of children formed a circle around her and began chanting.

"Ring around the mutants,
Hiding in the ruins,
If they're red,
Shoot them dead,
All fall down!"

A woman came out of a doorway on the other side of the street and yelled at them. The children laughed as they ran away.

"I'm not a mutant," Maeve muttered.

The building the man had described was not difficult to find. It was huge, stretching out far from the street with a number of boarded up entrances flaking green paint. The bricks, dark and red, had spalled in places, and the arches at the main entrance spoke of better days long past.

As she approached, a few men with rifles watched her until noises from within the building distracted them. An older woman, screaming curses, shoved a small girl out of the doorway.

"Get out of here! If you can't do the work, I've no use for you."

The girl tumbled down the steps in front of the building, landing on her hands and knees.

"What about my things?" the girl pleaded.

"You don't have any 'things.' Not anymore. Now get lost before I set the guards on you."

With tears running down her face, she looked up at Maeve, then stood and limped away.

"You there!" The woman stood at the top of the steps with her hands on her hips, still yelling. "Yes, you. The freak."

Maeve looked behind her. There was no one else nearby.

"I'm talking to you, mutant. If you can do a decent bit of work, I might be able to find a hot meal for you. I've recently had an opening."

Maeve looked up at the woman. "Is there a man here named Jarek?"

"Yes, not that it matters to you. Do you want the work or not?"

"I can work."

"Then let's get on with it. I don't have time to stand around here all day."

"And I'm not a mutant."

"Makes no difference to me as long as you can do what needs to be done."

The woman led her into a room with a half dozen cots.

"Nobody's using that one now. You can put your stuff under there. I'm Matron Elizabeth. Address me simply as Matron. I run this place, and if you want your meals you'll do as I say."

The matron put Maeve to work right away at cleaning and doing laundry. The hot meal promised at the end of the day was as described, but with little else to recommend it.

There were four other girls under the matron's supervision. They said little to Maeve, or each other, that evening. Only the youngest, Jenna, offered any sort of greeting. Her thin frame barely filled her worn clothes.

There were dark circles under her eyes and bruises on her arms.

During the day the girls were seldom together, each off in a different part of the building performing their duties. Most of Maeve's work consisted of cleaning up after the soldiers who came and went. For days the routine continued. Maeve pieced together bits of conversation and orders given to the girls to determine that Jarek stayed on the uppermost floor of the building. That alone wasn't much help as it had numerous rooms. Many were empty; some had desks, others the remains of machinery now stripped of anything useful. With access limited by her duties, she couldn't even guess at Jarek's location. As another morning came, Maeve despaired she might never find him.

The girls were stirring in the room where they slept when the matron yelled, "The food cart's here early, Jenna."

Jenna sat upright in her cot revealing a fresh bruise under her left eye. "What?"

"You'd better get it up to Jarek while the food's still warm."

"Can't someone else take it? I always have to do it." Jenna's eyes darted to each face in the room. "Please," she said, starting to shake, "I don't want to go back up there."

"You'll do as you're told," the matron commanded, slapping Jenna with the back of her hand, "or you'll end up back out on the street."

She bent over Jenna, but before she could bring her arm back to strike again, Maeve said, "I'll go."

Matron Elizabeth straightened up and faced Maeve. "You?"

"I can push a cart. Just tell me where to go."

"All right." She turned to Jenna and said, "But don't think this means you're out of hot water, girl!"

Rubbing her face, Jenna said quietly, "I can show her the lift."

"And how to get to the offices."

"Yes, Matron. Come with me, Maeve. I'll show you what to do."

Jenna led Maeve down the hall to a hand-operated lift. "We use this to get the cart to the upper levels. The rope works a pulley to raise it. Work it in reverse to get the cart back down. Go up the steps there," she said, pointing down the hall. "When you reach the third floor you'll see the lift to your left. Take the cart down the hall past two large sets of doors. There will be another set past there with red paint on them. That's where you deliver it."

"Thanks. I think I can find it."

"Before you go, can I ask you something?"

Maeve shrugged. "I guess."

"Why do you want to take my place? I'm grateful, but nobody wants to be around Jarek."

"He may have hurt someone I knew. Someone special. I need to find out if he's the one who killed him. Do you know if a man named Aiden was brought here?"

Jenna shook her head. "I've never heard the name, though we're told little of what goes on."

"I'd best be going," Maeve said, taking a deep breath, "before Matron comes out and sees us still here."

"Be careful," Jenna said, putting her hand on Maeve's arm. "Very careful. And thanks."

Maeve nodded and went up the stairs. By the time she'd reached the third floor, the cart was already waiting. The rusty wheels squeaked as Maeve pulled it from the lift and pushed it down the hall. There were many rooms on each side, but only one with doors painted red. They were partially open, so Maeve went in. A large, muscular man, dressed in dark leather, stood next to a table covered in maps. He turned toward Maeve as she entered.

"What do you want?"

"Are you Jarek?"

"Me? No. I'm Krieg."

"I'm supposed to deliver this to him."

"He'll be here soon enough." His eyes followed Maeve as she brought the cart into the room. "Just set it up and get out. And take the old dishes away."

About that time a taller man, thin, and with short hair walked in. Maeve assumed he must be Jarek.

"Krieg! It looks like the Shadow Mountain complex is good ... what's this mutant doing here?"

"She brought the food up," Krieg said.

"Well, be quick about it," he said to Maeve. "And while you're cleaning up, you can dispose of that trash in the corner," he added, pointing to a small pile of clothing heaped on the floor. "I'm tired of looking at it."

Maeve held one of the pieces up in front of her. It was an overshirt, the material coarse and brown except where stained a dark red. It was familiar - it was Aiden's. As Jarek and Krieg discussed the maps, Maeve walked around the room, holding the rough cloth next to her, a vacant look in her eyes. Eventually Krieg noticed, nudged Jarek, and pointed to her. Jarek rolled his eyes and threw his pencil down on the table.

"Girl!"

Maeve didn't respond.

"You, there! I asked you to take away the trash, not dance with it."

Maeve stopped and turned toward Jarek. "It was you, wasn't it?"

"Another brainless mutant," Jarek mumbled. In a louder voice he said, "What are you babbling about?"

"You killed him. You killed Aiden."

"Aiden?" Jarek looked at Krieg.

"The singer," he replied.

"Oh, yes! The singer. This Aiden was a friend of yours?"

Maeve closed her eyes as her grip on the overshirt tightened.

"I see," Jarek said. "More than a friend."

"Why? Why did you kill him?"

"Why? He was uncooperative. And quite stubborn even though we asked so little of him. We were even willing to pay."

"I don't understand."

"All we wanted were a few kind words about the Alliance while performing his act. Tell the good people in the villages how the Alliance provides for their protection, that they should cooperate with us. I even suggested he do a song about our valiant efforts to secure the region."

"He would never sing about killing or battles."

"As I discovered. He did have a rather naive attitude about such things. Our next thoughts were to educate him on the benefits of seeing the Alliance in a better light."

"So you beat him."

"Let's just say we were a bit more direct in our efforts to persuade him. Unfortunately, we became so direct that he was persuaded to death. His body, however, provided a means to obtain the cooperation we desired, so it wasn't a complete loss."

"You didn't have to kill him!"

"I agree completely! I would think a singing a simple ditty would have been far less painful."

Krieg and Jarek looked at each other and laughed.

"And I can see that you miss him, which I completely understand. If it's male companionship you desire, I'm certain Krieg would be delighted at the opportunity to become better acquainted. And should you survive, which is unlikely, I'll hang what remains of your writhing mutant bones in the middle of that rat-infested village as a reminder about who controls this part of the world."

As the two men stood in front of her grinning, Maeve's heart pounded. She dropped the shirt and took a step backward.

"You know, I really shouldn't lie," Jarek said. "I'm going to hang you there whether you survive or not."

Krieg smiled at Maeve, though it was not a friendly gesture. She turned to run, knocking over the cart and falling on top of it, sending plates and food flying across the floor. As she tried to get away, one of them grabbed a handful of her hair.

Maeve screamed, "Get off me!" She fumbled for anything to hold onto, anything to stop them from dragging her back. Draped over the cart, she felt something in her fingers, and gripped tightly. They laughed while lifting her up, her feet dangling in the air. She squirmed and thrashed trying to break away. Though not able to escape, her feet again touched the floor. With one arm covering her face, she twisted with all her strength, swinging the other as hard as she could. At the edge of her fist, a silver arc turned crimson as it passed through Krieg's throat, then stopped as it sliced deep into Jarek's arm.

Krieg fell to the floor, his life draining away accompanied by the ugly gurgling from his neck. Jarek winced as Maeve pulled the blade from his flesh. Maeve looked at her hand, as surprised as Jarek to find a small knife there. She stood in front of him, unblinking, the sound of her heart resonating in her ears, her lungs unable to breathe.

Holding his arm, Jarek yelled through clenched teeth. "You wretched freak! I'll gut you with my bare hands!" As he took a step toward her, his heel hit the oozing blood and slid out from under him. He fell, striking his head on the cart, and landing in a crumpled, moaning heap next to Krieg.

Maeve stepped back, then peeked out of the doorway. Down the hall to her left she heard voices. The hall to her right was silent. She ran that way until trapped by a dead end with not even a stairway for escape. She doubled back, taking a passageway off to the side. The heavy footfalls of the guards were close behind. Then a voice, barely audible over the pounding pulse in her ears, called out.

"In here!"

Maeve spun around, trying to figure out where the voice was coming from. She saw a girl in one of the rooms waving to her.

"Quickly! In here!"

A girl, younger than herself, sat at an old metal table, a chain leading from her ankle and fastened to its leg. She motioned frantically for Maeve to come into the room as the approaching footsteps grew louder.

"Hurry! Squeeze yourself behind that cabinet, between there and the pipes in the corner - and don't make a sound."

With the guards only seconds away, Maeve did as the girl commanded. It was a tight space, even for her small frame, but she wiggled behind the heavy cabinet, pushing against the cold drainpipes. She stopped and held her breath as the guard entered.

"Did you see a girl run past here?"

"Somebody went by," the girl answered, "But I didn't see who it was."

"You'd better be telling the truth," he said, looking around the room. "She's stabbed Jarek and Krieg, and Jarek wants her back. It would cost your life to help her."

A drop of blood on the floor caught the girl's eye. "Search," she said, waving her hand in the air as she moved her foot over the red spot. "There's no place for anyone to hide."

The guard grunted, then backed out of the door. He signaled to another guard and said, "This way!" After they ran down the hallway, everything was quiet.

"You can come out now."

Maeve squirmed out, closed her eyes, and took a deep breath.

"You stabbed Jarek and Krieg?"

Maeve's hands were shaking, her voice quivering. "The big one, Krieg - I think I've killed him."

The girl smiled. "I knew if the guards were after you there was a good chance you were a friend. I was right. Do you have a name?"

"Maeve."

"Maeve," she nodded. "I'm Nahria."

"Thanks for saving me."

"You're not safe yet. You'll have to leave here as quickly as you came. The guards won't be fooled for long."

Maeve shook her head. "I'm lost. This building is like a maze. And I've never been in this part before."

"You won't be able to escape out the front, that's for sure. Go down the hall in the direction the guards came from. There is another long hallway leading off to your left. At the end of the hall is a room with a window that opens to a roof below. The window is high. You'll have to jump to reach it. If you can get through it, drop to the roof below. There is a ladder leading to the ground at the far end. I've seen it from other rooms where they've kept me. I've even thought of escaping that way myself, if I ever get out of these chains."

"What do I do then?"

"Stay off the roads and run as fast as you can."

"Where?"

"Anywhere."

"Is there something I can do for you?"

Nahria held up her chained leg. "No."

"Perhaps I can come back for you."

"Worry about yourself first. Besides, Jarek's group moves around a lot. They'll be taking me away soon."

"They?"

"The Alliance. Or Jarek. He works for them. It all amounts to the same thing."

"But—"

"You should go. Now!"

"I won't forget how you've helped me."

"If you don't leave now, it will all be for naught. Now go!"

Maeve ran to the door, then glanced back at Nahria. "Go!" she said, waving her hand.

The hallway to the left was just as Nahria had described, but the window at the end was higher than Maeve could reach. The sound of footsteps grew louder. The hallway was a dead end, and the guards would soon be there.

She tried to jump, but fell short. There was an old wooden bench against the wall. She dragged it beneath the window and stood on it, but leaping upward from the wobbly bench only sent her tumbling to the floor. She needed a ladder, or steps, or something. She looked back at the bench. Or a ramp.

She leaned the bench at an angle against the wall below the window, just as the guards turned the corner. She got as much of a running start as she could and ran up the bench, reaching for the window frame. Maeve got one hand around it and was able to pull herself up and sit on the sill. The bench fell to the floor.

When she looked down, her heart sank as she saw how high the window was above the roof below. She doubted that she could jump that far.

A bullet ricocheted off the bricks around the window.

Yes, she could! She dove through the window, her eyes half closed.

Part of the old, flat roof gave way beneath her as she landed, helping to cushion her fall. As she tried to stand, Maeve could hear the guards inside the building. At the far corner of the building were the two metal loops at the top of the ladder leading to the ground.

Maeve scrambled across the roof, reaching the ladder just as the one of the guards leaned out of the window. She swung her leg over the edge searching for a rung. Finally getting her footing, she started down. The rusty ladder shook. As her head dropped below the roofline, a spray of bullets chewed at the stone capping the building's walls. The ladder ended at the top of the first story, so Maeve hung from it for a moment, then dropped into the weeds, tumbling as she landed.

She stood up and looked around, gasping for air. There were a few small houses to her left and an open, sandy area to her right. Straight ahead was the forest, and that was where Maeve headed.

No sooner had she reached the edge when the sharp popping sound of rifle fire erupted behind her. The bullets ripped through the leaves over her head, cracking against the heavier branches. She didn't know where she was or where she was going; she knew only that she couldn't stop.

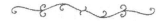

Maeve's eyes opened slowly. It was morning, and a light mist drifted through the forest where she had awakened. Her clothes were damp, but the coolness of the air was refreshing.

Her whole body ached as memories of the previous day's adventure returned - the fight, Nahria, the escape, and eventually collapsing in the dark forest. Gradually, she eased herself upright. Maeve looked down at her hand, the small knife that had torn Krieg's throat still clenched within her fist. During her entire ordeal, she had maintained her grip on the tiny weapon. She pried her fingers open, the dried blood cracking like old glue as the knife fell from her hand.

She looked around. Nothing was familiar. There were no sounds, not even a bird greeting the rising sun. Droplets of water clung to the leaves above her, glistening like jewels. She pulled them down and placed the moist leaves into her parched mouth.

She began to walk. The sun had been in her eyes when going to find Jarek. Now she made sure the sun was at her back.

Maeve wandered through the forest until it opened to a grassy area dotted by a few parched trees. In time, even the grass gave way to rock and sand, shimmering in the heat. The sun beat down on her as she stumbled along, with only the occasional dust devil for company.

Toward the end of the day, she approached a wooded ravine. She thought the trees might offer cover, if she had the strength to get there. When she reached the edge, Maeve took a step forward and her legs collapsed on the steep, uneven ground. She tumbled down, then down again, coming to a silent rest at the bottom of the hillside.

When she woke again it was nearly dark. There was a noise in her ears like a wind that never stopped. Almost too weak to move, she pushed a hand in front of her and felt a coolness engulf her fingers. It was water. Suddenly alert, she pulled herself toward it, scooping it into her mouth, rubbing it over her face. Maeve didn't know if it was safe, and she didn't care.

Once her thirst was sated, she rose to her feet. Even in the diminished light, she could see moss and flowers. In the near distance the source of the noise was visible; it was the falls. She was back at the glade where she and Aiden had sat together; the place of her first kiss on an evening when Aiden had sung only to her.

She walked toward the falls, trying to picture him there. The water shimmered under the rising moon, its rush growing louder. The mist chilled her skin as she walked under the rocks, just as Aiden had done.

Maeve stood behind the falls and gazed through the streams tumbling from the rocks above. The moon's pale light danced in the undulating water. She held out her arms, immersing her hands, still stained with blood. She rubbed them together, washing until her pale skin was clean. She watched the play of water and light on her hands for a moment, then closed her eyes and walked into the falls, the coolness startling her body. As she opened her eyes again, she gasped. In front of her stood Ghabrie, silhouetted by the moon.

"I see you took my advice."

Maeve shook her head. "Advice?"

"Not to end up like Aiden."

"Oh." Maeve lowered her head. "Only just."

"We'll build a fire. You can dry yourself next to it."

Ghabrie gathered a few twigs and small branches into a mound on the mossy point jutting into the stream. With a bit of tinder and flint, she had a fire going in short order, adding more wood until it cast a warm, orange glow over the banks.

"Here," Ghabrie said, offering Maeve a few pieces of fruit and a slice of dried meat. "You need to—" Maeve grabbed an apple, taking nearly half in the first bite.

"I was going to say eat, but I think you've figured that part out. Slow down, though," Ghabrie commanded. "There's plenty."

"Sorry," Maeve said as she chewed. "I haven't eaten anything for a while."

The food disappeared quickly. Maeve washed her fingers in the stream, then held her hands near the flames to warm them. Leaning closer to dry her hair, she hummed softly as Ghabrie prodded the fire.

"Is that a song Aiden taught you?"

"He didn't really teach me. He didn't have time. I was trying to remember the words."

"Make up your own. I don't think he would mind."

"They wouldn't be beautiful like his. That song is all I have left of him. It's all I have left of anything."

"I have something for you," Ghabrie said. "It's a pack with a proper bedroll and a short sword suitable for your size and strength. They're on the stump up the hill where you came in with Aiden."

"A sword?"

"It's a good weapon. It nearly killed me. I think you'll find it useful."

"I ... I don't want to fight. I want to see Kendra. I want to sell herbs and soap in a little shop like we planned. I want to sleep in a soft bed, not under a tree."

"It wouldn't be good to go near Kendra, at least for now. You have a price on your head; Jarek saw to that. They may use Kendra to get to you. Anyway, you're a warrior now. Others may come to test their skill against you."

Maeve laughed. "A warrior? I can't fight. I don't want to fight! Don't I have a choice?"

"No matter what you face in life, you will always have a choice." Ghabrie took a deep breath. "But that doesn't mean you'll like the choices you're given. You get to pick from what fate hands you. And as far as being a warrior, that is how people see you now. You've slain Krieg, maimed Jarek ... even attacked me."

"And ended up with my face in the dirt for trying!"

"Would you charge me again like that?"

"No. That would be stupid."

"Then you're learning."

"And I've learned that I'll have no peace as long as Jarek is alive."

"Losing the use of an arm is not something he's likely to forgive."

"If I stay here, it's only a matter of time before he finds me, and I'm not sure I have the skills to survive. I wouldn't have escaped this time if Nahria hadn't helped me."

"Nahria?" Ghabrie turned to Maeve and grabbed her arm, the fire reflecting in her eyes. "Did you say Nahria?"

"Yes, a girl, a little younger than me. She told me how to escape."

"Why didn't she come with you?"

"She was chained to a table. I don't know why."

Ghabrie placed her hand along the side of Maeve's face and closed her eyes. "It's her! She's still alive! Did Jarek say where he was going to move?"

"He did say something about the Wastelands - a cave in a mountain or something."

Ghabrie ran her fingers through her hair, then pounded her fist on the ground.

"Did I say something wrong?"

Ghabrie calmed herself before replying. "No. You've helped more than you can imagine. Would you help me find Jarek?"

"I'm not ready for that. I would probably be more of a hindrance than a help."

"I'm not so sure that's true, but I understand. Where will you go?"

"Back to the Northlands, for now. I may not have many friends there, but I should have fewer enemies."

"You have more friends than you know."

"Who would be my friend?"

"Anyone who's had to deal with Jarek, for a start. Or any woman who's felt Krieg's hand."

"When I'm older and stronger, and if Jarek is still alive, then perhaps."

"All right. But you still have a decision to make. Will you go as Maeve, the flame-haired warrior? Or Maeve, the shy herb-peddler?"

Maeve lowered her head and shrugged.

"Whatever you choose, you will always be welcome here."

"Thank you."

Maeve gazed at the swirling reflection of the moon in the stream, her eyes unfocused. Ghabrie leaned over to see her distant expression.

"You're thinking of Aiden, aren't you?"

"He was the only one."

"The only one?"

"Everyone else looked at my hair and saw a mutant. He knew right away I wasn't."

"Some people look, others see," Ghabrie replied.

"What if he really was the only one? What if he was the only one who will ever see me for what I am?"

"Then your life would have no meaning, no purpose. You may as well give yourself up to Jarek and be done with it. But you already know this isn't true."

"I do?"

Ghabrie smiled, perhaps for the first time Maeve could recall. "There are at least two of us here."

Maeve smiled back. "I suppose."

Ghabrie leaned back against a log. "I should rest now if I'm to get an early start after Jarek, and Nahria if she is still with him. You may stay here as long as you wish. You need the rest, too."

"That's kind of you, but it's time to leave. If anyone is coming for me, I want to get as far away as possible … until I choose to face them."

"There's food in a bag wrapped up in the bedroll. You should at least take that."

"I will. Thanks."

Ghabrie nodded.

Maeve walked up the path and stopped at the stump. She picked up the bedroll and put her arm through the rope tying it together for a sling. She looked at the sword, the gleaming hilt poking from its sheath, glistening in the light from the dying fire. She glanced back at Ghabrie who was facing away from her into the moonlight, sitting with crossed legs, her arms on her knees. Maeve picked up the sword by the hilt. She held it up and felt its weight. She closed her eyes and sighed.

"Good choice," Ghabrie shouted.

Maeve looked over her shoulder, but Ghabrie had not moved. *How did she know?*

With that, she slid the sword between her belt and skirt. Then, taking one final look at the charmed glade where she had once sat with Aiden, Maeve pulled back the vines that guarded the entrance to the falls and slipped into the darkness.

SAND

Michael Wombat

Under an impossibly azure sky, the cutter Jack's Bitch sailed at a steady ten knots, her single mast fore-and-aft rigged, her two headsails swollen by a foehn wind, thrusting her way across the fast sand that layered the scorched desert of the Wastelands. The only sounds were the hiss-tick of the wide wheels, fitted to enable the vessel to sail oceans of sand as well as those of water, and the occasional shout from the crew.

The desert wind was hot and dry. It curled my hair beneath the sweat-stained old baseball cap that sat uncomfortably over my antlers; it tugged at the white square of cloth that covered the back of my neck; it made my nerves jump and my skin itch. Its constancy nagged like an unsatisfied lover. It could not possibly get what it wanted, this wind, but it incessantly worked at my skin, trying to make me ... different; trying to erode that which makes me Ghabrie. It whistled through the rigging, modulated, singing without melody. It reminded me that no matter how many friends I might have, or how many people love me, in the end I will die alone. Some things we must do alone. Dying is one of them. The desert wind whispered that truth in my ear even as it grazed my cheek.

To starboard the beautiful Shadow Mountain shimmered into the blue, forming a barrier to more temperate country beyond. Wisps of cloud on the high ridges betrayed the strong katabatic winds that raged high above the vessel. As Jack's Bitch drew abreast of a rocky promontory that provided refuge for a swarm of wolf spiders, the captain beside me bellowed orders. Crew scrambled to lower the sails. The cutter glided to a stop.

Silence, save for the song of the wind and the creaking and ticking of the wooden hull under a burning sun. I adjusted my irises as I gazed out across the sunbright ripples of sand.

"Bloody hell, Jack," I growled. "There's nothing here. I swear if you're double crossing me your entrails will soon be your extrails." I had heard that threat once in an old movie that Alphaeus had shown us, back in the shipping yard, and had been waiting a long time for an opportunity to use it. Had it really only been a few months since I had left? It felt like years, and yet the world had turned only enough to change freezing winter winds into this furnace-scour that drove sand into every body crevice. I had begun this quest so full of confidence, so cocksure that I would find Nahria and bring her home safely. Two seasons on and still I had not found her.

David had told me more than once that I was a hero. That this quest of mine had led to freedom for many who, without me, would have been doomed to horrific slavery and experimentation. I did not feel like a hero. I did not care about those people. I cared only about one person, and still I had not found her.

Most of the time these days - ever since Planck had ruined both his hand and his katana - David remains back at base, an old boatyard on the outskirts of Forlorn Hope, to rehabilitate those we have rescued, helping them quietly back into the world so that they can live their lives in peace, out of sight of the Alliance. That last waif, what was her name, Kayera? She should be settled by now. When I get back from this trip David and I will set out together once more. He has a memory to pursue.

The captain's brown leather face almost sneered. "No double cross, Merz Ghabrie," he pronounced my name wrongly, stressing the second syllable. At one time I would have rounded on him for that, but David had taught me that a calm manner was usually more productive than anger, and I let it slide. Captain Jack attempted a conciliatory smile. His teeth were rotten, and his breath reeked.

"I'll go no closer," he said. "The entrance is in a fold t'other side of yon promontory." He gestured towards the wolf spiders. "No one will be working there in the heat of the day; you should be able to stroll inside while they're all at siesta. But get out before dusk; I'll come back then, as we agreed, and wait no longer than thirty minutes after the sun goes. And be careful. The sand's black round there."

Black sand was an everlasting reminder of the Blast. Intense heat had shattered rocks, releasing tiny explosions that had produced a fine black sand. Over the decades it had mostly disappeared, mixed into or covered by normal sands, but in some sheltered places, like the cove behind the promontory, it remained. Black sand could burn skin due to the high amount of energy it absorbed from the sun. It was also highly radioactive.

I reached out to the speck that rode the hot currents high above the promontory. The windhover's eyes showed me no activity behind the outreach of rock. Time to go. This time, please, let my sister be there. She had been gone far too long. I strode across deck to the rope ladder.

"Oi!" the captain shouted me back. "Payment. Now."

"If I pay you now, how do I know that you'll come back?"

"If you don't, how do I know that you'll come back?"

"Because I'm me," I tried.

He gave me a condescending look and held out his grimy paw. I sighed, and rummaged in my pack. Where was it?

"Are you sure you wouldn't rather have Radbegone?" I asked, and he spat on the deck. He was a filthy scoundrel, but in desperate times I could not be picky about my companions. My fingers brushed a smooth object deep in the pack and I pulled it out: the Leader's skystone, still in its ridiculous cumbersome frame. I handed it over. The captain held it up to the sky and squinted through the translucent stone. He grunted in satisfaction.

"What the hawntch have you framed this with? It's uglier than a hatful of arseholes," he sneered, and began pulling at the ugly frame, trying to remove it. He looked up at me. "Why are you still here? Off you toddle. See you at sunset." He took his dagger from his belt and tried to prise the skystone out of the casing.

I clambered down the ladder. My boots sank into the bright sand. The windhover keened as I approached the promontory of rock. At the shoulder of the outcropping, where the black sand began, I reached into my pack for the Radbegone and sipped from the flask as I gazed back at the sandship. The crew were hoisting the sails.

The intense white flash stabbed my eyes first, followed by a swiftly blossoming ball of fiery orange and ebon black. The sand danced beneath my feet. The explosion was colossal and Jack's Bitch was entirely swallowed by a vast fireball of destruction.

The shockwave knocked me flat on my back before the roar of the explosion reached me, an ear-shredding crack followed by a continuing rumble. I could no longer see the windhover and cast my mind, finding nothing but emptiness in the sky above. Small objects covered the blue above – pieces of shattered timber, glowing metal shrapnel, burning cloth, and body parts. They arced up slowly before starting to fall.

I stood, stumbling a little at a pain in my back. The sandship had become a roaring inferno that spewed greasy smoke into a towering column of black against the blue cloudless sky. The skystone – or rather the casing around it – must have been booby-trapped. The Leader had intended that little surprise for me, surely, in case his cronies failed to capture me in the woods that long ago night. Instead, Captain Jack and his crew were all gone in an instant. So much for dying alone.

My ears heard nothing save for a high ringing sound, and I reached up to rub them. My fingers came away wet, and red. I reached out for the windhover again, but sensed nothing. Still, there was little time to worry about that for the moment. Every pair of ears within the complex would have heard the explosion, siesta or not. I had to move quickly.

A final glance at the inferno that had once been Jack's Bitch told me there would be no survivors. I rounded the promontory at a run, my feet sinking slightly into the hot black sand. Some fifty yards ahead I could see the entrance to the complex, a thirty foot square opening set into the rock face, exactly as Maeve had described it. As I got nearer I slowed down, and moved closer to the shoulder of rock to my left. My luck was holding – there was still no sign of life. I edged along the rock wall towards the entrance.

Three dead wolf spiders lay on the ground close to the opening in the rock. As I stepped across one of the bodies the Geiger went crazy. I quickly moved back, and the clicks fell to a more bearable level. I moved around to give the corpses a wide berth, warily watching the opening ahead. Still no-one had come to investigate the explosion. I crept forward again, and again the Geiger went berserk.

It seemed that a field of intense radiation extended about ten feet from the entrance. I had never experienced such a sharp change in rad-levels before. The level beyond the margin would kill me within a minute, were it not for the Radbegone. Even with an extra dose, I would have ten minutes at the most. "Cheers, David," I said, raising my flask in thanks to the man who had given it to me, and took a deep gulp. There was still no movement inside. I strode across the radiation threshold and entered the complex. The Geiger shrieked. I turned it off, and set the timer on my watch to ten minutes.

<10:00>

The room was clearly a workshop. The air smelled of fuel, precious fuel. The Prometheans would have plenty, of course they would. Posters on the walls advertised various entertainments – for Aiden or Hurricane Lizbet, mostly. Others gave safety advice, or shone with inspirational quotes: *The only difference between a good day and a bad day is your attitude.*

"Stuff it up your greasy hawntch," I muttered.

Shelves held tools and boxes. Most of the floor space was taken by two motorcycles and a strange winged contraption. I wound around them. At the far side of the room, between large stacks of metal drums, was a closed door. I put my ear to it, but could hear nothing.

<9:07>

I took a breath and turned the handle, tensed, ready for a swift roll backwards should danger wait on the other side. The door swung in easily a few inches then stopped, blocked by something on the other side. I listened again. Silence. I put my shoulder to the door and pushed hard. The door opened reluctantly, pushing some obstruction behind it out of the way as I opened it wide. The brightly-lit room beyond was large, running easily two hundred feet to the far end, and was perhaps half as wide. I stepped inside. The first thing I noticed was the people. The room was full of them.

<7:52>

They lay sprawled on the floor, fallen in heaps, collapsed across desks and tables. One of them had blocked the door so that I had had to push it open. I bent to feel for a pulse in the man's neck, but there was nothing, no sign of life. I examined another body close by, but he too was dead. I knew without checking that not one of the people in here, some thirty or forty of them, would still be alive.

<6:40>

I crossed to a desk nearby. The woman who had been sitting there had fallen across it. A hot drink still steamed by her left hand. I pulled a sheet of paper out from beneath her right hand. She had been writing.

Dear Amanda, I hope we'll be finished here soon, honey. Just two more—

Whatever had killed these people had been sudden, snuffing out this woman's life mid-sentence. What did that mean for Nahria? Maeve had suspected that Jarek had brought Nahria here, to this research site hidden way out in the desert. Was Nahria lying here somewhere amongst the still-warm corpses, killed by whatever had ended all these lives so swiftly? I closed my eyes and relaxed my mind as best I could. Please, please let me sense her …

There! Nahria was alive! A sob of relief escaped me, and I realised that I had been holding my breath. I could still see her, only as a shifting shadow at the edge of my mind, half-hidden by purple and green mist, but she was definitely there.

<5:07>

A loud bang from behind me startled me into action. I threw myself to the side, rolled and twisted to my feet, bow drawn and arrow notched, aimed towards the source of the noise. I had expected a Promethean guard, but the youth I saw was anything but. He stood behind a sheet of glass; a window to a small room at the side of the vast hall. He was precariously thin, and filthy. He banged once more on the glass; my hearing was settling back to normal now. I walked over, lowering my bow.

As I neared I saw that his grey eyes held a pleading look. I also noticed that he was not alone. A girl, so like him that the two must be related, half hid behind him and peered out at me. It was hard to tell under all the dirt, but she was maybe a year or two younger than Nahria.

<3:59>

"Was it you? Did you cause the blue light?" the youth shouted through the glass.

I shook my head. "What happened?"

"There was an earthquake, an explosion maybe, ten minutes ago. It must have broken something up to the left there." I looked where he was pointing. The far wall was covered with tech; dials and knobs, pipes and screens spaghettiing its entire surface. Near the floor, a blue light throbbed. A low hum pulsated with it, slowly rising in pitch.

Jack's Bitch. The explosion that had killed her must have shaken the bedrock enough to cause damage to the sensitive machinery inside the complex.

"We saw a flash of blue light that pulsed out from there, and everybody just collapsed. All of them, all at once," the youth continued.

"But not you?"

"Maybe we're shielded in here, I don't know. Can you help us get out?"

"I was told there was a girl here. Nahria by name. Have you seen her?" I examined the door to the room while I continued talking. It was locked. A hatch allowed small objects to be passed through: mainly food for

311

prisoners, I guessed. Next to it four rotating dials enabled a four-digit combination to be set. Find the right one and the door would open. I tried four zeroes. No good.

<2:36>

"You're Ghabrie," the boy said. I stared at him, amazed.

"Yes! You know me? You have news?" One-two-three-four did not work either.

"We met your sister. She was locked in here with us until two days ago, when they took her away. She told us about you. She said you were coming for her; that you would save her. I see that her faith was not misplaced."

Four-three-two-one also failed to unlock the door.

"Do you know the combination?" I asked. Nine-nine-nine-nine: no.

"Sorry, no. You'll just have to try all the possibilities."

"Kind of on a countdown here. The radiation on this side of the glass is deadly. I have maybe ..." I glanced at my wrist.

<1:21>

"... five minutes before I have to leave," I lied. There was no point in upsetting the two prisoners yet. And besides, maybe I underestimated the strength of David's Radbegone. Maybe.

"Then try a few more and leave. You can come back for us later. We're not going anywhere."

"Hear that rising whine? I'm not sure, but that does not sound like a happy noise. It sounds to me like something somewhere is getting ready to go off bang. I'd rather not be here when it does, and I'm radding certain that you don't."

"Ghabrie, listen. You have to save yourself. You have to leave us."

"No, I—"

"But before you go, know this: your sister left a message for you."

"What?" I paused, stunned. There were words from Nahria?

"She left a message," he repeated. "She made me learn it, in case I ever met you. She said *'I still live, sister. I live, though I am carried like a leaf on a stream I know not where. I know that you still follow, and I hope you will find me. Please come soon.'* I know well the bond between siblings," he hugged the girl to him, "And I know that she had faith that you would save her. She is why you have to leave us now. You cannot fail your sister."

<0:21>

"Hawntch it!" I cursed. I pushed the remnants of Radbegone into the door hatch. "Both of you take a good gulp of that. It'll keep you safe until you get outside. I hope." I turned and walked away.

"Farewell, Ghabrie!" the youth called after me. "I hope that you find her!"

<0:08>

I turned, and screaming as loudly as I could to dispel a demon of fear, I sprinted towards the cell door. I launched myself into the air and hit it feet first with all the force I could muster. There was a loud crack. My legs and back shuddered with pain, but the door fell inward.

"Come with me if you want to live!" I commanded, and the three of us ran full pelt towards the exit. The high whine behind us reached a pitch almost impossible to hear. Above it I heard the youth beside me, dragging along his silent sister by the hand, shout "But how will we cross the desert? Do you have transport?"

"My ride home blew up," I yelled back. "But I have an idea!"

313

THE OASIS

Rebecca Fyfe

The squirrel leapt from the tree and swooped down to land softly by my feet, folding its bat-like wings against its side. My gran had once given me a book about animals that showed a picture of a flying squirrel. Those squirrels from before the Blast didn't have wings like this one and they didn't actually fly; they just sort of glided on flaps of skin that stretched between their forelegs and hind quarters. The Blast had changed a lot of things. I'd never seen a squirrel without proper wings that allowed them to fly, to take off from the ground and soar through the air as easily as any bird.

I wish I had that kind of freedom. My wings were more like the ones those former squirrels had possessed. It meant I could only fly if I took off from somewhere high enough and if I could catch the air currents long enough to get some real lift. Of course, it also made it easier to hide my mutation and blend in when I came across others.

Fortunately, I didn't encounter too many people out here in this oasis I had found. It was a small partial island, with a lake on one side that curved, forming a crescent around the lush vegetation in the middle which was, in turn, surrounded by desert, or what others called the Wastelands. I think I was the first person to ever find this place, maybe because my gliding ability made it possible for me to cross a lot further into the Wastelands than anyone else. The sand dunes gave me leaping off points.

Some might think it was crazy to venture into the Wastelands alone, especially not knowing whether there was any end to them or if they just stretched on forever.

But after my parents were killed by a group of Scavengers, I figured it was safer not knowing what lay ahead of me than staying where I was.

Scavengers were groups of people who stuck together only as long as it paid off for them. They looted and pillaged, taking from those who couldn't protect themselves, those who weren't strong enough to fight them. Scavengers stayed close to places with small populations. If the population of a community was large enough, they could band together and chase out the Scavengers. But in small communities like the ones my parents and I had lived in, there were not enough people to do anything about the Scavengers. There was nothing but hope that they didn't kill you when they eventually came to take everything you owned.

My parents weren't fighters. The only reason they had lived long enough to raise me was because my granny had spitfire in her blood, or at least, that was what she called it. She was tough, the feistiest person I'd ever met. But she had died of the Sickness when I was just ten. Most people from her generation had already succumbed to the Sickness, even if something else had not killed them beforehand. Granny had lived longer than most, probably because she was too stubborn to let the Sickness take her right away, not when she knew I needed her.

I was named after Gran. Well, that's what my parents told me, but I had never heard anyone call her anything other than Gran or Granny so I couldn't be sure. My parents called me Mags. It was short for something, but I can't remember what it was short for. Gran always called me her little Magyk, but that was just her pet name for me.

My parents had only lasted a few years after Gran died. Despite our low rations forcing us to skimp on food, they didn't appear to be falling ill to the Sickness the way my granny had. They taught me to read, and my dad was always bringing home a book or two when he went out to barter for more rations. He mostly did manual labor in exchange for food and water. He once told me about libraries. He told me that he had found some that still had books in them, but he couldn't bring too many back with him at a time, because it would be dangerous to carry so much when he already had to protect the rations he was bringing home.

I read everything I could get my hands on, learning about the world the way it was before the Blast. Sometimes I'd daydream about living in that world. It seemed to me, from the stories I read, that people back then didn't realize how easy their lives were. But on my more melancholy days, I'd wonder if things would get so much worse in the future that there'd be a girl looking back at right now and thinking that we had it easy. I learned, from my reading, that another of my mutations was called a photographic memory. If I read something, I could bring it back to mind, in perfect detail, whenever I needed it.

This place I'd found was my oasis. I'd read about this type of place in a book when I was about ten. There was running water here, clear enough to drink. There were nuts here too. And there were fruit trees. I hadn't had fresh fruit since I was a toddler. My parents would have loved it here. Granny would have been suspicious of it though, afraid we'd all grow too soft if we stayed.

There were animals here too, and, in order to hunt them, I fashioned myself a bow and arrows out of some branches, thankful that I had thought to pack some twine and my knife before leaving for the Wastelands. I didn't have anything to fashion the arrowheads with so I just whittled the ends of my wooden "arrows" into sharp points. It took me most of the first week practising before I was any good at shooting at anything. But, after more tweaking to my bow's construction and spending a couple of months in my oasis, I had become proficient with my bow and arrow.

I still felt a twinge of guilt every time I caught some small creature to cook for my dinner, so I frequently caught fish from the lake surrounding my island instead. None of the fish I caught looked anything like the ones I read about in books. I suppose those fish had all died off by now or mutated into the multiple-eyed, brightly colored and dual-tailed creatures I caught from the lake.

The rumbling of an engine startled me from my reverie. I'd only heard the sound once in my life. Fuel was scarce, so few vehicles could be found that were still functional.

The morning sun was just beginning to shine as I rolled to my stomach, lying in the grass, and propped my head up on one elbow, trying to figure out which direction the sound was coming from. The tree beside me beckoned, so I quickly scaled its branches to get a better look around.

In one direction, I could see over my little oasis and beyond it, to the Wasteland, that spread further than my sight could reach. In the other direction, closer to the edge of the oasis, I could see that it was not one engine I heard, but three. Two specks on the desert sands moved towards me while one kept pace in the air above them.

I'd seen these in books. The hang glider had a small motor on the back, and the person hooked into it looked petite, with short hair. Or perhaps it was a tight helmet. The two specks on the ground became clearer as they moved closer, and I recognized them as a dirt bike style of motorcycle.

How had they managed to cross the Wastelands? Very few people ever had enough fuel to power a vehicle for any length of time. And they'd found my oasis — would they be friend or foe?

In my experience, strangers were dangerous. My parents had always hidden me away whenever someone had approached our dwelling. And their deaths only served to prove their point about people bringing danger with them.

But my oasis was a small one. There was no way they would pass it by, and no way that I could hide myself for long. I gathered my things and hid them down by the water's bank, in a small opening I'd found in a tree shortly after I had arrived. I kept my knife and my bow and arrows with me, climbed to the highest branches of a nearby tree and waited to greet my unexpected company.

The hang glider reached the oasis first. She landed not far away, where the trees formed a barrier between the Wastelands and this little slice of paradise. I peered from behind one of those trees, trying to glean any information I could about these people before they noticed me.

She took her goggles off and I noticed two very small, pointy antlers on her head. I gasped. Even as sheltered as I had been, I had heard about her. She was a legend, one I didn't think was real until now. The legend had something to do with one of the few government enclosures that still existed. It was said that she had destroyed it, leaving the agents to the mercies of their former prisoners. She was always searching for her sister.

Still, I wasn't truly sure it was her until the kestrel swooped down and landed on a tree branch above her head, emitting three sharp screeches as if scolding her for landing first. With the arrival of the kestrel I knew without any doubt that it was her; it was Ghabrie.

As the two motorcycles pulled to a stop near her, I held out my arms, stretching my wings, and glided down from the top of the tree, landing softly in front of them. I raised an arrow to point at the group. If they were surprised by my mutation, none of them showed it. Their expressions remained guarded.

Ghabrie raised her hands up partway. "We're not here to steal from you or harm you. My friends here just got out of a bad situation and are looking for a safe place."

I don't know why, but I wanted to trust her. Maybe it was all those stories about her helping people. I slowly lowered my bow.

"It's safe here. And there's plenty if you want to stock up on food and supplies before you move on." I tried to make my voice sound strong and confident, but I knew I was out-numbered if they weren't friendly.

I walked back towards my camp, hearing their footsteps behind me. I sat down on my favourite rock and rested back on my arms, waiting for them, affecting as casual a pose as I could muster.

"I'm Mags," I said, as the three of them joined me. "Take a seat," I indicated the area around me, with several large, flattened stones and a tree stump. "There's plenty of fruit if you're hungry."

I studied the two with her as they munched hungrily on the fruit, juice dripping down their chins. The boy looked to be about my age, maybe a little older. It was difficult to tell under all the grime. He was really skinny too, definitely hadn't been eating much. His grey eyes, when they met mine, were full of steel. The child looked like a mini version of him. So they were related. She kept looking at me with big, haunted eyes. What had these two been through to get those looks in their eyes?

"Do you know if there are any settlements nearby?" Ghabrie asked, not touching the fruit. For the first time since she'd arrived, I noticed how tired she appeared. There were dark shadows under her eyes. I wondered what things her eyes had seen.

I pointed in the direction of the small community I'd left behind to come here. "There's a settlement that way, but it's small one. It's frequented by Scavengers. I wouldn't recommend going there."

I looked out at the horizon in the other direction. "No one seems to know what there is to find out there, in the rest of the Wastelands. I was heading in that direction when I found this place. This seemed as good as any to stay. There's food and water, and it's peaceful."

Something briefly passed through Ghabrie's eyes as I said the word 'peaceful'. Maybe it was longing.

"Are there any government facilities left in the settlement you left?" Ghabrie asked.

"No, people are on their own out there. There's no government left as far as I've seen."

"What about a girl? About your age, with dark hair? She might be going by the name Nahria, in the company of a one-armed man called Jarek. Have you seen her?"

"Kids in my village rarely survive to my age. I'm sorry, but I haven't seen anyone like that."

I let them stay overnight in the oasis. I spent the night in the tree's branches, but I didn't sleep much. I realised, as they drifted off to sleep below me, that I had grown unused to being near people. The soft sounds they made as they slept were at once strange to me and yet comforting.

Twice during the night, the little girl woke up screaming from nightmares, and her brother soothed her back to sleep with a gentle voice.

When morning came I rose before the others and caught some fish. It was almost prepared by the time they awakened. Ghabrie ate slowly, as though cherishing each bite, while the other two ate as though they would never be full. I watched those troubled eyes as they ate. What would they find when they left here? Would Scavengers get them? Or would they succumb to the heat and dehydration of the Wastelands?

Without even realizing that I had come to a decision, I said "Stay." All three sets of eyes looked at me. I looked at Ghabrie. "You said they were looking for somewhere safe. It's safe here." I looked at the two haggard strangers. Gran would want me to do this.

"It's also lonely." I looked at the boy and the girl. "I'm not entirely certain I can trust you yet, but I've heard of your friend Ghabrie here, and from what I hear, she can be trusted. So I'm extending that trust to you. There's plenty to go around here. I can teach you how to look after yourself, and we can all look after each other. There's safety in numbers."

The boy's steel-grey eyes looked deep into mine, as though trying to read my thoughts. He nodded briefly. And with that small motion, my life was forever changed. I could feel Gran smiling down at us.

SHESHWAHTAY

K J Collard

Two Horns was up to his shenanigans again.

"Give it here!" Red Foot screamed at her older brother. "Give me the doll!" She chased after him as he danced around her, holding the delicate, hand-made cornhusk doll just out of reach.

"You'll have to fight harder than that to get it, Little Sister. Catch me if you can!" He followed his taunt with a teasing look, and took off at a sprinter's pace down the foot path toward the creek.

Red Foot's shoulders slumped as she watched her brother's slim build vanish into the wood. The last thing she could see before he disappeared under the dark canopy was the flame of his unruly, red curls. "Awww, forget it. You're not worth it, Two Horns," she said as her defeated gaze shifted downward. She balled up her tiny fists and hollered after him, "You'll be back for dinner anyway!"

Summer was giving way to autumn. The leaves had just started to turn magnificent shades of yellow and red. The sun took its leave earlier and earlier each evening. Nights brought that undeniable, crisp smell of impending winter. Yet somehow everything seemed colder than past years. I feared the effects of the Blast were finally beginning to creep into our home. I'd spent thirty-seven years on this mountain, and I could feel things were changing. There was more of a bite in the winds that blew into our home. The skies were more grey. And winter was still a long way off.

As I sat on my front porch, I could not help but beam at the tableau surrounding my young cousins. Two

Horns had been born eleven years ago with both middle fingers gracefully extended. His recklessly carefree attitude was with him from the day he was born. But where Two Horns was antagonistic and playful, Red Foot was creative and loving. Their personalities could not be further apart on the spectrum, but their twin-like looks made it undeniable they were related. I loved my young cousins It did my heart good to see them act like children. The reports coming from our sister community in The Valley painted a very bleak picture of the world that they would inherit.

"One day, Two Horns will learn better than to tease you. Now, come here, Red Foot," I coaxed, unable to control the urge to hug her.

Red Foot's face broke into smile. "I love you, Ahma!"

I cherished every time she called me Ahma. The name I was given at birth was Third Rosemary. I was named to honor my mother, Second Rosemary, and her mother Rosemary before her. The first time Red Foot used the endearment, she was nearly four years old.

"You know my name is Third Rosemary. Why do you call me Ahma?"

"Sometimes you're like my Mama. But you're more fun. You're just an Ahma instead," she'd said cheerfully. Now at eight years old, it was all she ever called me.

Red Foot giggled as she made a beeline for my lap. I gathered her up and gave her the tightest of squeezes. She buried her face in my shoulder, her red curls tickling my nose. Her naked feet swung back and forth as she landed on my lap. I looked at the giant birthmark on her leg. Its dark bloody hue took up most of her ankle and calf. The heart-shaped nevus continued onto the top of her foot. I suspected that some places in this post-Blast world would view her mark as a sign of witchcraft or demon possession. There was even talk of human mutations. I didn't know what was false or what was true about most of the stories that we heard from The Valley, but here, tucked away in the mountains, I was content that Red Foot didn't have anything to worry about. We were nearly impossible to find.

I loved the sanctuary our home offered. Our ancestors had lived here and blessed this land for hundreds of years. Maybe that's why the societal fallout all urban areas suffered after the Blast didn't come close to touching our home. Buried deep in the wooded mountains, nature provided a buffer for us from other people. Even though time continued as normal, it seemed like everything here was slower. People breathed easier. Our culture continued on in harmony. As electricity and communications broke down globally, we offered thanks to the mountain for protecting us. When the chaos erupted and the panic embraced, we continued with our lives as we had for hundreds of years, as if nothing had changed. Our mills were powered by wind and water. Our homes were heated by fire. The mountain provided everything our tribe needed just as she always had. It was only recently that our trackers were having a hard time finding meat and that our crops were not as bountiful.

Every once in a while an outsider made their way here. These adventurers usually found us by following the cart paths here from our sister village. Even though we were a tight knit, isolated community of nearly six hundred people, we were open and friendly to travelers. We would listen to their stories and share ours with them. We would offer them food and lodging. Some stayed. Some left. That's just the way it was. Our cannon was fairly simple: 'Take what you need. Give what you can.' If someone felt that they could follow those rules, they were invited to stay. Most were searching for something better out there and chose to go their own path. Especially since the Blast had changed societies, people moved on far more often than they stayed.

"Ahma, please tell me the stories about your marques again," Red Foot begged, breaking me from my reverie. She trailed her tiny fingers up and down my arm, tracing the black whorls and lines. From warriors to storytellers, our tribe used tattooing to recount our life stories on our skin, each symbol holding specific meaning. It was a reverent act. No marque was considered lightly, and all marques were to be met with approval from the Elders.

"Which story would you like to hear first?"

"This one Ahma!" Red Foot squealed with joy as she pointed to a marque that was a permanent cuff around my wrist.

"Well, this one was because the Elders recognized my musical gift. This marque shows the music that Gold Leaf wrote when I sang for your parents' wedding ceremony."

"What song is it, Ahma?"

"This song is called 'Song of Wind'. It's also the song your mother used as a lullaby for you and Two Horns when you were just tiny things. Tiny pink little babies."

"I don't remember Mama singing."

"Probably not, but I bet your brother does. He also helped to take care of you when you were no bigger than a loaf of bread." It seemed impossible how fast children grow up.

"I was tiny, Ahma. But I'm a big girl now," Red Foot said with a gigantic smile. "What's this one with the three branches?" she asked as she pointed to my temple and cheek.

"It's three sprigs of Rosemary. That is because I am Third Rosemary. My mother was Second Rosemary. My grandmother was Rosemary. We were all born with black hair and green eyes."

"And you can talk to the animals, Ahma. Just like your mama and oldmama."

"Yes, love," I said giving her a quick hug. "We all have an understanding with the creatures of the mountain. Rosemary experienced it first. Right after the Blast. She passed it to Second Rosemary, who ended up passing it to me. That's how I have it now."

"Rosemary died." Red Foot said plainly. "And Second Rosemary is sick and old. That's why she stays in the main lodge with the Elders, right Ahma? So they can watch after her?"

"Exactly right."

"And the Elders can see the future."

"Not exactly. Ever since our village was born, the Elders have been able to receive images. Their interpretations can be different. And nothing is ever set in stone."

"What will happen if you don't have babies, Ahma? What if you don't have a Rosemary? What happens to the Rosemarys?"

The question caught me off guard. "I don't know. I suppose the gift is returned to the earth or maybe another branch of our village inherits it."

Red Foot seemed satisfied with that answer. She grinned and steered my attention to another marque.

"And this one, Ahma. What is this one?" She pointed to the crook of my elbow.

"That one?" I teased, knowing she was asking me to recount her favorite story.

Her fingers traced the outlines of a rock face and a heart with a jagged tear down the middle. "Yes!" Red Foot squeaked and wiggled with excitement. "The one where the Elders were going to promise you to a boy and you told the Elders that you would throw yourself from The

Seven Hills before you'd be married to anyone and Elder Seventh said your wants meant very little and ..."

"Feel free to stop and breathe, Red Foot. You silly little one!" I teased her, ruffling her hair. But she was right. I was to be betrothed to a boy I could never love. When Elder First asked why I was so opposed to the match, I was forced to reveal my long time love for someone else. And even though I confessed my feelings to the Elders, I didn't disclose his name. It would only have caused further embarrassment for me, for I believed he had no suspicion of my affection.

"And that was the first time the Elders ever released someone from being promised. Because you loved somebody else?"

"What I said came from my heart. I never meant to be difficult. I didn't even realize I was making village history by objecting to the match. I just loved someone else very, very much. No one else before me challenged the Elders when it came to matches. But there was no room in my heart for someone else to be my soul's partner. It would have been so unfair to that poor boy, don't you think, Red Foot?"

"Oh, yes Ahma! And there was never another boy the Elders wanted to match you with?"

"Oh, there were plenty of boys," I said with a smile, remembering all the meetings I'd had with the Elders after my mini-revolt. "And they certainly wanted to. But I think Elder Fourth understood better than the other Elders that my heart already belonged to someone else. I think she made sure that the Elders never tried to match me again." I lowered my voice and leaned in close to Red Foot's ear. "I think Elder Fourth held a secret love herself."

"Why didn't Elder Fourth marry her love?"

"I'm not sure, little one. Sometimes love is tricky and messy. Sometimes it's better to walk away from it than embrace it. I think you'll understand better when you add some years to your age."

"Maybe I'll be an Elder. Elders can be chosen any age. Elder Fifth is younger than you." Red Foot said.

"Yes, love. Maybe you will be an Elder someday. I think you would be a very caring and thoughtful Elder."

"Why aren't you an Elder, Ahma? You're so smart."

"I'm not sure I'd be a good choice, love. Although," I teased, "maybe I will be an Elder. I'll move into the main lodge, sit in boring assemblies, and decide who YOU marry."

Red Foot's laugh bubbled up like a fountain. Her eyes sparkled along with her smile, but like a cloud across the sun, her joy turned to thoughtfulness. "I hope I marry a boy as magic as yours. One day you'll tell me all about him."

"He was a kind of magic, huh?" I mused. The boy I never saw again, I added silently.

A loud blast from the center of the village alerted us to the start of the Eldermoon dinner. Once a month the Elders hosted a dinner at the main lodge, which the entire tribe was invited to attend. I shuffled Red Foot from my lap. "Scurry now. Find your mother and father. Tell them I'll see them after the meal."

Red Foot was nearly out of sight when she called back over her shoulder. "I will! I love you!" And then she was gone.

I headed into my cabin to grab my shawl. I knew once the sun went down behind the peaks of the mountains I called home the temperature would drop. While retrieving the shawl, I spotted a small box tucked in the corner of my trunk. Most times I forgot it was there, but for some reason Red Foot's inquiries of my marques had left me in a nostalgic mood. I picked up the box and opened it. The treasure inside was just as I'd left it. A small beaded bracelet nestled itself between my fingers as I twisted my wrist back and forth. It was the only token I kept from my grandmother. The tiny wooden beads had letters carved into them that spelled the word PATIENCE. I pressed the beads to my lips and whispered, "Thank you Rosemary for giving me words I would need every day."

I tucked the beads back into their box. Dinner was waiting.

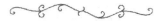

The monthly Eldermoon dinners coincided with the full moon. They gave the tribe time to celebrate one another as individuals and as a community. Since the moon provided enough light to see deep into the evening, most dinners became all night events. Games were played and stories were shared. News from our sister village in the Valley was relayed. Betrothals were announced, and deaths were mourned. Weddings were planned, and babies were presented to reveal their names. The fellowship shared at Eldermoon dinners was something that kept us connected to the earth and to each other.

I shared the Eldermoon dinner with my mother, Second Rosemary. She birthed me late in life, so the age gap was painfully apparent. As her body continued to fail, her mind remained sharp as a skinning knife. Although I knew the Elders worked closely with our healers to keep her comfortable, I feared the cough in her chest would only grow worse throughout the winter. All too soon, the tables started being cleared and the Eldermoon dinner was over. I kissed her on the forehead and promised to visit again within the week.

I kept my promise to Red Foot to find her after I helped to clear away the meal, and I found her with her mother, Short Willow.

"Where is Dark Cloud?" I asked.

Red Foot piped up. "Daddah is helping other men with Five Pine's shed. Where's Two Horns?"

"I'm not sure. Maybe he headed home already."

A dark look of concern came over Short Willow's face. "We haven't seen him. I thought maybe he returned to your cabin and attended the dinner with you. You haven't seen him?"

"No. I had guessed he made his way back home and shared the meal with you."

"Let's ask around. Maybe someone has seen him." Short Willow clasped her daughter's hands. "Red Foot, head up to the Elders' Table and have them post the question."

"He's fine, Mama. But I'll ask the Elders." Red Foot headed toward the front of the main lodge, her red curls bouncing with each step. There was no sense of urgency in her pace. I doubted she understood the full gravity of this situation.

"We'll find him, cousin. He's most likely lost track of time and forgotten his stomach." I put a comforting hand on Short Willow's shoulder, knowing what little peace it would offer until Two Horns was found.

After it was determined that no one attending the dinner had seen Two Horns, Red Foot was sent to fetch Dark Cloud and inform him that Two Horns was missing. The entire village sprung to life. People of all ages came together to form search pods for Two Horns. Dark Cloud came running with several friends bearing torches.

I ran back into my house to grab my protective shoulder skins to ward off the night chill and my supply pack. It contained everything I could need for an overnight camp on the mountain. Maybe nothing in it would help. I prayed we were all over-prepared and over-worried about nothing.

By the time I sprinted the round trip back to the lodge, the search pods had begun heading out in groups of three. Every five minutes another would leave. If Two Horns had doubled back, this was the best way of making sure he was found. I took my place and went out with the fourth wave.

Thirty minutes later a single shoe was found. It belonged to Two Horns.

I placed my hands on the ground and closed my eyes, reaching out with my soul to the surrounding animals. They could offer no assistance, although they promised to continue the search and spread the word of Two Horns' disappearance.

Deep into the night and through to the early morning, shifts of people scoured the mountainside for Two Horns. Each passing hour brought no sign of the boy. Short Willow was nearly inconsolable. Red Foot did her best to comfort her mother by insisting, "Two Horns is fine. He's with the Bird-Woman." Dark Cloud hadn't stopped to eat or drink since the news broke of his son's disappearance. He'd gone out with more search pods than anyone. Even our best trackers had no clue where Two Horns was. As the sun rose and set again, no one from the tribe was able to find even a hint of him beyond his lonely shoe.

That setting sun stole our hopes with it. The cold night winds pushed in. It was as if the mountain mourned with us.

The second night again yielded nothing. Conditions continued to deteriorate as cold and fog moved in. The search had to be abandoned.

Near the creek was a cave that Two Horns loved to explore. Several blankets and a skin of water were left inside the cave's entrance on the off-chance that Two

Horns was lost inside, exploring. We thought that if he'd lost his way in the woods, maybe the familiar landmark would help him find his way home.

Day after day, hope evaporated and joy diminished.

No signs were found. Just that lonely shoe.

Two Horns had simply vanished.

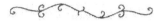

The forest was turning lush and green. Signs of rebirth and renewal surrounded me. The warm spring rain collided with the still-warming earth, and a tiny layer of fog blanketed the mossy ground. I knew I'd find him at the creek. Thankfully, I wasn't wrong.

"David," I said as I moved to sit beside him on the felled tree next to the giggling waters.

"Rose," he said. His smile was wide, but his eyes were a touch sad.

"What is it?"

"I'm leaving. Soon."

"Already?"

"There's something out there. I can feel it. Someone needs help."

They never stay for long. I put all my effort into memorizing everything about him. His careless dark hair and the way it fell over his forehead. His intensely dark eyes. Eyelashes so thick that they resembled charcoal lined eyes. His voice that was a little too gruff for his twenty-eight years. I wanted to remember everything about him. I knew once he left, he'd never find his way back. And I was desperately in love with him.

I knew all he saw was a seventeen-year-old girl who was a little too thin with messy, wind-tossed black hair and dirty, naked feet. During the handful of days he'd spent with the tribe, we'd only shared a cupful of words. For me, it was enough.

"Stay until the Eldermoon dinner tomorrow night. You can set off with the full of the moon to light your way."

He shook his head. "I've already said goodbye to the Elders."

The words were on the tip of my tongue. Words that begged him to stay. Words that maybe could have changed his mind. I dropped my eyes to the mossy earth and said nothing.

"Make sure you take care of them here, Rose. They're gonna need you."

David stood up and brushed the tiny pieces of broken bark from his pants. He grabbed his satchel, packed with supplies. "I'm glad we met."

With a brave face, I replied "Me too."

And I watched his figure get smaller smaller as each step took him farther away.

The memory faded to white as my shoulder shook. "Ahma! It's time for the Eldermoon dinner," she said. "Wake up. The Bird-Woman is on her way."

Red Foot had carried on about the Bird-Woman since Two Horns' disappearance. Short Willow was worried, but I reminded her that we all deal with grief in different ways. Red Foot was firmly convinced that Two Horns had found a friend beyond our village. It seemed there was no negative impact, so we let her have the fantasy of her brother's imaginary friend and protector. "They will be running out of food, Ahma!"

I righted myself from the nap I'd taken on my front porch. My head still foggy from my favorite dream, I smiled at Red Foot with heavy eyes. "I'm right behind you, love. Although I doubt the dinner will be short on food."

Although a full moon-cycle had passed since the disappearance of Two Horns, life in the village had resumed its daily patterns. I alone left my home every night to ask the earth and animals to continue the search. Every night I came home with no information, and every night I felt a bit weaker. There was a sighting of a group of young men and women with tattoos similar to our marques traveling through the Valley, but no evidence of Two Horns.

Red Foot grabbed my hand and we went to the Eldermoon dinner. The loss of her brother seemed to have matured her. She no longer skipped but walked with purpose. Her posture was more square. But despite her newfound maturity, her enthusiasm for life was undiminished.

The monthly Eldermoon dinner proceeded much like the ones before it. Business among the tribe continued to move forward despite the giant hole that remained. As the dinner was winding down, the door to the lodge burst open.

"MOTHER!" The voice was familiar and full of joy.

Everyone held their breath and turned to the door.

Two Horns, holding a tiny cornhusk doll, came barrelling over the threshold.

Short Willow jumped from her table and crashed into Two Horns in the middle of the floor. Dark Cloud and Red Foot weren't far behind. The entire family was mobbed by people from the village. No one attending the dinner held back their tears of joy at the reunion.

I stood up as I noticed a figure in the doorway. The full moon backlit the figure of a slender woman. She stepped into the main lodge and I could see her more clearly. The marques on her face resembled those we practised in the tribe. Her rugged clothing included skins and feathers, and there were trinkets from urban areas decorating her neck. She was beautiful and wild. Her eyes showed that she lived a life far more difficult than her youthful features suggested. She started to speak in a language I couldn't understand, but something about her felt familiar. I walked over to her and clasped her hand. My animal connection recognized her. We could talk to each other with our hearts.

My name is Third Rosemary. What is your name?

My name is Ghabrie.

I can't thank you properly. There are no words. You've brought my cousin back to his family. How can we repay you?

I don't want thanks. I'm crossing the earth looking for my sister. Your cousin was in the wood and couldn't find his way back. He was lucky I found him when I did. He was weak and dehydrated. We helped him find his way back.

Her choice of words didn't escape my notice.

We?

As if by earth's magic, Ghabrie sidestepped, and a new figure walked into my line of sight. As he stepped into the glow of the room, I nearly lost my legs. His hair was shorter. A rugged salt and pepper beard covered his sun damaged face, and crow's feet painted the corner of his eyes. And yet despite all the changes, one undeniable feature hadn't changed. The dark chocolate eyes framed by even darker lashes.

There is a feeling that is stronger than love, more encompassing than longing; a feeling that is bigger and more intense than desire or want; a feeling that leaves a deeper hole in your chest than simply missing someone. A feeling that overwhelms with joy, weeps for time lost, and cherishes the potential of the future. It's a feeling that crushes every emotion into a singular, overpowering moment. My tribe had a word for this feeling.

"Sheshwahtay," David said in his unmistakable gruff.

My eyes overflowed. "Sheshwahtay," I replied.

Twenty years of putting my feelings aside was finally at an end. As if magicians had performed the perfect illusion, he was standing in front of me. Without realizing I'd been walking, he was suddenly a mere breath away. He caught my face, and I noticed for the first time that the fingers of his left hand were stiff and inflexible. The fingers of his right twined deep in my hair, and he planted the perfect kiss on my mouth.

I broke the kiss and leaned back to look in his eyes. "You're not leaving again?" I asked.

"Not this time, Rose. Not ever."

As my senses started to return, I realized cheers and whistles were coming from my tribe. I turned to look at Elder Fourth. She was simply smiling as if she'd known all along. She stood slowly and deliberately. The tribe fell silent.

"A tribute, then. To our new friend. For finding that which was lost. Twice over. Let there be huiskee toasts in her name, for she is well and truly a brave warrior."

A grand cheer went up, and Ghabrie looked uncomfortable. I remembered she didn't know our words. I grabbed her hand and translated.

My tribe thanks you for bringing back Two Horns and David. The tribe celebrates you as a warrior.

I want no thanks. I simply want to find my sister.

Hmmm. The animals spoke of a girl with dark hair and marques like yours who came through the valley village. She traveled beyond here with a group of other men and women, towards Pandora and beyond.

Wait, towards Benanti Peak? I went there before in search of her. The complex there was abandoned.

Perhaps it no longer is? I wish you would stay for a while. Rest from your travels.

I appreciate your kindness. But each minute is critical. I have to find her. I'm not complete without my sister.

I understand. I wish you well, friend. And may the mountain protect you.

I gave her hand a tiny squeeze and kissed her forehead. I knew we would be linked through the earth from here forward. *Call out to the earth and animals if you need assistance. I will do what I can.*

Thank you, Ghabrie bowed deeply. She then turned and headed into the night, her figure's shadow outlined by the full of the moon.

I turned back to see David surrounded by people clamoring to welcome him back and youngsters eager to meet the dark stranger. I waited in the background. I knew I had the rest of my life to give to him.

He was finally mine to love.

THE BALLAD OF ASH & HUM

Alison DeLuca

Part 1 - HUMAN 273

Lying on the tiny bunk, Hum searches for files about Ghabrie on an ancient laptop. His head is pillowed on Ash's broad chest. Hum knows his cerebral enhancements must be digging into the older boy's ribs, but Ash just murmurs, "You've read that stuff 'bout fifty times already."

Hum closes the computer and sits up, rubbing his hardware. "Just thinkin' I musta missed something."

Ash smacks Hum's head and follows with a one-armed hug. Hum ducks into the embrace. The hardware on his neck, surgically attached when he was five, covers the last part of his neck tat: HUMAN 273. Wires and smartchips stretch over the numbers and two of the letters so only HUM is visible. Now no one remembers his original name.

"Whacha think eternity means?" he asks Ash. "I mean there has to be an end somewhere, right? The rock can't keep going on and on."

Hum thinks about infinity a lot. Dirt and stone surround Pandora Alliance that lies underground. No one knows what lies above their buried city. Thanks to his enhanced neural wiring, Hum can call up an exact picture of the entire facility, rotate, flip the image, and figure the fastest way to get from one port to another, including airshafts and what Ash calls 'smuggler tunnels' - passages known only in Alliance legends.

These mental images come to Hum as music, a strange symphony of bytes and constant input. No one quite understands the constant tune in his head, although Ash comes closest to hearing the crackles and whines of Pandora's song. The melody uses zeroes and ones instead of notes, wires and hardware for instruments.

Ash stands and twists his back. When he doesn't move for long he becomes restless. His enhancements are all physical: strengthened bones, perfect eyesight, the balance and poise of a dancer. HUMAN 272 is tatted under his long hair, but only Hum gets to see it.

They are bred to perform perfectly together. Ash is all hard muscle and sinew, ready to spring to action when Hum makes the call. One theorizes, the other acts. It il up ti dates how things have always been.

Hum leans back on his elbows to watch Ash whirl into a series of kicks, always stopping just short of the walls and door in the tiny space. Ash is a large feline boy, carelessly flicking dark hair out of his eyes – Hum watches and wishes he could keep the snapshot superimposed on his pupils forever.

Ash lands on one foot. "C'mon," he declares. "I'm hungry."

"You're always hungry - y'used up double rations last night." Hum follows Ash anyway. He always does.

"Well, hack in and get me triple," Ash laughs. A passing tech glances at him, her eyes filled with admiration. Hum can't blame her. Her name is Bhari – the girl who always wears something around her neck tied onto a knotted string. Whatever it is lies hidden under the collar of her shirt.

In Hum's mind there is no one prettier than Ash with his long black hair and lazy limbs like those of a jungle cat. Bhari is not the only one who turns to watch Ash move through the dim halls of Pandora.

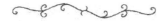

Dinner is phytoplankton soup grown in the vats on the lower levels of Pandora. The place was built near underground cenotes before the PBA event. Historical information is scratchy at best, and when Hum hacks into those files, the music filters through a constant waterfall of white noise.

Regulated airshafts blow a warm, sticky stream over Hum's body as he and Ash eat the soupy mix in their bowls. It is a VitD day to prevent rickets, so the atmosphere is extra humid as a result. Hum is used to the sweat in the creases of his bony knees. Perhaps this is what it will always be for him – agar soup and VitD days in an endless cycle. Ash will eventually sexbond with Bhari or some other tech, leaving Hum behind to his dirty, messy, hacky work in the dying computers of the Alliance.

Because the mainframes are dying. Power is constantly diverted away from the intranets to military ops and crowd control. Worse, Alliance hardware is dying as well, slowly corroding as each PBA cycle passes.

The cacophony of the downward spiral hurts Hum's hardware. It makes panic rise in his throat, makes him want to find the nearest smugglers' shaft and bust his way into it, and crawl up to the Surface where no one goes anymore. The idea of a Pandora blackout is horrifying, especially since Crippen seems to deny it could ever happen.

Ash nudges his elbow. "One more bite," he whispers. "Bleeding Alliance, Hum! Eat your damn food before you keel over – again."

Hum gives him an automatic two fingers. It's how things play out with them. Watch your partner's back while flipping each other off. With an exaggerated groan to make Ash laugh, Hum digs his fork into the green goop and spoons some up.

As he sucks it into his mouth, already wincing from the salt, a red flash combined with a howl of loud music temporarily obscures his vision. Hum's loaded fork clatters onto the table, spraying soup over his shirt.

Ash curses again. "You're such a driftbag! That's the third Henley this week ..." His voice dies out, and he squints at Hum. "Got something?"

Hum rigged his hardware several VitD cycles ago to buzz him at the slightest input of any new bytes related to Ghabrie. He turns to Ash, who picks up on his urgency at once. "Your room," Hum whispers.

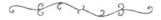

They sit next to each other on Hum's bunk. Ash holds out his wrist, and Hum plugs in. He and Ash spend hours in their neural hook-up to exchange ideas and practice their moves. Hum uses his expanded mental powers to shunt a mapped interface to Ash – shows him the weakest points of the landscape and the easiest way into an imagined enemy's camp. It's all happening in War Games, of course, not reality. They've won the Alliance trophy three cycles in a row before Hum decided another win would make them too visible.

When the port is complete, the familiar expansion fills Hum's brain with layered, exquisite harmony. Hum can now use two points of view, his own and what Ash sees. It's as natural as breathing: their own warsong.

"Check out this message." Hum brings up the red alert he hacked in the dining hall. There is an attachment:

<Ghabrie/info/new/PDA.53/Prometheus.gif>

Hum's heart thumps as he plays the gif. It is sharp and hi-res, showing a girl who holds a bow. Face paint marks her rounded chin and intelligent forehead. Weary eyes glare from heavy, shapely eyebrows. There's a hoop, jagged as an old cog, thrust through one ear. A bird sits on her shoulder, feathers mottled brown and white. Actual light from the sun casts shadows where Ghabrie's hair laps her cheek.

The gif plays through several times. The girl lowers her bow, tilts up her face as a signal, and the kestrel spreads its wings. Obviously the hawk is about to take flight, but the gif ends before it leaves her shoulder. Hum would love to see the hawk launch into the air and fetch the victim of the girl's bow.

"Beautiful," Ash whispers.

"Yeah. She's amazing." Hum knows the girl in the file is Ghabrie, even though there's no timestamp on the actual gif. The kestrel, the face markings – it is definitely her.

The boys turn to each other. What they have always hoped for has actually come true – they have received proof that Ghabrie exists. Her kestrel is real. And she's out there, walking around on the crust of rock far above them.

Just as Hum is about to pull up the intranets and compare the gif background with large-scale maps or anything he can find pre-PBA, another mental alert comes in via his hardware link, accompanied by high-pitched sirens indicating extreme danger. Ash screws up his eyes and covers one ear with his free wrist in a hopeless attempt to block it.

"What the hell?" Hum frowns as a long stream of data follows the alert. There are texts, in-house iMails, reports, agendas – a huge dump of information, all classified to the point of being highly illegal.

Hum prepares to unplug and wipe all the data, but Ash covers Hum's hand, the one jacked into Ash's wrist. "Look," he says.

"If we're caught, they could break us apart," Hum begins in a furious tone. His voice dies out as he reads the most recent report. It is written as a business letter. Crippen is in the cc: list. The cold, technical language does not mask the blind fear behind the words: Pandora Alliance is losing power and has less than three VitD periods left before the entire installation goes dark forever.

Hum's jaw slackens with fear. Crippen is not gearing up for defense of the facility after all. The General plans to go on the offense by attacking another Alliance, to pirate their food and safespace. A frenzied scan through the rest of the information tells him that he and Ash head the list to carry out a secret find-and-destroy mission. Their three wins in succession all those cycles ago have brought them to Crippen's attention.

Ash yanks his wrist free of the bond and covers his face. The sudden break of the neural link makes Hum hiss with pain. He would like to smack Ash or at least give him an ear-flick, but he softens when he sees the slumped lines of his partner's body.

With a groan Ash scrubs his hands off his face and turns to Hum. "We have to get out of here," he whispers. "Ghabrie's gif shows the surface is habitable. If we find the shaft upwards and escape, we can contact her. There has to be some kind of leftover infrastructure on the Surface you can hack to make contact."

"Have you met me?" Hum indicates his scrawny chest and thin legs with a contemptuous wave. "I'd never make it out, let alone survive on the surface." Blindly he feels for his friend's wrist, lets his little finger hover over Ash's port. "You could do it, though. I'm close to finding the entrance to those smugglers' tunnels so we could bypass the EMO's, get you past Military…"

Ash seizes Hum's chin in a harsh grip. Slender fingers grind against Hum's jaw "No way. It's either both or none."

The moment has grown in intensity. Hum can barely suck in oxygen. He burns with the excitement of their discovery and the suspicion everything is about to change.

Ash's eyes flick over Hum's face.

A thought Hum has never allowed Ash to see – even in their closest bonds – flares with impossible hope. Could Ash? Does Ash? Will Ash?

The silence between them becomes warmer, more intimate. It is unbearably exciting. Just as Hum is about to make a dumb joke to break the tension, Ash's eyes flicker down again. *Bloody hell*, Hum thinks. *He's about to kiss me, and I'm going to let him.*

Their faces tilt symmetrically, preparing to slot their mouths together. Ash's breath is warm on Hum's cheek, warm splinters of salty soup and pent-up desire.

A loud rap on the door shatters the moment into shards of embarrassment. Guiltily the pair slide apart on the bunk. Crippen himself sticks his face around the door. He must have just come from Maintenance – the man's hair is even shorter than usual, and his cheeks have the shiny look of a fresh shave.

Crippen's pale eyes dart over the scene. "Evening, ladies," he snaps. "Both of you, my office, oh seven hundred."

"Why?" Ash blurts out the question.

One thick eyebrow rises at the audacity. "Guess you got to come and find out. Lights out in five tics – Ash, you come along with me."

There is no chance to defrag what just happened between them. Hum watches Ash rise from the bunk to follow Crippen. Ash's eyes bore into Hum's with intensity before the door closes and Hum is alone.

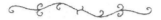

In the darkness, Hum accesses the files again under several layers of encrypted protection. No one must discover what he and Ash have accessed. He organizes the information, processes the data, and runs several different scenarios. From this he learns:

The Pandora Alliance has three VitD cycles left of potable water if they recycle all body fluids.

There are two PBAs left of sustenance if they eat all the canned food, including the expired stuff.

Power will go down after the third VitD cycle due to increasing usage.

The result will be a huge wave of disease and eventual death.

Most terrifying is the awareness on the highest security levels. Crippen already knows the timeline.

Hum wipes his eyes with the back of one hand and runs another scenario, one utilizing all the scraps of pre-PBA history he has ever found and squirreled away in his hardware-augmented brain. Suppose a civilization is on the brink of disaster. What's the reaction of the people in charge?

The answer is swift and brutal, a crash of dissonant music from his hardware. Leaders save themselves.

How? Hum queries.

Hoarding supplies. Creating private shelters. Eliminating useless population mass.

Stifling his gasp, Hum realizes Crippen isn't merely going to attack another Alliance. The General wants casualties, and Ash is first on the list.

Ash wakes like a soldier: instantly, bounding upright with hands ready to defend himself. "Don't break my hardware," Hum whispers, leaning over Ash with one hand braced on each side of his friend's body. "We gotta do this on the sly."

Ash's eyes darken as they focus on Hum. "Bloody Alliance! I nearly broke your arm! Do what?"

"Get out of here. Gimme your wrist." Hum ports into Ash and uploads everything he has learned about the future of Pandora as well as his own conclusions.

His partner closes his eyes, looks flattened from the weight of what's about to happen. "Ghabrie," Ash whispers.

The one quiet word makes Hum want to kiss Ash more than ever.

"Gonna be impossible," he comments. They will have to find the smugglers' tunnels, follow them to the military shaft, and sneak out.

"Nah." Ash grins. "Not impossible. I got you."

The original purpose of the smugglers' tunnels is lost. Maybe the passages were put there when the Alliance was built in order to cart down supplies, or added later by some revolutionaries before discovery and execution.

Hum runs more analysis and finds the two most likely places for the tunnel access point: one is behind the lower level farms, conveniently located behind the agar tanks; the second, and more likely option, is straight off the military install.

He huffs during the exchange of information, all done on the silent interchange network. Ash picks up on his mood at once, their interactions seamless. After working with someone on the neural networks for years it is easy to move as one unit.

Ash throws a longing glance in the direction of the agar tanks. "Why even waste time," he whispers. It is not a question.

"Yeah. Lead on." Hum follows Ash as quickly as he can through the low lights of the hushed Alliance.

At the outskirts of Military, Hum catches Ash's sleeve in one fist. "About to hit the point of no return," he says. It is true – what they are about to do is highly illegal. If they are caught… but Hum will not allow himself to think of the waterboarding, the nerve torture, the synapse rewires they'd be forced to undergo.

Ash never hesitates. He holds out his wrist and Hum plugs in.

A - <I handle the guards once you get us in. Two at each end, right?>

H - <Yeah. Looks like personnel cutbacks are already in place.>

A - <How you gonna head off the system-wide alarm?>

H - <Hack into heat signature. Gonna make Military think it's Crippen and his partner out for a midnight stroll.>

They grin at each other. There's something new between them, an underlying consciousness. Everything is about to change. Perhaps that is why Ash suddenly cups one broad palm around the back of Hum's neck, sliding his thumb at the base of the hardware, to pull him in for a quick, breathless hug. "Like holding a bundle of twigs," he murmurs into Hum's ear.

"Big lump of cheese," Hum retorts. The sarcasm covers the tiny sparks of electricity racing through his bloodstream that have nothing to do with neural bonds or enhanced abilities. Ash pushes him back to look into his eyes. With their recent hookup Hum can almost read his mind: *You make it out alive, no matter what happens.*

S'funny, he signs back. *Was about to say the same thing.*

Lips firm, Ash jerks his head at the door to the Military enclave. Hum ports into a hidden sidewire running between the entrance and the mainframe. A few tense moments later, the door slides back with a hiss.

Making the hand signal for Hum to wait, Ash enters Military. There are a few grunts followed by the hushed sound of several large bodies slumping onto the floor as Ash takes them out. It is Hum's signal, and he lopes inside at a half-crouch.

Ash stands inside, his mouth open, features blue under the spears of crystal light from the ceiling. Hum moves next to him, and their hands touch, fingers twist together.

This is the first time they have been inside Military. The place is huge. The enclave yawns like a cavern, those blue streams of light descending from a canopy far overhead. If Hum were not so furious about the wasted resources he would be overwhelmed.

Ash tugs him forward, points without a word. There are boxes lined against the walls among banks of humming instruments, each crate marked with spray-painted letters. FIGS, one reads. MREs. SALT. SMOKED AGAR. ALMONDS. It is a fortune in survival calories.

Another pull on Hum's fist. Ash brings him to the crate marked FIGS, and Hum grimaces. "Hungry now? Really?"

"Get in there and hide. I still have to take out the other two guards."

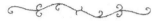

Waiting in the dark is horrible. Any moment the lid of the crate could be ripped off, framing the nightmare vision of Crippen. Hum can visualize it, see the man's piano-key teeth spread in a taunting smile, a hunting blade in his fist. *My last view better not be of that idiot*, Hum thinks. Nightmare visions sear his mind: a guard's club striking, blood, brains, chips of bone, the final twist of agony.

No. No. It can't happen.

When the lid opens, Hum is flooded with warmth when Ash peers in, his usual cocky smirk lifting one corner of his mouth. Hum climbs out, a few figs clinging like leeches to his dirty shirt. "Actually got it right, huh?" Hum says.

"You expect anything less? C'mon, kid, I'm taking you out in style." Ash reclaims Hum's fist and they run between banks of humming instruments. Hum is tempted to inspect the machines, but there is no time. "Tell me where, buddy."

Hum rotates his mental image of the Alliance, adding the newly discovered portions of Military. The most likely entrance to the smuggler's tunnels is behind a crate of Hardtack, which Ash moves aside easily. Smooth muscles ripple under his shirt as he works. There is a grid screwed into the wall behind the crate. Hum feels for the omnitool in his backpack, and when he finds it he digs at the rusted screws until they come out of the wall. Ash is ready to lift the heavy metal out of their way.

They breathe easier once they are in the tunnel. It is lined with old tiles, some marked with nearly indecipherable graffiti.

We did not deserve this, one reads.

Who gave you the right? another proclaims.

Some just show crude pornography. Humankind never changes.

The space is tall enough to walk upright, but Ash urges them into a jog. Hum ignores the ache in his chest and forces himself to keep up. After a while the graffiti dies out, and the tiles are scarred with other marks: smoke and the dark kiss of blood. They have ventured into a place no one has seen since the Blast.

Hum's musings end with the tunnel. It stops at a wall of bricks, but there is a set of rungs bolted into the wall. They are going to have to climb to freedom. After a terse argument Ash cuts him off and boosts him up first.

"Course I gotta take the rear," Ash grumbles. "Think you could survive an attack? 'Sides, maybe I'm nervous to be the first one to reach the surface, ever think of that?"

I might love you, Hum thinks, but doesn't say. They climb in silence, punctuated only by their gasps for breath. When Hum simply cannot go any further, Ash calls a halt. Hum clings to the rungs until Ash maneuvers his body over Hum's, bracketing his thighs so Hum can rest his aching muscles against his partner's warm chest. They drink warm pear juice stolen from the kitchens and eat flax crackers from the pockets of Ash's cargo pants. When Hum nods firmly, determined to make it, they resume their ascent.

At the point when he thinks he can move no longer, Hum's palm finds a flat stone instead of the next rung. He hauls himself up and manages to flop onto the floor, coughing and retching, trying not to vomit up the pear juice. Ash jumps off the rungs to his side, circles

Hum's shoulders with warm arms. "Just breathe," Ash orders. "Breathe for me, baby."

"I'm not a kid," Hum manages to choke out. He breaks free, stands, and gives Ash a weak punch.

They are in a huge space, dark and echoing. Hum echolocates with a few experimental stamps of his feet. Ash immediately produces a flashlight and holds it over their heads to reveal what looks like an empty waystation.

Not quite empty – Hum's quick ears pick up a hollow space in the far corner. He beckons to Ash, and they scurry through the dark like those cockroaches that blunder everywhere in the Alliance kitchens. There, behind a pile of rubble, Ash sweeps back a veil of dust and reveals double doors with thick glass windows.

"What is it?" he whispers.

There is no place to port on this level. Hum brushes off more dust and explores the cracks with careful fingers. He cannot pick up an electric signature anywhere, and after a few moments he realizes why. Excitement makes him speak louder than he should. "Think it's designed to run on counterweights and balances, like one of those old grandfather clocks we learned about in pre-engineering."

"You learned about." Ash shoves him just hard enough to make it count, soft enough so that it is friendly. "I wasn't paying attention. But do you think it still works? Whatever the hell it is?"

"One way to find out." Hum's finger hovers over a brass button set into a surprisingly ornate panel scarred with age and more graffiti: *This sucks. Angelo 6/16. Never Forget.*

With a deep breath Hum pushes the button.

There is a whirr of ancient machinery from inside the closed device. Hum is able to follow each rattle and clank, giving him a picture of what lies inside: an analog system of cogs and pulleys. He hears them grind into motion, allowing a large object to descend to their level. A flash goes off inside his hardware, and he turns to Ash, lips trembling with excitement.

"You won't believe this. It's an elevator. We can just…"

"…just waltz in and ride on out of here?" Ash chuckles, a rich sound. "Buddy, I thought we'd be dead by now, and you're telling me we can shoot to the surface in style?"

Hum laughs too. "Guess I'm stuck with you for a bit longer." The double doors open a crack before they stick, wedged several thumbspans apart.

"Now it's my turn. Outta the way, shortie." Ash widens his stance, gets his fingers through the crack, and pulls. Hum tries not to look at the way Ash's muscles bunch under his shirt and how the ragged material sticks to sweaty skin. With a few grunts Ash gets the doors open wide enough to reveal a dark space inside.

Ash flashes his light and recoils. The tiny space is packed with what looks like the final load of refugees to the Alliance level, except they have been inside the elevator for a long time. Radius and ulna bones slide out of a surprisingly intact jacket, emblazoned with PENN STATE. The words are meaningless.

"They're just bodies," Hum says as much to himself as to Ash. "We can deal with it for however long it takes."

"Unless the elevator gets stuck on the way to the Surface …" Ash shakes his head. "No, you're right."

"'Kay." Hum picks up his backpack. "Apray voo."

"No, apray voo, monsewer."

They bow at the waist to each other before Ash catches Hum's hand. His eyes sweep over Hum's face in a curiously intent gaze. "Just … just for luck. That's all it is."

Before Hum can respond, Ash kisses him with a mere brush of chapped lips. His breath is sour as he clutches Hum's hips. Standing in front of an elevator cab filled with corpses, Hum gasps and dares to deepen the kiss. When Ash's tongue slides against his, Hum has to throw one arm around his friend's neck, since the darkness is wheeling around him. He might faint. He might actually faint.

"You little sonsabitches!"

The shout cuts into their shared silver bubble. A powerful lamp slices through the black space. It blinds Hum, but he recognizes the voice.

Crippen.

Hum's neural wiring kicks into high gear. There is only one chance. Crippen will not leave until he has a victim. If he and Ash both go in the elevator they're boxed-up prey, ready for the killing shot. Crippen will tear them both apart. Those facts cut through Hum's enhanced consciousness like razors.

"Get the hell out of here." Hum pushes Ash, a vicious onslaught. He tries not to cry at his friend's expression – eyebrows raised, lips slick and parted from their kiss. "Go on – you disgust me, filthy driftbag. I'm sick of you following me everywhere."

Gathering all his strength, he hits Ash again in the center of his chest so hard the boy falls into the black room, tripping over the skeleton wearing the PENN STATE jacket. Instantly Hum hits the brass button. Please, please, please, he prays. Please.

There is a shot behind him and the whine of a neural bullet spinning in its chamber. Hum sobs aloud as the doors close on Ash's face, soft with shock, through the thick, smeared windows. It's the last view before the tiny cogs and gears whirr into motion and the elevator ascends.

Another whine and a red flash as Hum's hardware shorts out. He has a quick snapshot of Crippen's fury and Bhari's calm face bending over him before everything turns to white noise.

Part 2 – Knotted String

Bhari knows something is going on in the Alliance. She is not enhanced, so she cannot port in and investigate. Still, there is a new edge to Crippen's orders, the way his eyes slide around in their sockets like peeled eggs in a bowl. Without enhancement she has had to rely on her own skills of observation; keeping still and quiet so that no one notices her. People tended to reveal secrets when she was tucked behind a malfunctioning mainframe with her hands in its guts. Bhari is good at being silent and nearly invisible while the uppity-ups argue about disappearing rations and the oncoming blackouts.

Her unease has not led her towards action. She is used to being a mouse, to observing instead of doing. Ash, for example – she watches his long limbs and slender feet, the muscles sliding under silky skin. She does not want to touch. Part of her is broken, she is convinced of it, and she hopes to avoid a future sexbond. The idea simply has no meaning for her.

It is much more satisfactory to be on a job, to figure out the schematics as well as several solutions before deciding on the simplest and best one. The job before her now lies in an old dentist's chair, strapped down at wrists, knees, and ankles. Hum's neck is free, since Crippen has plans for the kid and he wants Bhari to carry them out.

"Anything?" Crippen spits.

"Still asleep. Those neural charges are strong." Bhari speaks absentmindedly, her fingers probing Hum's enhancement. It is a complicated braid of wires and scars covering the tat and the top of his spine. She strokes Hum's motherboard, a 2x2 flat box providing enough power to drive a quadruple charge to Hum's neurons.

Unenhanced brains run on 12 volts, which isn't enough energy to notice and retain all items in a crowded room. The low electrical charge explains human persistence of vision and optical illusions.

Hum's network, however, has 48 volts. His brain is a self-sustaining system with race-pattern power, so idle thoughts constantly recharge his batteries. Bhari has never seen anything so beautiful in her life.

"Get the box out of his system now." Somehow Crippen has edged right up behind her to speak right into her ear. "Unhook him."

Bhari gazes up at him from her crouching position next to Hum. "Why?" It is the first time she has ever questioned a direct order.

"What did you ask me?"

"This is a beautiful job." Bhari indicates the delicate platinum bands laced with gold. "Why destroy it?"

Crippen's face floods with sudden red, a maddened bull of a man. Once he had told Bhari that his son ran away from him straight into the spinning blades of the VitD fan. "Because he didn't listen!" he shouts now. "He didn't listen!" He swallows, breathes heavily. "Just get those wires out of him or I'll do it myself."

"Okay." It would be kinder in the long run to disconnect Hum gently. The sudden shock of disconnect could kill the kid.

She elevates Hum's head, searches for the place to start. There should be a knot of connectors right below the hypothalamus. It would suck when she made the first moves, but she can move slowly, take Hum down to her mental level in several stages.

Her tiny pliers and screwdrivers, as well as her omnitool, are spread out on the attached tray. Bhari selects the first instruments and gets to work, unspooling tight controllers and headers from the silver slots drilled into Hum's head.

He doesn't wake until she's on the fifth connection. Hum wakes with a howl, eyes flying open and spittle on his chin. "What!" he shouts. "What are you doing to me?"

"Chest restraint," she says. "Crippen! Are you listening? Get him stabilized or I won't be able to …"

The entire room plunges into darkness so complete Bhari can taste it: metallic and tinged with fear. For a moment the unimaginable cubic meters of earth above them crush her with their mere presence. What if there's a structural failure and the Alliance caves in?

Crippen saves her by switching on the search lamp mounted on his rifle. "We don't have time for this." His words are matter-of-fact as he pushes her to one side, sweeps her instruments off the tray.

There is a moment of shocked incomprehension before Bhari realizes what he is going to do. Blinding rage makes her gag as she chokes out the words: "No. Don't. No. General Crippen, stop." And, above all, the desperate question, "Why?"

"I'm saving the Alliance," Crippen states quietly. He had been just as calm when he had saved Bhari from Ivenko, a driftbag who thought slaps and punches were foreplay. "Gonna cut off the expendables and take the survivors into Military until we can regroup, get the power back online." Crippen sniffs before he brings the butt of his rifle down on Hum's motherboard.

The kid howls, a horrible sound filled with loss and unimaginable pain. Bhari covers her skull with both arms. By the time she raises her head, the room is dark again and Crippen is gone. His final order for her to take care of it echoes in the heartbroken darkness.

"Gray. Slow – it's so slow." Hum's voice is cracked, harsh from his prolonged screams of agony. "I've got nothing. Can't port in, can't move like an EMO, don't even have a name …"

"What the hell are you talking about? You have a name." Bhari supports the kid with one arm around his waist. Their flashlight dots the hallways, intersecting with similar blue beams as terrified Alliance inhabitants rush to unknown destinations.

"No. Hum was the first three letters – my hardware covered the rest. Now… now I'm just Human 273." He stops, tugs at her backpack. "Got a deathcharge? Anything? Just do it. You heard Crippen. I'm expendable."

"Bloody Alliance, shut your mouth until we get inside the Farm." Bhari drags him inside the dark space, interspersed with the gentle glow of grow-lamps whose batteries have not run out yet. "Now. Tell me what happened to Ash. How did you find that elevator leading up to the Surface?"

Hum nods, nearly falls from the effort. "We were supposed to escape. Together. We were going together."

"Yeah." Bhari straightens, puts one hand on the small of her back to ease it. "Well, now you've got me instead. There's another escape hatch, right? And I think you know where it's located."

His eyes slit as he answers, "I knew about the hatch because I was enhanced. I could port in and use the intel to create a plan – but now I have nothing."

"Don't act like a baby." Bhari wants to slap him until she remembers the marks Ivenko left on her, bruises and black eyes. "Hum. Listen to me. You've got the same as I do – a perfectly good working brain. I've done okay with it so far, and now you've simply got to deal."

"No." His gaze is firm, lips compressed, all decision and whipcord. She can see why Ash is so attracted to the kid. "I'll give you the coordinates, but you're going alone. At least I got Ash out of this hellhole."

Bhari realizes she is going to have to be merciless, even cruel, to save the little idiot's life. "Got him out? And for what? He's drifting around on the surface right now, facing – who knows what he has to confront. Mutants? Fire? Or just meters and meters of dust?" A prickle in her nose tells her they just ran out of time to argue. "Tell me, right now. And you're coming with me. No arguments."

Hum considers and Bhari bites her tongue. Any second Crippen could burst in, bellowing orders and the decision that she and Hum are both expendable. "Okay," he finally says and points to the agar tanks.

The hatch behind the tanks is older than anything Bhari has ever imagined. When she and Hum are inside, she sees the passage is lined with bricks. The walls, once white and glossy, are now broken and soiled with filth. They have just enough room to walk upright in the tunnels. Every fifty meters there's another flight of stairs pitched at an impossible angle. The steps are also broken or, in some cases, missing altogether. Sometimes she has to stop and use her stolen karabiners to haul them to the top.

After what feels like several days of hopeless slogging in the dark, Hum's breath catches. "Need to …" She just manages to catch his arm in both fists before he pitches forward.

Bhari allows them both a mouthful of water from her pack, plus half a flax cracker each. "How're you doing?" she asks.

He is slumped forward, head cradled between thin arms. "Gray," he repeats. "Slow."

She can only imagine what it would be like to lose most of her mental capacity, to have the ability to port in and out of the whole Alliance and get shut out. "You didn't lose everything," she soothes. "My engineering thesis was on residual intelligence. The powers you had should still be traced in your brain cells – you just have to find new ways to access them. They'll be slower than you're used to, but they're intact."

He grunts, a sound of disbelief. After a few minutes she repacks and stands up. "Keep going," she orders.

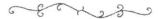

Their next stop is when they nearly fall off a long flight of stairs. One karabiner fails and breaks, nearly pitching them into a large pit of broken bricks. In the darkness they look like teeth. Hum shouts it was her fault, she didn't place it correctly. Bhari feels her hand curl into a fist, senses the exact amount of drive and power necessary to punch him in his stomach for some blessed silence and the end of Hum's nagging.

Two breaths, three. Bhari recaps the water bottle. "Let's keep going."

At the next stop she lets him sleep for a few minutes. While he's out she trickles some of their precious water over the wound on the back of his neck. For the most part the blood has dried, but Bhari can see the tattoo: HUMAN 273.

Asleep, he looks very young. Long eyelashes cast fanned shadows on his sharp cheekbones in the beam of her light. She steels herself and wakes him, stands and hefts the bag to her shoulder.

"I know, I know," he grumbles, getting to his feet.

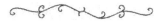

They climb in silence, their breath whistling in the stale air. A landfall could bury them under massive tons of rock. They could hit a pocket of carbon dioxide. Bhari tries not to think about those possibilities. Moving through the darkness is awful, eerie. Strange shapes seem to rush at them as her brain creates sensory images out of black deprivation.

Bhari thinks she sees her old boyfriend, his hand swept back to crack her across one ear. It is not until Hum's arm shoots out and catches her elbow that she realizes what was about to happen.

Every muscle in her body shaking, Bhari switches on her flashlight and shines it ahead. The floor in front of them has caved in, and she has nearly fallen into the hole. She turns to Hum, her eyes widening. "How did you …?"

"Echolocation," he whispers. "It's coming back." A huge grin splits his face. "It's coming back! I can sense the passage of time, too – run a mental clock. Uh, you were right. I guess."

She nods, digs in her pack. "Can you estimate how far we have left?" The water in the bottle sloshes as she holds it up. "Will this get us up to the surface?"

Hum studies it, purses his lips. "Depends on how destroyed the stairs are up ahead."

Bhari holds the bottle to her cheek as though the moisture could leach through her skin. "It'll worsen the closer we get to the blast."

"Oh." Hum closes his eyes, breathes. "We've probably got to double the time between rest-stops."

"Can you time it? Tell me when we should stop?"

He nods.

During the next few climbs Bhari realizes she has put her life into the hands of a damaged enhancement. Her mind tries to trick her, to tell her that he is drawing out their travel periods. Surely they should be stopping by now? She makes herself count to a hundred, a thousand, ten thousand.

At last Hum calls time. They slump, exhausted, against the wall, and he tells her they can only have one sip each of the warm water.

She nearly hauls off and slaps him but manages to tamp her fury. Bloody Alliance, Ivenko influenced me more than I knew, Bhari thinks.

Reality wobbles in and out in the pitch black. She sees floating squids, luminescent whales. Hum hands her a few flakes of phytoplankton, and she nearly knocks the food out of his hands to avoid a nonexistent shoal of eels.

"Time to move." His voice is thick with exhaustion. She and Hum get to their feet and keep going.

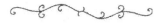

Hum's second warning comes too late. Bhari trips, and the bag flies off her shoulder. There's a sickening thump. All their supplies fly out, skittering in the dark. They have to go on hands and knees to find what is left. When Bhari discovers the flashlight and turns it on, the beam shows just how close she came to pitching into another cave-in under their feet. As it is, their water and extra food have disappeared into the hole and are lost.

"You go," Hum declares. "Find Ash, and tell him – tell him…"

"We're both going," Bhari insists.

"I saw how you looked at him." Hum's tone is accusing. "You can sexbond with him once you Surface."

"What?" Bhari slumps. Any second Crippen could come after them, or the whole shaft could implode. "I – Hum, Ash is a beautiful guy, but… but…"

"But?" he prompts, fierce and young.

"I'm not made that way," she confesses. "Prefer tech to people, to be honest. I… I admire beauty, but there's no desire behind it." It is the most personal thing she has ever divulged.

Hum lets his head fall back against the wall of the shaft. The white bricks are covered with mold, but he does not seem to notice. "He'd be better off with you," he whispers.

She is about to tell him he is strong too, and she could not have made it this far without him, when the ground underneath them rumbles. Far below there is an ominous creak, a prolonged grumble from the earth itself.

"Alliance drift!" Bhari swears. "What the hell was that?"

Hum jumps to his feet. "Explosion." His lips pull back from his teeth. "In the Alliance. Gonna cause aftershocks."

They run, the slim beam of the flashlight picking up the tunnel. There are more holes now, and they have to weave to avoid them. Hum's breath whistles in his chest, and Bhari can almost feel the boy's pain.

There's another rumble below, and Bhari loses her footing. As she goes down, the flashlight skitters out of her hand. A moment later there is a tiny thud, and they are left in the dark.

After so much running and urging Hum to keep on moving, Bhari is at the end of her strength. She hears someone cursing worse than a seasoned EMO, and after a minute she realizes the voice is her own. "This is it." Bhari slumps against the wall. "I'm sorry, kid. We're at the end of the adventure – looks like we lost this round." Maybe she can find a sharp edge to take them both out so they do not have to suffer the slow horror of death by thirst and hunger. Or maybe…

Her hand moves under the hem of her shirt, finds the knotted string. There's a whistle on it, the one Crippen gave her when he rescued her from Ivenko. *Keep this on you so I can reach you,* he had told her at the time. *Anyone touches you, sound the whistle and I'll be there.* If she blows it now, would the EMO's find her and Hum? Put bullets through their brains to end the suffering?

"No." Hum shakes her shoulder. "No, Bhari. Look!"

He takes her hand and points ahead, angled up to where the Surface must lie. Ahead of them in the black there's a distinct rectangle – the outline of an open door.

It is the first time either of them have seen the sky.

Wiping away her tears, Bhari scrambles up from the floor. Holding Hum's fingers, she follows the boy and heads towards the little square of blue.

As they get closer a small shape soars across the framed view of the Surface. Squinting fiercely, Bhari can just make out what it is. The shape appears to hover in the wind a moment, and emits a klee-klee-klee of victory: the triumphant call of a kestrel.

363

Part 3 – Surface

When Hum emerges from the tunnel with Bhari's arm firmly tucked around him, no one is there. She tilts her head back, perhaps to feel actual wind on her face, and Hum nearly weeps at all the color around them. Trees covered with moss stretch overhead and as far off as they can see. The silence is broken only by their footsteps as Bhari prods him forward.

They are still in a desperate position. All their supplies were lost in the dark during the explosions, and at any moment Crippen could emerge with his neural rifle. Neither of them know what to expect from this new land – hordes of mutants or pockets of deadly radiation. They have no food, no water. Neither of them is enhanced.

Hum realizes that he is at least able to lead them in a straight line, following the flight of the kestrel they saw from underground. The air is so fresh it is intoxicating, cold and pure in his lungs.

Bhari asks him to echolocate for water, for human life. Each time his signal returns – nothing but trees.

And there is more. Hum's neck has begun to itch in a deadly, sickening way. He knows some sort of infection has started where Crippen knocked off the hardware, boiling under the inked letters of HUMAN 273. Screwing his eyes, Hum ignores the pain until the white noise returns to his ears, the scratchy song of disease.

His inner clock ticks up several hours before the light fades and he slumps to the ground in the woods. There are leaves heaped underneath them, and more moss. "Leave me," Hum begs Bhari through chattering teeth. "Waste of effort." She shakes her head, and it strikes him how calm she always is. Her forehead never lines with worry – she simply sees what has to be done and does it.

"Find Ash," Hum whispers. The white noise increases in volume.

Even now her face does not reveal panic. "Inner clock still working?" Bhari asks.

"What? Yeah, I guess so."

"Blow on this every six minutes." She pulls the string off her neck and presses a tube into his fingers, slotted with holes at top and bottom – a brass whistle. "I'm going to fan out, see if I can find Ash or some help."

Ghabrie. Is she among the trees, sliding through shadows with her hawk on one shoulder? Is Ash with her? Hum nods and takes the whistle. Through the scratches in his brain he hears her boots crunch through the leaves. Even Bhari's footsteps are filled with determination.

His inner clock begins the countdown, rewinding numbers flashing red inside his eyelids. When they reach zero, Hum puts the whistle to his lips and blows. At the thin sound the peeper frogs suddenly stop courting each other. The effort nearly makes Hum vomit, and he realizes just how badly off he is. His neck is on fire, and he moans.

Air moves against his cheek, and suddenly a dark figure is bent over him. "Bhari," Hum croaks. "Not working – just go and find him. Find Ash."

"Hey," the dark figure whispers. "Hum. I'm right here." Someone feels for the whistle on Hum's neck and blows it again – two sharp blasts. Hum is lifted by corded arms, held against a hard chest. He whimpers as the movement jostles his neck, and the person tells him sorry, says he will bring him to the camp as quickly as possible.

After that there is a confusion of motion and heat, interspersed with flashes of vision. Flames, with people seated around the fire. Grumbles from a bird perched on someone's shoulder. Intelligent eyes under heavy brows; Bhari's face, and her clipped speech as she talks to another girl.

And above all, black hair slipping over Hum's shoulder as he's put down in some sort of bedroll before strong, broad palms frame his face and a boy kisses Hum's cheek again and again as though he never wants to stop.

Ash.

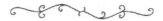

Part 4 – Ash and Hum

"It won't work as well as what you used to have, but you'll be able to port in." Bhari brushes Hum's hair back and fiddles with the wires, her gaze intent on the tech.

"Looking good." Across from them, Ash grins and leans back on his wrists, his teeth white in a huge grin.

"Port into what?" Hum huffs. "It's not as though there's an intranet handy."

"Thank you, Bhari," Bhari says pointedly, although one cheek dimples.

"My man, grumpy as always." Ash hits Hum's foot with his own, until Bhari yells at them to knock it off while she works.

"Hey." The girl Ghabrie squats next to them, and instantly Ash stops fooling around. Her face is tired but filled with determination. "We're reclaiming tech each day. You might be the key to finding – finding someone very important."

They all know whom Ghabrie means. As she turns around to shout for her hawk, Hum catches a flash of the girl's own tat: HUMAN 76.

"Ready?" Bhari nudges him, and he nods. There's a pop at the base of his skull, and Hum is flooded with input. Above all, there's the music he's grown used to, the constant dance of information and analysis.

Hum cannot find the words to explain. "Yeah?" Ash asks. "That good, huh?" With a flourish he holds up one fist, an offering to port in.

Hum jerks up the frayed cuff of his jacket. Next to him he can feel Bhari holding her breath. Hum ports into Ash's wrist, and it is as though they have always been together.

"Looks like it's holding up." Bhari rises and jams her screwdriver into one beltloop. "I'll calibrate in a few hours, test the ports and make certain everything's working." With a final wink, she follows Ghabrie into the woods.

Nothing left, Hum thinks, except to test out the connection levels between me and Ash.

H: <*Didn't mean it. Didn't mean anything I said by the elevator. Just had to get you out of there.*>

A: <*I know. Gonna beat you up over that later, though.*>

H: <*I. Ash.*>

A: <*I know. I know.*>

Slowly their lips touch, slotting together as Ash deepens the kiss. The music flows between them, a sweet ballad filled with something like hope.

WE MAKE THE FUTURE

Lisa Shambrook

"Is there nothing else you can locate in your files?" Ghabrie grumbled. It was hot, as hot as a wolf spider's sandy armpit and Ghabrie could barely hide her frustration.

Hum ran his thin fingers through his long hair as he shook his head. "What else do you expect me to find?" His sigh made guilt churn in Ghabrie's belly. "I've searched everything I've got left, and it's not a full system, you know that!" He glanced up at Ash.

"Nothing about Nahria?" Ghabrie insisted. "Nothing more at all?"

He shook his head. "Nothing more than you already know."

Ash placed a protective hand on Hum's shoulder. "He's tried everything."

Ghabrie scowled and glared as Bhari threw her a frown. She held up her hands. "I'm done. It's fine." Ghabrie got to her feet. "There's nothing more I can do sitting around here. Tomorrow I move. Anyone who wants to come with me is welcome, but don't get in my way."

Thirty-Six flinched and Bhari wrapped her arms tightly around the broken creature. "Of course we're coming!" she sounded indignant. "We're not simply a group of waifs and strays you've picked up. Thirty-Six will follow you to the ends of the earth. You asked Maeve to join you once before and now she's come all this way to be here. As for the rest of us, well, without us how would you be learning more about what happened deep underneath?"

"But you haven't located Nahria."

"Nor have you," shot back Bhari.

Ghabrie cast a look of pure venom and stalked away. "I'm relieving Maeve of her watch. Be ready to move in the morning if you're coming."

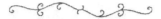

From the cleft in the hills, Ghabrie had a clear view of the entire terrain. All except the area behind the cliffs, but Thirty-Six had recovered enough sensing ability in rehabilitation to warn them if anyone tried to sneak up from behind. She let out a sigh and pushed the feeling of guilt back down into her stomach where she could pretend it was pangs of hunger. She gazed down at her group moving in the woods below, their safety in her hands and their trust given unconditionally. She swallowed, true hunger twisting in her belly like a dagger.

A sharp cry from the skies brought her to alertness. Kee, kee, kee and Ghabrie shielded her eyes from the burning sun to watch her kestrel circle. His movements were smooth and his glide soft upon the currents, but his watchful gaze was trained and his pitches deliberate. She followed his direction and rose to her feet. Shimmering on the horizon was a figure, a dark hulk of a man, and beside him loped a creature large enough to be a wolf. Ghabrie pulled in a sharp breath and hopped down the scree like a mountain goat, reaching the wooded hollow before the others heard a sound.

On her silent order six bodies melted into the trees, hidden amongst brush, moss and thorns. Only the cry of the kestrel offered a sharp warning of company.

"I know you're here." The man was large, bigger than Ash. He loosely held a two-foot knife. "And even if I didn't, how long do you think it would take Freddie here to sniff you all out?"

"I see you've learned how to do up a zip," Ghabrie's voice was uncharacteristically soft and teasing.

The man chuckled and ran stubby fingers up the front of his jacket, his fingernails clicking against the zip's metal teeth.

"How did you find us?" asked Ghabrie, stepping out from behind a tree.

"Taking no chances, I see," he said motioning to the shimmer of the blade in her hand.

"There's a bow trained on you too, and a strong mind melding with your hound." Ghabrie's hand rested on her dagger. "No chances. How did you find us?"

"Followed your windhover."

"Not possible, he's veiled!"

The man chuckled again. "Exactly how I followed him, and you. Every time I tried to sense him I was blocked by a huge, solid wall. I just needed to keep that wall on the horizon."

"How did we not sense you? How did Thirty-Six miss you?" She flung an annoyed glance at the crop of rocks hiding her comrades. "How long have you been following me?"

"That's not the question you should be asking." He whistled and his dog jogged back to his side.

"Why have you been following me?" Ghabrie tried.

The man gave a small nod. "I know where Nahria is."

Ghabrie gasped. She had not felt Nahria in a while. That scared her. She had crossed hills and valleys, scoured mountains and deserts in her quest to find her little sister; a quest that seemed to have lasted countless seasons. She had been focussed on the emotions that called to her, the colours that tinged her world. She could see Nahria or at least feel her. Colours beckoned, purple and black the most, pain and fear, until just recently her colours had dimmed and faded. They'd moved to dismal grey and bruised mauve and spiked in red and gold before softly switching to the green of a meadow; the kind of green Ghabrie had never known except in stories handed down through the ages, stories told by old Alphaeus and those who'd survived the Blast. She knew it was the green of life, of lush grass and she had no idea what the colour meant. Her sister had faded to an imaginary green and she had lost her again. Here and now, though, the wild man claimed to know where she was.

She could not speak.

Freddie whined as the man let a backpack fall from his shoulder. Wary, Ghabrie stepped back. Maeve moved out of the trees with Ghabrie's bow notched and aimed. The man raised his hands and kicked the bag forward. "You saved my life, Ghabrie, I'm not about to screw you over. I also know you're not a myth, not a wraith or a ghost, but flesh and blood like the rest of us. I know too that you need help. Have your tech guys look inside."

Bhari emerged from behind a tumble of rocks followed by Ash and Hum. She moved cautiously towards the bag on the ground. She gazed at it for a moment, her eyes twinkling at the thought of something new, anything to stimulate her mind more than the occasional routine tuning of Hum's enhancements. She dropped to her knees but hesitated.

"There's no booby-traps. I just don't know what to do with that lot." The man motioned to the rucksack. He kicked an area clear of pine needles and cones and lowered himself to the ground. "I can do stuff, but not this stuff."

Maeve kept her bow trained on him, but relaxed her grip as Bhari plunged her hands inside the bag. "Where did you get this?" Bhari asked pulling out a small metal cylinder and smoothing a tangle of blue and white wires through her fingers.

"Is that …?" Hum's eyes grew wide as he reached for the cylinder and measured it against the port in his wrist.

Bhari nodded. "A storage device – and there's more. A keyboard. Ugh!" She screwed up her face as she extricated the keypad from the mess of personal items inside the backpack. She ignored the man's grin and brandished the console. "Like I said, where did you get this?"

"And are you being followed?" asked Ghabrie, glancing at the trees surrounding them.

Maeve tightened her fingers on the bow.

He shook his head. "Freddie saw to them."

"Them?" asked Ash.

"The rats, the tunnel rats."

Hum flinched. "Underground?"

"Yep, from underneath, but no match for me." The man chuckled.

"We're from underneath too." Hum blinked and gazed at the cylinder resting on the warmth of his palm.

Bhari placed a warning hand across the bullet sized chamber as he held it to his port. She bit her lip. "Is it safe?"

"That's what I'm asking you." The man cleared his throat. "I didn't kill anyone to get it, not this time. The Resistance is everywhere, underneath, on the surface, in the hills and this lot were keen to get rid of the tech before it got discovered in their possession." His long fingers drew absent circles in the dust on the ground. "Cievette said –"

"Who?" Ghabrie's curiosity surged at the familiar name.

"Cievette, one of the tunnel rats, sewer rats – though a good looking one." He licked his lips." She was keen to get this intel out there, above ground – and to you. Thus, here I am." He spread his hands with a flourish that looked out of place from the muscular man sitting cross-legged on the ground.

Ghabrie watched as Bhari and Hum investigated the hardware, their faces hidden behind Bhari's dark curtain of hair. She nodded. "Go ahead, it'll be safe."

Ash opened his mouth to protest, but Hum had already plugged the drive into his wrist port.

"What can you see?" demanded Ghabrie.

"Give him a minute!" said Ash, falling to his knees and placing his hands protectively on the boy's shoulders.

"The Alliance – not Pandora – the Promethean Alliance, the one more desperately searching for Ghabrie." He shook his head. "It's muddled. And … Stein?"

Ghabrie flinched as Bhari grabbed the keypad and tapped, ignoring Hum's wince as a screech whined through the still air, setting off Freddie. The dog jumped up and paced. She worked rapidly unplugging a connection, spitting on it and plugging it back in again. Hum sat up straight.

"Nahria!" he cried. "She just flashed across the images. I could tell it was her!"

"Why? How?" Ghabrie paled.

He shook his head. "Between pictures of you, they know you're looking for her."

"Where is she?" asked Ghabrie her fingers trembling, "What else do you see?"

"There are names, places. The Benanti Institute. It says the Promethean Alliance moved out months ago – it's abandoned. The information is so corrupt – it's hard to say what it all means – but someone's there, up in the mountains in the remains of the institute."

Freddie barked but the large hand on his neck calmed him. "It's okay, boy." The man turned to Ghabrie. "I know who's up in the mountains."

Ghabrie bit back the emotions that swam through her mind and faced him. She'd had enough of this cat-and-mouse guessing game. She strode forward until her scuffed boots were toe-to-toe with his. She glared down at him, swallowed the bile in her mouth and curled her lip. "Tell me everything you know, and everything Cievette told you."

He laughed, which settled the dog who dropped down beside him, and he cracked his knuckles. "I know that the institute was lost to the Alliance. Then rebels took it. When the rebels found it looted and empty another group took it. This group stole from the Alliance, so they're not exactly advertising their whereabouts, but their leader is regrouping, or hiding, one or the other, up there. Or so I believe."

"And what does all this have to do with Nahria?"

"I think you told Cievette about your sister; it wasn't something you shared with me." He raised an eyebrow. "Nahria's with them, up in the hills. With Jarek and his men."

"Jarek!" The name spewed from Maeve's mouth like a poisoned waterfall.

"The Jarek you escaped from?" Ghabrie stared at her.

Maeve shook her head. "I don't know, but there can't be too many with that name who are on the run from the Alliance. Whatever you decide to do, Ghabrie, I'm right there at your side."

"We go now. Right now." Ghabrie looked along the rag-tag line of mismatched comrades in the wooded glade.

Bhari still sat, head bent, dark hair swathing her features as usual, working on the cylinder that was still ported to Hum. Hum had relaxed back into Ash's arms, as mental images and code flooded his mind. If she wanted tech, Bhari and Hum were a necessity. Muscle – and loyalty, if Hum was part of her group – came courtesy of

Ash. Maeve's red hair burned like her eyes, boring holes into Ghabrie's face as the girl stared at her with pure intensity, and Thirty-Six stood, slightly lost, to the side, but determined to accompany Ghabrie, her redeemer, to the ends of the earth.

"I'll come with you if you'll have me. I'm bored. I could do with a little adventure." Freddie yipped as his owner stood and invited himself into Ghabrie's band. She did not object. The man grabbed his backpack from Bhari's feet and slung it over his shoulder on top of a bigger bag fixed to his back. "It's early, and we've got a lot of miles to cover. You lot ready?"

Ghabrie grinned, and electricity tingled down her spine. For a moment she recalled sneaking away in the early hours, many moons ago, with only her kestrel swooping and offering company. Maybe this time, with friends and comrades, she would find her sister and her journey could end. Ghabrie was tired of travelling, but not tired enough to stop, not yet. "C'mon, let's go!"

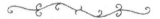

The sun burned down, and the sparse woodland opened out into desert and rough dirt tracks. After a while there was nothing behind them, nothing in front, and barely anything but scrubland and faraway mountains either side. Ghabrie stopped to take a swig of water from her canteen and glanced up at her kestrel.

"The windhover's keeping watch," the wild man's deep voice comforted her and Ghabrie looked at him.

"So, what is your name?" she asked.

His lip curled in amusement. He shook his head. "I have no name."

"Since you won't tell me, I'm going to call you Eastwood." She flashed him a grin as his appreciative laugh bellowed beneath the hot sun. "And, Eastwood, thanks for not giving me up – to the Hybrid." Ghabrie flushed a little as he regarded her.

"You didn't really need saving and I think you saved me right back before you disappeared. Do you know how hard it is to get an explanation from a dog?" Ghabrie smirked. He smiled and continued. "I've been meaning to ask, if it's not too personal, what happened to the gash across your stomach? It was deep and I thought you were dead."

"That was the plan." Ghabrie glanced down at her stomach and ran a hand across her leather corset fingering the slash within the material and deep abrasions over the buckles.

"Was it superficial?"

She shook her head. "No, it was deep."

"Then you needed stiches?"

"I should have, but it healed."

"On its own?"

"It took time, it was painful, but it healed. I have a scar." If Ghabrie had been about to say anything else she was interrupted by a bark and a squeal loud enough to raise the dead. They both swung round to see what had spooked Freddie.

"Something's coming!" yelled Thirty-Six.

"What is it?" cried Ghabrie.

Thirty-Six shook and whirled about on the spot, her feet creating a dusty whirlwind. "Over there, beyond them mountains. Something's coming!"

"On bikes, quads … and there's something else? Chasing someone … something?" Eastwood tried to sense more.

"No!" Ghabrie told him, "Let Thirty-Six do it, let her sense." Ghabrie coaxed the girl as she stared into the far distance.

"Men." Thirty-Six closed her eyes and screwed up her forehead. Her teeth chattered and her skinny body quivered. "Four of them, but I can't see what they're chasing. They're hunting dogs, and something else I can't make out. They're closing."

Ghabrie peered at the mountains and sure enough a plume of yellow dust rose from the foot of the peaks. She closed her eyes and freed her own mind. Colours of panic and fear, indigo and black, blurred together and noise rushed through her brain. Not Nahria. She opened her eyes. "We need to move, get out of here! They're coming this way, fast!"

The group took off down the hard, dirt track, but the noise and dust cloud got closer and louder. There was no cover near and no way to avoid confrontation.

Bullets whipped past Ghabrie's head. Engines growled and roared and what sounded like hooves pounded the ground behind them, echoing across the plains. "Stop!" shouted Ghabrie. "At arms!"

The group fell to their knees and pulled weapons, turning to face the oncoming commotion. A figure leaned forward across the neck of a strange beast as it galloped hard, accompanied by two hurtling dogs, one dark, one light. Bikes scrambled behind them and loud whoops and catcalls thundered in the dusty air. The thick, grimy cloud behind the bikes rose like a blustering sand-storm. Ghabrie screamed "SHOOT!"

"At what?" yelled Ash. "At the weird thing or those chasing it?"

The sandstorm whipped away her answer as she released a volley of arrows and bullets flew from Ash's pistols. Suddenly a huge explosion, a fireball of angry red and orange, knocked them all sideways.

The bikes whirled into the air through charred, black clouds of oily smoke. They crashed down onto rock and dirt. Metal, skin, bone and blood flew through the air, and beneath the ringing in her ears Ghabrie heard loud guffaws beside her. She turned, scrabbling to sit back up, dirt in her fingernails and blotches of colour in her eyes, to see Freddie licking his master's face. Eastwood wielded a hefty gun. A colossal black cannon that rested on his arm, smoking from the wide muzzle that pointed at where the bikes had been.

The galloping creature still bolted towards them, its terrified eyes as wide and bulging. Ghabrie scrambled to her feet as the ugly animal began to slow and the rider, red and sweaty but with a wide grin, sat upright. The woman whooped "I am Fury!" she yelled, her voice cracking with effort. "I am – oh hawntch!" she cursed as her top hat fell to the ground.

The lumbering beast drew to a halt. The animal wheezed and coughed and stood shakily on wide legs. The girl patted him furiously, praising him and promising him a song. Then she glanced up and at the group assembled before her. "I am Fury," she gasped, "… I am Glint!" this time her introduction was a little more restrained as she puffed then she stared at Ghabrie and squinted. "Oh, I know you!" she panted.

"It's been a while." Ghabrie nodded, shaking her head to try to get rid of the infernal buzzing.

"And thanks for the BOOM. Smith could have outrun them – perhaps – but you know, thanks anyway." Glint grinned and whistled through her teeth. She smudged more dirt across her face as she wiped her forehead. "So, where are we heading?"

"What the … What is that thing?" Maeve could barely take her eyes off the beast. "Is that an overgrown mutant sheep or what? I mean, I've seen a sheep before and that's so not one."

Glint grinned even wider. "Smith's a llama, crossed with a bunch of I-have-no-idea, and then mutated. He don't care what you call him, as long as he gets grass, water and a song every now and then. Do you sing?" Maeve's face fell, and Glint gazed at Ghabrie. "Did I say something wrong?"

As Thirty-Six crept up to the great beast, Maeve allowed a smile to curve. Thirty-Six gently ran her fingers through the llama's thick fur and leaned close to sniff the creature. She recoiled and the whole group laughed.

"He 'aint had a bath in a good while but when you need something warm to snuggle up to on a frozen night, you won't care what he whiffs of!" Glint slid off Smith's back. Maeve handed her the top hat, which gleamed for a moment as the light touched it. "We okay to join you, just for a bit? It looks like Maddie and Samson are good." Her two dogs were frolicking with Freddie as though discovering a long lost friend. "And I think we owe you big. I've been alone longer than should be and I could do with some company, and not the sort that was chasing me."

Freddie had indeed taken to Glint's companions and even the llama no longer seemed a threat to the huge grey dog. Glint appraised Ghabrie's friends. "You look hungry and tired. If we travel for a while longer, when the sun drops behind that peak there'll be an outcrop of rocks and a stream. Danger's gone for now, especially with that bazooka of your man's, and I've got food enough to share. I've not long come from the Tour."

"I'm not her man – or anyone's – but we've something in common. You got soup?" Freddie whined as his man spoke. "Barleybean …?"

"… glop!" finished Glint and chuckled. "Need to warm it up; and I've got muskrat too." She nodded towards the saddlebags on Smith. "We'll eat tonight." She gave Ghabrie a look. "David?"

"He found what he was looking for."

"But you still haven't. You still searching for your sister?"

"I am. Got a good lead, too. It's where we're headed now."

"Can I come?"

Ghabrie grinned. "Join us, Glint." She gave a mock bow and Glint tipped her top hat. "Let's head for that sunset."

Maeve smiled as Glint helped Thirty-Six up onto the shaggy llama's long back. "… and I might even have a little song for Smith."

As they later rested amongst a hidden crop of rocks, Glint fed them all. Barleybean glop and roasted muskrat tasted like the food of kings as the sun faded and night's indigo blanketed the world. As stars glittered Maeve sang, and bittersweet remembrance filled the little creek.

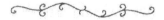

Feet ached and even Smith faltered as rocks and scree clattered beneath his hooves. Only the dogs and Ghabrie seemed surefooted enough to push past the blistered pain barrier.

"How are we even sure she's here?" Ash puffed as he hauled Hum's slim frame along beside him.

"We're not." Ghabrie refused to turn and deftly jumped across a narrow ravine.

"I … I can't be sure of the information," Hum could barely speak. "So much corruption –"

"But we keep going," said Ghabrie, her eyes focussed ahead. "I've been here before."

"And she wasn't there then." Bhari's voice travelled on the cool breeze that floated across the mountains.

Ghabrie shook her head and stopped. "No, no she wasn't." She glanced up at her kestrel circling on the currents and then faced her crew. "She wasn't. Neither was she out in the Foreman Wilds, or underneath in the tunnels. I didn't find her in the domes or in the temples or in any of the laboratories I tracked down. Glint met me heading out here the first time after her father's death." She looked at Glint and her eyes softened. "Then David helped, and no, we didn't find Nahria but we found others, and I determined I would never stop until I found her. When I got here the last time, the place was abandoned. It looked like prisoners had been there, the same as the old zoo down beyond the Tour, but this time there were no notecards, no clues – nothing! We had to start again." Ghabrie's voice rang out clear echoing over the snow-capped peaks. "It was the same when I searched the old mansion where Maeve was being held; nothing and no one. But people have seen her; they've passed on messages, and kept me going. Nahria knows I'm looking for her. She's waiting for me!" She flashed her eyes at Hum. "Your intel says this place is not yet finished – and nor am I."

"So we keep moving," said Maeve, "We keep going until we find what we're looking for."

"If she's still alive," said Bhari, glancing sideways at Ghabrie. "You can't see the future and we don't even know if she's still alive."

Ghabrie's shoulders broadened as she raised her head and met Bhari's eyes. "I can't see the future, or read it, but what I do know, is that I can make it. I make the future. And my future is with Nahria."

Bhari nodded, her expression full of respect. "Then we're with you, no matter what."

The going was tough. Glint gave up Smith for Thirty-Six and Hum to ride, and she walked with Bhari.

"Your windhover's circling lower." Freddie loped beside his master. "Your windhover's seen something," said Eastwood.

"I know." Ghabrie paused and closed her eyes. Green, meadow green, flooded her mind and she gasped. A wall hit her, flashing through her mind and throwing up a barrier that struck as Ghabrie tried to see past it. She grabbed her head and winced.

"I feel it too!" cried Thirty-Six leaning forward on Smith's back.

"What do you feel?" asked Ghabrie as her kestrel called from the sky.

"Someone's there, someone with power, someone like me." Thirty-Six slipped off the llama and hurried forward grabbing Ghabrie's hand. "Follow me!"

"I – I know the way!" stuttered Ghabrie, but she followed Thirty-Six down the dusty pass into the shadow of the mountain. Tears stung as a gale whipped through the narrow gorge and Ghabrie struggled to push against both the wind and the barrier that fought with her mind.

Bottles, abandoned equipment and broken tools, detritus left behind during a quick exit, littered the way and a sign hung loose from a rusty nail. The word: NANTI announced itself in chipped and faded paint like the broken and abandoned place that it named.

"I feel pain!" wailed Thirty-Six.

"Whose pain? Yours, or...?" Ghabrie's desperation peaked as her voice rose.

"Yours."

Ghabrie stopped and planted her feet firmly in the dusty sand. She had no idea her emotions had surfaced so strongly, and for a moment she tried to bury them with the roiling guilt in her belly. She closed her eyes and concentrated, but her own anxiety engulfed her. Fear clouded her vision as apprehension and stress kicked her in the gut. She could not feel her sister and hated having to rely on someone else, even Thirty-Six. Colours danced but they were colours of trepidation, nerves, fear, anger and bravado. Blues and reds blurred with black and gold – and orange burned beneath them all, a fire of bravado and courage. Her eyes fluttered open and she regarded her comrades. They stood beside her, brave and lost, scared and valiant, daring and heroic. The colours radiated about them and Ghabrie attempted a lopsided grin.

"We've nothing to lose," she said quietly, but firmly. "Let's find out what's hiding from us."

Thirty-Six tightened her fingers around Ghabrie's then let go and stepped forward with Freddie loping beside her. "I have a connection! It's fragile, but it's there."

The kestrel called again, his cry echoing across the range, far away into the Shadow Mountain. Ghabrie whistled. He descended in a spiral and glided through the gorge to land on Ghabrie's leather clad shoulder. Hope surged through the girl as she gently kissed his feathers and followed Thirty-Six with fierce determination.

The iron gates – solid, riveted doors built into the rocks – hung open, broken and bent. The group moved through them, in single file, and only Smith's feet plodded with a gentle thud on the parched, cracked earth. Glint, crossbow at the ready, moved ahead of Thirty-Six, who refused to carry a weapon. Ghabrie slid alongside her with an arrow notched and her dagger glinting at her waist. Beyond the gates the valley within the mountain spread before them and for a moment Ghabrie felt a stab of homesickness. The valley stretched between two mountain ranges, protected from both the elements and attack. A sheer cliff dropped on the south and huge steel battle walls rose from the mountain edge in the north. Ghabrie lowered her bow and raised her hand to halt her troop. She listened intently but only the sound of the wind answered as it shrilled through the peaks.

"Where is everyone?" hissed Ash, holding one of Ghabrie's pistols at shoulder level.

Bhari clutched Ghabrie's knives, and Maeve let her fingers caress the hilt of her sword as she leaned against Bhari. The two girls echoed Ash's question and gazed around the settlement.

"It feels like an ambush." Eastwood tightened his grip on his cannon. "I have grenades ..."

Ghabrie shook her head. Ash scanned the walls and scoured the mountain, searching for mercenaries ready to gun down the intruders. He shook his head. "There's no one here."

"There is!" whispered Thirty-Six. "But not what we're expecting."

"Is Nahria here?" hissed Ghabrie, her fingers turning white as they clutched her bow.

"Someone like us is," said Thirty-Six.

Maddie growled and hung back beneath Smith's shaggy body, but Samson put his nose to the floor and began sniffing. "Careful, boy," warned Glint.

Concrete buildings filled the far side of the valley, blocky and stout, with flat roofs and barred windows. Green grass, meadow-green grass, rolled down the empty slope before them. Ghabrie could not get over how much it looked like home, except they had never had truly green grass. Home's grass was yellow, ochre and gold, like full grown corn and maize. Further down this valley, a field of gold peeped from behind the furthest buildings and Ghabrie's eyes widened.

"Wheat, they're growing wheat!" She shook her head. "Right up here in the mountains, they're growing wheat!"

"I think the Alliance was using this site for more than just food experimentation," said Eastwood. "So, back on your guard, Ghabrie."

"Months ago there was no sign of food up here." Ghabrie lowered her bow as Eastwood moved in front of her.

"You can't be too careful."

"But there's no one here, it really is abandoned," she said.

"Someone's tending those crops and keeping this grass low and watered," he said.

"Ash, do you see anything, anyone?" asked Ghabrie. "Hum, anything new?"

Ash shook his head and Hum's eyes glazed for a moment as he searched memory banks for any new data. He shook his head too. Ghabrie examined the area, scrutinising the buildings and scanning the plethora of doors that she knew led into tunnels and laboratories within the mountains. The last time she had been here most of the doors had been broken or left wide open, and for a moment fear swarmed inside her head. It was not that long ago she had been navigating other corridors searching for Nahria and come across a nemesis. She had finished Dr. Stein, but Dr. Stein had not been the only technician who had worked on her. The closed doors and the labs behind them still sent shivers down her spine, and her tattoo tingled on the back of her neck.

She lifted her bow again and waved her group forward. "If there's something or someone here, we'll find them," she said, and they walked as quietly as they could in the company of three dogs and a llama.

A surge of emotion washed over Ghabrie and she flinched, at the same moment Thirty-Six indicated a small crop of buildings. Freddie and his master took the lead, closely followed by Bhari and Ash. Maddie and Samson padded at their flanks, and Maeve covered the rear of the group, twisting and turning at the back with an arrow ready to loose from her bow. Freddie sniffed and whined at the closest door. Eastwood turned the door handle and pushed the door open with a loud creak. He cared nothing for caution; he strode through the doorway, disappearing into shadows beyond with his huge gun held aloft. Freddie followed but the others waited and worried outside, until Freddie barked and the two emerged with a couple of elderly men shuffling in front of them.

Freddie licked the hands of the newcomers and wound his lean body about their legs. Ghabrie could not stop the twitch of a smile at the terror on their faces. When they saw the rest of the group, the two men raised their arms and stood as still as they could on shaky legs. Ghabrie hid her smile and made sure her blades were shining and evident as she strode towards them.

"Who is here?" she demanded. "Besides you."

They paled at the sound of her voice and one collapsed to his knees as Ghabrie's kestrel screeched from her shoulder.

"Oh, Birdwoman," he began, "treat us well."

The other man tried to help him up while he gazed at Ghabrie's antlers. "She is treating us well, we're not dead!"

"You speak wisely," said Ghabrie. "Who lives here?"

"Not many of us. We're nomads. We roamed… and now we're here." The first man climbed back to his feet. "This is a place of peace and rest." He thrust his hands out. "As you can see, we live in peace."

"No weapons, armoury?" asked Ghabrie.

The second man glanced towards the building next to the entrance and Ghabrie swung round. She gestured to

Ash and Bhari to investigate. As they strode towards the grey hut, its door opened and three more unarmed nomads filed out, nervously.

"We farm and we look after each other. We take in the sick," said the second man.

"Names?" asked Ghabrie.

"Thom, and he's Derick," said Thom, "Are you just passing though? Except we're way out of the way for anyone just passing through…"

Ghabrie pointed at the mountain doors – the doors that led to research facilities. "Are the labs back in use?"

"You know about the labs?"

She nodded. "Are they still in use?"

He shook his head. "Mostly empty, they took most stuff when they left," explained Thom. "We're just farmers, trying to stay out of the way up here."

"How many of you?" asked Glint.

"A few dozen, maybe fifty." Derick blinked and stared at Smith. "We keep sheep and goats – but I 'ent never seen one of them!"

Glint grinned. "Bet you haven't at that."

"So, passing through?" asked Thom again.

Thirty-Six moaned and Ghabrie glanced up at her still astride Smith. Ghabrie could feel the same pull, the same emotion, as Thirty-Six murmured, "It's strong."

"I'm searching for someone."

"We have all sorts here, come from all over. We're a haven, of sorts." Derick still gazed at the llama. "What is that?"

"Couldn't tell you," said Glint.

"I'm looking for a girl like me," said Ghabrie, swallowing hard. "Nahria." The two men swapped a look and Ghabrie's hackles rose. "She looks a little like me and –"

"There's a girl by the name of Nari," said Derick ignoring the elbow that jabbed his side.

"Nari?" Ghabrie's breath caught in her throat.

"Uh-huh, came with a band of men. They was injured, most of them. Some died." Derick glared at Thom as his elbow spiked his side again. "I don't owe them nowt! Hawntch, they took some of my land!"

Thom stepped forward. "They're not to be trifled with and the girl's a tough nut."

"Have they hurt her? Is she hurt?" Ghabrie held her breath.

"Hawntch! No one would hurt her! Jake won't let no-one touch her!" Derick shook his head. "But when Jake goes, there's gonna be none to watch her."

"Jake?" Ghabrie felt Maeve stiffen as she moved from the back of the group. "Who's Jake?" Ghabrie asked.

"Jake's their leader, but he's no use." Derick scowled at Thom. "He's not, not now. He got injured, and wounded bad."

"What's wrong with him?" Maeve's voice pitched a little on the high side and she cleared her throat. "What happened to him?"

"There must have been a knife fight," said Derick. "Blades and blood. He only had one weapons arm."

Maeve's intake of breath made Ghabrie place a hand on her shoulder.

"That's how he lost most of his men. Blade brawls." Thom joined in.

"And when they got here they took the best stuff," said a man arriving with Bhari and Ash. He was interrupted by one of the women.

"They tried taking women too, but we weren't playing their game." She spat on the ground and Derick laughed. The two women linked arms and Derick winked, more relaxed now.

"Nowt separating you two, 'ent happening!" he said.

"The girl?" Ghabrie prompted.

"She's with Jake, he don't let no-one near her," said Derick.

"Is she cuffed?" asked Maeve.

He shook his head. "She don't need no cuffs, she's his by choice."

Ghabrie's mind swayed.

"I feel her," Thirty-Six murmured.

"So do I," whispered Ghabrie. A sharp pain stabbed her temple and she flinched. Green flooded her brain again and she pushed her mind forward. She recoiled once more as the green flashed like molten explosives and hit the barrier before her. Frustration coiled in her stomach along with daggers of guilt and loss. She tried not to show her anguish and fought back the tears that pricked at her eyelids. She clenched her teeth and her words hissed. "Where's Jake and Nari?"

The scruffy nomads indicated further down the slope to a clutch of small cabins set against the rocks and what might have been a waterfall had there been any rain. "Down there," said Derick, "They're not us, not our group. They took from us, but as they was injured we let them stay." His voice trailed off. The small unkempt nomads wouldn't have stood a chance against any aggressive take over. "We let them stay…"

Maeve hurried forward and Ghabrie matched her pace.

The mountains shadowed the settlement, but the blazing sun shone across the narrow fields and the lush grass beyond, which clearly benefitted the institute's new inhabitants and modified crops. Faces appeared at small windows and some the grubby settlers wandered outside to watch with guarded interest. Ghabrie's eyes flickered across the people, amazed at the ability of humankind to seek out and grab anything they could in these desperate times. The doors into the mountain labyrinth, some still loose, but several fixed and newly hung with shiny bolts, continued to haunt her but she tried to keep her attention on her footsteps and the trickling stream running between the cluster of lodges ahead.

Ghabrie squinted against the sun. Down by a narrow rivulet that dribbled from the stream sat a man on a rock, clasping a knife between his knees. His head was bent as he cleaned the blade with one hand. He either had not heard their approach or did not care. The knife glinted in the light and blinded Ghabrie for a moment as a guttural cry came from beside her. As blue and black spots cleared from her vision, Ghabrie saw Maeve bolt across the grass towards the man. The redhead's sword shrieked as she unsheathed it. Ghabrie opened her mouth to yell, but could not manage a sound before Maeve's blade plunged deep into the man's chest.

A scream of rage echoed through the mountains and the burst of mental wrath literally knocked them all to their knees. Ghabrie tried to stand again as shock hit her almost physically in the chest. She had had no idea that Maeve's fury carried a mental edge.

But Maeve was flat on her back too, and as Ghabrie stood, blinking, she saw that the small freckled warrior was now overshadowed by a girl. The girl held a knife to Maeve's neck and anguish echoed in waves as the girl wailed. Behind them both, the man known as Jake clutched at his chest with his good arm. He weakly tried to pull the sword from his chest, but blood oozed and pain paled his face. He whined and the girl astride Maeve turned back to him. She dropped her dagger and leaped to his side to cradle his head in her hands.

Ghabrie felt the blood drain from her own face. "Nahria?" her voice squeaked.

The girl ignored her as she stroked the man's bristled face. Maeve jumped to her feet, her face flushed and incredulous. "Nahria?" Maeve echoed Ghabrie's cry.

As blood seeped through his shirt the man stared at Maeve and tried to speak. His words burbled and splashed. "I underes … timated you … Mutant. Should never … never have let you go." Jarek's face screwed up in pain. "To be killed for a song … not the way I'd have chosen."

Maeve stared at Nahria. "Why are you with him?" Her words spilled in disbelieving gasps. "Nahria! Let him go. Let Jarek go! This is vengeance for Aiden and everyone! Nahria?"

Ghabrie moved to Maeve's side, her eyes never leaving her sister's face. "Nahria, I'm here." But she wasn't ready for the venom which attacked her as Nahria glared.

"You left me!" she seethed, "Left me with those animals. Stein and Planck…and those…" She spat upon the dirt at her feet. "Those creatures. You left me after promising you never would."

"I didn't leave you!" she sobbed. "I'd never leave you!" Her protests bounced off the mountain's sheer cold face. "They took me … they rescued me, but I tried to get to you, I tried! You know I tried! You saw me try!" Ghabrie stared, shocked, as Nahria hugged Jarek close, his blood soaking and staining her sister's jeans.

Nahria wailed again when Jarek gurgled as life left his body. Nahria's howl of agony shattered the stilted silence.

"Nahria!" cried Maeve again, pushing her red hair back and gesticulating wildly. "You saved me from him. What happened? You wanted him dead too!"

Nahria slipped to her knees on the bloodstained grass. Tears dripped down her nose. As Maeve stepped closer, Nahria moved her bloody hands through her own hair pulling it away from her face, revealing tattoos that decorated her temples and neck. Nahria bared her teeth like a feral animal and Maeve landed on her rear.

Ghabrie hurried to help the redhead up. "Nahria, I don't understand."

The girl on her knees glared and Ghabrie felt purple and black engulf her like a thunderstorm. She struggled to stay on her feet as the colours assaulted her.

"You don't understand?" Nahria struggled to breathe for a moment as rage simmered. "You left me. You abandoned me." She left no space for Ghabrie to interrupt. Her words spilled into the colours that almost blinded Ghabrie. "You know what they did! Pain. It hurt so much, I screamed for you. Torture. Implants and no sedation." She pulled back her hair again and bared her neck. Silver slots and implants raged, embedded within red scars at the top of her spine next to the tattooed number at the base of her neck. "We were both experiments, but without you it was worse. You got away. You escaped. So they wanted me!"

Ghabrie tried to speak but her sister's storm was too great.

"Stein tried to kill me, but I was too strong. She said I was like you. She said I was stronger, but they still wanted you. So I became stronger. I fought and as I fought, they, they ..." her voice faded. "They hurt me. They hurt me more. Because of you, they hurt me more."

"We tried to find you," Ghabrie's words sounded small. "They went back for you when I was too sick, but you'd gone. I went back, but there was no one there."

"You left me." Nahria met her gaze. "Demons. They took me to a mountain where demons rose from thin air. Where humans were no longer humans but just damaged experiments."

"I tried to find you. I went everywhere." Ghabrie turned to her comrades and heads nodded vigorously. "You even left me a message with the children out near the black sand, and I've been searching ... I've been searching everywhere ..."

"Everywhere except where I was," Nahria's words stung. "Jarek found me though, not you. He rescued me and the others. He kept me safe."

Maeve shook her head, her auburn hair glimmering in the sun like flames. "He didn't! You told me you wanted to escape! He didn't save you, or the others. They became ... he sold them ..."

Nahria shot a venomous look at Maeve and Maeve's mouth closed. "He saved me."

"He abused you!" cried Maeve. "You helped me escape, but you couldn't get away because he'd chained you up! Look at your wrists, the scars!"

"He saved me," she hissed, "He didn't want a mutant. His chains kept me safe. No more experiments, no more pain, no more, no more ..." Nahria began to cry. "He loved me. When the Prometheans came for me, he saved me, he loved me. He protected me."

A small voice rose from the back of the group as Thirty-Six stepped forward hesitantly. "He saved you because of your value. I was saved once too, but it took your sister to liberate me!"

"No!" wailed Nahria. "Jarek loved me, he loves me! He told me he'd changed!"

"Serpents don't change," muttered Ghabrie.

"You were worth something, that's what they loved about you," said Thirty-Six.

Nahria's eyes flashed. "You're right, I am worth something!" She clumsily rose to her feet. "I am. I'm strong. They taught me and Jarek made me strong. He was taking me to Stein, but this time they'd have protected me, they'd have let her help me, but they'd keep me safe. Stein can make me even stronger. She can enhance me even more," said Nahria baring her wrist and showing a port, stray wires and a narrow interface amongst silvered scars. "But this time on my terms ..."

"Stein is dead. I killed her." Ghabrie stared at her sister.

Nahria released another strangled cry. The men who had gathered behind her began to advance towards Ghabrie and her comrades, but Ash and the rest of Ghabrie's friends held their weapons ready and the men halted behind Nahria.

The unexpected noise that then erupted from Nahria threw Ghabrie and Maeve back to the ground, and Ghabrie found herself buried in an assault of roaring colours. She gripped Maeve's arm and struggled to stand. Maeve fell backwards again, unable to withstand the onslaught. Ghabrie shook her head and opened her eyes, trying to concentrate on her little sister. She could barely make sense of Nahria as the mental offensive grew. Then she felt hands grip her shoulders, and she could stand as Thirty-Six and Eastwood joined her. Another mind joined them as Glint threw her abilities in with theirs and they tried to block the violent anguish and fury that stemmed from Nahria.

The power struggle shook the ground and the wooden cabins shuddered. Ghabrie felt tears wet her cheeks. Her brain threatened to implode with the surge of colour and emotion that rained down upon her. Ghabrie tried to get closer to Nahria. Thirty-Six struggled to overcome the girl's mind. Glint tumbled to the ground and Ghabrie felt Eastwood's fingers slip from her shoulder as he too fell to his knees. Ghabrie gazed almost blindly, seeing people mill about. She saw Bhari, Ash and Hum huddle with their heads together, and Freddie dance agitated as his owner crawled back to him.

Nahria intensified her fury, and vicious purple-black thunder cracked in Ghabrie's mind. Nahria walked steadily across the grass, the meadow-green grass, and stood eye-to-eye with her sister. Mental fire whirled in blues and purples and black, and Ghabrie felt her throat begin to tighten as her sister's hands closed around her neck. Thirty-Six, still at her side, stared at Ghabrie in wide-eyed horror and stumbled, and as Ghabrie began to turn blue Nahria threw the exhausted, nameless waif to the floor.

Ghabrie grabbed at the air, feeling life steal away, then latched onto Nahria's wrists and with physical contact managed to break her psychological connection with her sister even as Nahria's rage choked her.

A great clanking noise pounded, and a door screeched as it begged for oil and regular use. "It looks like I was searching for the wrong sister." The nightmare voice sent shivers down Ghabrie's spine and she truly believed the pits of hell were calling. "I'll let her destroy you, H76, then I'll reward her with everything I would have given you!"

Ghabrie struggled to gain breath, as her sister's hands tightened around her throat, and battled valiantly to stay conscious. She let go of her sister's wrists and grabbed desperately at her torso. Her fingers tingled and shook as they brushed against her corset and belt and she found what she was looking for. She jerked out the knife; the dagger Xanthe had given her, the dagger she had used to kill Stein. She thrust the dagger into Nahria's stomach, inwards and upwards, at exactly the moment that Hum plugged himself into the port on her sister's wrist.

Nahria's hands squeezed tighter and Ghabrie felt her life leach away, the colour of death seeping like grey lake fog into her mind. Then, when she thought she was ended, Nahria's fingers slackened and Ghabrie gasped for breath as every colour under the scorching sun invaded her brain.

Nahria collapsed and Ghabrie rolled away, tears streaming from her swollen eyes. She clutched at the earth as life returned, as sight flooded back and the assault of colour faded away. Her chest rose and her breath shuddered as sobs erupted. Her blurry vision began to clear. "Nahria ..." her hoarse voice croaked and cracked. "Nahria." She turned over on the ground, and stared at the body slumped beside her. "No, no, NO!" her voice cracked painfully. "Nahria!"

"Hold her," Bhari, ever sensitive, her voice breaking too, "Ghabrie, hold her. She may not have long."

Ghabrie roughly wiped her tears away and scrambled to her sister's side. Nahria gulped with pain and blank eyes.

"What did I do?" She clasped Nahria in her arms, her prize, her beloved, her meaning for life, and wept. A clear keening call echoed throughout the mountains and, as Freddie inched forward to lick Ghabrie's face, the kestrel dropped from the sky to land beside the sisters. "This can't be! I make the future, I make it, not this ..."

"I see, I see, Ghabrie, I see you ..." Nahria whispered.

"I'm here," Ghabrie assured her and tightened her grip.

"I'm sorry." Nahria's voice slid and faded like a retreating mountain mist. "I see ..."

Ghabrie's eyes travelled to her sister's hand and to the port. "What are you doing?" she demanded as Hum and Bhari leaned close.

"She can see," murmured Bhari.

"See what?"

"Everything. Everything that was on the intranet that we can still access. She has a port, they gave her a port," said Bhari.

Ghabrie followed the port and the wire to Hum. He spoke quietly. "I'm showing her. Images, stories, you – everything in my memory banks of you. Stories of Nahria's worth, your search, her experimental value, how the Prometheans searched for you both ..."

"I see you," Nahria's dying breaths came fast and her eyes struggled to hold Ghabrie's. "I'm sorry. I know now … I can see … you didn't leave me."

Then her breath stopped and Ghabrie's throat closed up once more. Her scream and her anguish were as silent as her tears.

The nightmare voice cackled again from the mountain door, and a woman sauntered across the grass. "You've lost everything, H76. There's only one way out now, one way to end all this pain. And you know what it is."

Ghabrie clasped her hands over her ears and screwed her eyes shut. She could not bear to look at the source of the voice. "Stein is dead. Stein is dead!" Ghabrie's lips moved but she could not hear herself speak.

"Don't listen!" cried Hum panic rising in his voice as he gently unplugged himself from Nahria's cold, pale wrist. "Don't listen to her!"

Ghabrie's wail finally broke out of her throat, a cry of such torment and grief as was never before heard. It echoed across the mountain and through the desert plains. Those who heard that anguished scream of black despair spoke of it until the day they died.

Ghabrie's bloodstained hands left imprints in the dirt as she collapsed beside her sister. Stein's laugh rattled through her and Ghabrie felt she had nothing left to give. The doctor's voice burned into her mind. "You could have been immortal. You could have been pure!" Her words boomed against the mountains and through Ghabrie's head. "You were pure. You could have been the new order of life …"

As her words spewed out, Ghabrie's rage swelled and she rolled away from her sister. Struggling to her feet she grabbed the cannon from Eastwood and raised it to her shoulder. "Stein is dead, I killed her!" She stared in disbelief at the woman facing her down. Doctor Stein stood – very much alive – before her. A bolted metal plate concealed her left eye, and a cage of enhancements circled her neck and half her skull. Ghabrie released a crazed cry, but as she prepared to shoot, a shadow emerged from the doorway behind Stein. Ghabrie's nemesis crowed. "Welcome, Human X. Human 76, meet the New Order of Life."

"Don't shoot!" rose a cry from amongst the nomads. "Don't shoot him!"

"Pri, are you crazy?" yelled a man as a woman sprinted out of the crowd towards Ghabrie.

"Don't shoot him!" screamed Pri.

Ghabrie lowered the cannon, but kept her eyes on the lumbering figure behind Stein.

"He's the same as you, Ghabrie!" yelled the woman.

Ghabrie cast a quick glance her way in disbelief then raised the cannon again. "He's not the same as me, that's a monster!"

Human X growled and the predatory sound caused Ghabrie's finger to twitch against the trigger. The woman called back into the crowd. "Rob, help me!" Then she raced towards the monster and Stein. Ghabrie watched out of the corner of her eye, one eye still on Stein. The man in the crowd shrugged and sighed, and finally after shaking his head, hurried to catch Pri.

Stein screeched at the huge creature. "Kill her, kill the girl! Destroy Human 76, destroy Ghabrie!"

Ghabrie lined Human X in the cannon's sights but Pri was directly in the way of her shot. Her delay allowed the giant the time to throw out electrifying mental fire which hit Ghabrie once more full in the chest. The cannon hit the ground and Ghabrie creased up, bending with pain and blinding red hot sparks of colour. Purple swathed her and the pain increased as she fought to stand and bear it.

She caught a glimpse of Human X, his eyes white, glazed and unresponsive, lumbering towards her, continuing to attack her mind, bringing pain that threatened to annihilate her. Her comrades lifted weapons, but their arrows fell to the ground well short of their target and bullets skewed past the huge man.

Ghabrie's grief turned to raw fury as Stein bellowed at the creature. Her heart pounded as she tried to take control of her anger. She closed her eyes to override the pain that coursed through her and focused. As the pain receded and purple switched to blue, then turquoise, she gained strength and power within her mind. She felt the mental ripple that told her that her friends were doing the same.

A flicker of yellow pricked her mind and she opened her eyes. Thirty-Six stood by her shoulder, her eyes focused on the giant. Ghabrie glanced to her other side expecting to see Glint, but the girl was gone, replaced by Eastwood and his flexing muscles. Bronze and tawny gold flashed across her sight and she heard her kestrel shriek. She gazed up into the blue and gasped as two birds of prey shot across the sky, dancing amid the currents and streaks of caramel and amber. Her kestrel and a magnificent hawk spread their wings and plunged towards the monster. She barely had time to think as Human X sent another lightning bolt into her brain and she had to refocus on the attack.

Human X staggered closer, his white eyes terrifying and veins bulging across his bald head. Amid the purple haze of electricity and pain, Ghabrie watched the birds whirl about the creature and she concentrated. "His eyes, his eyes!" she sent her words into her bird's mind, feeling the windhover's understanding as both birds flashed tawny gold and dived towards the man's eyes and exposed scalp.

For a moment Human X faltered again and Pri yelled like a woman possessed from the battle's side-lines. Talons and beaks pecked and scratched and wings beat across the giant's head and he lost control, his arms flailing wildly as he sought to protect himself. But Stein's hypnotic instructions pushed through and he punched the air with tight fists.

The hawk rebounded off his knuckle like a cannonball. It tumbled and screeched and Ghabrie watched the bird strike the ground amid a cloud of dust. It was Glint that rolled out of the dust. She rolled to her feet to scream like a harpy knocked off her broomstick.

Ghabrie added her own war cry, and now, having seen Glint embrace her hawk, she realised there was more to her windhover. She had no idea how to become her bird of prey, as Glint had done, but power burst through, newfound control and dominion roused inside her and she willed her own bird to fight.

Her kestrel's battle cry, echoing over the mountains, rallied her friends and now they concentrated on Human X, directing all their mental abilities at one place. His power was strong, but chaotic, and they began to sense a chink. Every time Pri yelled, her shout rising above the echoes from Stein, the demon broke contact, just for a second. "Ael!" she screamed, "Ael ..." The word opened a thin crack in his attention and Ghabrie forced her advantage.

Her allies centred their mental flames and storms and aimed, focussing together. The colours lit up their minds, and as Pri and Rob reached the huge man he grabbed his head and let out a convulsive cry of his own "Get out, get out, GET OUT!"

Pri threw her arms around the man and Ghabrie saw that his eyes looked normal once more. The attacks on her mind stopped suddenly. She had no idea what manner of thing had been inside the man called Ael, but she'd been through enough at the hands of the Prometheans to recognise that she and her friends had forced it out. She would talk to him soon enough, but with the immediate danger gone, she slipped back to her sister, trying to ignore the devil-doctor that stood behind Ael.

Grief surged once more as she sank down beside Nahria, now cradled in Hum's skinny arms. Blood stained Nahria's black top like a patch of sweat, but it was Eastwood who noticed. "I've seen this before," he said and Ghabrie stared at him.

"Seen what?" she asked.

Freddie licked Nahria's prone, still body and whined at her lack of response. "Her blood's on your hands and where you speared her, but nowhere else. It should be soaking into the ground, pooling beneath your sister, covering Hum with blood ..."

"But it's not," said Ghabrie.

"I've seen it before," he said.

"You have?" said Ghabrie staring down at her belly and smoothing her hand across her abdomen. Her attention returned to Nahria.

"They wanted us both to be immortal," Nahria's words were indistinct and barely more than a breeze, but Ghabrie heard every syllable. "Lucky, I call it, or maybe inspired."

"Nahria?" Ghabrie could scarcely breathe. Nahria opened her eyes and gently felt her own stomach. She pulled up her shirt and revealed a bloody mess – but no wound. Ghabrie's grin spread across her whole face, lighting up her eyes and making her tears shine like crystal. Nothing else mattered as Nahria carefully sat up.

Stein sneered her disdain as Human X fell to his knees, dust rising as his hands hit the ground, and the scientist instead closed her own eyes and faced the group. She reached behind her collar and touched something then set her sights back on Ghabrie. "Don't let me ruin the reunion. But don't for a second think I haven't learned a thing or two myself."

Hum shivered and moaned. "I feel her. She's connected to the intranet! She's enhanced!"

Eastwood picked up his cannon. "I'll enhance her to smithereens!" He aimed, but the mechanism seized. Sensing his frustration Freddie sprinted towards the scientist, followed by Maddie and Samson, but an unseen jolt threw the hounds backwards as if they had been shot. They whimpered and limped back to safety.

Nahria took Ghabrie's hand and squeezed it. "We're a force. They made us —she made us — let's give it back!"

The sisters rose to their feet and closed their eyes. The energy from Stein that hit them made them recoil and shook them to the core, but they remained standing. Colours flew about Ghabrie's head and for a moment she wasn't sure they'd be able to withstand the attack. Purple, crimson and black flashed and exploded from Stein's hands and the sisters were flung backwards, landing in a heap with Eastwood, Glint and Thirty-Six.

"Where the hawntch did she get that kind of power!" hissed Ghabrie. "I swear I killed her!"

"Then kill her again!" Eastwood's words flickered around Ghabrie's head, sparking scarlet and orange.

She grabbed Nahria's hand and they both leaped to their feet. She felt her sister's fear course through her as Nahria's fingers tightened inside her hand. "We can do this!" she whispered.

Fire swirled from deep within, rising like a phoenix inside her veins, and dragon flames curled about her head. Rage churned like a tsunami and every mental ability burned. She felt the surge bounce off her mind from Nahria too and they stood facing Stein.

Behind them power fizzed and flickered, dogs snarled and wings beat and she knew they weren't on their own.

An electrical pulse cracked through the air, and they simultaneously blocked the charge as amaranthine and bittersweet bolts exploded in the space between them. Sparks detonated, scattering bursts of energy and Ghabrie conjured up every malevolent thought she had ever had. Steel-grey hail showered Stein and she shrieked as the pellets struck her. She returned fire with white bolts of electricity and cackled "I don't need a helmet now! You'd better take cover!"

Ghabrie allowed her fury to ride the storm, rising like a kestrel protecting her young, and her sister read her mind. Together they cast wrath ignited with the ache of rage and their onslaught hurled Stein to the ground. The doctor scrambled up and spread her fingers and arced her arms before releasing a powerful barrage of energy. The dogs yowled and the birds squawked in terror.

Ghabrie felt Nahria slip from her fingers and she glanced through the blitz of pain at her little sister. The girl knelt at her side, her head bowed and pain creasing her face. She tried to speak but Stein's offensive curled her own stomach and bored into her brain. She recovered her vocal chords and launched a scream, a war cry, a rallying call, a last desperate urge to fight. Nahria sprang back to her feet and Ghabrie joined her.

Chaos danced about them, violet and charcoal and crimson and sapphire. Nahria clasped her sister's hand and Thirty-Six pushed forward from behind them to counter the offensive. Stein stepped back and Nahria leaned close to whisper in Ghabrie's ear.

A smile flickered across Ghabrie's face; she let go of her sister's hand and stepped back. "She's all yours, Human 77," she said.

Stein waved her arms theatrically and opened her mouth to speak. Nothing came out and confusion contorted her disfigured face. Nahria offered back the same melodramatic wave and Stein dropped to the ground in a cloud of yellow dust.

Stein lay still. The cloud of dust settled, and murmurs skipped across the crowd. Nahria shook her head commanding silence. "Wait," she commanded, her voice ringing in the stillness.

Silence fell, like the calm across the ocean before a storm, then an ignition clicked, echoing through the mountain and a deafening boom split the air. Stein exploded. Her augmentations detonated and splintered, and her body disintegrated like ice beneath a blow torch.

"My enhancements are better than hers; I connected her off switch to her default self-destruct." Nahria laughed grimly. "Now, she's dead, truly dead. We killed her."

Ghabrie threw her arms around her little sister, tears welling and love engulfing her. Nahria hugged her back tightly.

"I thought I'd lost you," whispered Ghabrie into Nahria's hair. "I thought you hated me."

"I did, until I saw. I thought you'd lost me," replied Nahria, muffled against her sister's shoulder.

"Never," said Ghabrie, "never again."

They held each other, warmth flowing through them and for the first time Ghabrie's mind filled with green, meadow-green, a beautiful, honeyed golden-green.

Nahria broke away from her hug. "I think I need to apologise to Maeve, and meet your friends, and go home." She hugged Ghabrie tight again. "I miss home and Xanthe. I might even try some huiskee!"

"I'm not sure I want you all grown up, little sister," said Ghabrie, wiping the mist of tears from her eyes.

The two girls reluctantly separated and turned to the raggle-taggle group of friends that watched, each nursing their own bruises. Ghabrie could not wipe the smile from her face and her grin got even bigger as her kestrel swooped to brush Nahria with his feathers. He settled on Ghabrie's shoulder and lost his balance for a moment as Nahria stopped dead, eyes wide and smile gone. Ghabrie's brow furrowed and with apprehension rolling like a whirlpool she followed her sister's gaze.

Nahria spoke with incredulity. "And, what the radding hell, is that? I have never in my entire life seen a creature like that before – is it a sheep, or a camel, or, no seriously, what exactly is that?"

EPILOGUE

Michael Wombat

The sisters' companions had left them as they journeyed home, taking their leave one by one, each going their own way. Now only Nahria and Thirty-Six accompanied Ghabrie as they rounded the last crag and strode the dusty track towards the shipping yard gates. They were singing and smiling, happy to be home, marching to the beat of their lively air.

The roof of the shipping container was hot against Planck's belly. He rested Constant on the corpse of the old man, Alphaeus, and brought up the targeting system in his ocular. In the sky above he heard an avian cry; *kee kee kee!* It seemed that he had been mistaken about this particular 7-series' ability to shapeshift. Ghabrie's head steadied at the centre of the cross-hairs as the targeting compensator took effect. He drew in a breath, held it, and triggered the plasma bolt.

All hail the Brotherhood. All hail the Alliance.

AUTHOR BIOS

Alex Brightsmith

Alex Brightsmith was born and raised in Bedfordshire and defies anyone who was not to place it on a map. Bedfordshire is so obscure even its own residents struggle to agree which region it belongs to, and its legacies have been a resistance to categorisation and a lasting fondness for sprouts.

Alex has published two character-driven contemporary thrillers that lay the foundations for a series featuring traceuse, thief and potential government agent Kathryn Blake, but is also readily distracted by flash fiction in a range of genres and by the development of an epic fantasy set around the Khyran provinces and the Tormaben plains.

Web: www.alexbrightsmith.WordPress.com
Twitter: *@BrightsmithGamp*

Denise Callaway

B. D. (Brenda Denise) Callaway was born in the summer of 1972 at McCurtain Memorial Hospital and spent most of her childhood growing up in Broken Bow, Oklahoma. Denise left upon graduation in 1990 to attend Southeastern Oklahoma State University. This course of study was interrupted by marriage, parenthood, and a military tour in the U.S. Navy. She returned to university studies in 1994, except this time at East Central University in Ada, Oklahoma, where she pursued a degree in accounting, then later in education focusing in mathematics. In 2003, she began teaching in a small school nestled in the Kiamichi Mountains of Oklahoma. Three years later, she moved to central Oklahoma where she continues to teach and has gained her Masters.

Denise began writing as early as the 5th grade and encouraged by her family, friends, and teachers continued to put pen to paper over the next 30 years. She is currently focused on writing fantasy fiction and has written various short stories and poetry from multiple genres. She presently lives in central Oklahoma with her two cats Loki and Sophie and within short reach to her daughter in college and family in southeast Oklahoma.

Web: *lostinafieldofdandelions.wordpress.com*
         poeticwonderer.blogspot.com
FB: *www.facebook.com/fieldofdandelions*
Twitter: *@denise_callaway*

KJ Collard

"When given the choice of geeking out or keeping it together, always geek out. You may find some spectacular new friends." ~ KJ Collard

KendallJaye Collard has lived all her years in central Illinois. She was bitten by the writing bug in high school when she took a creative writing class simply to fill her schedule. Since then she's created worlds, spun tales, and breathed life into poetry. Leaning on the darker natures of the human soul, she manages The Darker Playground blog where she posts poetry, short stories, and her #TwitterShort Challenges. She believes that if her writing connects with one other person, then writing it was worth it.

KJC currently geeks out over Supernatural, Chicago Cubs baseball, The Walking Dead, and Game of Thrones. She believes Severus Snape is one of the most beautifully written characters of all time. She might love bacon more than you.

Web: *www.thedarkerplayground.blogspot.com*
Twitter: *@KJCollard and @drkerplayground*

Alison DeLuca

Alison DeLuca is the author of several steampunk and urban fantasy books. She was born in Arizona and has also lived in Pennsylvania, Illinois, Mexico, Ireland, and Spain.

Currently she wrestles words and laundry in New Jersey.

Web: *www.amazon.com/Alison-DeLuca/e/B004Q7IE3I*

Michelle Fox

Michelle Fox grew up under her covers in the space between sleep and awake. With a #7 mechanical pencil, she trapped her nightmares in a hard-cover journal and vowed never to speak of them again. Years passed, and life continued. She got married, went to college, and had two beautiful children. But the hard-cover journal constantly called to her; stalking her every move and reminding her of a past she wished to forget. For the sake of her sanity, Michelle has now broken her vow. The demon described in Human X is inspired by one of the many nightmares she wrote about in that journal.

FB: *www.facebook.com/chelle87fox*
Twitter: *@Chelle87Fox*

Rebecca Fyfe

Rebecca Fyfe, an author with stories in several anthologies and collections, is a mother of seven children and, having lost over 145 lbs. of excess weight, blogs about health and fitness at SkinnyDreaming.com. She graduated with a BA in English Literature and an AA in Child Development. She is a Californian who married an Englishman and now resides in Great Britain. Rebecca created and runs the Chapter Book Challenge which runs every March, and, when not writing short stories or children's stories, she's busy creating urban fantasy novels, full of her own special blend of magic. She gets her inspiration from her five daughters and two sons. She is the founder of Melusine Muse Press.

Web: *www.rebeccafyfe.com*
FB: *www.facebook.com/rebeccafyfe*
Twitter: *@beckyfyfe*

Jeff Hollar

Jeffrey Hollar was born in Lima Ohio at a very young age and in humble surroundings. He describes himself as an author/poet, father, husband, and a Klingon/Ferengi hybrid. He considers himself to be a writer without genre and a specialist in short fiction. Developing a love for reading in his early life, Jeffrey read anything and everything he could get his hands on. First published at the age of seven in his school newspaper, Jeffrey has periodically continued that trend.

While his work has appeared in numerous anthologies as well as collections of his own short and serialized fiction, Jeffrey has made it quite clear he has no intentions or interest in writing The Great American Novel. Work commitments, family obligations, as well as a predilection towards laziness and sloth have relegated his writing to the aforementioned formats.

There remains hope he will one day overcome at least some of these distractions and again publish a book or seven.

Web: www.amazon.com/Jeffrey-Hollar/e/B00A7VMTWO

Nick Johns

Nick enjoyed travelling as a child. From Barsoom to the Courts of Chaos, via Rivendell and Camelot, with Biggles and Captain Nemo, he saw sights and met characters that still jog his elbow when he is writing. This is a disadvantage when editing books and professional publications, but rather less so when writing advertising copy. He is a Welshman living in exile in Northamptonshire with his wife and a cat given to bouts of peristeronic homicide. He collects information of infrequent utility. Due to a chronically short attention span, he now writes flash fiction almost exclusively.

Web: talesfromatightrope.blogspot.co.uk
www.amazon.co.uk/Nick-Johns/e/B00GZZFAPY

Miranda Kate

Miranda Kate is a Freelance Proofreader/Editor who loves helping authors with their writing in whatever capacity they need. She is published in multiple flash fiction anthologies. Miranda is currently working on her own novels, but finds editing other writers' stories far more enjoyable.

Web: *manuscripteditingservices.weebly.com*
           purplequeennl.blogspot.nl
Twitter: *@PurpleQueenNL*

M S Manz

MS Manz writes things. Most of those things are stories, and some of them are even good.

Web: *msmanz.com*
FB: *www.facebook.com/MSManz*

Julia Rios

Julia Rios is a writer, editor, podcaster, and narrator. Her fiction, non-fiction, and poetry have appeared in several places, including Daily Science Fiction, Apex Magazine, and Goblin Fruit. She was a fiction editor for Strange Horizons from 2012 to 2015, and is currently the poetry and reprints editor for Uncanny Magazine and co-editor with Alisa Krasnostein of Kaleidoscope: Diverse YA Science Fiction and Fantasy Stories, and the Year's Best YA Speculative Fiction series. She is also a co-host of the Hugo-nominated podcast, The Skiffy and Fanty Show, a general discussion, interview, and movie review show. She has narrated stories for Podcastle, Pseudopod, and Cast of Wonders, and poems for the Strange Horizons podcast.
Twitter: *@omgjulia*

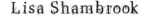

Lisa Shambrook

Lisa began weaving intricate stories inside her imagination from a young age, but these days her words find themselves bursting forth as flash fiction, short stories and novels. As a sensory writer, she delves into sensitive subject matters that will lift your spirit and steal your heart.

She was born and raised in vibrant Brighton, England, and living by the ocean heavily influenced her lyrical and emotional writing. She works with the senses, description and colour, and her readers will easily visualise the narrative. A wife and mother, Lisa draws inspiration from family life, faith, memory and imagination. Since having her first of three children, Lisa has lived in Carmarthen, West Wales, another town rich in legend and lore.

Lisa is also highly creative and co-owns an Etsy shop, Amaranth Alchemy, with her daughter Bekah, where they breathe new life into old pages and create bookpage gifts and art from old, worn, torn and abandoned books.

Lisa's debut novel 'Beneath the Rainbow', its sequel 'Beneath the Old Oak' and the final Hope Within novel 'Beneath the Distant Star' are all available in paperback and eBook at Amazon.

Web: *www.thelastkrystallos.wordpress.com*
           www.lisashambrook.com

Bekah Shambrook

Bekah Shambrook is a multi-talented proponent of self expression which manifests in the areas of awe-inducing makeup artistry, inspired and inspirational cosplay, a burgeoning interest in the realm of acting and performing arts, as well as a plethora of handicrafts. She embraces creativity as essential to existence and has yet to decide that any particular artistic outreach trumps another.

Web: *bekahshambrook.wordpress.com*
Twitter: *@bekahshambrook*

KR Smith

K. R. Smith is an IT Specialist and writer living in the Washington, D.C. area. While mainly interested in composing short stories of the horror genre, he occasionally delves into poetry, songwriting, and the visual arts.

Web: *www.theworldofkrsmith.com*
Twitter: *@wokrsmith*

Steven Paul Watson

Born and raised in the hills of Eastern Kentucky, Steven is many things: a writer, artist, amateur photographer, and avid outdoorsman as well as an all-around self-proclaimed geek.

His love of writing includes soul-chilling science fiction, fantasy, and all things supernatural/horror. But his true passion is steampunk/alternate reality.

Attending more than a handful of conventions a year (And one day maybe even in a costume), he stays close to his geeky roots. When out in nature, Steven enjoys running multiple 5Ks a year and hiking the hills near his home. There is no better way to stoke one's imagination than being outdoors in the wilderness having real adventures that feed the ones he puts on the page.

Web: *stevenpaulwatson.wordpress.com*
FB: *www.facebook.com/Steven-Paul-Watson-212171268917291*
Twitter: *@ashviper*

Michael Wombat

A Yorkshireman living in the rural green hills of Lancashire, Michael Wombat is a man of huge beard. He has a penchant for good single-malts, inept football teams, big daft dogs and the diary of Mr. Samuel Pepys.

Abducted by pirates at the age of twelve he quickly rose to captain the feared privateer 'The Mrs. Nesbitt' and terrorised the Skull Coast throughout his early twenties. Narrowly escaping the Revenue men by dressing as a burlesque dancer, he went on to work successively and successfully as a burlesque dancer, a forester, a busker, and a magic carpet salesman. The fact that he was once one of that forgotten company, the bus conductors, will immediately tell you that he is as old as the hills in which he lives.

Nowadays he spends his time writing and pretending to take good photographs. You are encouraged have a good laugh at his pathetic blog or his photographs, but most of all please go and mock him mercilessly on Twitter or Facebook. Michael Wombat has published over one book. Other authors are available.

Web: *cubicscats.wordpress.com*
FB: *www.facebook.com/wombatauthor*
Twitter: *@wombat37*
Photograph by Dotty Cook.

Made in the USA
Coppell, TX
10 July 2021

58780199R00245